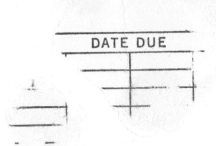

DATE DUE

GREAT
LOVE STORIES
from THE SATURDAY EVENING POST

Other books in this series

GREAT WESTERNS
from *The Saturday Evening Post*
MYSTERY & SUSPENSE
Great Stories from *The Saturday Evening Post*

GREAT LOVE STORIES

from THE SATURDAY EVENING POST

EDITED BY JULIE EISENHOWER

THE CURTIS PUBLISHING COMPANY INDIANAPOLIS, INDIANA

CONTENTS

INTRODUCTION

In researching *Saturday Evening Post* fiction of the past half-century for *Great Love Stories*, the words to the popular song "What the World Needs Now Is Love Sweet Love" often echoed in my mind. The world has always needed love. In our generation, in a small yet significant way, *Post* editors met this need by invariably including a love story among the four or five fiction selections each week. Many of the well-known authors of the twentieth century who wrote regularly for the magazine—Kurt Vonnegut, Jr., Pulitzer Prize novelist Oliver LaFarge, Sinclair Lewis (whose first *Post* story in 1915 earned him $9.17) and playwright-novelist Garson Kanin—turned their pens to love and are represented in this *Post* anthology.

Because *Great Love Stories* is the product of so many fine literary minds, it is a remarkable statement about the universal quest for love—how some respond to love, how it affects their lives, and how the love one feels for another changes year by year. The words written by the *Post* authors are often more poetic, or dramatic, or even more clever than the ones we use in communicating our love to others; but they speak vividly to the reader because they capture the different depths of emotion one experiences when one loves.

For example, sweet and even sentimental is Oliver LaFarge's beautifully written story "Runaway Honeymoon." Far different are the cynicism and quick-paced tempo of "The Bonfire," John O'Hara's story of a young widow. And for sheer melodrama, one can

read Edmund Gilligan's gothic romance, "The Wedding of Marie Rose," which begins:
I saw her pace the wind-rippled beach near her doorway, a tall lean woman gazing at the ruins and over the sea.

If any one theme emerges from this volume, it is that love is never static. Undoubtedly, the love one feels for others undergoes constant changes. Often the changes are painful. One discovers that the fresh young love described with sensitivity in Dorothy Thomas's "Love Is a Proud and Gentle Thing" cannot remain unblemished. The ability to feel what your loved one feels is not possible 100 percent of the time, no matter how passionately in the beginning one watched for and wondered about every sigh or shrug. Inevitably, one realizes that the fourteenth or sixteenth month "anniversary" was not noted or exclaimed over.

Perhaps the greatest death to love is indifference—numbness to another's emotions. The bittersweet story, "Night for Love," by Kurt Vonnegut, Jr., is the saga of how wishes for what might have been can atrophy the growth of love. Another classic story about the lack of communication between husband and wife is "Lightning Never Strikes Twice" by Mary Roberts Rinehart (a popular *Post* author from 1909 to 1955). The most grotesque example of the death of emotions is John Cheever's "The Geometry of Love." Cheever describes a man who gambles desperately to insulate himself from the cold terror of the disintegration of the love he feels for his family. His solution is to reduce his way of life to a series of mathematical equations.

Anne Morrow Lindbergh, in her book *Hour of Gold, Hour of Lead,* addresses the question of how to face a tremendous emotional loss. When the firstborn son she loved with all the love in a mother's heart was kidnapped and killed, she learned that, despite the pain, "to grow, to be reborn, one must remain vulnerable—open to love but also hideously open to the possibility of more suffering." Her message to others is that "the seed of love must be eternally resown." The stories in the *Post* anthology do not directly proclaim the view that one must constantly renew love. But, after reading the stories of pure, young love; of unreality and fantasy; of cynicism and bitterness; and of indifference, one concludes that indeed love must be "resown."

Great Love Stories From The Saturday Evening Post fills a need most people experience—the desire to learn more about love. It is a beautiful book which stretches the mind as well as the heart.

In the course of researching over one hundred years of literature in the archives of the *Post*, the following members of *The Saturday Evening Post* staff aided me in finding stories and "missing" authors.

Jep Cadou
Roberts Ehrgott
Rosalyn Fox
Astrid Henkels
Jean White

GREAT
LOVE STORIES
from THE SATURDAY EVENING POST

ROADHOUSE WOMAN

WILLIAM E. BARRETT

Jerry Lawlor sat on the right side of the brick cabin and watched the long road which lay like a dropped rope across the mountains. The driver of the truck, who had picked him up on the highway, was not talkative, but when they crept slowly up a steep grade east of the pass, Jerry shifted his guitar case on the seat beside him and the man glanced at him.

"You one of them cowboy singers?" he said.

"Some of the time."

The driver considered that. "Seems like you're headed the wrong way," he said slowly. "Seems like Denver would be better. They got a lot of nightclubs up there and a lot of radio."

Jerry shrugged. "There's nothing in any city that I want."

"There's nothin' where I'm goin' neither."

"There'll be something."

They left it at that. Jerry Lawlor was nineteen and there wasn't anything that he felt like talking about to anyone. He had been young and strong and he had known glory. He had ridden the rodeo circuits from Houston and San Antone to Cheyenne and Pendleton, and he had won his share of prizes. In Madison Square Garden, New York, he reached the end of the glory road with a horse on top of him. When he got out of the hospital he came West again to report to his draft board, overdue and underweight. They hadn't been interested in him. After that, he bought the guitar.

The truck picked up speed beyond the pass, rolling down into the

1

golden glory of the aspens, finding the straight road of the valley where chili peppers hung in scarlet strings on small houses and huts. There was a smudge of smoke in the sky; then a couple of shabby filling stations and a sign proclaiming the existence of a town and naming it. It was PATATA.

"Reckon this is your town," the truck driver said. "I'm hauling to a wildcat up beyond. Ain't nothin' between here and there."

"Good enough. Thanks."

Jerry swung down from the truck on the main drag. It was about three blocks long, with a motley collection of stores, bars and eating places. All the buildings were old, weather-beaten; mostly frame. There was a church steeple off the drag to the right, with the foothills crowding close behind it, shelves of rock angling upward with the hint of space behind them. There was no motion-picture theater and there were no TV aerials in sight. Jerry approved that. There had to be entertainment of some kind, probably his brand. At the edge of town he found what he was seeking.

There was a low, rectangular building with a sign that identified it as GARCIA'S PLACE, proclaiming in Spanish that it was a place of refreshment and of entertainment, with music, dancing and three kinds of beer. Jerry Lawlor read and spoke Spanish, after a fashion, as he played the guitar. He had learned from men who, like himself, followed the rodeo trail. There was much time in which to learn skills, and few skills to learn, along that route. A man concentrated on the few that he had a chance to learn and, if he was interested, he became pretty good.

The light was dim in Garcia's. A big, barnlike room extended back from the bar. In the afternoon it was merely a resting place for shadows: at night it would be a dance hall. There were tables ringing the open space, and an upright piano on a raised platform midway between the bar and rear wall. Jerry photographed it all in a glance; then faced the only two people in the place—a slender, dark-haired girl behind the bar, and a big man who sat on a bar stool with one elbow resting on the bar. They were looking at him, silent, curious. Jerry was not interested in girls at the moment. He addressed himself to the man.

"You the boss?" he said.

The girl's scornful laugh cut across the inquiry. "He is not the boss," she said. "He is the lazy man who drinks when other men work." Her eyes rested on the guitar case, then lifted to Jerry's face. "You are the musician? You want a job?"

"You guessed it, sister."

The man laughed, and there was scorn in his laughter for an Anglo who sought a job in a place that was Spanish. The girl glanced at him and her chin lifted.

"This is not the place for the man with many dollars in his head," she said. "It is the place for poor men with money in their pockets, poor men who earn the money by digging the potatoes and baling the alfalfa and doing the things that a man must do."

She spoke to Jerry, but he knew that the words were intended for the man at the bar. Jerry waited. The girl shrugged her shoulders.

"To play music is to work too," she said. "We need the musician. The boss plays the guitar, but he is too busy to do it. You will show me what you do."

She moved lazily out from behind the bar and strolled toward the piano platform. She was small and she moved with arrogant grace. Her blouse was red and she wore a wide-swinging skirt of green and yellow. Her black hair was straight, uncurled. She jumped lightly to the platform and seated herself on the stool. There were two chairs, and she waved Jerry to one of them. The piano was incredibly scarred and scuffed, but her fingers called square-dance music out of it. Jerry drew the guitar from its case. He tuned it, watching her; when she nodded to him, he came in. He could play square-dance music in his sleep. She let him carry it, abandoning the piano to dance around the platform. She snapped her fingers.

"*Bueno*. Now you play Spanish, yes."

"*Si.*"

He smiled at her. For no particular reason he was beginning to like her. He warmed up on *Carmen* music, a little "La Paloma," some Cuban rumba; not caring much what he played, so long as it had a Spanish beat. The girl undulated her body, scarcely moving her feet. He dark eyes glowed and there was a dazzling whiteness in her smile. She went through a pantomime of snapping her fingers for a while without snapping them; then she snapped them once.

"I think yes," she said. "You sing?"

"Some."

He trailed his fingers over the strings, reaching for something. She leaned toward him. "Spanish," she said.

He gave her *Adios, Mariquita Linda*. It was something he had learned from experts, from homesick vaqueros who put heartbreak into it. He did not think of it as a love song until the girl went back to the piano. She leaned toward him, commanding his song for herself, playing her own accompaniment to a soft, velvet-smooth voice. It was easy to sing with her, and to her.

He had forgotten the man at the bar. He was aware of him suddenly, with no time to prepare for him. The girl's fingers crashed the keys and her singing broke on a frightened cry of "Pedro!" The big man vaulted to the platform and there was blind, blazing anger in his broad face. Jerry pushed his chair back, but he had no chance of gaining his feet. The man wrenched the guitar from his hands and the heavy arms swung it like a club.

Jerry went down under it with the dark depths opening before him, bright lights swinging high. The girl's voice was a sound in Spanish, indistinct and far away, a thin sound on the edge of silence.

There was daylight behind a cracked and dirty shade when Jerry awakened the first time. The light hurt his eyes and he closed them again. The next time he opened them, the girl was in the room. He stared at her for several moments before she was aware of his regard. She looked startled then, her eyes widening.

"Ah, you have decide to live. I was thinking maybe you are a corpse that breathes." She crossed the room swiftly. "What can I do for you?"

He blinked, struggling with a confused memory. He had vague pictures in his mind of the girl bending over him, doing things for him; many pictures, all of them blurred.

"How long have I been here?" he said.

"Days. You are very sick. You have the doctor one time."

He struggled to sit up, but the effort was too much. In that brief struggle, however, he had a view of the room—a narrow room with one window. It was night and there was a small lamp lighted on a dresser. There was an iron bed and a chair and the cot on which he lay. He was suddenly embarrassed, as only a youth of nineteen who lived in a man's world could be embarrassed.

"You—you took care of me," he said.

"But of course. Certainly! There was no one else. It was my fault that you are hurt."

He had to close his eyes again. "How?"

"I was very stupid. The big buffalo was angry with me, so he beat you. It is the way of a man, and I should know it."

He did not want to talk about "the big buffalo." He did not want to talk at all. The girl understood. "I have the kitchen," she said. "I will get the soup for you. It is good to have when you are sick."

He was not certain that soup, or anything else, was good to have. He had disordered memories of nausea and vomiting and racking pain. He was embarrassed again. He tried to find a sequence of events in his memory, but there was nothing but the one vivid picture of a big, snarling man and a lot of scattered dream, or nightmare, sequences. His fists clenched, but it was an effort to clench them. He could not have killed a fly with them.

The girl came back with the soup, and he could see her clearly now. She was prettier than he remembered; round-faced, with large dark eyes and full, beautifully shaped lips. Her skin was dark ivory with rose tints in it.

"How did I get here?" he said.

"The man who brings the beer came. He is big, strong. He carry you to my place. It is not far."

Jerry wondered, as he ate the soup, what would have happened to him if the girl had not taken him in. As far as this town was concerned, he was just a tramp without money. Disaster had fallen on him before he got a job. The girl sat on the chair, her hands clasped around one knee. She seemed delighted that he was able to eat.

"I have prayed for you," she said simply, "and now I know you will be all right."

She took the soup bowl away and he heard her washing it in the kitchen. When she returned to the room, she asked him if there was anything else he wanted. He shook his head.

"Only your name. You didn't tell me," he said.

She smiled, pleased with him. "Maria," she said; "Maria Gonzalez."

There were, probably, a million girls named Maria Gonzalez, but she gave her name pride and dignity and a certain beauty in the way she spoke it.

"I am Jerry Lawlor," he said.

"Jerry!" She weighed the name on her tongue and rejected it, frowning slightly. She found the name again in Spanish and her eyes lighted. "I will call you Geromo," she said. "I like that. But it is very late. Good night, Geromo."

She turned out the little light and he heard her undressing in the darkness. He did not look toward her, wanting to do so, yet respecting something that he could not put in words; the fact, perhaps, that this was the only privacy Maria Gonzalez had and that she had shared it with him because he was helpless.

He lay staring at the ceiling for a long time after her regular breathing told him that she was asleep. He was remembering the big man now as a human creature, divorced from the nightmare, a fat lounger at a bar, loafing while other men worked. Before the last horse, Jerry might still have gone down before a man that big, but the man would be hurt first; he wouldn't just hit, he would be hit. Remembering how it actually was, Jerry felt his jaw tighten. In the nightmare, man and horse had been confused in his mind, but there was no confusion now. He did not hate the horse.

The girl slept late, long after the light grew strong behind the cracked shade. When he heard her stirring, Jerry rolled over and faced the wall. He did not turn around until she spoke to him. She served him a breakfast of ham and eggs. It surprised him to discover that he was hungry and that food tasted good.

"There is not much to do in daytime at Garcia's," she said, "and I work most at night. I play the music. I sing. I dance a little when I feel like it. There are other girls to dance. This week the wife of the boss, Dolores, is sick, and I go there in the afternoon too."

He did not ask what she did before she came to Garcia's. It didn't matter. Somewhere she had learned to play the piano, and the accomplishment gave her rank and station. She could wait on tables when she was needed or serve drinks from the bar, but she was a musician, an entertainer. In a Spanish town all distinctions were important.

After the girl left, Jerry tested his legs. He walked up and down the room, rested a while, then walked again. His shirt had been laundered and was on a hanger behind the door. There were blood-stains on his trousers, but they were faint. Maria had tried to remove them. He dressed slowly, painfully, when the girl left again after supper, and he walked up and down in the darkness outside. Maria's two rooms were in a lean-to addition to a shabby frame house west of Garcia's. There was a family with children in the main part of the structure. He considered that fact thoughtfully. A sick and helpless man in Maria's rooms was one thing; a convalescent was something else.

Maria was cheerful when she came in late that night. She sensed his depression and she made conversation. She told him the legend that was older than the town; the legend of the Indian maiden who jumped from the high point of rock beyond where the Catholic church now stood because her lover was of another tribe and she could not marry him.

"It is beautiful," she said; "more beautiful than sad, no? But it is not funny. Love is never funny."

She tried to tell him something funny. From the beginning of the town, this country was a place of potatoes. Men sought oil and uranium without finding what they sought, but a man, if he worked hard, could make his living from the potato.

"Because this is true," Maria said, "the name of this town is Patata, which is the potato that is Spanish. But it was not so in the beginning, no!"

In the beginning, she explained, men called the town San Patata, which, in Spanish, is Saint Potato; but that was changed when the first priest came.

"The priest said to them that this is a sin, that the potato does not go to heaven. And the men ask him, very serious, how they make a living in heaven if the potato does not go there."

She laughed softly, delighted with her own story. "It is a joke," she said, "but nobody laughs. With the good Spanish joke, everybody laughs tomorrow, not now. With this, even the priest laughs tomorrow, but the name of the town is changed. That is funny, no?"

Jerry admitted that it was funny, and he laughed with her, sharing her enjoyment, but the things that he wanted to say to her had to wait till tomorrow, if their laughter did not. She was already reaching for the light. Her eyes were soft for a moment, looking at him.

"It is good that you are happy, Geromo," she said. "And now, *buenas noches*."

He turned his face to the wall, and there was warmth in him, and nameless longings. He was an orphan, raised by an uncle and an aunt to whom he was a Christian obligation and a duty, but never an object of affection. He had known few girls, and those few shyly, inarticulately, self-consciously. He lay awake long in the darkness, conscious of every creak and rattle of the iron bed when Maria moved. He wondered if what he felt for her was love, and how a man could know. He was feeling something—something that ached inside of him and kept sleep away.

In the morning after Maria was gone, he walked in the yard. He sat on a dusty crate when he tired and he looked at the sloping rock that rose behind the town.

It was not so difficult as he thought that it would be to climb that rock. There was a street with an easy grade that passed the Catholic church, and a curving path beyond it. He rested often, but in less than three quarters of an hour he had climbed it. He stood on the edge of a cliff that dropped sheer to a dry creek bed a hundred and fifty feet below. Jerry turned away. He did not think about the Indian girl who was supposed to have jumped down there. He didn't believe any part of the story. He had known many Indians and he just couldn't imagine it.

He lay with his hands behind his head for an hour after he returned to Maria's, staring at the ceiling. She was all around him, in the things she owned and wore. There was a small crucifix on the wall and there were two highly colored lithographs of the Holy Family and of the Virgin of Guadalupe. There was a pink garment not long enough to reach her knees. It was lying across the bed that she did not have time to make before she left, so he knew that it was her nightgown, or whatever it was called, the something in which she slept. Her powder was spilled on the dresser top, and it had a strong scent. There was a green ribbon on the floor.

Jerry knew all of those things, and where they were, without looking at them. There was something else; a fountain-pen gift box on the dresser top near the spilled powder. He rose suddenly and picked it up. The pen inside was cheap, like the box, a ball point that, obviously, had never been used. He went on a quiet search for paper. Everything that she owned was in the two rooms. She did not own much. There was no paper. The calendar on the kitchen wall advertised a filling station. None of the months had been torn off. He tore off the month of January and wrote slowly, laboriously, on the back of it.

"Dear Maria," he wrote, "thanks. I won't forget. Someday I'll do something for you."

He hesitated; then signed the note, "Geromo."

There were two crumpled dollar bills that he had not owned in the right-hand pocket of his trousers. He did not discover them until he reached the highway. He stood for a moment, weighing pride against his necessity; then he walked back and placed one of the bills on the table under his note. He kept the other one because he was unsure of himself now in strange territory without the guitar.

A truck that was hauling pipe picked him up and he didn't ask where it was going. It was going somewhere.

Jerry Lawlor lived. He washed dishes and he swept floors and he did odd jobs where he found the jobs, sleeping wherever he was permitted to sleep, eating whatever was given him to eat. When the winter closed down on the western slope, he was working for a man named Lindstrom in a town of six hundred people. Carl Lindstrom operated a hotel of fifteen rooms, which was never filled to capacity even in the summertime. He had beds and warmth and food. He could afford to offer a handyman his necessities for whatever the man could do.

At first, there was not too much that Jerry could offer him. As the weeks went by, however, Jerry's body came slowly back to life. He shoveled snow then, and he cut kindling, and he did odd jobs of carpentry.

When he had developed new muscles, Jerry fought grimly with a big man named Pedro down snow-covered walks, and lashed into him with the ax that split the piled lengths of wood. At night sometimes he thought of Maria, but not often; when night came, he was too tired for thought. The big man was a job that he had to do, a score that he had to even, a fight that he had to fight. He could think of him through the day, and the thinking gave his muscles a goal, a reason for being, an objective needing strength. He ate well and he slept well; he worked hard and he grew.

The winter was long and with the spring he went out with a highway crew that repaired the ravages of winter. He was the lowly member who kept track of tools and hauled water, ran errands and did innocuous things such as restoring fallen highway markers to their proper places. By June he was driving a truck for a highway contractor, and in July he went into the woods, with all other available manpower, to fight a forest fire. The fire lasted for ten days and he stood up to the work, the smoke, the loss of sleep, the irregular meals, the fatigue of forced marches, the danger. He knew, when the fire was out, that he was whole again.

In early August, after the fire, he went to Denver with one of the trucks. He had money in his pockets and sound working clothes. He went down on Larimer Street where the pawnshops are and he priced guitars. He found one with a deep, mellow tone, a black one that felt right under his calloused hands. It was better than the one he had had when he went to Patata. He held it, savoring the moment, proud in the knowledge that he could afford it. Then he saw the wristwatch.

It gleamed brightly from a box lined in velvet, small, bright, feminine. He thought of Maria, seeing her, seeing the watch on her slender arm. She did not have a watch. There wasn't a clock in her two rooms. She never knew what time it was, save by a certain instinct that told her to go to work, to eat, to go to sleep. Jerry pointed to the case.

"How much is that?" he said.

It cost more than the guitar. Jerry looked at it. He could buy it. He laid the guitar on the counter, turning his back on it. He lifted the tiny box containing the watch. There was hardly any weight to it.

"Wrap it up," he said.

He went back to the highways and a man's work. The summer sun stained his skin and the labor swelled his muscles. He had a sure feeling about Pedro now, and he did not have to think about him. He could take him when the time came, and he would. He thought more often of Maria. He had a present for her and he was patient.

It was the fall once more when Jerry Lawlor came back to Patata. The aspens were gold in the passes and the chili peppers were scarlet strings on the small houses and the huts. His job had come to an end with September, and he rode the back trail as he had ridden out, hitching a ride with a trucker. He stood on the main drag and he looked at Garcia's sign in the distance. It was late afternoon, too early for her to be going on the night trick yet. It wasn't reasonable that the wife of the boss would still be sick. Maria would not be working in the afternoon.

He strode out swiftly, slowed with the sudden thought that she might be gone from Patata; then speeded up again, impatient to know. The house and the yard were as he remembered them. No one had moved the crate on which he used to sit. Everything, like the Spanish joke she had told him, was tomorrow; nothing ever got done today. He knocked on the door.

She was no longer young. The year had taken some of the rose tint from the ivory of her skin. Her eyes were not so bright and her mouth not so full. She was thinner and no electricity flowed from her. She opened the door and stood there, her clothes hanging limply on her. She did not know him.

"Don't you remember me, Maria?" he said.

"No." She stared at him impassively; then she leaned suddenly forward, her eyes widening in recognition. "Geromo! It is not possible!" Her hands darted out, her fingers digging into the hard ridges of his forearms. "I am so glad for you," she said. "I am afraid that you are dead."

"I could have been once."

There was swift fright in her eyes. "Why you come back?"

"Many reasons. To see you."

"No. Sit down, Geromo." She did not invite him in. Nothing was as he had planned. Jerry sat beside her on the crate. "You are strong," she said. "You have come back to look for Pedro. You must not. It was not his fault. He is a good man. I made him jealous and I knew it. It is the way of women."

Jerry knew then. He frowned, not looking at her. "He is a bum," he said curtly.

"No! You do not understand. One man digs the potato, makes a little money, gives it to a girl. It is all he has, very little. Another man says the little money of the potato is not enough for his girl. He has a big dream. He wants her to have many pretty things."

Jerry's fists tightened. "So he's a bum, without even potato money. He doesn't give her anything."

Maria's hand rested on his. "A woman does not care, my Geromo. It is good for her that he wants her to have many things. That is very good for a woman."

"It makes it easier for him too."

She shook her head. "No! It is harder for him, harder than to dig the potato."

There was patience in her voice, pleading in her eyes. She wanted him to understand, but Jerry Lawlor couldn't understand. He made a slashing, impatient gesture with his right hand.

"O.K.," he said harshly. "That's a Spanish joke. I'll laugh tomorrow maybe. He plunged his hand into his pocket. "I wanted you to have something pretty too. I brought you a present."

"A present?"

She turned to him, startled, and her voice was a child's voice, surprised, excited. He placed the tiny wrapped box in her hand. She stared at it for long seconds; then her hand closed on it possessively.

"I must have light to see it," she said. "It is getting dark here." She rose swiftly, hesitated a moment. "You come in with me, Geromo," she said.

He entered the room behind her, the room that he remembered so well. She turned on the small lamp on the dresser. The crucifix and the two lithographs were still on the walls. His cot was gone. So was her narrow iron bedstead. The room had a double bed now. The precious *Certificado de Matrimonio*, in a dime store frame, hung below the lithograph of the Holy Family. Maria was tearing the wrapping from the box.

The wristwatch was gleaming glory against the dark velvet, a thing of flashing reflection, of daintiness, of femininity. Maria looked at it, hypnotized. Her eyes lifted slowly to Jerry's.

"I have never seen one so beautiful," she said. She thrust her left arm out. "Show me how it works, Geromo."

He wound the watch, and his fingers trembled when he fastened the strap clasp on her wrist. She held the watch away from her, looking at it, turning it one way and then another. She held it against her ear and listened to it tick. The clasp fascinated her and she played with it, opening it and snapping it shut.

"Geromo," she said, "I cannot talk."

He could not talk, either. The thought came back to him that he had known a year—that to enjoy the enjoyment of Maria was better than anything that he could have for himself. She took the watch off and put it on again, frowning slightly as she struggled with the clasp, smiling when she mastered it. She sighed at length, removed the watch from her wrist and replaced it carefully in the box. She held it, looking at it, then extended the box to Jerry.

"Geromo," she said, "you have made me very happy. All my life I will remember."

He stared at her, not comprehending. When he did not take the box, she tried to force it into his hand. "Someday," she said, "you will have a girl and you will give her this."

11

"I gave it to you."

She raised her face to him. Her eyes were wet. "It was very sweet. I will think of it and it will always be my present, Geromo. It will always be mine and I will think of it."

"You've got to keep it."

"No. I cannot." She shook her head slowly. "Never in all of his life can Pedro give me this. It is what he wants to do, Geromo, and he cannot do it."

There was finality in her voice. A fact was a fact and it could not be altered. When she looked at him there was mystery in her eyes, and the excitement was gone. She was no longer a child; she was a woman who knew that she was a woman, and that he was a boy. Jerry accepted the box reluctantly, respecting something that he could not understand.

"Is there anything that I can do for you?" he said.

She smiled at him. "But no, Geromo. You have done more for me than you know. I will always love you a little."

She kissed him, holding his face between her warm palms for a moment; then she walked with him to the door.

He stood on the highway, waiting for a truck, and the lights were on in the town. He thought briefly of Pedro, no longer hating him, no longer caring. Yesterday was over and everything was tomorrow. This Pedro, whatever he was, had found the love of a woman. It was something that Jerry had yet to know.

It was a long wait for the truck, and he thought about Maria, understanding for the first time the gentle sadness of *Adios, Mariquita Linda* which he had learned from the vaqueros. His hand closed around the small package in his pocket.

The yellow lights of a truck gleamed on the highway then, and he raised his hand to them.

BONNY BELLE

FRANK BUNCE

Ol' Maw Skinner had just begun her screaming when the boy came in. Bonny Belle saw him before the vigorous jolt of Wanda's elbow against her ribs reminded her that she was not supposed to look around during services. She saw that he had on a newish sweater that looked as if it would burst at the shoulders if he moved around too much; she saw that his shirt tonight was uncomfortably buttoned at the throat and cinched with a bright, newish necktie. Especially she saw the square set of his jaw and the hard glint of his eyes, and she tingled.

"The daring thing," she said softly to herself. "He's going to sit right up here again. That daring thing."

She smoothed her dress down over her knees. It was a dress that had been given to her by one of the faithful back in Coldspring, Missouri, but she was pleased with it. It was long and trailed out behind like the dresses she had seen on women going into theaters in Dallas and such places, and it made her look at least two years older. She hitched up her coat—a gift from one of the faithful in Little Rock—so that the fur collar would show to better advantage, and she gave the curl that hung down across the center of her forehead a quick twirl with one finger.

"Don't you dare look around," Wanda hissed. Her face twisted away briefly, returned, wearing a scandalized expression. "He's coming up the aisle. He's going to sit up here behind us again tonight. Don't you look around at him."

"I'm not looking around," Bonny Belle said. "I haven't looked around tonight, yet." She let her head pivot very gradually to the left, as if it were on slow cogs; a trick she had practiced ever since she was small and had been scolded for not paying strict attention to the services. Her eyes shifted, in their guarded sweep, from Mrs. Skinner to the small band of the faithful, dominated by her mother, kneeling in front of the altar; went on to her father, slouched into a plush-covered chair by the organ, his head bowed into his hands; attained finally to the wide middle aisle. She seemed looking at Ol' Grandmaw Hedges, who had sprung up; but she saw many other things. From a corner of her eye she saw the boy coming up the aisle, walking clumsily and with his eyes fixed straight ahead of him, and level. She saw a black-haired girl three benches back crane to look at him, then turn back to her, Bonny Belle, with a sudden flare of animosity in her eyes. She saw that the boys and girls paired off in the back of the tabernacle were giggling and nudging one another, and that other people were looking at the boy and discussing him. All this Bonny Belle saw while she was dutifully looking at Ol' Grandmaw Hedges. Then she turned her face back front.

Just at the end of the bench where Bonny Belle sat, the boy stopped. He stood there a moment and then crowded in, stepping carefully over Wanda, who was making scandalized noises, across Bonny Belle, and dropped into the wide vacant space between her and one of the faithful, a certain Tompy.

Bonny Belle sat frozen. Even her breathing stopped. She had never dreamed that this awful boy would push in and sit down by her. She had thought he would sit down on the bench behind and maybe lean over and try to talk to her, as he had the night before. She would have known how to handle him if he had tried that again. She could just sit straight and stiff and refuse to turn around, refuse to answer a word. But up here by her he might do anything. He might try to hold her hymnbook. He might even, the daring thing, try to put his arm along the bench behind her as Bonny Belle had seen some of the boys doing with some of the girls in the back of the tabernacle.

But he didn't. He crowded Tompy over, so that there was a space between himself and Bonny Belle. Two inches, anyway. Tompy made an indignant noise, and the boy turned to look at him. Systematically, with concentration, he set to work to look Tompy down. Bonny Belle saw Tompy's eyes rolling and a shrinking look grow up in them as the boy kept on staring, and she tingled all over with an emotion that was new to her, that was sinful and delightful. Tompy was sweet on her, and everybody knew it. The boy knew it, and he was looking Tompy down. It was almost like seeing them fight.

14

She kept her face turned to the front, but she used her eyes and all her senses skillfully to gather in impressions of what was going on around her. The girls and boys in the back were still tittering. Many other people were watching and saying things to one another; about her and the boy and Tompy, she knew. The black-haired girl three benches back was tossing her head and looking the other way and pretending she didn't care. Bonny Belle gathered in impressions of the boy too. He was an immense thing: he was twice as big as anybody else. He smelled faintly like soap; he smelled good and healthy and washed up. His yellow hair was nicely slicked back, though the ends of the short hairs at the side, just over his near ear, were rebellious; and his cheek was smooth as a girl's. There was a dent in his nose, as if he had been hit there.

Tompy satisfactorily subdued, the boy turned around to look at her, and Bonny Belle immediately made herself oblivious of him. Up front, she saw, the faithful had begun talking. Nothing of this had any surprises or any novelty for Bonny Belle, nor, consequently, any interest. She knew just how the meeting would go, she knew just about what her father and her mother and the others who preached or testified would say and do, for this revival and this meeting were reiterations of countless others she remembered from the time when she had been so small that her father had had her sit with him on the platform as an example of one of the little children of whom the Kingdom was to be comprised. She had enjoyed sitting there because it had made her feel superior to the children in the towns they went through, superior to Wanda and the children of the faithful who boarded them, more important than anyone else except her father. When it was decided, finally, that she was getting too big and too naughty to exemplify a little child anymore, she was degraded to the front benches along with the other faithful, and she found that tiresome. In the past year or so, something else had entered to add to her discontent; a feeling that her life was different from that of other girls, that it was missing in things they had as a natural right. She saw them coming into the meetings with boys, and sitting with them, and going away neatly paired off after services, and she got cheated; though she dared say nothing about it to either Wanda or her mother, though she hardly dared admit it to herself. The most she allowed herself to wish for was that her father would quit evangelizing for a while again, so that she and her mother and sister could settle down somewhere and be like other people.

Up front, the talking in tongues was drowned as the organist struck into a hymn. The choir caught up the hymn, and Bonny Belle's father signaled the congregation to rise. Bonny Belle took a hymnbook out of the rack on the back of the bench ahead of her. She stood up. The boy stood up, too, and one of his immense brown hands reached out to grasp a corner of the book.

Bonny Belle's breathing stopped. She couldn't sing. She couldn't think. Her knees began to tremble, so that she was afraid she would have to sit down. She was aware of Wanda's excited hissing in her ear, of Wanda's horrified eyes and the prod of Wanda's elbow into her ribs. That awoke her to the scandal of her position. She tugged the hymnbook toward her. The boy held on. His strength was unbelievable. He held the book just by one corner, with a thumb and one finger; but he held on, tug as she would. She shook the book furiously, and he held on. She let go of it, and he held it back up in front of her with all the solicitude as if he thought she had let go of it so he could hold it for her.

Bonny Belle grew angry. She grew so angry that everything turned red in front of her and her fingernails itched.

"You give me back my book," she said. He said nothing. He continued to hold it for her. His eyes looked dangerous; his lips were pressed so tightly together that there were white spots at the corners. She felt cornered and terrified and wildly enraged. "Give me back my book," she said. "You haven't got any right to hold my book. Nobody asked you to hold my book. Nobody asked you to sit up here, even. You're not supposed to sit here."

"Anybody can sit anyplace in this tabernacle," he said. "We all helped build it. I helped build it myself. I hauled saw logs for it."

The singing stopped. Everybody sat down. Bonny Belle sat down. The boy sat down with his shoulder touching hers. She moved over, crowding Wanda. The boy moved over, too, or he let himself spread, or he did something mysterious, so that his shoulder came back to touch hers.

"You can't crowd me like this," Bonny Belle said. "You can't just push yourself in like this, even if you did haul saw logs for this church."

"Can I help it if I take up a lot of room?" the boy asked.

"I'm going to tell mamma," Wanda hissed, from her other side. "You're talking to him, and people are all looking. I'm going to tell mamma right tonight."

"My name is Pete Williams," the boy said. "I got a lots of kinfolks around here, so don't get me mixed up with the Williamses that live in town here, or the Williamses over on Piney Ridge. I live in Bitter Creek Hollow. I got a place of my own."

"I never asked you what your name was, or where you lived," Bonny Belle said.

"I know your name," the boy said. "I asked Mrs. Peters, at the store, this morning. It's a sweet name. I think you're a purty sweet girl too. Last night was the first night I came to this revival. I stood in the back and saw your hair and couldn't keep from looking at you, even when I couldn't see but just your hair. It's like these hills in the fall when the leaves turn red."

Bonny Belle sat straight up, indignantly. "My hair is not red. It's auburn. Several people have said my hair is not red but auburn."

"Then when you turned around once, I saw your face," the boy said, going on as if she had not spoken. "It was so white and purty, you looked like an angel. I had to get up close before I saw you had some freckles. That made me feel better about you. You couldn't talk much to an angel."

"You can't talk to me," she said. "You'd better listen to the prayer and testimony. That's what you're supposed to come to church for."

He did listen while Brother Below and Brother Jordan prayed and testified. But when Brother Willis, who roared, began to testify, he started in again.

"I saw Tompy going home with you last night. He was making out that he was talking to your father and mother, but he was getting up as close to you as he could. He's working it smooth."

"Tompy never has gone home with me," she said. "Nobody ever goes home with me. Not with me, I mean. There are always about seventeen people who go along with my father and mother, and I have to go home with them. So you'd better not try it, even if you do work it smooth."

"You just keep a-talking," Wanda hissed, from her other side. "I'm going to tell mamma."

"I'm not going to try it," the boy said. "I can't work things smooth. And anyhow, I wouldn't want to go home with you if there had to be seventeen other people along. There wouldn't be anything I could say to you."

He listened to her father preach for a while. He waited till the altar call was given and the services grew noisy again; and then he said, "Don't you ever go anyplace besides to church, Bonny Belle?"

"I go lots of places," she said. "I used to go to school in almost every town we came to, but my grades got mixed up, so that nobody could tell what classes I belonged in, and they took me out. Now they send me to the post office for the mail, and to the store, and I get butter and eggs and things from old Mr. and Mrs. Tillson, out in the country, for Mr. and Mrs. Harris. We are staying with Mr. and Mrs. Harris. I go to the post office every morning about ten, and then

I usually go out to get eggs or something from Mr. and Mrs. Tillson."

"I've seen you going out to Tillson's. My place is right along the road, down in the valley to your left just after you turn the bend. I'm going to be around town tomorrow morning. I'd rather walk you to Tillson's than walk you home. There wouldn't be seventeen other people along."

"I don't need you to walk me to Tillson's," she said. "I can walk myself, thank you."

He let himself spread, so that she was crowded over into Wanda. His jaw came out. "This is a free country. Anybody can walk that road. We all built it and keep it up. I helped scrape it this spring."

He got up and went away. She saw him pushing through the people standing in the back, and going out of the door.

Up front, the organist interrupted the praying by striking into a hymn. Everybody took hymnbooks and stood up. Bonny Belle took a hymnbook and stood up. Tompy stood up. He looked back toward the door and then reached out to take hold of her hymnbook. She jerked at it and got it away from him easily; Tompy's hand drooped, and he looked shamed and scarlet.

Bonny Belle's father gave the benediction. People bunched in front, to shake hands, to talk to the new converts. It grew late, and several of the lanterns were blown out as a warning to people that they must be moving along. Bonny Belle's father look the last lantern and led the way out, many others trailing, Tompy among them; Tompy sticking quite close to Bonny Belle while pretending to be talking to her father. Tompy was playing it smooth.

Wanda was going to tell on her. Bonny Belle knew that from the way she kept sniffing all the way along, and braced herself for it. Somehow, she didn't care. Somehow, she even looked forward to it. Something strange had come over her; a kind of glow that made the walk to Mr. and Mrs. Harris's, the leisurely good nights to people at the gate, the prosaic business of going upstairs and getting ready for bed, even the prospect of being scolded, exciting and wonderful.

Wanda did tell when their father and mother came in to hear their prayers. But the effect was disappointing. Their father paid no attention. He was weak and shaken and withdrawn, as he always was after he had preached, oblivious of all things terrestrial. Their mother only looked at Bonny Belle in wonderment, and then said briskly:

"Pshaw! She's only a child!"

"I'm sixteen," Bonny Belle said.

Their father knelt then to pray. Their mother prayed, and then they. Then Wanda attacked again:

"She talked to him, too, mamma. They just talked, talked, talked all through the meeting. And people were all looking."

"I was just trying to get him to shut up," Bonny Belle said. "I did get him to listen to some of the prayer and testimony. He was real good then."

"She told him where we were staying. He told her his name and where he lived. She knew he didn't belong up there, but she didn't try to put him back where he belonged."

"This is a free country," said Bonny Belle. "Anybody can sit any place in that tabernacle. They all helped build it. He hauled saw logs for it. All that's the matter with Wanda is he didn't talk to her. He didn't even look at her. He just walked right across her."

"Children, children!" their mother said, and left, clucking dismally, in the wake of their father.

Bonny Belle decided, before she went to sleep, that she wouldn't let him walk her out to Tillson's. He was too bold. She didn't know anything about him. He was too big and too pressing; he made her feel cornered. And anyhow, he probably wouldn't try. He probably had been just talking. He wouldn't even be in town in the morning.

But he was. He was in the post office when she went after the mail; he was standing with some other boys in front of the pool hall when she passed it on the way out to Tillson's. The other boys laughed when Bonny Belle came close. He didn't. He kept his eyes on her, scowling, with the white spots showing at the corners of his mouth. And when she came opposite him, he fell into step with her.

She walked fast. He kept up easily; he only had to take one step to her three. She went faster, until she was almost running, but he kept up without any trouble, with an ease that made her furious.

They went to the end of the sidewalk and then out into the road. They started up a long hill, with Bonny Belle still walking as fast as she could.

"You better slow down," he said. "Keep on like that, and you'll be plumb winded before you get up this grade."

She said nothing. She wasn't going to let him inveigle her into talking to him. She'd show him. She broke into a trot, kicking up puffs of dust every time she put a foot down. Her breath failed and her legs got heavy. She tottered.

"Take it easy," he said; his arm went through hers. It offered support like a rock, it felt friendly and good. He helped her to a bridge near the top of the hill, and set her down on a rail of it. He leaned back against the rail and slid his arm along behind her. "Take it easy," he said. "I'm not agoing to eat you up."

She waited till her breath came back. Then she said, "I don't know anything about you. We haven't been introduced. I'm not old enough to go with boys."

"I'm not agoing to hurt you," he said. "Nobody could hurt you. Nobody would want to do anything but do things for you, and make your eyes shine."

She sat still, looking away from him. She sat marveling at the wonderful warmth that crept over her; at the longing she had to take his great yellow head in her arms and rock it gently.

"My place is just down that valley," he said. "I got a hundred and sixty acres, mostly cleared up, and good, tight buildings. The house ain't maybe what a girl would just go crazy about, but if she'd come, I could make things better for her in a year or so. You can see the roof from here—that stone chimney sticking up."

"I've seen it from the curve," she said. "I thought it was a nice house." She let herself look at him. His face in the sunlight had a yellow glow like his hair; it seemed radiant and purified. She saw big transparent drops on his forehead, and suddenly she wanted to serve him, to do something for him, to give him back gift for gift. She brought out her handkerchief from her sleeve and wiped his forehead. "You're sweating," she said.

She felt him tremble. His arm fell away from her. She was amazed; incredulous, that she could shake him like that, so easily as that.

"Listen," he said; he talked as if he had a mouthful of hot stuff. "You don't know how you make me feel. Anything you say—anything you do. I didn't know it was going to be like this. Some of the boys told me there was a purty little redheaded preacher's daughter at the revival. They bet me I couldn't make her talk or walk her anyplace. I took them up on it. I didn't know——"

She slid down off the bridge rail. He took a look into her face and stopped talking suddenly. She had never been so mad in her life. She snatched up her market basket and went off up the hill.

He came after. "Listen," he said. "You got the wrong idea. You didn't let me say what I meant."

"Go on!" she choked. "Go on away from me! You're not going to talk to me! You're not going to walk me to Tillson's! Not on a bet!"

He caught her arm. "I'm not talking to you on a bet. I'm not walking you to Tillson's on a bet. I'm talking to you and walking with you because I like you. That's what I meant to say. That's what I was going to say when you got mad. You got a temper like the devil himself."

She stopped and turned on him. She hit him in the chest with both fists, several times, as fast as she could.

"Go on! Go on away!" she said. "I hate you! I won't have you with me! You leave me alone!"

She ran to the top of the hill. She ran down it, around the curve almost to Tillson's.

When she looked back, he was nowhere in sight.

She stayed mad. She was so mad all day that she ached. Only when, as the meeting was starting that night, she figured out what she would do to him did her rage dissolve. She waited till he came in and stood talking to some people at the back; looking at her now and then, she knew, though she did not permit herself to look back at him. Then she moved over quite close to Tompy, pretending to ask what the next hymn would be. Tompy stuttered, Tompy grew red and began to sweat. And then Bonny Belle took out her small lace handkerchief and very daintily flicked his forehead with it.

"You're sweating," she said.

She did not let herself look around until she had the handkerchief back in her sleeve and everything about herself readjusted nicely. Then she saw the boy coming up the aisle, walking fast; his eyebrows frowned so far down over his eyes that she was frightened. She quivered. But he didn't come up to her bench. He didn't even come up to the bench behind hers. He stopped three rows back and sat down by the black-haired girl, who got red, then pale, and then smiled at him. The organist just then launched into a hymn, and everybody rose. The boy took a book out of the rack on the back of the seat ahead of him. He held it for the black-haired girl with all the solicitude in the world, and over the top of it his eyes glared into Bonny Belle's.

Bonny Belle began to feel sick. The lanterns seemed to dim, and black patches formed on the walls and against the altar and the platform.

"I'm not feeling well," she told Wanda. "I'm feeling bad. It's my stomach. It's something I ate. I'm going home. You tell mamma."

She went out by the side door. Going down the steps, she stumbled and fell. She picked herself up and ran as fast as she could until she got to Mr. and Mrs. Harris's. She went to bed and lay there without seeming to think anything, without feeling much, until long after her mother had been in to see about her and give her medicine, until after Wanda had gone to sleep. Then she began to get things straightened out. Everything was all her fault. She had a temper like the devil himself. She would tell the boy so and let him walk her to Tillson's in the morning to make up for it. He'd still want to. He didn't really like that black-haired girl. He couldn't, much, or he'd have sat by her before and held her hymnbook. He had been only pretending, as she had been pretending with Tompy. She'd see him tomorrow and explain things. He'd be in front of the poolroom or along the road somewhere.

But he wasn't. She went all the way up the hill, all down it to the curve, without seeing anything of him. And there she stopped. Far down in the valley to the left was his house. It was long and low and weatherbeaten, with a great stone chimney at one end; it was tiny and cool among great oak trees and brown patches of steamy fields. Just off the curve, a road wandered down to it, and to Bonny Belle that road presented irresistible temptation.

Not that she was going to his house. She assured herself of that, in shocked negation, at every step down the road that led to his house. At the first brook she determined to turn back, but a ford of stones challenged her and she crossed over. A little farther a patch of oak and maple trees seemed so cool and peaceful from a distance that she was lured on to them. And from that grove the house was visible.

Now that she had come so far, she told herself, there was no sense in turning back without at least having a look in. It would be interesting to see how he kept house. In guilty haste, so that no one could see her from high up on the road, she went across a young cornfield and a meager grass lawn to the house.

It pleased her. It had a wide cool porch in front and a cool small porch in back, both with new neat steps leading up to them. There was a front room, a kind of parlor, that had real wallpaper on the walls and two rocking chairs drawn up before a center table with a hanging lamp over it. There was a kitchen papered with building paper, and a bedroom papered with old magazines. And then there were two rooms that seemed to be used for nothing but a woodshed and a storeroom for rusty tools and such. Surprisingly, the place was neatly kept up, though when she got to looking around, she saw that some of the corners had been neglected; and she doubted if the beds and the kitchen stove had been swept under since Christmas, if then.

She found a broom and cleaned out some of the corners; wishing, meantime, that she had time to do some scrubbing. A pile of dirty dishes on the kitchen table attracted her. She yearned to them; put aside temptation, and then weakly yielded. She built up a fire in the kitchen stove and set over water to heat. While she waited for it to boil, she stirred biscuits and parboiled some salt pork that she found in a barrel.

Then she decided that, since she had gone so far already, she might as well make a dinner of it, so she peeled and fried some potatoes, and made flour gravy and coffee.

Watching so many things at once kept her occupied, and she was amazed to hear a clock in the parlor striking twelve. That threw her into a panic. She put the dinner up into the warming oven, whisked off the dish towel she was using for an apron, and made ready to leave. But just then she heard a harness jingle in the yard and the boy's voice hollering, "Whoa!"

She ran to the kitchen door and looked out. He was just going into the barn behind two mules. Bonny Belle ran through the house to the front door and out onto the porch. There she remembered her market basket, and scurried back in for it. When she returned to the door, he was coming up a path that commanded a view of both sides of the house. She was trapped.

She dodged back into the kitchen and stood there shivering as if she were cold. She heard him tramping heavily into the wood room adjacent. He threw down something that shook the floor, and came on into the kitchen. At sight of her, he stopped, gaping.

She had had time to get ready for him. "Tillson's haven't got any eggs today, and I came down to see if you had any eggs. For Mr. and Mrs. Harris. Tillson's haven't got any eggs today," she said.

He said nothing. He continued to stare at her. Strange golden lights began to dance in his eyes when the sunlight caught them.

"Have you got any eggs?" she said.

He did not answer. He went to a pail that stood on a shelf behind the stove and got a drink. He began to roll up his sleeves, looking meanwhile at the stove, at the clean dishes, at the dinner warming in the oven.

"I thought you might have some eggs. Mr. and Mrs. Harris have me get their eggs from Tillson's because they're fresher and cheaper than in town. But Tillson's haven't got any eggs today. Their hens have quit laying for some reason."

"You didn't come here after eggs," he said. He poured water into a wash pan and began to wash, slowly and seriously, as if he were thinking out something.

She began to feel frightened. "All right, then. If you don't want to sell any eggs, you don't have to. I'll go get them some other place."

"You're not going any other place," he said positively. He straightened and wiped his face and turned around to her. "Not till I get ready to go with you."

Bonny Belle felt cornered. She saw that there was no escape for her. It was a long way to the road and other people.

If she tried to run, he would soon get her back. One of his steps was as good as three of hers.

"I don't know what you mean," she said.

"I mean the only place you're going is to Bealeville with me. Right after dinner. Bealeville's the county seat. They give out marriage licenses there. It looks to me," he said, with golden lights dancing in his eyes, "as if we'd better get married, shore. People would talk if you got to coming here for eggs, when everybody knows I ain't got a hen on the place."

Bonny Belle warmed. She got mad all over. "I didn't know you didn't have any hens on the place. I just asked. I'm not going to Bealeville with you. I'm not going to marry you. I'm too young to get married. You haven't even asked me. We haven't even been introduced. How are you going to get me up to Bealeville, anyhow? It's twelve miles."

"I've got a car," he said. "I've been using it the past couple years just to cut wood, but I can make it run. You sit down and eat while I spruce up a little. And don't try to run off, or I'll come out and get you, even if I haven't got a stitch of clothes on. I'm not hungry, for some reason."

She wasn't hungry either, but she ate at the biscuits and gravy while he filled a tub and retired with it and some fresh clothes to one of the storerooms. A little later he came out wearing creasy blue pants and a white shirt open at the throat and a white sweater with a letter on it that made him look like a football player.

"Come on," he said.

She blazed: "You just think you can order me around. I'm not going with you. I'm not going to get married, when we haven't even been introduced, or you haven't asked me, or my father or mother or anything. You take a lot for granted."

"I can't work things smooth like Tompy," he said. "I just bust in and get things done. Your folks will like me all right after they get used to me. You'll like me all right. I know just the way to handle you. Come on."

He took her out and set her down in the shade while he drew on some greasy coveralls and did things to the car, lovingly, with infinite patience. And finally he got it to going.

"You just take me up to Tillson's," she directed, when she was installed in the seat beside him.

"I told you where I was taking you," he said, and, with the canny foresight of a veteran flivver driver, urged the car to an uproarious spurt for the twisting grade that led up out of the valley.

Just after they strained up into the main road, they passed a farmer in a wagon.

The man stared at them so hard and then halloed so lustily that the boy stopped and backed up to him.

"Listen, Pete," the farmer said, his eyes bulging as he looked from one to the other of them. "I don't know just what you're up to now, now, but you're agonna get into it if you go back to town like that. Her folks and the Harrises has got scairt and called the shuriff. They'll hold you and put you in jail, sure as shootin'. You know how Anse likes you, anyhow."

"I'll go the old road," the boy said; and just over the crest of the hill, swung left on a road that was thick with buck brush and corduroyed with decayed sunken logs in the marshy places.

"Who's Anse?" Bonny Belle asked him.

"The sheriff. He's my cousin, but he doesn't like me any too well since I took the top off from his jail."

"You what?" said Bonny Belle.

"I took the top off from his jail. He.put some friends of mine in there just for having a good time on the Fourth, and I got them out. I got a pry pole and took the roof off."

"Oh," she said, and shuddered, seeing plainly now how hopeless her position was, how impossible it would be to get away from such a monster. She kept silent for a difficult mile or two, and then she said, "You're going to get in jail yourself, for taking me like this. It's against the law to take a girl without her consent."

"I don't care much," he said. "Anse feeds well. He doesn't like me, but he's a good feeder."

Twice the old road twisted across the new. And each time the boy stopped the car well back from the new road and went ahead to reconnoiter before crossing. Bonny Belle was delighted by that. It was like something in a book. She began to enjoy herself so thoroughly that she was sorry when they coasted down into Bealeville and pulled in to the curb in front of a drugstore on the square.

And there a sudden change came over the boy. He ceased to look like one who busts in and does things. He sat with his eyes on his feet, playing with the key on the dashboard.

"Listen," he said, in a subdued voice, at last. "We'd better go in and get the license. Come on."

"I'm not going to do it," Bonny Belle said. "I told you I wouldn't. You can't make me do anything here. If you try to, I can scream, and people will come running."

His jaw came out. "I don't care about people. I can go in and get the license myself. It only takes one to get a license. And after I've got it, you'd better be here, or I'll come after you, people or no people."

"Getting the license won't do you any good," she said. "I won't marry you after you do it. You can maybe drag me up in front of a preacher or somebody, but when they ask me if I'll have you, I'll say, 'no, no.' I have something to say about getting married. I've seen people married."

He was bothered. He tugged open the door on his side and put a foot out. But he got no farther.

"Well, what are you waiting for?"

He began to sweat all over—on his hands, on the back of his neck, on his cheeks and forehead.

"Listen," he said, very low. "I could make you do it, some way, I reckon. But I'd rather you'd do it because you wanted to. I wish you'd come."

Before she could answer, a car that had raced into the square stopped just ahead of them with a loud screech of its breaks. From it a tall man with a gun on his hip and a star on his shirt leaped out. He swaggered up to their car, planting himself in front of the boy, staring from him to her, grinning with tight lips, little golden lights dancing in his eyes.

"Wal, Pete, I shore got it on you now," he said. He didn't look mad, but he looked stubborn and terrible. "Been waiting a long time and now I got you right where I want you. This here stunt will put you in the coop for a long time. Long enough to teach you some sense."

He produced a chain with a handgrip on one end, and reached out for the boy's wrist.

The boy did not move. But Bonny Belle did.

Astoundingly, to herself, she put her hands upon the boy's shoulders and yanked him back into the car. She reached over him and banged shut the tinny door of the car, to the peril of the sheriff's extended hand.

"You let him alone," she said. "You're not going to put him in the coop. He hasn't done anything to be put in the coop for. I came with him myself. I got him to take me. I worked it so he would. We came up here to get married, and there's no law against that." She took the boy's great yellow head into her arms and held it. He seemed stupefied, he seemed helpless and childlike, and she rocked him gently while over his vast breadth of shoulder her eyes blazed at the sheriff so murderously that he went back a step. "You let him alone," she said. "He's mine. He's just what I want."

THE AWKWARD AGE

DOUGLAS CARMICHAEL

Tom Reimer carefully kept his eyes on his plate to avoid his father's slowly budding curiosity and speared another piece of bacon. Here it came.

"Coming fishing today, Tom?" his father asked.

Tom shook his head. "Thought I'd go exploring along the shore. Maybe find some good crystals somewhere."

"Aw, what do you want with a bunch of old rocks?"

Tom eyed his brother Eddie with brief disapproval. Kids Eddie's age never did seem to want to be alone.

"We'll see you at lunch, then," his mother said. "I'm going to park on the porch with a book."

That would make a little sense, Tom thought, if he had anything worth reading. What fun his father and Eddie saw to sitting in a rowboat under a hot sun in the middle of the bay all morning, hauling in a sluggish fish now and then, he couldn't see. It wasn't as if they went out to sea where they could catch something interesting. Huntly Harbor and its little hotel, whose elderly proprietress seemed almost alarmed at the presence of guests, were not his idea of a vacation spot. He'd rather have stayed home at Earlstown, near Doris.

Doris would probably be spending the day at the club with the gang, playing tennis and lounging around the pool in her white bathing suit. He'd hardly ever seen her alone, except for a few minutes when he took her home, barely long enough to kiss her good

27

night. Of course, she was always his date. She used to run her fingers through that tangled hair of his and tell him he was cute. But with half a dozen other people always along——Tom thought of the breezy letter tucked in the folds of one of his shirts where Eddie wouldn't find it. It would be fun to go back to school and see Doris again, but he'd bet she didn't miss him. Seniors they'd be this year. It made him feel a little dignified already.

He stuck a rock hammer in his belt and strolled carefully down the village street, trying to ignore the twangy-voiced natives on the store steps. With all the overalls around, Bermuda shorts made you feel like a summer visitor in a cartoon, even if they were the most comfortable thing for the weather and you wore a conservative sport shirt and tucked it in, instead of one of those gaudy, flapping, Hawaiian things Eddie liked. It was like being on parade till you reached the end of the houses.

North of the back beach there was a wooded point that he hadn't been to yet. It had a ten-foot band of bare rocks between trees and water, like all the coast here, except where it was marshy at the tidal creeks, and there might be some quartz crystals tucked away in a vein somewhere. It would be nice to find some pretty enough to set and give to Doris. Dick Potter might manage a setting for him in metalworking. Doris would bubble over when she got them.

Tom crossed a damp field to the seaweed-littered sand, empty now, though pocked with the marks of beach fires. Clambakes were one of the few good things about this hole. A few yards away the beach ended among sloping ledges cracked and seamed by the water that now lapped at their fringe of barnacles. Gray-green water, shot with sun over the rocks and shading to deep blue farther out. It was a good day, blue and crystal over the sea, with the scrubby blue-green firs above the rocks smelling hot and spicy. It almost made you not mind being alone.

Around a corner the woods changed from the scrubby firs to tall, scattered pines. Tom climbed up to the floor of the woods for easier walking and stopped a moment in awe. The place was like something in those poems Mr. Lansing made them read. He could see for a long way through the trees, and all the ground and the boulders and hummocks on it were covered with bright green moss. There were wisps of other moss, feathery stuff, trailing from the pine-tree branches, and the branches were high enough so you could walk around. They swayed in the breeze and made a soft, sighing noise that went with the regular slap and gurgle of the waves. The place even smelled mossy, warm and rich and dark-earthy, with just a tang of salt. Broceliande? Was that the magic wood he'd seen the name of somewhere? Tom walked over the moss almost reverently, trying to swallow all the wonder of it. He came to a soft bank flecked with sun and shade, and lay down and stretched his legs out delightedly.

There was a bright, tinkling sound that didn't seem to fit the sleepy blend of pines and water. It puzzled him as he lay half asleep, and he lifted his head to look around.

A girl was coming through the trees, swinging along with an easy stride over the velvet moss. The tinkling was coming from little silver bells hanging on her bracelets. She was wearing a short pleated skirt and halter of bright green with a silver belt. She had blond hair around her shoulders, and her skin was light, and she looked happy.

She was so perfectly right for the woods that it was like a poem again, and as if he were in the poem himself, Tom found himself playing his part. When she came near he got up from his green couch and knelt on one knee, waving his arm in a gesture that would have dusted the ground if he had had a plumed hat. "Welcome, lady," he said, and was surprised at the firmness of his voice. No hint of the embarrassing squeaks that he dreaded and Doris laughed at. "Are you the queen of this place?"

The girl had stopped a few feet away. She was slim and short, not much above his nose, and her eyes had green lights in them. Her mouth was grave. "What makes you think so?" Though lower, her voice was as silvery as the bells on her wrist.

"You walk as though you owned it."

She smiled beautifully. "Then I am the queen. And who are you?"

"The shepherd boy."

"Youngest of three brothers?"

"Unfortunately, the older of two."

"You're handsome enough to be the youngest. I forgive you."

She stepped forward and held out her hand, palm downward. Still in a dream, Tom put it to his lips, like someone in a movie. Its gentle pressure brought him to his feet, and the girl was looking up at him almost arrogantly.

"Will you stop with my hand? The last shepherd boy was braver."

"What man dares, I dare." Heaven knew where that line came to him from.

With his heart pounding, Tom took her by the shoulders and kissed her. He met the pressure of her lips as long as he dared, as long as the script for the scene could possibly call for. When he let go, she stepped back and looked at him contemplatively.

"You kiss well," she said, almost in surprise.

Tom felt his cheeks getting red. The long practice with Doris now seemed a waste of time. "How many shepherd boys have there been?" he countered and felt his voice rise dangerously high.

The girl laughed. "You're the first to find the point here."

"Is there any king of the point?"

"No king either. You know what it means to kiss the fairy queen, though."

"Death?" Tom tensed for some surprise.

"Not quite so bad. But you have to serve her seven years, come weal or woe."

"Such service would be an honor."

"You talk by the book," she said. Again his face burned, and she must have seen it, for she hurried on. "What's your name, shepherd?"

"Tom Reimer."

"Then harp and carp, Thomas, harp and carp along with me. Till I've shown you all my ain countree."

She held out her hand, but he hesitated. "Harp and carp?"

"Don't ask me what it means. It's a line from some ballad. A fragment. Come on."

She took his hand and led him off over the moss. They climbed heaps of carpeted boulders and peered at the hollows beneath them. She showed him a little amphitheater in the greenness and a brook that ran into the sea through a miniature canyon in the rocks that they leaped across. There was a tiny beach at the brook's mouth, and when they turned up stream they came to an open glade in which stood a gnarled old apple tree with Red Astrakhans almost ripe on it. The girl's name was Fay Morgan, and she lived in a house beyond the point. Her father owned it. The air was warm, and the wind stirred the branches of the pines way above them, and far above the branches there were billowy white clouds.

It was late when Tom looked at his watch. Fay saw the glance. "You're the shepherd boy, not Cinderella," she said. "Stay in character."

"Even shepherd boys have stomachs. And families," he added gloomily. "How do I get back to the world?"

He had been sitting quietly with her hand in his on the side of the rugged glen where the brook welled up from a spring. She led him to the top of the knoll behind them, where the moss gave way to dry grass and juniper.

"There are three ways. All maddeningly symbolical, probably." She pointed first to the field of daisies and devil's paintbrush that shimmered white and red at the edge of the trees a few yards away, on the far side of the point from town. "You can cross the field to the road and have easy walking, but it's pretty far. The shortest way is the way you came, if you don't mind scraping over rocks and getting scratched by the brush. And there's the third way, winding through that patch of ferns and across the marsh. It won't develop your character, but maybe it's the prettiest."

Tom hesitated, not knowing quite what she meant. "Do you prefer prettiness to character?"

She planted herself in front of him provocatively. "Do I look like the wholesome type?"

She must be what books called a coquette. If he couldn't picture his family's questions if he came late to lunch—"I'll take the middle path," he said. "Do you come to the point often?"

"I told you I was queen of this country. And I hold you in my thrall. Remember?"

He walked through the bed of ferns, sweet-smelling and dry against his legs on the hillside, sweet and cool on the edge of the salt marsh that guarded this place of magic from the world. Almost imperceptible, the path twisted across it on some thread of firmer ground and brought him out on the highway near the village. "Held him in thrall." Where did she get words like that? He knew them, but he didn't use them. She must be older than he was; he hoped not too much. Maybe she was playing with him, but she was wonderful, and it was fun to play. And in the stories the shepherd boys married the queens and lived happily forever after.

Eddie was proudly exhibiting four cunners, the fruit of his morning toil. "Bet you didn't get anything as good," he jeered.

"Nothing but granite." You kept quiet about the fairy queen. It was hard enough to let necessary information about dates with Doris out for family discussion.

They had come to Huntly Harbor for two weeks, and one had gone. Only seven days for Fay before he'd have to go back to town. Yet he was due to serve her seven years. Were the days like the days in the Bible, just symbols? And what came at the end of them? Back to school and Doris? Tom shut himself up that afternoon to answer her letter, but he couldn't think of much to say. If he told her about the point, she'd think it was a good place to bring the gang for a wienie roast.

Eldon Point it was called, he found out from the hotel woman. He went there again the next morning, taking the path through the marsh. He didn't like being so exposed to view, but there was no one in sight, and he whistled as he walked, some violin thing he'd heard that kissed you and tore your heart out at the same time. He found his way back to the bank where he'd dozed off yesterday, but today he kept alert, and soon he heard the silver bells again. Fay was coming over the moss, in white shorts this time, but with a green scarf holding back her hair. He ran to kneel before her, and she laughed and raised him up, and they kissed again. She'd brought her bathing suit, and they changed in a hollow and went swimming from the little beach, racing out to an orange lobster float and back. She beat him the first time, but then he poured his strength into his best crawl and overtook her twice running, till she called it quits. They lay on the warm sand and talked about movies, and boats in the harbor, and books they'd read when they were kids, and even religion and politics. Once or twice they talked about love, but neither mentioned anything about it but hearsay, and tacitly they shied away from it. Fay was beautiful stretched out on the gray sand.

"Tomorrow?" Tom asked when he got up to go.

"Tomorrow."

It was a glorious week, even though it was hard to invent excuses to the family for going off by himself every day. Tom could see his father was a little hurt, and it hurt him when he thought of it, but it couldn't be helped. He invented a much greater interest in rocks than he felt, and chipped off a few very ordinary samples every day on his way back to the hotel. Lucky his family didn't know anything about minerals. Eddie dismissed his absence as good riddance, and his mother took it all with her usual serene calm.

But Fay. Fay was wonderful. They swam and loafed in the sun and played hide-and-seek, stalking each other through the woods like young animals. It was fun to track her by footprints in the moss before the spongy stuff slowly rubbed them out. One day Tom brought sandwiches from the hotel, and they ate by the brook and had the whole day together. One time when they were swimming, she splashed him, and he ducked her, and she came up in his arms spluttering and clinging to him while he kissed her wet face a lot less formally than on their daily meetings. They kissed a lot after that.

One day it rained, and Fay brought a book of poems, which they read huddled in one of the dank little caves among the boulders. He'd had some of the poems in school, but they made more sense when Fay read them. Some of them even made sense when he read them. Tom wondered if he was in love with her. He supposed he was, because she was wonderful and he wanted to be with her all the time, and he'd never felt that way with Doris or anybody else, but it hurt because there didn't seem to be any future for it, and at seventeen there isn't really anything you can do about love except make plans and hope. Love then is only a heartfelt longing for a reality that's vague and distant.

The day of their seventh meeting they sat on the highest part of the shore, throwing pebbles at a lobster float bobbing in the green water.

"You're whipping those stones over as if you had a personal grudge against the poor thing," said Fay. "Why so quiet, Thomas?"

"I've got to go home tomorrow afternoon." Home would be exile.

Fay tossed a stone up and down in her hand and then pitched it into the water without aim. "Where is home?"

"Earlstown. Ever hear of it?"

"Occasionally. I've been going to college at Radnor."

Tom's throat felt dry. "What are you now?"

"A senior."

There it was. He'd known it all along and tried to ignore it. Radnor was a smooth place, too, and beside it high-school kids were—kids. Radnor was near home, and he knew girls who went there.

Fay's hand was on his. "We still have a day."

One day as a gift from the queen. He looked to see if she was laughing at him, but there were no signs. Maybe—maybe better not think of it. He heard himself talking again, one part of him listening to another.

"There are twenty-four hours in a day. What's the point like at night?"

"Still magic. Do you want to find out? We could dance around the apple tree in the moonlight while the ghosts try to look like shreds of fog."

One evening at least. Tom thought about it at lunch, rehearsing lines of burning eloquence he knew he'd never be able to deliver. It was Eddie who was eloquent.

"By the way, I found out where Tom's been going," he mumbled as he attacked his apple pie. "He's got a girl. A regular queen."

"You little sneak!" The word sounded dirty as Eddie used it, something to be wiped away.

"She's old, though," Eddie went on. "Must be as old as Aunt Marion. I saw them this morning."

"Marion's only twenty-one," said Mr. Reimer.

"Old enough."

For Tom it was. He could see the significance sink into his parents, see the moment of alarm in their eyes, the determination to be tactful and understanding, just what the columns in the papers for the parents of adolescents advised. They wouldn't use the words "crush" or "puppy love," but they'd be thinking them.

They followed the strategy he expected. "I was in love with one of my teachers once," his mother was saying. "I cried for two days when he married the school secretary."

"Why didn't you tell us you'd found a girl, Tom?" asked his father. "You could have had the car any time, if you'd wanted."

Policy 16-B according to Doctor Morton. Keep it out in the open where you can see what's going on, gain the child's confidence.

"Thanks, dad, but everything here is walkable. No need to bother you."

They meant well, but he felt naked in front of them. There were things you had to do alone. He parried their questions and they let the subject drop. The affair would be all over tomorrow anyway, they'd be thinking with relief. No danger of entanglement. No need to interfere to break it up. Eddie, though. The brat must have trailed him through the marsh and hidden in the scrub. Fortunately, he couldn't have been close enough to hear anything. Tom took him aside and gave him a lecture on brotherly duties, backed up by a few threats and the promise of a share of his next week's allowance for good behavior. It was all right for Eddie to spy on him and Doris with the gang around, but privacy had to be respected.

To add to the day's problems there was a letter from Doris scolding him for not having written her something passionate she could show to her friend, Judy Adams. He supposed when he got back he'd be dependent on Doris for dates again, unless he wanted the trouble of digging up somebody new, so he scribbled down a few empty phrases to comply. Plague take Doris! All she wanted him for was a jewel in her glittering entourage or whatever she wanted to call it.

Tom pleaded weariness and went to his room early, but he pulled his clothes on again and sneaked downstairs as soon as he was sure Eddie was asleep in the other bed. His parents wouldn't approve of a moonlight rendezvous, so he hadn't mentioned it to them. They wouldn't forbid it; they'd just suggest he take Fay to the movies over in Hamilton. Why they'd think a parked car afterward was better than the shore, he didn't know.

The village was deserted. A heavy fog had rolled in, faintly luminous with the moon, and the air was warm and damp and almost opaque. The path through the marsh felt squushy underfoot; the tide must be high.

Fay would be waiting for him, Tom thought. He wondered how

much waiting she would do. Radnor was only twenty miles from Earlstown. They could see each other weekends. Perhaps the folks would even let her stay at the house. He could take her to football games and dances at the club and picnics when the leaves were red. It would be fun to show her off at school in front of Doris and the others. He could even picture himself with her at a prom at Radnor, him in his tux and her in a green gown with a big skirt. It would have to be green. And probably everyone would wonder what cradle she'd robbed. But if she didn't like him, why was she waiting for him this muggy night?

On the point the fog was so thick he could see only a few feet among the trees, but he heard the jingle of silver bells ringing clear against the deep bass of the surf. He groped toward them until he could make out a whiter, denser ghost among the wraiths of fog. Fay's moist hair was against his cheek, her face in the hollow of his neck.

"Oh, Fay, Fay, Fay, I love you!" a husky voice was saying. There. It was said.

"I know," she whispered. "I thought maybe you did."

"Well?"

"You're challenging me to do something about it?"

Tom let go of her, feeling suddenly miserable and defeated. "I suppose so."

Fay took his hand and made him sit down beside her. "What do you want me to do about it, Tom?"

"I don't know. Have dates this fall after we go back. Go steady, perhaps. What more can we do?"

He felt rather than saw the trouble of her silence. "I was afraid it might turn out like this," she said slowly. "I suppose I should have done something to stop it, but it was too late. You know I'm older than you are, don't you, Tom?"

"Never mind telling me how much I'm just a kid."

"It's my fault. If you were just a kid, there'd be no problem. You were cute, and fun to play with, and this point is a never-never land."

"Never, never. That's it."

"Let me go on. I should have known it might stop being play for you, and that we'd get back into the world. Playing here is the middle path. I guess I owe you something, Tom. Nobody has a right to stir up someone else's emotions and do nothing about it. If you want me to, I'll be your girl, steady or any time you need me."

"What's the Princeton guy with the red convertible going to say about that?"

"There isn't any king. I told you that before. Just a few also-rans."

35

"What are you trying to do? Force me to be noble and kiss you good-bye?"

He felt her stiffen. "That would be pretty cheap."

"Yeah, I suppose it would."

"I'm not in love with you, Tom, but you're awfully nice. Tell me what you want and I'll do it. Think it over and tell me tomorrow, if you'd rather. There are problems, but we can get around them."

He was holding her close and kissing her again, and somewhere that triumphant violin music was tearing at him. It made a chill go down his back, though the night was as warm and soft as Fay's arms. It seemed like a long time before he needed to talk again. "Shall we dance around the apple tree?"

"Let's have a swim first. There are good waves."

They changed in the dripping shadows, and the moss was like a wet sponge under their bare feet. They had to cross the brook to come to the beach, and the high tide was surging wave after wave, up through the little canyon. Fay jumped across, but as Tom followed, his foot slipped on the spray-wet rock and he fell into the cleft. An incoming wave swept over him and pounded him against the rough stones and tried to drag him back to sea as he clung gasping to the ledge. In a moment Fay was climbing down to help him, and a new wave tore at her. It knocked her legs from under her, but she was able to keep her grip. When it was gone, she reached him a hand and they dragged themselves back out of reach and lay panting on the ground.

"Thanks. If you'd waited a minute, you'd have had no problems." Tom sat up gingerly, waiting for the pain in his bones to subside. Fay had a dark smudge on the front of her bathing suit. He cried out in alarm.

"It's from you, I think." She was sitting up and putting gentle fingers to his ribs.

He looked down and discovered a big raw place on his chest, and his knees were scraped and sore. Fay's legs showed dark scratches too. He moved his own leg and was relieved to find it respond.

"Are you all right?"

"I guess so." She rubbed her bleeding leg against his. "This would be a good time to make you my blood brother if you wanted."

He moved his leg away. "I'm holding out for something better."

Wearily they limped back up the brook to cross it at an easier place and wash their hurts in fresh water. Somehow there seemed little to say. They put on their clothes again and said good night. It took a long time. Fay's hair was wet and stringy, but her eyes caught the glimmer of the fog, and he loved her.

In the morning Tom waited till Eddie had gone downstairs before getting up and swabbing his scrapes with iodine again. It stung, and he felt stiff and sore when he moved. It was too bad he hadn't been able to rescue Fay, instead of the other way around. It didn't fit the pattern of queen and shepherd boy. He tried to hide his stiffness from the family, but he did tell them he had to go and say good-bye to Fay. He thought his mother looked a little relieved. Wait till she saw how things developed. Fay was his for the asking.

But did he want to ask? Everything seemed different this morning. The fog had passed, and the air had a touch of fall to it. There was red on one branch of a maple. Things were changing again.

He thought of the last week with Fay, how he had acknowledged her as queen, how she had shown him the point and read poems to him and pulled him out of the water.

She was waiting for him in the meadow by the apple tree, dressed in green again, with her hair bright in the sun. She held out a red-streaked apple to him. "The first undeniably ripe one of the year."

"No worms?"

"Not on Eldon Point."

They took alternate bites of the tartness that set their teeth prickling, and pitched the core into the brook.

"Do you feel like dancing?"

Tom shook his head. "I've left a trail of gore all the way from the hotel."

"My hero. Lie down and I'll weave you a garland. When do you have to go?"

"After lunch."

"Will I hear from you, Tom?"

"Sometimes, I guess." He didn't know how to put it. "Fay, you're wonderful, and I wish we could stay like this."

"But?"

"There's too much difference. You'd always be the queen and I'd be the shepherd. You teach me things, and you take care of me, but a queen ought to marry a prince."

She put a circlet of daisies on his head. "I could crown you. Or you might be a prince in disguise."

He took the circlet off and turned it over in his hands. "If you crowned me, you'd still be queen, and if I'm in disguise I can't throw it off yet." He dropped the wreath and jumped up. "Oh, darn it, Fay, it was only a game."

She stood looking up at him. "I'm sorry, Tom. But someday you'll grow up, and the difference will be gone. If I'm still here then, you could try coming back."

"Sure. I'll come." He paused and dug at the ground with his foot. "Only listen. Will you come to one dance with me this year?"

She laughed. "Any one you want."

"I'll write to you then. Good-bye, Fay."

"Good-bye, Tom."

He kissed her and then knelt and kissed her hand.

When he turned to go, he didn't look back, but went down to the awkward path along the rocks by which he had first come. Behind him he heard silver bells fading away.

Back at the hotel it was time to pack. He noticed the unmailed letter to Doris lying in his drawer and tore it up. She didn't need him, and he didn't need her any longer. Sometimes a man was better off alone.

THE GEOMETRY
OF LOVE

JOHN CHEEVER

It was one of those rainy late afternoons when the toy department of Woolworth's on Fifth Avenue is full of women who appear to have been taken in adultery and who are now shopping for a present to carry home to their youngest child. On this particular afternoon there were eight or ten of them—comely, fragrant, and well dressed—but with the pained air of women who have recently been undone by some cad in a midtown hotel room and who are now on their way home to the embraces of a tender child. It was Charlie Mallory, walking away from the hardware department, where he had bought a screwdriver, who reached this conclusion. There was no morality involved. He hit on this generalization mostly to give the lassitude of a rainy afternoon some intentness and color. Things were slow at his office. He had spent the time since lunch repairing a filing cabinet. Thus the screwdriver. Having settled on this conjecture, he looked more closely into the faces of the women and seemed to find there some affirmation of his fantasy. What but the engorgements and chagrins of adultery could have left them all looking so spiritual, so tearful? Why should they sigh so deeply as they fingered the playthings of innocence? One of the women wore a fur coat that looked like a coat he had bought his wife, Mathilda, for Christmas. Looking more closely, he saw that it was not only Mathilda's coat, it was Mathilda. "Why, Mathilda," he cried, "what in the world are you doing here?"

She raised her head from the wooden duck she had been studying.

Slowly, slowly, the look of chagrin on her face shaded into anger and scorn. "I detest being spied upon," she said. Her voice was strong, and the other women shoppers looked up, ready for anything.

Mallory was at a loss. "But I'm not spying on you, darling," he said. "I only——"

"I can't think of anything more despicable," she said, "than following people through the streets." Her mien and her voice were operatic, and her audience was attentive and rapidly being enlarged by shoppers from the hardware and garden-furniture sections. "To hound an innocent woman through the streets is the lowest, sickest, and most vile of occupations."

"But, darling, I just happened to be here."

Her laughter was pitiless. "You just happened to be hanging around the toy department at Woolworth's? Do you expect me to believe that?"

"I was in the hardware department," he said, "but it doesn't really matter. Why don't we have a drink together and take an early train?"

"I wouldn't drink or travel with a spy," she said. "I am going to leave this store now, and if you follow or harass me in any way, I shall have you arrested by the police and thrown into jail." She picked up and paid for the wooden duck and regally ascended the stairs. Mallory waited a few minutes and then walked back to his office.

Mallory was a free-lance engineer, and his office was empty that afternoon—his secretary had gone to Capri. The telephone-answering service had no messages for him. There was no mail. He was alone. He seemed not so much unhappy as stunned. It was not that he had lost his sense of reality but that the reality he observed had lost its fitness and symmetry. How could he apply reason to the slapstick encounter in Woolworth's, and yet how could he settle for unreason? Forgetfulness was a course of action he had tried before, but he could not forget Mathilda's ringing voice and the bizarre scenery of the toy department. Dramatic misunderstandings with Mathilda were common, and he usually tackled them willingly, trying to decipher the chain of contingencies that had detonated the scene. This afternoon he was discouraged. The encounter seemed to resist diagnosis. What could he do? Should he consult a psychiatrist, a marriage counselor, a minister? Should he jump out of the window? He went to the window with this in mind.

It was still overcast and rainy, but not yet dark. Traffic was slow. He watched below him as a station wagon passed, then a convertible, a moving van, and a small truck advertising Euclid's Dry Cleaning and Dyeing. The great name reminded him of the right-angled triangle, the principles of geometric analysis, and the doctrine of proportion for both commensurables and incommensurables. What he needed was a new form of ratiocination, and Euclid might do. If he could make a geometric analysis of his problems, mightn't he solve them, or at least create an atmosphere of solution? He got a slide rule and took the simple theorem that if two sides of a triangle are equal, the angles opposite these sides are equal; and the converse theorem that if two angles of a triangle are equal, the sides opposite them will be equal. He drew a line to represent Mathilda and what he knew about her to be relevant. The base of the triangle would be his two children, Randy and Priscilla. He, of course, would make up the third side. The most critical element in Mathilda's line—that which would threaten to make her angle unequal to Randy and Priscilla's— was the fact that she had recently taken a phantom lover.

This was a common imposture among the housewives of Remsen Park, where they lived. Once or twice a week, Mathilda would dress in her best, put on some French perfume and a fur coat, and take a late-morning train to the city. She sometimes lunched with a friend, but she lunched more often alone in one of those French restaurants in the Sixties that accommodate single women. She usually drank a cocktail or had a half-bottle of wine. Her intention was to appear dissipated, mysterious—a victim of love's bitter riddle—but should a stranger give her the eye, she would go into a paroxysm of shyness, recalling, with something like panic, her lovely home, her fresh-faced children, and the begonias in her flower bed. In the afternoon, she went either to a matinee or a foreign movie. She preferred strenuous themes that would leave her emotionally exhausted—or, as she put it to herself, "emptied." Coming home on a late train, she would appear peaceful and sad. She often wept while she cooked the supper, and if Mallory asked what her trouble was, she would merely sigh. He was briefly suspicious, but walking up Madison Avenue one afternoon he saw her, in her furs, eating a sandwich at a lunch counter, and concluded that the pupils of her eyes were dilated not by amorousness but by the darkness of a movie theater. It was a harmless and a common imposture, and might even, with some forced charity, be thought of as useful.

The line formed by these elements, then, made an angle with the line representing his children, and the single fact *here* was that he loved them. He loved them! No amount of ignominy or venom could make parting from them imaginable. As he thought of them, they seemed to be the furniture of his soul, its lintel and rooftree.

The line representing himself, he knew, would be most prone to miscalculations. He thought himself candid, healthy, and knowledgeable (who else could remember so much Euclid?), but waking in the morning, feeling useful and innocent, he had only to speak to Mathilda to find his usefulness and his innocence squandered. Why should his ingenuous commitments to life seem to harass the best of him? Why should he, wandering through the toy department, be calumniated as a Peeping Tom? His triangle might give him the answer, he thought, and in a sense it did. The sides of the triangle, determined by the relevant information, were equal, as were the angles opposite these sides. Suddenly he felt much less bewildered, happier, more hopeful and magnanimous. He thought, as one does two or three times a year, that he was beginning a new life.

Going home on the train, he wondered if he could make a geometrical analogy for the boredom of a commuters' local, the stupidities in the evening paper, the rush to the parking lot. Mathilda was in the small dining room, setting the table, when he returned. Her opening gun was meant to be disabling. "Pinkerton fink," she said. "Gumshoe." While he heard her words, he heard them without anger, anxiety or frustration. They seemed to fall short of where he stood. How calm he felt, how happy. Even Mathilda's angularity seemed touching and lovable; this wayward child in the family of man. "Why do you look so happy?" his children asked. "Why do you look so happy, Daddy?" Presently, almost everyone would say the same. "How Mallory has changed. How well Mallory looks. Lucky Mallory!"

The next night, Mallory found a geometry text in the attic and refreshed his knowledge. The study of Euclid put him into a compassionate and tranquil frame of mind, and illuminated, among other things, that his thinking and feeling had recently been crippled by confusion and despair. He knew that what he thought of as his discovery could be an illusion, but the practical advantages remained his. He felt much better. He felt that he had corrected the distance between his reality and those realities that pounded at his spirit. He might not, had he possessed any philosophy or religion, have needed geometry, but the religious observances in his neighborhood seemed to him boring and threadbare, and he had no disposition for philosophy. Geometry served him beautifully for the metaphysics of understood pain. The principal advantage was that he could regard, once he had put them into linear terms, Mathilda's moods and discontents with ardor and compassion. He was not a victor, but he was wonderfully safe from being victimized. As he continued with his study and his practice, he discovered that the rudenesses of headwaiters, the damp souls of clerks, and the scurrilities of traffic policemen could not touch his tranquility, and that these oppressors, in turn, sensing his strength, were less rude, damp, and scurrilous. He was able to carry the conviction of innocence, with which he woke each morning, well into the day. He thought of writing a book about his discovery: *Euclidean Emotion: The Geometry of Sentiment.*

At about this time he had to go to Chicago. It was an overcast day, and he took the train. Waking a little after dawn, all usefulness and innocence, he looked out the window of his bedroom at a coffin factory, used-car dumps, shanties, weedy playing fields, pigs fattening on acorns, and in the distance the monumental gloom of Gary. The tedious and melancholy scene had the power over his spirit of a show of human stupidity. He had never applied his theorem to landscapes, but he discovered that, by translating the components of the moment into a parallelogram, he was able to put the discouraging countryside away from him until it seemed harmless, practical, and even charming. He ate a hearty breakfast and did a good day's work. It was a day that needed no geometry. One of his associates in Chicago asked him to dinner. It was an invitation that he felt he could not refuse, and he showed up at half-past six at a little brick house in a part of the city with which he was unfamiliar. Even before the door opened, he felt that he was going to need Euclid.

His hostess, when she opened the door, had been crying. She held a drink in her hand. "He's in the cellar," she sobbed, and went into a small living room without telling Mallory where the cellar was or how to get there. He followed her into the living room. She had dropped to her hands and knees, and was tying a tag to the leg of a chair. Most of the furniture, Mallory noticed, was tagged. The tags were printed: Chicago Storage Warehouse. Below this she had written: "Property of Helen Fells McGowen." McGowen was his friend's name. "I'm not going to leave the s.o.b. a thing," she sobbed. "Not a stick."

"Hi, Mallory," said McGowen, coming through the kitchen. "Don't pay any attention to her. Once or twice a year she gets sore and puts tags on all the furniture, and claims she's going to put it in storage and take a furnished room and work at Marshall Field's."

"You don't know *anything*," she said.

"What's new?" McGowen asked.

"Lois Mitchell just telephoned. Harry got drunk and put the Barbie doll in the blender."

"Is she coming over?"

"Of course."

The doorbell rang. A disheveled woman with wet cheeks came in. "Oh, it was awful," she said. "The children were watching. It was their Barbie doll and they loved it. I wouldn't have minded so much if the children hadn't been watching."

"Let's get out of here," McGowen said, turning back to the kitchen. Mallory followed him through the kitchen, where there were no signs of dinner, down some stairs into a cellar furnished with a Ping-Pong table, a television set and a bar. He got Mallory a drink. "You see, Helen used to be rich," McGowen said. "It's one of her difficulties. She came from very rich people. Her father had a chain of Laundromats that reached from here to Denver. He introduced live entertainment in Laundromats. Folk singers. Combos. Then the Musicians' Union ganged up on him, and he lost the whole thing overnight. And she knows that I fool around but if I wasn't promiscuous, Mallory, I wouldn't be true to myself. I mean, I used to make out with that Mitchell dame upstairs. The one with the Barbie doll. She's great. You want her, I can fix it up. She'll do anything for me. I usually give her a little something. Ten bucks or a bottle of whiskey. One Christmas I gave her a bracelet. You see, her husband has this suicide thing. He keeps taking sleeping pills, but they always pump him out in time. Once, he tried to hang himself——"

"I've got to go," Mallory said.

"Stick around, stick around," McGowen said. "Let me sweeten your drink."

"I've really got to go," Mallory said. "I've got a lot of work to do."

"But you haven't had anything to eat," McGowen said. "Stick around and I'll heat up some curry."

"There isn't time," Mallory said. "I've got a lot to do." He went upstairs without saying good-bye. Mrs. Mitchell had gone, but his hostess was still tying tags onto the furniture. He let himself out and took a cab back to his hotel.

He got out his slide rule and, working on the relation between the volume of a cone and that of its circumscribed prism, tried to put Mrs. McGowen's drunkenness and the destiny of the Mitchells' Barbie doll into linear terms. Oh, Euclid, be with me now! What did Mallory want? He wanted radiance, beauty, and order, no less; he wanted to rationalize the image of Mr. Mitchell, hanging by the neck. Was Mallory's passionate detestation of squalor fastidious and unmanly? Was he wrong to look for definitions of good and evil, to believe in the inalienable power of remorse, the beauty of shame? There was a vast number of imponderables in the picture, but he tried to hold his equation to the facts of the evening, and this occupied him until past midnight, when he went to sleep. He slept well.

The Chicago trip had been a disaster as far as the McGowens went, but financially it had been profitable, and the Mallorys decided to take a trip, as they usually did whenever they were flush. They flew to Italy and stayed in a small hotel near Sperlonga where they had stayed before. Mallory was very happy and needed no Euclid for the ten days they spent on the coast. They went to Rome before flying home and, on their last day, went to the Piazza del Popolo for lunch. They ordered lobster, and were laughing, drinking, and cracking shells with their teeth when Mathilda became melancholy. She let out a sob, and Mallory realized that he was going to need Euclid.

Now Mathilda was moody, but that afternoon seemed to promise Mallory that he might, by way of groundwork and geometry, isolate the components of her moodiness. The restaurant seemed to present a splendid field for investigation. The place was fragrant and orderly. The other diners were decent Italians, all of them strangers, and he didn't imagine they had it in their power to make her as miserable as she plainly was. She had enjoyed her lobster. The linen was white, the silver polished, the waiter civil. Mallory examined the place—the flowers, the piles of fruit, the traffic in the square outside the window—and he could find in all of this no source for the sorrow and bitterness in her face. "Would you like an ice or some fruit?" he asked.

"If I want anything, I'll order it myself," she said, and she did. She summoned the waiter, ordered an ice and some coffee for herself, throwing Mallory a dark look. When Mallory had paid the check, he asked her if she wanted a cab. "What a stupid idea," she said, frowning with disgust, as if he had suggested squandering their savings account or putting their children on the stage.

They walked back to their hotel, Indian file. The light was brilliant, the heat was intense, and it seemed as if the streets of Rome had always been hot and would always be, world without end. Was it the heat that had changed her humor? "Does the heat bother you, dear?" he asked, and she turned and said, "You make me sick." He left her in the hotel lobby and went to a cafe.

He worked out his problems with a slide rule on the back of a menu. When he returned to the hotel, she had gone out, but she came in at seven and began to cry as soon as she entered the room. The afternoon's geometry had proved to him that her happiness, as well as his and that of his children, suffered from some capricious, unfathomable, and submarine course of emotion that wound mysteriously through her nature, erupting with turbulence at intervals that had no regularity and no discernible cause. "I'm sorry, my darling," he said, "What is the matter?"

"No one in this city understands English," she said, "absolutely no one. I got lost and I must have asked fifteen people the way back to the hotel, but no one understood me." She went into the bathroom and slammed the door, and he sat at the window—calm and happy—watching the traverse of a cloud shaped exactly like a cloud, and then the appearance of that brassy light that sometimes fills up the skies of Rome just before dark.

Mallory had to go back to Chicago a few days after they returned from Italy. He finished his business in a day—he avoided McGowen— and got the four o'clock train. At about four-thirty he went up to the club car for a drink, and seeing the mass of Gary in the distance, repeated that theorem that had corrected the angle of his relationship to the Indiana landscape. He ordered a drink and looked out of the window at Gary. There was nothing to be seen. He had, through some miscalculation, not only rendered Gary powerless; he had lost Gary. There was no rain, no fog, no sudden dark to account for the fact that, to his eyes, the windows of the club car were vacant. Indiana had disappeared. He turned to a woman on his left and asked, "That's Gary, isn't it?"

"Sure," she said. "What's the matter? Can't you see?"

An isosceles triangle took the sting out of her remark, but there was no trace of any of the other towns that followed. He went back to his bedroom, a lonely and a frightened man. He buried his face in his hands, and, when he raised it, he could clearly see the lights of the grade crossings and the little towns, but he had never applied his geometry to these.

It was perhaps a week later that Mallory was taken sick. His secretary—she had returned from Capri—found him unconscious on the floor of the office. She called an ambulance. He was operated on and listed as in critical condition. It was ten days after his operation before he could have a visitor, and the first, of course, was Mathilda. He had lost ten inches of his intestinal tract, and there were tubes attached to both his arms. "Why, you're looking marvelous," Mathilda exclaimed, turning the look of shock and dismay on her face inward and settling for an expression of absentmindedness. "And it's such a pleasant room. Those yellow walls. If you have to be sick, I guess it's best to be sick in New York. Remember that awful country hospital where I had the children?" She came to rest, not in a chair, but on the windowsill. He reminded himself that he had never known a love that could quite anneal the divisive power of pain; that could bridge the distance between the quick and the infirm. "Everything at the house is fine and dandy," she said. "Nobody seems to miss you."

Never having been gravely ill before, he had no way of anticipating the poverty of her gifts as a nurse. She seemed to resent the fact that he was ill, but her resentment was, he thought, a clumsy expression of love. She had never been adroit at concealment, and she could not conceal the fact that she considered his collapse to be selfish. "You're so lucky," she said. "I mean you're so lucky it happened in New York. You have the best doctors and the best nurses, and this must be one of the best hospitals in the world. You've nothing to worry about, really. Everything's done for you. I just wish that once in my life I could get into bed for a week or two and be waited on."

It was his Mathilda speaking, his beloved Mathilda, unsparing of herself in displaying that angularity, that legitimate self-interest that no force of love could reason or soften. This was she, and he appreciated the absence of sentimentality with which she appeared. A nurse came in with a bowl of clear soup on a tray. She spread a napkin under his chin and prepared to feed him, since he could not move his arms. "Oh, let me do it, let me do it," Mathilda said. "It's the least I can do." It was the first hint of the fact that she was in any way involved in what was, in spite of the yellow walls, a tragic scene. She took the bowl of soup and the spoon from the nurse. "Oh, how good that smells," she said. "I have half a mind to eat it myself. Hospital food is supposed to be dreadful, but this place seems to be an exception." She held a spoonful of the broth up to his lips and then, through no fault of her own, spilled the bowl of broth over his chest and bedclothes.

She rang for the nurse and then vigorously rubbed at a spot on her skirt. When the nurse began the lengthy and complicated business of changing his bed linen, Mathilda looked at her watch and saw that it was time to go. "I'll stop in tomorrow," she said. "I'll tell the children how well you look."

It was his Mathilda, and this much he understood, but when she had gone he realized that understanding might not get him through another such visit. He definitely felt that the convalescence of his guts had suffered a setback. She might even hasten his death. When the nurse had finished changing him and had fed him a second bowl of soup, he asked her to get the slide rule and notebook out of the pocket of his suit. He worked out a simple, geometrical analogy between his love for Mathilda and his fear of death.

It seemed to work. When Mathilda came at eleven the next day, he could hear her and see her, but she had lost the power to confuse. He had corrected her angle. She was dressed for her phantom lover and she went on about how well he looked and how lucky he was. She did point out that he needed a shave. When she had left, he asked the nurse if he could have a barber. She explained that the barber came only on Wednesdays and Fridays, and that the male nurses were all out on strike. She brought him a mirror, a razor, and some soap, and he saw his face then for the first time since his collapse. His emaciation forced him back to geometry, and he tried to equate the voracity of his appetite, the boundlessness of his hopes, and the frailty of his carcass. He reasoned carefully, since he knew that a miscalculation, such as he had made for Gary, would end those events that had begun when Euclid's Dry Cleaning and Dyeing truck had passed under his window. Mathilda went from the hospital to a restaurant and then to a movie, and it was the cleaning woman who told her, when she got home, that he had passed away.

CALCULATING WOMAN

PHYLLIS DUGANNE

This manuscript which they were reading in the high-ceilinged room overlooking Manhattan's East River would be the sixteenth play in which Linda Merwin and Harold Joyce had acted together, the seventh written for them by Albert Hutchinson. Their first joint appearance, in 1935, had not had equal billing; Linda was already a star, and Hal an unknown young actor. He was four years younger than she, though gossip usually increased the difference.

How old is she now? She must be crowding sixty . . . Linda Merwin was forty-seven; she had been on the stage, in the public eye for thirty years.

She was reading aloud, her lovely cadenced voice rising and falling, deepening and becoming light as gossamer—her lovely, celebrated voice.

"I think Bertie's done it again," Hal said, when she had finished. "A slight mishmash of Midnight and Dark Hour, but why not?"

"Why not, indeed?" she murmured. "If it's good once, it's better the umpteenth time." She pretended to read, " 'Albert Hutchinson's latest vehicle for the Joyces is witty and trenchant, as always.' . . . Who'll we get to play Iris, Hal? Polly couldn't do it."

"Um," he said. "She wouldn't be very good, would she? Needs someone really young."

"And with fire," said Linda. "Me, at twenty."

It was Linda who selected Clare Copeland from a dozen actresses who read the part. She was young, and she had the fire. Fire of ambition, of avidity for everything life might offer, and fire of talent.

"She isn't very pretty," Hal commented.

"No," agreed his wife. "She's merely beautiful." He made a face, and she added, "You wait and see. The girl has bones and the kind of beauty that comes from within. She can act beauty. She could play Helen and make the audience believe in the Trojan War."

A week later, Hal said, "You were right about Clare, Linda. I went over that second-act scene with her again this morning. She was wearing baggy slacks and a quite dreadful striped shirt, and suddenly—remember where she crosses and looks out the window?—she was radiant."

Linda Merwin nodded her golden head.

The part of Iris was a small one—in Albert Hutchinson's plays for the Joyces, all the parts except their own were small—and one afternoon when Bertie dropped in to watch rehearsal, Linda said, "Why couldn't you switch some of Margaret's lines to Iris, Bertie? That rainy-day speech, for instance."

Clare Copeland's smoky agate eyes flashed to the face of the leading lady. "That's most awfully generous of you, Miss Merwin."

Linda echoed, "Generous? I think it will improve the play. . . . Do you agree, Bertie?"

Three days before opening night, Linda came into the theater where they rehearsed to see if she had left her handbag. No rehearsal was scheduled for that hour, but on the dusty, empty stage, with heating pipes and ropes and a whitewashed brick wall for scenery, Harold Joyce and Clare Copeland were standing. Hal was speaking his own lines from the play; Clare was speaking Linda's.

She checked her first impulse to call out, "What goes on?" and, standing in the shadows, became completely absorbed in listening to them. Clare was in her customary slacks, though today she wore a boy's pale pink shirt, crisp and becoming to her pallor. Hal, in his well-tailored English clothes, looked even handsomer than usual; his black hair seemed thicker and more lustrous, his lashes thick and dark about his gray eyes.

" 'Kiss and make up?' " he said the familiar line, and Linda watched, and admired, Clare's hesitant, then jubilant, response to the question, and to the kiss. *I don't do it any better myself*, thought Linda, and then, no longer audience, but wife, thought, *Why, that little hussy is kissing my husband.*

Hal said, "Damn good, Clare," and Linda, in the voice that did not need to be raised to command attention, said, "Very damn good."

She thought that Hal looked uncomfortable.

Clare said, "Thank you, Miss Merwin."

Hal met Linda's eyes. "This young woman has learned your entire part," he explained. "I told her that you hadn't had an understudy in years, but she's a glutton for punishment."

"Understudies make me nervous," said Linda, smiling at Clare. "They always look at one with that pleading why-don't-you-drop-dead-or-something expression."

Clare laughed. "I know. I've been an understudy. Did you really think that I was adequate, Miss Merwin?"

"I'd grant you more than that loathsome adjective," Linda answered. "You're too young for the part, of course." She was still smiling as she added, "Experience keeps me from being too old for it."

No one, including the cast and the critics, was surprised by the applause on opening night. After five curtain calls, Linda took Clare's hand and led her on stage to take her bow between the Joyces. She had made the most of her part, as she made the most of everything within her reach. Inclining her head to smile at the young actress, Linda was startled and almost repelled. Clare's face, to the audience, was properly grateful and gracious, but her extraordinary agate eyes had an unpleasant glitter; her nostrils quivered like the nostrils of a—not frightened, but dangerous horse.

The Joyces did not wait up to read their reviews. At ten-o'clock breakfast, Hal picked up the top from a stack of newspapers, turned to the theater page.

"Little Clare must be feeling happy."

"Read it," said Linda.

" 'A young woman named Clare Copeland brings reality and richness to a minor role,' " he read. " 'Her voice has some of the qualities of the great actresses whom she could never have heard, the timbre of Bernhardt, an evanescent huskiness reminiscent of Mrs. Fiske. Miss Copeland, we prophesy, will go far.' "

Linda laughed. "Hal, you look positively fatuous! One would think you were the proud papa." They were sitting side by side on the sofa, and she reached out her hand and patted his knee. "I'm glad for Clare. She deserves it." She waited an instant. "Does it mention us too?"

Hal Joyce did not smile. He read the reviews with the careful enunciation of an actor trying out for a part. They were, as usual, unanimously good.

She continued to sit on the couch, drinking a fourth cup of coffee, while Hal took a shower and dressed. When he emerged from his bedroom, he had his hat on his head.

"I'm lunching out," he said casually.

Linda nodded. "Bertie's coming for tea around four-thirty." What a critic had once called her Bay-of-Naples eyes followed him to the door. Again it seemed to her that Hal was looking unusually handsome.

She stood up and crossed the pale, deep-napped carpet to the Directoire mirror above the bookcases, looked intently at her reflection. "Miss Merwin continues to be the most glamorous woman in the theater today. She can still seduce by the merest turn of her lovely neck; the ripple of a small tendon in her lovely arm suggests infinite rapture." Dennis O'Brien had written that the evening before, pounding his typewriter in a deserted newspaper office. Miss Merwin's mouth was ironic as, before the mirror, she executed a barely perceptible turn of her neck, gestured slightly with her right arm. *Miss Merwin continues to be*—— she thought. *Miss Merwin can still*——

Linda Merwin was prepared for a bad time ahead. In twenty years of marriage to an attractive, temperamental actor, there had been a number of bad times. It was not news when a charming woman fell in love with him; it was still in the man-bites-dog department for Hal to take his brief strolls off the marital reservation seriously. Linda knew that his interest and imagination were roused by Clare Copeland. She knew, far better than he, what steel Clare was made of. But she was utterly unprepared for his bringing Clare home to their apartment to share in the ritual tea which had followed all the opening nights of Bertie's plays.

Bertie had been there nearly an hour when they appeared. When, amended Linda to herself, they made their entrance. She knew her husband too well to study his face. It was Clare Copeland whom she did not know.

She said, "Why, hello," in a voice which registered nothing—not surprise, nor pleasure, nor displeasure. "Hal, take Clare's coat . . . Would you like tea or a drink, Clare?"

"Tea, thank you."

Her voice, Linda noted, sounded a bit more like Mrs. Fiske's than before O'Brien's review.

"Ran into Clare on Fifth Avenue," Hal was saying.

"A nice street," Bertie murmured. "I simply love the way it makes all those divine right angles. Much neater than Broadway."

So Bertie suspected that Hal was lying, too, thought Linda, handing Clare a teacup. Hal had said, weeks ago, that she was not pretty, and Linda had answered, "No. She's merely beautiful." The beauty was there now, deliberately hidden, like a latent fire, like a gift concealed from sight by its wrappings. She was a tall, thin girl who looked awkward, and then surprised and delighted one by her grace. Fencing and ballet lessons, probably, Linda thought. She did not wear makeup, not even lipstick, and again it was the absence of the obvious which arrested people's attention. She was wearing a nondescript tweed suit and a gray sweatshirt—and if, thought Linda, she should lift her face, and say, "Romeo, Romeo," one would see a cap of seed pearls on her brown hair.

Instead, Clare said, "Mr. Hutchinson, someday will you write a play for me?"

The brashness, the enormity of the question momentarily silenced even Bertie.

"Maybe in three years?" the girl went on. "I have a theory about 1960. For almost forty years, now, there's been nothing comparable in art or literature or the theater to the Twenties. I believe that the Sixties——"

"Really," Hal interrupted her. "I resent that, Clare!" He was smiling, but he did resent it.

Clare's grape-skin eyes did not flicker. "I don't mean that there haven't been individual flowerings," she said, easily. "There are three of them in this room. I mean a whole flood of flowerings— O'Neill, Fitzgerald, Picasso——"

Linda poured herself more tea while the vibrant young voice went on. She needed the tea. Clare Copeland might be young enough to be Hal's daughter, but Linda did not underestimate anything about her. She had intelligence; when she wanted it, charm. She had talent and, Linda suspected, complete ruthlessness. Hal, too, was listening, one layer of his mind thinking his own private thoughts—thoughts revealed by the brightness in his eyes, a smile on his lips. Linda had seen that look before, and always before, she had been able to contend with it.

"I must get along," Bertie said. "May I drop you off, somewhere, Miss Copeland?" He looked impishly at Linda, and she knew that he meant: *Off the end of a pier, perhaps?*

The second-night performance played to a packed and enthusiastic audience. For a second time, Linda Merwin observed and weighed Clare's response to applause. Hal often lunched at his club, especially during the first weeks of another successful play, but Linda was not surprised when, at a cocktail party, the club's actor president inquired, "You on a diet or something, Hal? Haven't seen you for ages."

The play had opened in February. One warm April Sunday, Linda telephoned Bertie. "I'm alone, and I hate being alone on a spring afternoon. Want to come and talk to me?"

He arrived carrying a green sheaf of florist's paper.

"Is it enough that Bertie comes, like an idiot, babbling and strewing flowers?" he asked.

"Darling!" said Linda.

He watched her arrange them. "How serious is it?" he asked.

"I don't know," she answered. "He's seeing a lot of her." She smiled unhappily. "Seeing her a lot," she corrected herself. "We both know Hal, Bertie. But this time I'm frightened."

Albert Hutchinson leaned against the pale gray mantel and looked at Linda without smiling. "You had just married Hal when I met you," he said. "Why couldn't I have met you before? Or wouldn't it have made any difference?"

"I love him," she said, in a matter-of-fact voice. The statement was a matter of fact—of fact absolute.

"I'm afraid that you do," he admitted. "I'm fond of the creature myself." The glint returned to his quick brown eyes. "Playwrights make better husbands than actors."

"And almost any women make better wives than actresses," she added. "I wish I'd had children."

"Corny," he told her. "Besides, you have Hal."

Linda Merwin, unlike Clare Copeland, was both pretty and beautiful. She could be, onstage and off, piquant, vivacious or almost classically beautiful. At this moment she was quietly, heartbreakingly lovely, thought Bertie.

"She has a lot to offer him," she said.

"Tripe," Bertie retorted. "I'm ashamed of you, Linda."

"Perhaps I'm selfish," she continued, in the same flat voice, flat as a Kansas prairie. "Let me talk, Bertie. Hal is younger than I."

"Give him a few more years and he won't be."

"Then perhaps I should give him the years that he is," she said.

"Dear heaven!" cried Bertie. "The renunciation scene! Has Hal asked for this?"

"We haven't mentioned it," she said.

"Don't," he advised, and for a few moments they sat in silence. It was difficult for him to imagine how any man, even Hal at forty-three, could fall in love with another woman when he had Linda Merwin. When he had been married to Linda for twenty years——

She was leaning forward, intently rearranging the flowers. Her slender hands, like everything about her, were exquisite. She did not look up when she spoke.

54

"You know, I picked Clare," she said. "When we first read the play, I told Hal that the part needed me—at twenty."

"It would be a lot better played." He laughed. "Linda! Think of a show that could have all the female roles acted by Miss Merwin at assorted ages!"

She shrugged. "Did I tell you that she has learned my part? Every line of it?"

"So could a bright parrot," he retorted.

Linda's gaze was level. "Don't underestimate her, Bertie. I heard her reading with Hal. She's good."

"I think you're losing your mind," he told her impatiently. He jumped up and crossed the room, took a cigarette from a box on the farthest table. Then he turned and faced her. "I've never said this, Linda, because you won't like it. You know it, though, deep down. Hal Joyce is no great actor. He couldn't play any part he's ever had, without you."

Her cheeks flamed. "That's not true, Bertie!"

"For whom, my love, are you blushing, then?" he demanded.

"It isn't true," she repeated stubbornly.

"Linda, you give him all his moments, all his laughs, all his emotions. You know how to make the audience look at him instead of at you." He grinned. "All the audience except me, of course."

"You're being absurd," she told him. "Why don't you make us a nice drink?" Her head turned at the sound of a door opening.

Hal Joyce was carrying a green paper cornucopia, with deep blue delphinium protruding from the top. Bertie turned quickly and disappeared into the butler's pantry.

"How lovely!" Linda said, in a bright, brittle voice. "Bertie brought me flowers too. Spring must be bursting out all over."

"Clare and I took the ferry to Staten Island," said Hal. "Believe it or not, she'd never done it."

"It must have been beautiful today," she murmured. "How was the skyline?"

"Still there," he answered. "Is Bertie making a drink?"

She nodded, and her eyes followed him somberly as he walked to the pantry. Bertie did not make himself a drink. He remembered an engagement and took himself off

"Don't mention it," Bertie had advised her. . . .

"Hal, are you in love with Clare?" Linda asked.

"I don't know," he answered truthfully.

"One usually knows," she said. He was silent, and she asked, "Is she in love with you?"

"She thinks she is."

"No," Linda murmured. Clare Copeland would know. She would probably know all her life what she wanted, and how to get it. Hal said nothing, turning his glass in his hand, swirling the pale liquid. *He's waiting for his cue,* thought Linda suddenly. *He's waiting for me to give him his next line.*

She did not know what the next line should be, and she felt the panic that she would have felt before an audience if she had forgotten.

"Let's go out tonight," she said. "Let's——" Her voice died. "Unless you have an engagement?"

"I have no engagement," he answered.

She put on a new dress that she had never worn, and he noticed it and complimented her. She remembered Clare Copeland's gray sweatshirt, and wondered if she had worn it today to Staten Island. It would not matter; clothes did not really matter. They had dinner at a French restaurant, and people recognized them and lowered their voices: "She's still very beautiful, isn't she?"

"How old do you suppose she is?"

"He's much younger, you know."

Perhaps Bertie had been right. Perhaps she should have pretended that she did not know. She could not think of anything to talk about but Clare. ("Do you want to marry her, Hal darling? . . . . Would you like a young wife and children? . . . Clare would not leave the stage: she could have a family and still go on in the theater.")

"Like to see a movie?" Hal was asking.

"All right," she said.

People did not have to talk, watching a screen. Young people held hands; young heads rested against young shoulders in the darkness.

In the theater, in the darkness, sitting beside Hal, she felt a sudden twinge below her shoulder, sharp as the thrust of a needle. Nerves, she thought; once, long ago, she had had neuritis in that arm. Minutes later, she made a faint, involuntary sound.

"Linda?" Hal's arm brushed the shoulder and she winced. "Are you all right?"

"Of course," she whispered.

The previous neuritis had not kept her from playing. Nothing ever had. Once she had gone through three of Bertie's always-strenuous acts with a temperature of one hundred and two, and played a matinee the next afternoon.

She took three aspirin tablets before she went to bed, three more in the early morning. At five she called Hal.

"I can't seem to sit up!" she said, her eyes wide with pain and fear.

He lifted her gently, piled pillows behind her bright hair, and called the doctor. He brought her breakfast, sitting in an armchair close by her bed, watched her. . . .

Dr. Michael Turner grunted. "You have a bursitis, Linda, and a honey." He was opening his case. "I'm going to give you a couple of shots."

"What kind of shots?" she asked suspiciously.

"One that will stop the bursitis, if we're lucky, and some morphine to let you sleep."

"No morphine," said Linda.

"That," said Doctor Turner, "is what you think."

"We have a performance tonight," she reminded him.

"Perhaps you'll play it, if you do what I say," he retorted. . . . "Phone me when she wakes up, Hal, and I'll come right over."

She awoke around noon, and it did not seem possible, but the pain was worse. Hal was sitting in the pale-blue chair. She struggled to sit up, and again could not. Hal telephoned the doctor.

He arrived in ten minutes, and stood looking down at her.

"Sorry, my dear," he told her. "But curfew is not going to ring tonight."

"Very witty," she muttered. Perspiration stood out in drops on her smooth forehead; her hair was damp about her pale face. "Mike, I've got to be all right by eight-thirty. We can't cancel the performance."

"Yes, we can," Hal contradicted her. "I've already told Howard."

Involuntarily, she attempted to raise herself, and gave a smothered cry. "What did you tell him?"

"That we'd probably have to cancel," he answered calmly. "It isn't your fault, Linda. Howard sent his love."

"I'll be all right," she insisted. "I always am."

"Your left arm, please," said Doctor Turner.

At four o'clock Hal was still beside her bed. "Don't, darling," he said, as she tried to move. "Do you want me to lift you up?"

She nodded. "It's got to go away, Hal. Isn't there anything else that Mike can do?"

"He's doing all he can," he said. "Linda, dear, don't look like that! Everyone misses a performance once."

She closed her eyes. She did not sleep now; she waited. It had to get better, just a little better. She kept on waiting.

"What time is it?" she asked finally.

"Nearly six."

She sighed. "Hal! What about Clare?"

"Clare?" Hal Joyce looked, for an instant, as though he had never heard the name. "Good Lord, Linda, don't think about Clare now!"

"She knows the part," said Linda.

He laughed. "You're not serious?"

"I certainly am," she answered firmly.

"She knows the lines," he said. "But you know that she couldn't play it."

"I think she could," Linda said.

He shook his head. "Honey, you're off your rocker. It must be the morphine. Clare can't play your part."

"She can't wear my costumes, but I bet she'll dig up something just as effective. Let's see. The first act——"

"Mad as a hatter," he interrupted indulgently. "Linda, granted she could walk through it, she's too young. It would be ridiculous."

"Get her here," said Linda. "Fast."

Hal did not move. "Bertie'd blow his top."

"Get Bertie, too," she said. "Please, Hal."

Bertie arrived first. "Brought you thirty pages of a new play," he told her. "That'll get you well."

"I'm perfectly well," she retorted.

"Except that she's in agony and can't move," said Hal.

"Bertie," Linda said, "Clare can play my part tonight."

Bertie's face turned pink; his mouth opened and closed.

"I told her it was the morphine," Hal said. "The doctor will be here soon and pipe her down."

"He'll do no piping until I'm ready to be piped," she stated. "You've seen her, Bertie. The girl is an actress."

Albert Hutchinson was staring at Linda. He wet his lips with his tongue. "Could I have a drink, Hal?" His mouth twitched. "Which are you, Linda," he inquired softly, when Hal had gone, "a very clever woman or a very reckless one?"

"Here you are," said Hal.

The doorbell rang. They heard the maid's footsteps, heard Clare Copeland's throaty voice saying, "I'm expected." Hal rolled his eyes at Bertie.

She was sorry that Linda was ill, Clare said, politely and coolly. She was quite calm; only the faint twitching of her nostrils betrayed any excitement.

"I'm not going to drop dead," Linda told her dryly. "I'll be able to play tomorrow night and you'll go back to Iris. Do you think that you can do my part tonight?"

"Yes, Miss Merwin," Clare answered.

"Linda, listen to me!" said Hal. "For one thing, I doubt very much whether Howard will permit it. Audiences come to see you."

"Us," she corrected. "And I think Howard will trust my judgment."

Bertie's silence was explosive.

"You'll have to do something about Iris, Bertie," Linda continued. "Couldn't you give some of her lines back to Margaret, and let Polly read it, if necessary? Will you call her?"

"You're quite sure," Bertie asked, "that this is the way you want it?"

"Do you want me to lie here thinking of an audience being turned away?" she demanded. "The commuters waiting for trains, all the people who bought their tickets——"

"O.K.," he said. "We'd better get moving." He looked at his watch, and Dr. Michael Turner appeared in the doorway.

Hal and Bertie and Clare were silent while he took Linda's temperature and felt her pulse. "Nice going," he told them ironically. "Why I didn't become a pediatrician or an anesthetist, I'll never know! Actresses! Actors! You're all crazy!" He opened his case. "This time, Linda Merwin, I'm really going to put you to sleep! You people get out—and stay out!"

It was bright daylight, when Linda awoke. She moved her arm tentatively, moved it more briskly. It was sore, but it was better.

She tried sitting up. The effort hurt, but she sat up.

She called softly, "Are you awake, Hal?"

He was wearing a dressing gown, an English one which she had given him, but he had shaved. "You're better!" he exclaimed.

She nodded. "How did it go?"

He grinned. "It was murder, Linda."

"What do you mean?" she demanded. "Did Clare fluff?"

"Clare didn't miss a cue," he answered. "In fact, she didn't miss anything. Miss Clare Copeland was the whole show."

"I told you!" said Linda. "I'll give you even money that she's starred next year. How was the audience?"

"They loved her," said Hal. "She even got the odd *olé* and a couple of *bravos*. I'll bring you your breakfast."

He brought her tray with a white orchid wrapped in waxed paper beside the plate of toast.

"Aren't you glad that you listened to me?" she asked.

"That, my love, is a difficult one to answer," he said. "Any chance of your going on tonight?"

"Why, of course!" she replied. "I'm fine. And no doctor is going to tell me differently."

"You'll do what Mike says, young woman," he retorted. "For

you, I would go through a repeat performance. But only for you."

"I don't understand you, Hal," she said.

"Get Bertie to tell you," he advised. "He was out front." He looked at the clock on her table. "He ought to be here on the next broomstick. Said he'd drop in around noon."

Linda's eyes were bright. "How did Clare look?"

"Haven't you told me so enough? Beautiful, of course, just as you prophesied. Mind if we change the subject?"

When Bertie appeared, Hal said, "I think I'll leave you two alone. Don't forget that she's my wife, Albert." He bent over and kissed Linda. "I'm lunching at the club, darling. I really am."

Linda smiled at Bertie, the smile of a good and happy child. And Bertie smiled back, a smile half small boy, half devil.

"It was a massacre," he said simply.

"Tell me," she said.

"Clare will be a great actress someday, if someone doesn't poison her coffee first," Bertie said. "I don't know her exact age, but somewhere, somehow, she has managed to learn all the tricks of the theater from Euripides down. All the nasty tricks, I mean. When a better scene-stealer is born, they'll have to write longer scenes. She upstaged Hal every chance she got, and once I distinctly saw her push him. She stole his laughs by charming little sideplays of her own. There's only one word to describe Clare Copeland, and I hesitate to employ it." He extended his arm. "Which hand may I shake, madame? Congratulations are decidedly in order."

"Whatever are you talking about, Bertie?" asked Linda.

"I told you yesterday that you were either very clever or very reckless. We can now omit the 'reckless.' Obviously, you knew what you were doing."

Linda said, "Honestly, Bertie, you don't make sense."

"Look, darling, this is me!" he reminded her. "Old faithful Albert. You don't have to put on an act." He chuckled. "Without undue immodesty, I may add that I helped a little. I gave her a pep talk when Hal wasn't around, and suggested a few small bits of business that would tend to rivet the audience's attention on her."

"Why, you wretch!" said Linda. "Why did you do that?"

He gave her a long, thoughtful look. "It's the Sir Walter Raleigh in me—only I'm playing the cloak, of course. I feel confident, Mrs. Joyce, that any threat to your marital happiness which Clare might have represented is ended."

Linda was very quiet. Then she said, "I do like you, Bertie."

"Good!" he said. "And you trust me?"

"Of course."

"Implicitly?"

"Implicitly," she answered, smiling.

"Then," he said, "answer me óne question, ere I perish of curiosity. Did you really have bursitis?"

"Why, Albert Hutchinson!" she exclaimed. "I don't know what you mean!"

He inclined his head. "I know what you mean, darling," he told her. "You mean that I'll never know."

DYGARTSBUSH

WALTER D. EDMONDS

John Borst was the first settler to come into Dygartsbush after the war. He came alone in the early fall of 1784, on foot, carrying a rifle, an ax, a brush scythe, a pair of blankets and a sack of cornmeal. He found the different lots hard to recognize, for there was no sign left of the houses. Only the charred butt logs remained, surrounding a layer of dead coals that the rain had long since beaten into the earth. The fields had gone to brush; the piece where he had had his corn was covered with a scrub of berry vines, rough grass, yarrow and steeplebush. Young poplars had begun to come in along the edge. But near the center of it he found a stunted, slender little group of tiny cornstalks, tasseled out, with ears that looked like buds.

Whenever the work of clearing brush seemed everlasting, he would go over and look at that corn and think how good his first crop, seven years ago, had looked. It was good land, with a southerly slope and water nearby. That was why he had come back to it. Other people were pushing westward; many of them Yankees from New England who had seen something of the country during the war or heard tell of it from returning soldiers. But John Borst thought it would be many years after their farms became productive before they would find a market for their crops. The war had taught him to prefer the things he knew and remembered.

After he found that his wife had been taken captive to the Indians' towns, he had joined the army. They had given him a fifty-dollar bounty and a uniform.

As soon as his enlistment ended, he volunteered from his militia class for the Levies and was assigned the land bounty of two hundred acres. This he had left with Mr. Paris, of Stone Arabia, who was now with the legislature in New York City, to sell for him on a commission basis.

If he were lucky enough to sell, he would become comparatively rich; but John Borst was a methodical man who did not believe in waiting for good luck. When he had his land readied again, and his house rebuilt, it would be time enough to think of buying stock and household goods.

He needed next to nothing now. He lived on his cornmeal and pigeons he knocked off a roosting tree at dusk each evening. All his daylight hours he spent in the field, cutting down the brush and arranging it for burning. He slept in a small lean-to he had set up the first day in. And it was at nights, as he lay in his blankets and watched the fire dying, that he felt lonely. He had had no inclination to remarry, though he knew of several men whose women had been carried off by the Indians who had taken new wives in the past year.

One of the Devendorf girls, living in Fort Plain, he thought would marry him if he asked her. She had been pretty plain about it too. She wasn't a bad girl either, and he had thought seriously whether he would not be wise to take her. But that would have meant building a cabin, first off, for her to live in; and, now that he was back on the land, he knew he would have begrudged the time spent raising one and the money necessary to hire help, since there were no neighbors to come to a raising bee. Besides, he had never got over his feeling that Delia would come back. He felt it more strongly here in Dygartsbush than he had in the past seven years.

At nights he would remember her in their one month of married life—cooking his supper for him when he came in; the way she knelt in front of the fire and handled the pans and dishes; sitting beside him fixing his clothes after the meal; getting ready for bed when he had stepped outside the last thing. He would come in to find her in her nightdress, combing her brown hair before the hearth, and the light of the red coals showed him the shadow of her body. She had been a long-bodied girl with fine square shoulders; she stood straight, even after a day of helping him in the corn piece. He did not think that the Devendorf girl would work the way Delia had and seem happy and gay in the labor.

He worked alone all through September. In October, when the dry winds began to parch the ground, he burned his land. Then, when he was ready to return to Fort Plain, three men turned up in Dygartsbush.

When he first sighted them, he went over to the edge of the burning for his rifle. There had been cases, during the past two years, of settlers who had gone back to their farms being murdered by Indians or renegades. But the men shouted to him that they were friends, and as they came nearer, he saw that one of them was Honus Kelly.

With Kelly were two New Englanders, named Hartley and Phelps, who came to look over the land. Honus explained that he had decided to sell his lot and that he had the selling of the Dygarts' also. As both these touched on John Borst's land, John spent a day with them, running the boundaries. Hartley and Phelps liked the country and suggested to John that the four of them raise three cabins, so that they could move in, in the spring.

John had not figured on building his cabin that fall, but the men had horses to skid the logs and it seemed like a good chance to get his house built without using cash. He spent half that night deciding that he would build his new house exactly on the site of the old one. When Honus Kelly asked him why, he replied that in 1776 it had seemed to him the best site, and he had found no reason to change his mind now. Kelly laughed and said it was just Dutch stubbornness, and Hartley said he thought it would make uneasy living; there might be ghosts around. "Nobody got killed here," John explained.

In the back of his mind, however, was the thought of how it would seem to Delia when she came back. With the cabin raised, the place would look to her the way it had the day he had brought her in the first time. "My, it's a nice house; it's a nice place, John. I think it's beautiful." He remembered her words, her fresh deep voice. That was the first time she had not sounded shy. All the way in she had been shy with him, so that he had wondered whether he had been too strong with her. He was a big, powerful, heavy man, and, like most slow-moving men, he did not realize his full strength.

They built the three cabins in the next three weeks, cutting and skidding the logs with the New Englanders' horses; and then John helped them burn their land with the brush standing; and then they left to file their deeds and return to New England for their families. They would come back, they said, as soon as the roads were passable.

"Ain't you coming out with us, John?" Honus asked him.

John said no. He would stay and do finishing work on his cabin and maybe fell some timber, over in the hardwood lot. He would want to put in wheat next fall. The price of wheat was bound to go up with the influx of new settlers.

Honus did not laugh at him. "You're right," he said. Then he added, "They're going to have a treaty with the Indians this month. They're going to ask for all prisoners to get sent back."

"That's good," John said. He stood stubbing his toes in the dirt, as if to settle his feet.

"Delia ought to be back next summer," Honus said understandingly. "They wouldn't kill a girl like her. They liked her." He turned to the two New Englanders. "I'd probably have my hair hanging on an Indian post right now if it wasn't for John's wife. She helped me get away after they took us. They killed every other man but me and my brother and John here. Delia's a fine girl; she'll make a good neighbor for your families."

John flushed. Phelps, the older of the two, said it would be fine for his wife to have a woman neighbor. Especially for his mother-in-law, who didn't like the idea of their coming. He would tell his mother-in-law about Mrs. Borst.

"Tell her she's pretty," said Honus. "One of the prettiest women I ever saw."

John did not flush again. It was a fact, not flattery. The younger man, Hartley, looked round the clearing as if he were trying to imagine what an Indian raid was like. "Must've been pretty bad," he said.

Honus said, "It was bad enough." And they left.

It seemed lonelier to John the day after they left. He had got to like them. They didn't seem like Yankees, especially. It would be good to have neighbors, he thought. Delia would like it. She used to say she liked people round, not that she liked to gad a lot, but just to hear and see them every week or so.

The rainy weather set in and he hunted him a deer and then spent time in his new cabin, chinking the walls. The men had had some paper, which he used in his window, and the inside of the cabin he fixed up with shelves like the old one; but these were made of split logs, like the benches. He would have to buy boards for a table, or buy a table secondhand.

He went out when the snow came, and worked at what he could find around Fort Plain, and then trapped a little. In the spring he had thirty dollars left of his bounty money and thirty-five dollars from trapping, over and above the cost of the traps. He bought a mare for thirty-five dollars, a heifer in calf for twelve, and three hogs for four dollars, at a bargain. With what was left he bought his corn seed, a log chain and a plow, and hired a man to help him drive in his stock.

It was a bare beginning, but he considered himself well off. He was starting his planting when the Phelpses came in: Phelps, his wife, one child, and Mrs. Cutts, his mother-in-law, a thin-faced woman with a dry way of speaking. John Borst got to like her pretty well.

The Hartleys came later, hardly in time to plant, and John Borst thought he would not make so good a neighbor. He said he was late because he did not like slush-traveling; he wanted to have warm weather to settle. He got John and Phelps to lend him a hand with his first field.

Mrs. Hartley was a frightened-acting girl, who seemed to take a fancy to John. She was always running over to the Borst place to be neighborly, offering to mend his things. Once she took some home with her when she found he was out. He went over next day to get them back and thank her, and, looking round her cabin, he thought privately that if Mrs. Hartley put her mind to it she would find so much work to do to catch up her own work she would not have time to take on his. She made him take back a loaf of bread, and when he got home he found that it was soggy in the middle.

But he had to admit that the sight of even Mrs. Hartley, who was a pretty-looking girl, for all her sloppy ways, made him lonely. Next day, though he could have put off the trip for another week, he went out to Fort Plain for flour and stopped in to see Honus Kelly. He asked Honus whether any women had been brought in from the Indian towns.

Honus thought quite a few had. "They most of them get left at Fort Stanwix." He seemed to understand how John felt. "Anyway, when Delia shows up she'll most probably come through here. I'll tell her you're back at Dygartsbush."

"Thanks," said John. He fumbled round for a minute. "Do you think there's any chance of her coming back?"

"Sure I do. I told you before, the Indian that took her treated her real good. Pete told you that too." Honus didn't feel it was his business to tell John the old Indian planned to make a squaw of her.

"Yes, you told me that." John Borst looked out the window. "I wonder if it would do any good if I went out looking for her. They say it's safe enough traveling in the Indian country."

"You'd probably never find her that way. She might turn up just after you left here and then you both would have much more time waiting."

"I guess that's right." Honus had told him that before too. Honus knew a lot about the Indian country. A man wouldn't have any chance out there finding out about a particular white woman. He said good-bye to Honus and went over to the store to do his trading. He bought himself some flour and a bag of salt and some salt beef. He didn't know quite how it was, but when he happened to see a new bolt of dress goods, he decided to buy some. Later, he decided it was because the brown striping reminded him of the color of her hair. He told the storekeeper's wife he wanted enough for a tall girl, about so high, and he held his hand level with his cheekbones.

He started back about two hours before sunset, though he knew that he would have to go slow the last part of the way, as the mare was still unfamiliar with the trail. It was after dark when he reached the outskirts of Dygartsbush, and he could see, off on his left, the light from the Hartleys' cabin, a single small square glow, appearing and disappearing among the trees with the mare's progress. He had a glimpse of Mrs. Hartley crossing the lighted space. She had her hair down her back, as though she were preparing for the night. The sight brought him a sense of intimacy, from which he himself was excluded. He had no companionship but the sound of the mare's hoofs, the smell of sweat, and the motion of her walk between his legs.

He did not see any light from Phelps', but he heard the child crying. The thin sound was muffled. John knew that the child and the grandmother slept in the loft. By the time he reached his own clearing the sound of crying had died away, and he was alone with the mare under a dark sky. He rode heavily, leaning his hands on her withers, paying no attention to the trail; and he was entirely unprepared when the mare threw up her head and stopped short, snorting.

She nearly unseated him and, as it was, his cheek struck painfully against her head. He started to kick her sides, jerking her head angrily, when she moved forward again of her own accord, but with her head still raised and ears pointed. Looking up himself he saw, at the far end of the clearing, a light in his own window.

It made a dim orange pattern through the paper panes. He could see no shadow of any person moving in the house, but a spark, jumping from the chimney mouth, caught his eye, and he guessed someone had freshened a fire on the hearth.

He stopped the mare and dismounted and got his rifle ready in his hand. Honus had told him that there were still a few Tories and Indians who had lived along the valley, who were trying to get back. Down in Fort Plain they had an organization to deal with them.

He knew how far the light reached when the door was opened. Before he came into the area he let the mare have her head and slapped her flank. She stepped ahead quickly, passing the door to go round to the shed. John lay down in the grass, with his rifle pointed.

The door opened, shedding its light over the mare, but there was no ambush from the field. A whippoorwill had started singing, but John did not hear it. A woman was standing in the door, looking out with large eyes at the mare. The beast stopped again, snorting uneasily, then moved on. The woman cupped her hands on each side of her face, to act as blinders from the light, and stepped past the mare. He could see her plain now. She wore Indian clothes, moccasins and skirt and a loose overdress. He could tell by her height who she was.

He got up slowly, a little uncertain in his arms and legs, walked over to her and leaned on his rifle and looked into her face to make sure.

But he knew anyway. She stood erect, looking back at him, her hands hanging at her sides. He did not think she had changed, except for her Indian clothes and the way she wore her hair in two braids over her breast. He saw her lips part to say, "I'm back, John," but her voice was the barest whisper. He shifted a little so that her face, turning with him, came into the light, showing him again, after seven years, the curve of her cheek and the tenderness of her mouth. Then he saw that her eyes were wet. Neither of them heard the whippoorwill still calling in the young corn.

At times, John Borst had the feeling that he and Delia had taken up their lives exactly where they were the night the Indians raided Dygartsbush. That night also, he had been coming home from Fort Plain with flour, almost at the same time. But then he had been afoot instead of riding his own mare.

That night might have been a dream—the burning cabins and the firing, and the rain. He had come into Hawyer's clearing just in time to see the Indians reach that place. He could tell by the fires that the Indians had surrounded every house. He had seen Hawyer shot in his door and Mrs. Hawyer hauled out of the house. The Indian had her by the hair and was dragging her, the way a man might lug along a stubborn dog to put it out for the night. Then they had spotted John, half a dozen of them, and he had set out to run for the fort.

He told Delia about it the day after her return—they had not done any talking that first night. He told her how he had got fifteen men to come back with him and they had found every house in ashes. They had picked up the tracks at the end of his lot, followed them for half a dozen miles. Then they had come back and buried the dead. That task had taken them the rest of the day. They had had to camp the night just off Hawyer's clearing, and it was sheer luck that John had waked to hear the crying of a little girl. He said if he had not heard it then Mrs. Dygart's daughters would probably have wandered off and got lost in the woods. When he found them they were walking away from the ashes of the Dygart house, because the seven-year-old one did not think it was theirs. She was hauling the little one along, trying to find their house. When they heard him coming they just crouched down, still as rabbits. Now, he said, they were with their mother who had been brought back by General Sullivan's army.

Delia had been crouching in front of the fire, like an Indian squaw, and while he talked she had suddenly got down on her knees, the way she used to do. It gave him a vaguely uneasy feeling to see the slow pink rising in her cheeks, as though she had corrected herself in a mistake. Now she lifted her face and her eyes regarded him with their old searching level glance.

"Did you think I was dead, John?"

He thought a while. "No. I didn't think so. But I thought I probably wouldn't ever see you again. I joined the army. There wasn't anything left for me here, and I didn't get back to Tryon County for more'n a year. Then I found out that Caty Breen had got back. She came back married to a man that had got himself exchanged. I don't remember his name. She's living up in Kingsland now."

Delia said, "I'm glad. She was so scared. They took her off from the rest of us, two Indians did." She turned her attention back to her cooking.

"Where was that?" he asked.

"Near the head of a river. I don't know what one. We went on to the Genesee, the rest of us, except for Peter Kelly and the Mitchel girl."

"They got back five years ago," John told her. "They ran away. Honus told me about it. He told me Pete hadn't heard anything of you."

"Honus was good to me, John."

"He told me how you helped him get away."

"What else did he tell you?"

John looked at her. "Why, I don't know. Just about how he got away. He kept telling me, too, he didn't think the Indians would hurt you any. He said the one that took you thought a lot of you. He had a comic name, High Grass, I think Honus said."

"Yes. High Grass. Gasotena."

She drew her breath slowly, and became quite still. He had noticed that about her in the one day she had been home—the way she fell into a stillness. Not silence, for she always answered him at once if he said anything. He did not know how to describe it to himself, but he supposed it was because she felt some kind of strangeness getting back to white people. Maybe, he thought, she felt strange with him. Seven years was a long time to be away from a man; maybe a woman got to feeling different about things.

He said, "It must be queer, coming back to me after so long. Must seem like taking up with a man without getting married, almost." He tried to say it in a light, joking kind of way.

But she whirled suddenly, lifting her face and looking closely into his. "What makes you say that?" He saw her lips tremble and become still.

"I didn't mean to make you jump. I thought, maybe, I'd seem like almost a strange man. Like, maybe, there was things you'd disremembered about me. Things, maybe you didn't like so well."

He could see her throat fill and empty.

"Did you think that last night?"

He felt himself coloring. "No."

"Are there things about me?"

"No," he said. "God, no." There was visible pain in her eyes. He was a fool, he thought. "Look out, Delia. That fat's catching fire."

She turned back to the cooking quickly and silently, and he looked down on her back. It always seemed to him the most homely thing in the world for a man to sit watching his wife bend to cook his dinner. She had done up her hair in braids wound round her head, but she still wore her Indian clothing. It was good to work in, she said. They couldn't afford to throw away good clothes. Now she was still again for a long time, and he thought she had gone off into one of her spells until she began to speak.

Then her voice was throaty and pitched low, and she seemed to have difficulty with her words. It was hard to hear her. One of the hogs had wandered up to the shed door and was oinking to himself and rubbing his hide against the doorjamb. Her words came through the sound of the pig and the dead June heat.

She said: "I used to wonder if you'd got caught. But they never brought in your scalp. I got to believe you were alive, John. Then after I'd been in the Indian town for a while I began to think I'd have to stay there all my life. We knew the army was coming. I thought it might come near, but it never did come near. Then, after a long time, it seemed as if I didn't have anything to hope for. I wasn't bad off like some other prisoners. The Indians were good to me, but it wasn't like white people being good to you. I didn't mind the work, John. Work helped, somehow, but no work you did was for yourself. No house belongs to any one person among the Indians. Their gardens are for the whole house, all the people in it. The squaws didn't ever plant flowers by their houses. I used to think about the little dark red pinks I planted just outside the door and wonder if they ever blowed."

Listening to her in a kind of fascination John heard himself say, "I don't know, Delia," but she went on quietly.

"I guess the fire scorched them to death. I looked for them when I came back, but it was getting near dark then, so I couldn't tell. I looked this morning, but there weren't any. Indians don't plant flowers, though they like picking wild ones. The children would pick wild ones and carry them round till they were dead and throw them away. I put some in water once to show them, but they never caught on. Sometimes I used to think maybe you had come back and was tending the pinks for me. But I knew that was silly, that you couldn't come back till the war was over." She drew a long breath. "I used to wonder and wonder about you, what you were doing, and who you were with, John. Did you wonder about me?"

"Yes."

"When they told me about the treaty and said I could go home, I was afraid, John. I thought, it's seven years and you haven't heard from me. I thought maybe you'd found another woman and married her."

"I saw plenty," he said. "I never had the urge to marry."

"I didn't know that. I wouldn't have blamed you, though. But I had to come back to find out. Ganowauges brought me. He knew the southern way better, and he said he'd bring me as far as Fort Plain. Most went to Fort Stanwix, I think. I asked him if we could come through here and he said we could do it. We got here just about dark, John. We came in the same way Gasotena took me away. We came out of the woods and we both smelled hoed land. Then I looked and saw the house, just the way it was, right in the same place. I was so frightened I could scarcely move. Ganowauges pointed to it and told me to go. I asked him if he would wait. I thought then I would go back with him if there was a woman in it. He acted kind of nervy and said he'd rather wait in the woods. I went to the house, John. I had to see what she looked like."

"She wasn't there, was she?"

Delia glanced at him in a startled way, saw his eyes, and tried to smile.

"No. First I thought maybe you'd taken her to Fort Plain with you. Then I went inside and I saw you'd been living alone."

"How did you know that?"

She smiled this time, to herself.

"I knew it was you too. I could tell because the way the tooth twig was laid against the sack of gunpowder. You always laid it standing up so the brush end would dry out. It was so much the same. I just sat down and cried. I didn't want to light the light because I wanted to get my crying done before you came. I forgot all about Ganowauges. I never even thanked him. John, did you build the house right here on purpose?"

He said, "Yes."

He saw her eyelids trembling, and got up and went out to wash. When he came in again she seemed peaceful. She had laid out their food on the board table. He said, "It's not so well fixed. But I'll get a glass sash before winter and a chest of drawers for you to keep your clothes in. I've got a little money left."

She drew a deep breath, looking round.

"It's all ours. John, I don't care if we're poor. It's no matter to me. All I want to do is work for you, and for you to be happy, and have you care for me the way you used to. I'm older than I was. I guess I show it. But I'm healthy and strong, still." Her voice trailed off.

He said, "You look all right." He felt strangely troubled. He could not tell why. He tried to talk about something else. "I'll have to take you over to the neighbors. They're Yankee people. But I like the Phelpses. I like Mrs. Cutts too. She's kind of like the way Mrs. Staats was, but she's sensible."

"Which one is she?"

"Mrs. Phelps' mother. She's elderly. Hartleys are always borrowing. You'll have to watch out for them. They mean all right. They're just shiftless." He got up. "Guess I'll begin mowing grass over in the swale this afternoon. We got to have hay for the mare and cow, next winter."

"We didn't have a cow and horse before, did we? It makes it seem more like a farm, even if we haven't got a glass window. When's the cow due?"

"They thought in September. I think maybe August. I had a chance to get her cheap," he explained. "I meant to get a window first."

"I'd rather have the cow. I used to make butter fine."

John went out, leaving her looking happy, he thought. More the way she used to be. He took his scythe and went toward the swale; but as soon as he entered the woods he made a circuit and picked up Delia's tracks. He found the Indian's plain enough. The Indian had been like a fox nosing the clearing. After Delia went toward the house, he had moved along the edge of the woods until he was opposite the door. There, in crushed ferns, John found the imprint of the Indian's body. He must have lain there for quite a while. Probably he had been there when John came home. John stood still, thinking what a plain mark he must have made. He didn't like the thought of it, even though the Indian hadn't done anything.

Delia came to the door with the bucket she had been washing the dishes in and threw away the water with a swinging motion, making a sparkle of drops through the sunlight. Then she stood for a moment, resting her weight on one hip, and staring after the way John had gone. He thought he had never seen her look so pretty as she did in her Indian dress. Just why, he wasn't sure. He thought maybe it was the strangeness of it—as if she was something he didn't really have a right to. After a moment she let her head bend, and then she turned and put up her arm against the jamb of the door and rested her forehead on it. She might have been crying.

Suddenly it came to John that he was spying on his wife. His face reddened, even though he knew himself alone and unobserved; and he went back through the edge of the woods, cut across to the swale, and set down the point of the scythe snath in the grass.

He began whetting the scythe. The high sound of the stone against the blade, the heat of the sun on the back of his neck, the waves of warm air shimmering above the grass, and the whine of a hot-weather bird all seemed to go together. He mowed with a full sweep. He prided himself on being a four-acre mower; but that afternoon he could not put his heart into the mowing. The image of his wife leaning her head against the doorjamb kept coming before his eyes to trouble him.

She became suddenly shy of the idea of calling on the neighbors and, after twice mentioning it, John let her alone. But next day, meeting Phelps, who had come over to mow his half of the swale, John thought it only polite to mention Delia's return. Phelps thought it was almost miraculous. He shook John's hand and vowed he would tell his womenfolk that evening. John explained that Delia felt shy about meeting people. She had no decent clothes yet. Just the Indian things she had come home with. Phelps said he understood, and they mowed all day without taking up the subject again.

But Mrs. Cutts was a curious woman, and made a point of passing through Borst's clearing on her way home from the berry patch on Dygart's knoll. With no warning, Delia had no decent chance of getting out of her way and, when Mrs. Cutts asked if she could come in, smiled hesitantly and stood aside from the door.

"It's a good thing for John you've come back, Mrs. Borst," said the old woman, sitting down. "My, the sun's hot. But I got some dandy strawberries. I'll leave you some. I've got a real likin' for John." Her keen old eyes examined Delia frankly. "Phelps—I always called him Phelps; he used to be my hired man—Phelps said you was shy about your clothes. Land sakes! If I was a part as pretty in them I wouldn't be living with my son-in-law."

She smiled as Delia flushed.

"You ain't very talkative, are you?" she asked, after a moment.

Delia got even pinker. "It's hard to be with people again—white people, I mean."

"It must have been hard," said Mrs. Cutts. "Did they burn everything you had?"

Delia nodded. "But I don't seem to mind it now. Not what happened to our place. We were lucky that way."

"Yes. John told me he was away. He said every other man but one and a boy got killed."

"That was the bad part, wondering what had happened to John." She walked over to the window. "I don't like to think about it, Mrs. Cutts."

"No wonder. Indians must be awful people. I expect they made a kind of slave out of you. They do that with their own women, I've heard tell."

"Squaws don't think they're slaves. So they didn't treat me bad by their lights. You see, I got adopted into a house."

Mrs. Cutts studied her shrewdly.

"You mean you was just like one of them?"

Delia nodded.

"I guess that's why you feel uneasy with white women. Listen, Mrs. Borst," she said, after a moment. "I don't know what happened to you out there. I don't want to know unless you want to tell me. . . I'm no gadder, if you want to. But I like John. You won't make him happy if you keep troubling yourself about what happened. It wasn't your fault, was it?" Delia shook her head. "You're healthy and pretty-looking, and you're still young. There's a long time ahead of you. It's not so easy for a woman to begin over as it is for a man—I don't know why. But you can do it if you want to."

Delia swung round on the old woman, who now had stooped to pick up her berries. "Give me a dish, dearie, and I'll fill it from my pail."

But Delia made no move to. She stared at Mrs. Cutts with painful intensity. "What do you think happened to me, Mrs. Cutts?"

"I don't know. It's not my business and I'm not asking. Don't you worry. My tongue's my own, and I keep it where it belongs." She gave Delia a hearty smile. "Now, where's a dish?"

Mrs. Cutts heaped the dish with the fresh berries and went out of the door. She was a dozen yards down the path before Delia thought of thanking her.

She ran after the old woman, who, by then, had her shawl over her head and was stumping along like a vigorous witch. Delia moved so quietly in her Indian moccasins that she startled Mrs. Cutts.

"I meant to thank you for the berries. They're lovely."

"You're real welcome to them," said Mrs. Cutts. "When you feel ready to, come over and see us. Bring John or come alone."

"Thank you. I'll walk along a way with you. It's time I went and told John to come to dinner."

"That's neighborly."

Mrs. Cutts did not speak. She thought maybe the girl would unload her trouble. She knew she had one, and the only way to get her to tell it was by keeping quiet.

But Delia walked also in silence. She was a good head taller than Mrs. Cutts. Glancing sidewise, the old woman could see thoughtfulness in her face. "Think of an Indian with that," she thought to herself, studying the round of the chin, the straight nose and reserved eyes, and the large mouth. They parted at the fork of the path without having said another word. Mrs. Cutts wasn't planning to say anything, but at the last moment she unexpectedly made up her mind.

"Delia Borst," she said, "just remember that there's some things a man is a lot happier for not knowing. It may be hard on you, but it's true."

"The man might find out sometime. Then what would he think?"

"I'd let him take his chance of it."

Delia looked over the top of Mrs. Cutts' shawl.

"But I love John," she said.

She made up her mind to tell him that night. When he came in from the swale half an hour after her, he could tell that something was on her mind.

She had been helping him all afternoon, raking his mowing of the day before into haycocks. She seemed to take pleasure in the work, and they kept at it all afternoon in companionable silence. But she didn't say anything until she had given him his cornbread and broth, and then she came at it roundabout.

"Mrs. Cutts stopped in this morning, John. We had a talk."

"She's a neighborly woman," he said. "Though she's kind of short-spoken."

Delia got the dish of berries. "She left these for us. I didn't like her at first, but, after a while, I thought she was nice." "She tell you about the way she broke her wrist?" Delia shook her head. "She will. She likes to talk about her troubles, but she don't let them hinder her from doing what she wants."

75

"She didn't mention it. We got talking about what men think."

"Did you?"

"She said it was better for a man not to be told everything by his wife."

John said, "I guess that depends on the wife."

"That's what I said." She finished her berries and sat still, leaning slightly toward him over the table. She had the look of taking hold of herself with both hands. They were folded on the table edge, so that when she leaned against them they fitted the cleft in her breasts. Her hands could feel the beating of her heart.

"You look worried," John said suddenly.

But she did not notice him. Her eyes seemed lost in the darkness gathering beyond the open door. There was a fringe of balsams beyond the swale and their tips were like small arrowheads in the line of pale light still showing under a west-moving bank of clouds.

They had not lit the dip. Their only light was from the fire. An exploratory June bug buzzed through the door, flipped on one wing tip between them, and hit the stone back of the fireplace. Delia shivered and turned her eyes to her husband's.

"John, I've been home most a week, and you've never asked me what happened to me in Onondarha."

"Where was that?"

"That's the name of the town I lived in. You see, you never even asked me that."

John Borst also had become quiet. His big hands, which had been resting on the table, he put into his lap. She could imagine them holding his knees. His heavy face with its slow-moving eyes stared back at her. She drew her breath slowly, thinking how kind it looked. She had never heard his voice sound the way it did when he spoke to her.

"I didn't ask you because I figured you would tell me what you wanted I should know. What's all right with you is all right with me. I've wondered what happened to you sometimes. I got crazy about it sometimes. But, now you're back, I don't want you to tell me what you don't want to."

She was surprised and touched. "Mrs. Cutts almost said the same thing, John. Do you know what I said? I said I loved you too much. Maybe it's bad to love someone too much."

"Maybe," he said. It sounded stupid. He could see her trembling. The lift of her chin toward him was a hurtful thing to see; the complete quiet of her struggle with herself.

"I've got to tell you, John. You can send me away then if you want."

"I won't never send you away."

She put out her hand quickly as though to stop his lips, then let it fall to the table between them. "I won't take that for a promise," she said. "You've got to listen. I can't bear you loving me unless you know. High Grass, the Indian that took me, got me adopted into his house. The women dressed me up and showed me how to make a cake and told me to give it to the old woman of the house. I didn't know what they said; I hadn't learned Indian then. You believe that?"

His voice sounded heavy. "Yes, I believe it."

"I didn't know I was getting married. I wanted to please them. I wanted to stay alive, so I could come back to you. I didn't know till night, when he came into my place. I didn't know it was his place till then. There were thirty people in that house all round me, John."

He didn't say anything. He didn't look at her. Her voice became more urgent.

"I couldn't do anything. Anything, John. I couldn't. I didn't think I could live."

"You did, though."

"Yes, I did." She sounded suddenly calmer. "After a year, I had a baby, John. He was the only thing I loved. I didn't love him, either. Every time I saw him I thought of you. I thought how you'd hate me."

"I don't hate you."

Her lips stayed parted. She licked them suddenly with her tongue, but even then she could not speak. After a while John got up. He turned to look out of the door.

"Where's the baby?"

"He died."

"You didn't leave him, did you?"

"No, John."

"That would have been a bad thing. Did you have any more children?"

"No." She whispered, leaning forward over the table. "I couldn't have come back, leaving a child, could I? And I couldn't come back with one. I thought, when he died, it was like Providence telling me I could come back. I knew I had to tell you, but when I got here, I couldn't, John. Honestly, I'm sorry."

He didn't notice her.

"This High Grass," he said. "What's he doing?"

"He went off on a war party. He didn't come back. They told me he got killed."

"My God," he said. "I can't do nothing."

He turned through the door abruptly, leaving her at the table. She sat alone for a long time. She could hear him walking round, but she could not move. She waited like a prisoner until at last he came in. He said, "Ain't you done the dishes?" But she only shook her head and watched him. "Come on," he said, "I'll help you."

She rose slowly, reaching for the dishes blindly. "Do you want me to stay?"

He turned on her, his voice heavy with sarcasm.

"Where in hell could you go to this time of night?"

An outsider would have seen nothing unusual in their relations. Delia herself sometimes almost persuaded herself that John was putting what she had told him from his mind. But, in a day or so, she would catch him watching her; and at such times something in his eyes made her feel whipped and humiliated. She accepted the feeling as part of the payment she would have to make for what had happened to her—that she had known all along she would have to make. A good woman, she thought, a Christian saint, would have died first. But Delia hadn't wanted to die; she had wanted to get back to John; now she must take the future with patience.

It was hard to be patient, living with John. Times were when she wanted to cry out, "Stop looking at me that way. I'd rather you'd whip me, if you wanted. I didn't do anything bad." While they were working together in the field, it was more like old times; or hauling the hay up to the sheds in small loads on a sledge. The rick built slowly, but when it was high, John sometimes grinned, pitching the hay up to her.

In the evenings was the time their reserve came between them. It arrived with the intimate darkness. She felt that he thought of her as just a useful body, something one accepted as one accepted the weather. But her resentment was less against him—she remembered how he had waited seven years for her and built the cabin where she expected it to be—than against the providence that had played tricks with her. It got so she prayed that it might be reversed, for even just one day.

One way he had changed was in laying down the law about their neighbors. He kept after her until she had made a dress from the calico he had brought. She could hardly bear to touch it, thinking of the impulse that had made him buy it at the very time of her return, and of what her return had resulted in. But he said he didn't want the neighbors to think he wasn't proud to show her off.

They made the visits one Sunday, she in the calico that felt like a cold rag touching her limply, he with his coat brushed. They went first to the Hartley house; to get the worst part over quick, John said.

Delia disliked them both. The man eyed her with open and curious admiration. The woman, in the one moment they had to be alone, asked, "Tell me, Mrs. Borst, are Indian men the same as other men?"

"Why should I know?" Delia asked frigidly.

Mrs. Hartley whinnied softly. "With the shape you've got. Oh, my! Listen, I'd like to see you dressed in squaw's clothes. Phelps said you come back in them. Would you show them to me?"

They were a strange couple to find in Dygartsbush, Delia thought; but she found the Phelpses nice simple people.

John was pleased the way the Phelpses took to Delia and she to them. He wouldn't feel easy about leaving Delia alone when he went down to Fort Plain, if she didn't have a place she could go to. Mrs. Cutts had said they'd be glad to have Delia visit them the next time he went down. The old woman had seen, with one look, that there was something between the Borsts; she guessed what had happened. She took John aside as they were leaving and said, "John, I want to tell you I think she's one of the best sort of women. You can see she's honest." Then she added, "When a person's young he or she's likely to set a lot of store in notions that don't amount to much when they get older." She gave his shoulder a sharp pat and sent him after his wife before he could think of a reply.

He walked silently and morosely until he and Delia were near home. Then he asked, "Did you tell Mrs. Cutts anything about you and that Indian?"

As she turned her head to answer he could see that she was close to tears. "No. I didn't think anybody but you had any right to know."

"I think she must have guessed about you then," he said gloomily.

Thank God, he thought, Mrs. Cutts wasn't a talkative woman. She was smart, though, and she had probably guessed it. He couldn't hold it against Delia. He watched her getting their Sunday supper, and then got down his rifle to oil it. He would have to go down to Fort Plain again soon and he thought he might as well go that week. Anything to get out of the house. He glanced up, to surprise her covertly studying him from the hearth. She turned her head at once, paling slightly. She made him think of an abused dog when she did that, and he felt a senseless and irrational burst of anger.

"What do you always want to be staring at me for?"

"I didn't mean to be staring at you. I didn't want to make you mad."

"I get sick of it."

She watched the fire. Then, "You hate me, don't you, John?"

"No. I don't hate you. But I can't stand that way you look." He

79

got up suddenly to replace the gun. "Don't start talking that way either."

"I can't talk at all, can I?" She turned on her knees to face him. "John, what sense is there in us living together like this?"

"Stop it. I'm going out. When you've got the supper ready I'll come in. I'm going to look at the heifer."

It was a feeble excuse. He felt ashamed. The heifer wasn't due for a couple of weeks yet. He tramped down to the shed and looked her over. He stayed there, fussing aimlessly about nothing, until he heard Delia's tentative call. When he entered the house, she was sitting on her side of the table, and he felt an impulse to say something that would make her feel better.

"I guess I'll go down to Fort Plain tomorrow," he said. "I've got to get flour, and I might as well go sooner as later. Maybe I'll hear something about my bounty land."

Neither of them believed he would hear.

"I'm sorry I talked that way," he said.

The corners of her mouth quivered.

"I know it's hard for you, John. It's hard for me. When you talk like that and look that way you make me feel like something dirty."

He relapsed sullenly into silence.

Though it was raining, he started next morning, letting the mare take her time, so that they reached Fort Plain toward noon. He did his trading before dinnertime, finding that the price of salt beef had risen like everything else. Flour was pretty near prohibitive, as far as he was concerned. Then he went round to Honus Kelly's to visit and ask whether there had been any news from Mr. Paris about his bounty land. Honus had gone out earlier that morning, he was told; no, no word had come for him from Mr. Paris. He might find Honus down at the tavern.

John didn't like to ask Honus's hired girl to give him food, and she didn't offer him any, so he went down to the tavern in a gloomy state of mind. Nobody was in the place except the landlord and a couple of women in the kitchen. The landlord came into the tap and said he could give John some cold pork. John asked for some, and ordered a glass of strap.

The landlord said, "Quite some rain, ain't it?"

John said it was.

"I been looking in my almanac." The landlord fished out a worn book from under the bar, flipped the pages to August with a licked thumb, and said, "Look what the bug-tit wrote down about the weather." John looked at the column of Various Phenomena for August, but the landlord read out the words, "Very hot. Hot and dry. Then he says Cooler winds. Way down at the bottom he's put in Wandering thun. showers. I paid two and a half shilling for this book. Why, hell, I could've wrote down that kind of stuff myself. And look at it rain and no thun.—that's what he calls thunder—neither."

John said it didn't look very good to him and asked for Honus Kelly.

"He come in this morning," the tavern keeper said casually. "He got Walrath, Pierce and the two Devendorfs, and they went off after an Indian that was in here."

John said, "That's too bad. I wanted to see him. Who was the Indian?"

A stout, red-cheeked woman brought in a plate of sliced fresh ham, bread, a cold roast potato with a slice of raw onion leaning against it. The landlord leaned over it as if to smell the onion. They looked desultory, like any two men in a taproom on a rainy afternoon. An investigating fly buzzed over from the window and the landlord slapped him down with the glass rag. Through the open door the sound of the eaves' drip from the low stoop continued steadily.

"Why, he acted all right when he come in here. Said he was heading south, and asked about the settlements. I said there was some people living in Dygartsbush." The landlord looked up. "Why, that's where you're settled, ain't it? I forgot. You don't come down much."

John left off eating. His big face leaned intently toward the tavern keeper's. "What was the matter with him?"

The tavern keeper poured himself a drink.

"Makes my stomach turn to think of it. He got a couple of rums inside and commenced acting big. I told him to behave himself. I said we killed fresh Indians round here, but he just slammed his hand-ax down on the bar and said he'd kill me if I didn't behave myself, the lousy old skunk! I didn't dast move out of the tap, and there wasn't anybody else to send for Honus. So I just waited, and pretty soon he got nervy and said he'd had enough, and I told him what he owed me. Then you know what he did? He hauled out a kind of funny-looking purse and I looked at it and said it was funny-looking, and he held it out for me to look at. Mister, it was the skin off a human hand. Looked to me like a woman's, honest-to-God."

The tavern keeper looked into John's flushed face.

"Makes you feel ugly, don't it? He paid me in British money too. I knowed then he was a genuine bad one. But I didn't tell him English money was worth twice York money. I made him pay straight, yes, sir. He paid me and went right through that door, putting that purse back in his coat pocket, and he clumb the fence and went into the woods. I tell you, I went right after Honus."

"How long was it before Honus got after him?"

" 'Bout an hour and a half. Honus has got the boys organized pretty well. I figure he'll pick him up before too long a time."

John spoke slowly, half to himself. "It's hard tracking in a rain like this one."

"Ain't it the truth? I hadn't thought of it. Still, Honus is good. Ain't any of these Indians has got away from him yet. The boys tell me about it, because they know I keep quiet. Tie 'em to trees, they say; don't hurt 'em at all. Only they use the neck-and-limb method."

The landlord had to laugh. Then he met John's eye and stopped short. "No offense, you know, mister."

John ignored him. "What did the Indian look like?"

"Why," he said, "looked like any Indian. He had on an old hat and a coat, he'd probably stole. Looked pretty old—he'd let his hair grow, and there was some white in it. But he was fat. I knew there was something about him. He had the biggest stomach you ever saw."

"Did he say what his name was?"

"Said he was Christian Indian. Christian boy, he said. Bet he was sixty years old. Called himself Joe Conjocky. Ever hear of him?"

John pulled out his purse. "What do I owe you?"

"You've hardly et."

John picked up his rifle and started. But he stopped in the doorway, and the tavern keeper thought his face was strangely set.

"Hey, you! Did you tell Honus how that Indian asked about Dygartsbush?"

"Why, no. Come to think of it, I guess I didn't."

"You fool!"

John went out. He didn't run, but his big legs took him swiftly along the muddy road to the barn. He saddled his mare, packed on his flour and beef and salt, reprimed his rifle, and led her out of the barn. It was still raining.

The wind was southwest, bringing the rain against their faces, and the mare flickered the first drops from her ears. He swung upon her and headed her home. He had a sick feeling in his insides: Twenty miles; a wet trail; and the Indian had started at about ten o'clock. John figured it would be past one, now. Even if he pushed the mare hard enough to founder her, he could not expect to reach his cabin before suppertime. Delia would be coming back from Phelps's long before that. He felt a sudden blaze of anger against the tavern keeper. If the fool had only had the sense to tell Honus, Honus would have headed straight for Dygartsbush when the tracking got slow. But Honus wouldn't hurry. He'd follow his usual plan of getting up with the Indian about dark and taking him by his campfire. That was safe and easy, Honus said; and it saved a man the bother of lighting a fire for himself. The one sign of intelligence the fool tavern keeper had shown was to recognize the Indian as a bad one. He couldn't help it, though, after seeing that purse.

John wasn't an imaginative man, but he could guess how it had happened. A woman alone in her cabin, maybe with a child, you couldn't tell, and her man away for the day, hunting, or gone in to a settlement. The Indian, mousing into the clearing, quite openly, to beg some food, and finding out she was alone. Sitting himself down in the cabin. The woman scared half to death getting his dinner. Him eating and watching her get more and more scared and cleaning his plate. Watching her clean up, waiting till she made a move to slip out.

The mare came to the first ford and nearly lost her footing. John jerked her up and kicked her across. The creek had risen since morning. The rapids were frothy and beginning to show mud. The rain fell into the gorge without much wind, but John could see the trees swaying on the rim of the rock walls. The scud of cloud in the narrow belt of sky seemed to take the gorge in one jump.

The mare was a willing brute, but she had always been a fool about her feet. John settled himself grimly to ride her. He managed to keep her trotting a good part of the time, sitting well forward and squinting his eyes to look into the rain.

He had told Delia to stay at Phelps's till he came home, but she wouldn't. She would start out in time to get home well before him. She said it was what a woman ought to do. A man ought not to come home from a long trip to have to wait for his food. She'd be there now, fixing the fire.

He seemed to see her kneeling in front of the fireplace, blowing the fire, pink-cheeked. And he could see the fat figure of the Indian trotting along through the woods for the clearing. Even a fat Indian could cover the ground; he'd have plenty of time to get there before dark. Delia wouldn't hear him. She wouldn't see anything either, not even his face in the window, because the panes were made of paper. She'd only hear the door squeak on its wood hinges; and even then she'd think it was John.

"God help her," John said, and the mare pricked her ears and he gave her a cut. He knew then that what had happened to Delia in the Indian country made no difference to him. It was what might happen to her before he could get home.

The ride became a nightmare for him. There was a lot of stony footing in the upper part of the creek section through which the mare had to take all the time she needed. It was nearly dark in the gorge. The wet sky in the narrow opening was just a color overhead, without light. He got off and walked at the mare's head, and they came to the turn by the beech tree and climbed the steep ascent to the flat land, side by side. The mare was blowing heavily.

John counted fifty to let her blow herself out, but she spent most of the time shaking herself. He swung onto her again and started her off at a trot.

On the high flats the woods thinned and, now and then, he got a canter out of her. They had more light, also, and in the west the clouds showed signs of breaking and he saw the sun once, nearly down, in a slit over the woods. Night came, however, when he was still three miles from home.

He thought he had made a mistake when he saw the light off the trail. For a minute it seemed to him that the mare must have done a lot better than he realized and that he had already reached Hartley's. Then he knew that the light was too close to the earth to come from Hartley's window. Someone was camping off the trail.

He cursed himself for not realizing it sooner, and brought the mare up hard and tied her to a tree. To be sure, he picked out the priming of his rifle for the second time and reprimed. Then he slid into the underbrush and began working his way up to the fire.

He had not gone fifty yards before he saw that there were five men sitting round the fire and he recognized Honus Kelly's black beard. They were hunched close to the flames, with their backs to a brush lean-to they had set up, eating bologna and bread.

John got to his feet and started for them, shouting Kelly's name. He saw them stop laughing and pick up their guns and roll out of the firelight, like a comical set of surprised hogs. When he got into the firelight he couldn't see any more of them than the muzzles of their guns.

"John Borst," roared Kelly, rising up. "What are you doing here?"

"Where'd that Indian get to?" John asked.

"Oh, the Indian. How'd you know about him?"

"I've been down to Fort Plain. I heard about him in the tavern. The fool said he didn't tell you the Indian was asking about my place."

Honus let out a laugh. The others, who had resumed their places, left off picking the leaves from their bread to grin too.

"You didn't think he'd get away from us now, did you?" asked Honus. "The Indian's all right. He's just a piece above us."

He sat down, pointing his thumb over his shoulder. Looking

upward, John saw moccasined legs hanging beside the bolo of a maple. The fat body was like a flour sack, three parts full, inside the old coat.

Honus Kelly, watching John's face, said, "Sit down. You'd better."

But John shook his head. He could hardly speak for a minute. He was surprised because he still wanted to get home. But he tried to be polite.

He said at last, "You boys better come back with me. It's only a short piece, and you can have a dry bed on the floor."

"No, thanks," said Honus. "We got a good place here." He saw that John was anxious to get on, so he rose to his feet and put his hand on John's shoulder and walked back with him toward the mare. "Delia and you won't be wanting a bunch like ourselves cluttering your place tonight," he said. Then he swore. "If Frank had told me about it, I'd have sent a couple of boys straight up to you. We had a time tracking him. It's been lucky all round."

John shook hands with him.

"You don't need to thank me," said Honus. "I always wanted to get even with that Indian. Don't you remember him? He used to hang out west of the settlement. Him and me had trouble over my trap line once or twice."

He watched while John mounted. Then he caught hold of the bridle to say, "We'll bury the rat. It's near the trail." He looked up, his eyes showing white over his beard. "You won't tell Delia?"

John shook his head.

"Best not," agreed Honus. "Well, good luck."

He slapped the mare's quarter and let her go.

It had stopped raining, but drops were still shaking off the leaves. There were no stars. The woods smelled of the rain, fresh and green. The air was light and felt clear when he breathed it, and the mare moved more perkily between his thighs. When she came into their clearing, John saw a light in the cabin window. He saw it with a quick uplifting of his heart, and he was glad now that Delia was pigheaded about being home before him. He remembered how it used to be before her return, coming home alone, and fumbling in the dark.

He rode by to put the mare in the shed and carried the load round to the door. It squeaked on its hinges as he pushed it open. Delia was kneeling by the fire, blowing it, her face flushed. She swung round easily. He had a quick recollection of the image he had made of the Indian entering. But her face wasn't afraid. It was only apologetic.

"I thought you weren't coming home, John. I let the fire go down. Then I heard the mare."

Her eyes were large and heavy from her effort to keep awake. He warmed himself before the sputtering fire, watching her struggle to get back her faculties. Suddenly she straightened up. "You're wet. You're hungry."

"I got delayed," he said. She went to the saddlebags, rummaging for food, and he said awkwardly, "I wanted to get some sausage, but beef was so dear I didn't have money left for it."

"Oh, John," she said, "I don't care." She started to heat water.

"There's a little tea, though, and half a dozen loaves of sugar."

"White sugar?"

"Yes. You'd better have tea with me."

"I don't need it."

He felt embarrassed and shy. He didn't know how to tell her what he wanted to. He couldn't say, "I thought there was an Indian going to bust in on you and I got scared. But Honus hanged him, so it's all right." That wouldn't explain it to her at all. She was looking at him, too, in a queer breathless, tentative way.

"You always used to like tea," he said. "You remember the first tea we had."

Her gaze was level, but her color had faded. Her voice became slow and her lips worked stiffly.

"You said, 'Will you have some tea?' "

John for a moment became articulate.

"No. I didn't say that."

"You did." The look in her face was suddenly pitiful.

But he shook his head at her.

"I said, 'Will you have tea with me, Mrs. Borst?' "

She flushed brilliantly.

"Oh, yes, John. And I said, 'I'd love to, Mr. Borst.' "

He needn't have worried about her understanding. It all passed between them, plain in their eyes. She didn't ask anything more.

THE WEDDING
OF MARIE ROSE

EDMUND GILLIGAN

Because a vessel may not be un-
loaded at St. Pierre on a Sunday, I had the day to myself and I spent
it by taking a walk out to Galantrie Head, where lies the abandoned
hamlet once called Galantrie. There the Atlantic tides pass and
repass between the French islands and Newfoundland.

Often enough, while taking my vessel into St. Pierre harbor, I had
looked at Galantrie, its bone-white walls askew and the falling ruins
of salt-scoured shelters for boats, long since removed to better
fishing grounds. Only one cottage stood sound and whole at the time
of my visit. In it Marie Rose had lived all her life.

When I halted on the hill, I saw her pacing the wind-rippled beach
near her doorway, a tall, lone woman gazing out of those ruins and
over the sea. In black curves a Breton cloak swirled around her. I gave
her a hail, a loud one to carry against the wind and the cries of gulls
over her head. When she turned I lifted my cap, and to this salute she
bowed. Although I had heard something about her, from time to
time, and knew that she lived alone, I had no reason to be sure of a
welcome. Yet she looked after me with such keenness that I took
good care to pass nearer on my return. I couldn't quite figure out
why I should wish to pass the time of day with such an elderly lady. I
fancy that her name had again risen far back in my memory,
crowded by tales of our Gloucester schooners and Gloucestermen on
the Grand Bank and among the islands.

When I saw that she stood between her doorway and her gate and gazed at me directly, I gave her the deep Newfoundland bow from the waist that my grandfather had taught me. He had been the third generation of our family to trade with the French.

She answered in the precise English of the convent school at St. Pierre. She glided forward, opened her gate and made a sign that I should enter. Even so quickly, I discerned that some quality in me had moved her deeply. The onrushing mood of her heart came into her eyes until they became suffused, like the eyes of a young woman in the way of lovemaking.

When I followed into the kitchen, I said to myself: *How very strange! She is stirred by tenderness.* I surmised that she might have remembered my grandfather. No, my name had no meaning to her.

She said, "Captain, you are a courteous young man, indeed. It is an event—a true event—in my life when a stranger pauses at my door. I have long been the only inhabitant of Galantrie."

I made a reply concerning her graciousness. She sat prim in an ancient, straight-backed chair that I thought had been made of rosewood. Wine and glasses were set out in my honor, and there were almond cakes from her oven. The blue day mixed mildly with the sea shadows changing on blue walls and the gleam of blue delft dishes upright on the mantelpiece. Next to a gold-rimmed cup of extraordinary size there lay a tool of our Gloucester fleet: a wooden bailer. On its scoop I read a vessel's name: *The Lark*.

Once more the remembrance of childhood began, and I recalled that in my father's boyhood *The Lark* had come home, her colors at half-mast for a young captain lost in a dory. *And how did it happen*, I asked myself, lifting my glass to her, *that he left his deck to haul fish in a dory?*

My striving memory told a tale of a doryman injured off the French islands. The captain had taken that man's place in the dory. A sundering gale had struck in. *The Lark* had had a brave afternoon of searching for dories. At nightfall she had found the captain's dorymate clinging to a trawl buoy. The captain had flung him that buoy, and then the gale had driven the dory off into the darkness. I remembered, too, that it had been a greenhorn blunder on the doryman's part that sent him slipping over the side.

"A safe voyage home, captain." Marie Rose touched her lips to the glass. It was only then I discovered the rare color of her eyes—the exact hue of meadow violets; and I recalled more of her. Those eyes had made her a great beauty, according to Armand LeMay, who had been my family's agent on the French island for half a century.

I rose to make my farewell, and I looked down at her, discovering traces of her beauty even in the sparse, untinted figure she had become. Her capable hands, long-fingered and reddened by a life-time of labor, lay in her lap, the left hand quite hidden by the right.

"On my next voyage, madame, may I have the pleasure of bringing you some Boston apples?"

She thanked me; then, seeing my hand held out, she made her farewell. On looking after her hand when it was withdrawn, I saw on her left hand a wedding ring, a plain gold band. She did not look up at me again. No, she kept her eyes on the ring. Upon it now her tenderness played.

When I told Monsieur LeMay of my visit he said, "Excellently done! You are more and more like your grandfather, captain, in politeness."

"If it is proper for me to ask, monsieur, isn't it true that Marie Rose has been married? I saw her ring. Where is her husband?"

He sighed in compassion. "It's her fancy—nothing more—that gives her the ring. Ah, the world—the world and love have passed her by, captain."

"You have never told me enough about her. What had she to do with *The Lark*? I've been trying to remember all this time and now I remember that her captain rowed to some shore through a terrible blizzard."

He told me that he had heard the story long ago from his mother, who had been in the convent school with Marie Rose and had been her good friend for many years. So it was from him, an able talker, I found out that, if the world had passed Marie Rose by, love had not.

Long before I was born Marie Rose stood one noontime in her doorway, searching the sea for her father's sloop returning. Winter had come early. Already there had been a gale, a harsh blow out of the east, driving hail and making ice. All the vessels had kept snug in St. Pierre harbor. The vessels working on the Newfoundland coast had taken shelter and they were keeping in it because the gale had not really blown itself out. There were signs that the storm would come scudding out again from the caverns of Langlade, the island lying in the east.

Her father's vessel had tied up safely in Fortune Bay of New-foundland. Because there was no way for her to learn those good tidings until the sloop itself appeared, she had her anxious hours. For some years she and her father were the only people left in the hamlet; therefore, she could not expect that another vessel, or a neighbor, might come by with the news that she desired.

"Ah, it will blow again!"

She spoke of the gale. At the time, she was nearly thirty years old and had long since become seawise, accustomed to the Atlantic and its changes. She knew well the work of the coasting vessels and could sit to the oars as well as any man. Now that she had read the signs of the gale to come, her anxiety for her father waned. She knew he would never venture out of shelter until the storm had passed for good.

Her dog came up to take a caress. Of the Newfoundland breed, black and thick-coated, the dog helped the family in much of its work. He had been trained in the usual way to draw a light cart. The leather harness lay snug over his chest and shoulders. In the migrating seasons of waterfowl, when the wild goose fell before her father's gun, the dog showed much skill in retrieving birds from the hurrying tide. Also he kept guard at night and called her when her father came down the path, lantern in hand, after his trading voyages.

The dog followed her when she set about her chores. She cleared away the shallow drifts of snow blown to her doorstep by the easterly; and she carried into the kitchen the coal and wood for her stove. During that time the wind off the sea chilled her so much that she returned to the cottage and there changed her woolen skirt for woolen trousers and the thick-soled boots of the sea trades. By noontime, the sands of the shore glowed so pleasantly that she walked there a while, the dog romping in and out of the sea.

Marie Rose spied a tramp seal in the green breakers. Those adventurers amused her. Self-exiled from the herds of the north, such vagrants revealed much interest in life ashore. They respectfully returned greetings by bobbing up and down and would often swim a mile along the beach to gain another wave of her hand. Sometimes she thought they seemed like schoolmasters, becomingly bald and whiskers drooping, their eyes requiring an answer to a profound question.

Abruptly, and with no politeness at all, the seal slid beneath the waves.

In searching for him in a casual sweep of the sea yonder, she saw a boat under sail—perhaps a dory. It appeared to be taking advantage of the flood tide to make a swift passage from Newfoundland to St. Pierre. Marie Rose paid small heed to it. Indeed, in the time it took her to retrace her way down the beach to her home, she did not again look out to sea.

At her doorstep, she stayed a while to take more of the sun because it had been hidden for so many days by the gale and was now likely to vanish again. She saw the sailing dory. It had come nearer. This change surprised her because it had been on a course that should have carried it nearly out of sight, much closer to Dog Island and the inward passage to the harbor.

"How strangely she sails!"

For a time the dory steered straight toward her. Because of this alteration, which may have revealed an intent to come ashore there, she walked down the path to the well house. There in its shadow she awaited the stranger's arrival.

The dory had now come close enough for her to see that it was neither a French boat nor one made in Newfoundland. No, its sides were higher than the sides of such craft, and it had a kind of massiveness, created by the forceful way it rode the seas, neither yielding lightly to the tide rips nor faltering when a breaker burst against the blunt bow.

A sun-streaked squall harrowed the sea and struck against the dory. Its sail blew up and flapped in and out of curves of spray. This new change sent the dory veering off, plainly out of control. The tide took hold of the dory, flung it back into a boisterous tide rip, and the rip flung foam and black water over the gunwales.

"But there is no man in it!"

She called her dog and, pointing to the distant dory, bade him watch over it until she returned. He understood this order clearly. He walked gravely to a dune near the well house and sat there, his deeplighted, amber eyes fixed on the dory. He carried himself in somber fashion and now and then lifted his right paw in a gesture toward the sea.

At the cottage Marie Rose took a sea glass—the long telescope of those times—out of its case, and, her back against the cottage wall, she trained the glass on the horizon. She brought it slowly down until she found the image of the dory. A man's head appeared above the gunwale. Dimly she saw his yellow storm hat and, under its brim, his eyes gazing, not at her or the shore, but in a curious downward look into the flow of ice and foam.

Even so far, and coming from a stranger in yellow oil clothing, the eyes signaled an appeal to Marie Rose, one that she could not understand. She lost the image. When she searched it out again, the face had vanished. The dory had swung all the way around again. Ice knocked at its sides.

Her dog had counted all these changes. He came closer to her side and stood nigh, his eyes set on the dory. Whatever were the images taken in by the dog, they kept him uneasy. A growl rumbled in his chest; he kept tossing his head, a sign to her that he was trying to see more.

"Jean," she said, "it is a living man, a stranger."

She kept her glass fixed on the dory. It seemed likely that there might be soon an explanation of its actions, something to quiet the fear in her heart. A cry of relief parted her lips. The man out there had done something that assured her; his arm appeared in a motion three times repeated. Three times the yellow sleeve glittered in the sun, now long past its noon.

"He is bailing her."

This conjecture soon ceased to satisfy her heart. Three heaves of a bailer meant nothing. Her sea knowledge proved that the dory had not shipped enough water to endanger it. Moreover, the sail kept thrashing, a shattered wing snapping into the blue. No man would risk his sail to clear a little water.

His next action told her more of his condition. He rose to his height in the dory and, by clinging to the mast, held himself up. He bent far backward, his face upturned, his arm rigid in a gesture that seemed one of anger or of appeal to the sky. The sail whipped down and wrapped him.

Marie Rose saw him immobile in that canvas prison; only his white-gloved fist stayed thrust, now against the black water, now against the blue sky. The sail unwound itself and blew away in two skeinlike parts, all tatters. The man's back gave a number of flashes, these from sunlight across his yellow jacket. After that, he lunged awkwardly forward and, once again, vanished under the gunwales.

"Dear God! He has fallen!"

Before ever she stirred from her place, she swept the sea with her telescope, hoping to find another sign of life on that glassy swell. She saw nothing, except the dory turning.

She had no time to seek help elsewhere. Indeed, considering the nature of the task so abruptly thrust upon her, she required no other help than time and strength enough to struggle against the tides and to escape the returning gale. She had been to the hard school and had the skill to carry out her rescue. Moreover, she had her dog, a vigorous, intelligent animal stronger than herself.

Between the well house and the highwater mark a boat lay on its side, its oars under the slanted thwart. She ran to it and righted it with one full heave of her body. At her signal, the dog stood by for the tying of the boat painter to his harness.

She shouted: "Jean! Go!"

He lunged forward, his paws spurting sand, his claws taking good hold. Crying out her signal again and again, she heaved with him until the boat slid into the sea. She drew the rope out of his harness and, calling him in, sat to the oars. She began to row strongly against wind and tide.

By chance of wind and tide, the stranger's dory changed course and sailed directly toward her, gliding forcefully up the seas and plunging hard. In quick glances over her shoulder Marie Rose saw the distance closing swiftly. She bore to windward to make their meeting smoother. Her boat ran too far that way, so that she passed the dory at such an angle she could not look into it. Backing her port oar, she turned her boat with the wind and, in a few strokes, lay alongside the dory, her hand holding to its gunwale.

Face down in a slush of hail and brine, the man lay sprawled. By striking out with his right hand, he kept trying to lift his head out of the water that lapped upon the bottom boards. He seemed unable to do anything with his legs.

She shouted, "Hold on! Hold on!"

She made the painter fast to the dory thwart and slid over the gunwales to his side. She passed her arms under his. In a fierce strain of thighs and legs, she heaved him forward half his length. She turned him over on his back and held his head between her hands.

Now she saw what he was: a man of her age, a ruin of frostbite, hunger, and of immense strength poured out against the gale that had darkened her windows. She struck away the slush freezing on his mouth. She cleared the closed eyes of frost; and then, fearful that he had died, she tore open his jacket and thrust her hand through his woolen shirts until she found his heart beating mildly to her touch. Even beneath all the folds of wool, her fingers encountered frost.

He spoke to somebody far away, to a doryman, pleading: "Greenhorn or not—I go with him! Can't spare a dory now."

Despite the violence of his thought, his voice quavered like the voice of an old man, boastful in a dream of manhood. He tried to make a gesture to back up his words. His hands failed. He had spoken in English yet not in the manner to which Marie Rose was used.

She bent over him. "Can you hear me?"

He sighed. He let his head fall gently against her knee, either in peace or in the loss of all consciousness.

She straddled the thwart and, by heaving with all her strength, she drew him nearer the bow, where his wooden bailer lay. Burned into its scoop, she read the words *The Lark*. She thrust it under his head. She took up the dory's painter and tied it to her boat, which she entered and began to row. The tide, coming to slack water, made her task easier. She towed the dory to the beach below her home.

The dory could not be handled. It was all she could do to tip it slightly so that his body turned nearer the gunwale, where she stood over her boots in the tide. She had to rest. Fear had tapped her heart and her strength. She stared down at the enigma of his face. The winter evening began to flow over it. Long shadows of the evening waned. Beyond the outer islands lighthouses began to flash; and the bell buoys, heaved now by the ebbing tide and a rising wind, clanged another note, keener and faster. Over far Langlade, the gray became black, foretelling the quick coming of the gale.

She had not the power to lift the man. Yet she had to do it. Already a new frost laced his storm hat. Again placing her arms under his, she drew him to the gunwale; then, marshaling all her force, she dragged him over the side. He slid heavily into the water.

"Oh, no! No!" This time he spoke in such weariness that it seemed to her he could never speak again; and yet at once his lips opened in a sigh so piteous that she cried out wildly in answer. Cleaving the sea noises of a tide splashing on shores of rock, her cry became a wail.

The dog took this cry for a summons and ran through the water to raise his paw to her. She took off the rope from the boat and harnessed the dog to the man's shoulders. She passed the rope round and round the man's waist. She held him by the arms and shouted to her dog.

By one unbroken pull in tandem, the dog straining at her heels, they dragged the man all the way up the beach, past the well house and to her door. She opened it and, joining the dog again, drew the man into the kitchen. That room was well warmed by a coal fire in the cookstove.

She pulled off his boots. Spurts of water came out of them. This dismayed her because it meant that boots and oil clothing had failed and his feet had been in chilling brine all this time, making the danger of frostbite even worse. Therefore she bathed his feet in warm water and rubbed them with her hands until a faint ruddiness appeared.

Out of her oven she took two bricks that always lay there in winter for the purpose she now required of them. She wrapped them in flannel squares and placed them close to the man's feet. She then removed all of his outer clothing. When she unbuttoned the chin strap of his storm-hat, thus revealing his forehead and close-cropped curly hair, she saw that his hair had much the same color as her own. His stubble beard, days old, seemed not red at all, it was so dark. Because of a deep line on either side of his bluntish nose, and another between his eyebrows, he had the look of a much older man, one of middle age, worn by sea toil and sea cares.

"Sir? Sir?" He made no sign.

Against the nightfall she lighted two lamps and again knelt by him. She bent far down and studied his closed eyes. Under the lids, inflamed by frost, his eyeballs moved in spasms.

She made tea, sugared it well, and put rum into it. She fed him with a spoon. At the touch, his lips opened so eagerly that the first portion went down well, and yet, after the second spoonful, she saw no swallowing action. She had to rub his throat briskly before she marked the passage of the liquid.

She held off. He had tried to lift his left arm and had failed. In response to the break of famine and thirst, he cried out clearly and without distress: "My vessel! Is she safe? Answer me!"

She did not think that he actually knew what he was saying or that he could receive an answer. She made none. Even so far gone, he had something on his mind—a great fear. It forced him to repeat his thought, this time in such a pleasing, calm tone that she answered boldly, wishing to comfort him, even at the cost of a falsehood. "Your vessel is standing off and on the headland. She is safe, captain."

She wiped his forehead and his mouth.

Either her words or her soothing hands sent a meaning to his searching heart. He let his head go gently to one side. He began to breathe naturally, no longer striving to take in gulps of air. He raised his right hand to his throat and fumbled at a leather cord there. He soon gave this up.

Marie Rose tried to give him more drink. She didn't succeed because he wouldn't open his mouth. A little later, in a voice that waned at once to a whisper, he said, "I am her skipper. John Darmody of *The Lark*. Gloucester. Let that be remembered. Do you hear me there?"

She answered, "Aye, captain! All of us hear you. Have no fear, sir."

"Fear!" She had, for once, made a clear communication to him. This word came scornfully from his lips, and the scorn twisted his lips into severity. Resuming the calm voice that had comforted her, he said, "I'd like to know just what there is to fear. I would, indeed."

The establishment of thought between them raised her hopes greatly, and she kept them so, even when he again refused to admit the liquid. He responded by a change in his breathing to such a hoarse rattling that her heart became faint with renewed fear. In trying to force his left hand away from an awkward position, she found it icy and inflexible. This was her first certain knowledge that frost and famine had stricken him so deeply in those days and nights on the Grand Bank or the Green, wherever he had been lost from his schooner. She uncovered his feet. Warmth from the enfolded bricks floated through her fingers, yet his feet had yielded to the paralyzing chill.

"Do you hear me, captain?"

Because she knelt by him the intense cold of the earth, working through the floor, began to hurt her knees. She could no longer let him lie there. Unable to carry him to a bed, she brought the bed to him, one from her own room, squeaking on casters. After struggling long against his unyielding body, she placed him between the sheets and covered him again.

Night had drifted over Galantrie Head. The unspent gale had risen. Sleet scraped at the windows. At times snow fell so thickly that flakes slid melting down the kitchen panes. Far away the breakers repeated the throbbing, cavernous melody that told of ice floes pushing in from the east. The wind frightened her. Yet it had been her lullaby.

Now, for the first time, his eyes opened. They closed so quickly that she couldn't see their color. This brief access of strength created in him another fancy, a dream, of such a nature that his empty expression changed to one of intensity.

"What vessel is that? Oh, I can't hear him! What's he saying, chum?" Even in his delirium, he sought an answer. He repeated his questions and turned his head sideways as if he were actually scanning the sea.

Employing the name of her father's vessel, Marie Rose replied in loud, pretended cheerfulness; "'Tis the *Mathilde* out of St. Pierre, captain. Aye, 'tis her. Now she signals: 'All is well.' "

His question had been ably said. Her answer had no effect, except the opening of his eyes, not in a lively way, but in a drowsiness. This hid any meaning that she might have found if his gaze had been directed toward her. He looked dreamily at nothing. The pupils of his eyes each held images of lamps. Upon the gray irises, night floated, whirled.

In an action that surprised her by its smoothness, he again reached into his sweater. This time, he drew up the leather cord. A tiny pouch of green leather came to the edge of his sweater and then fell outward rather heavily. A new intensity marked his next words. He made a plea. "Mary!" And: "Oh, my darling, give me your hand. Ah, how long it has been, Mary!"

He held out his hand in the pleading. Marie Rose gazed at it. Soon her tears, no longer to be held back, hid the hand from her sight. When he whispered the name again, she placed her left hand in his grasp. His hard fingers embraced her hand entirely. His eyes closed;

once more a degree of gentleness stayed on his mouth. A change came. His breathing increased in force. He began to breathe roughly through his mouth. This soon subsided.

Marie Rose tried to spoon the liquid into his mouth. She could not. She cried out to him. An uproar of the gale beat against the door and windows so loudly that he couldn't hear her. Nor did he perceive the gale. Even when the cottage shook, he lay in seeming peace.

She began to pray that help might come, although she knew that the only help lay miles away in the town of St. Pierre. It now seemed possible to her longing heart that her father might have made the crossing and might come to her. Yet she was aware that, even for him, the roads and paths to Galantrie were long since drifted over and difficult to pass. Nevertheless, she wished for the welcoming bark of her dog, lying outside the door. In the end she understood there were no reasons for such hopes. She bent over the young captain.

He began fumbling at the drawstring of the pouch. His failure made him complain fretfully. "Oh, dear! Oh, what luck!"

When he failed the third time, Marie Rose opened the pouch for him. He reached into it and, with a deftness that again surprised her, he took out something wrapped in a delicate blue paper. His hand passed over the object, surrounded it; and he held it closely to him.

He had to make keener efforts to follow the bidding of his far-inward thought. The line between his eyebrows deepened and a set of wrinkles came skeining across his forehead.

"Mary! Come close to me, dear. Oh, the time has come, thank God!"

He laughed in delight; yet no pleasure appeared in his eyes. They stayed blank. By a sudden enclosure of her in his right arm, he drew her down to him and, again in a laughing way, he said something about lips and breasts that caused her to flush and turn her eyes from him. He would not let her go, or he could not, so strong was his delusion. He held her even closer and, at last, brought her mouth to his. So they kissed; and the man and his kiss seemed very sweet to Marie Rose, who had had no other kiss of love.

Soon, in that passionate embrace, she felt his arm weakening on her shoulder. He had strength only for whispering, "Don't leave me, Mary."

And she answered, "I will never leave you, John." After speaking so, she kissed him and kissed in haste.

Now a solemn vision stirred him gently, and his eyes closed and opened again. "Aye!" he whispered in contentment, as if the vision contained the summertime and apple blossoms at home, and a bell chiming amid the song of red-winged blackbirds near a garden where he stood, and his white-gowned Mary advancing to him on the arm of her father.

More than ever gentled, he drew Marie Rose to him and said, "I love you, Mary. And I always will."

Marie Rose laid her hand on his forehead and kissed his frost-broken lips and answered, "I love you, John. And I always will."

He held her hand. His empty eyes staring away, he drew a wedding ring out of the blue paper by the last effort of his left hand. He placed it on her finger. He carried her hand to his lips and kissed the ring.

"Oh!" he said clearly, fondly, "oh, Mary, I am so happy now!"

Thereupon he turned his head toward the sea window, where the gale clanged in its darkness.

After a time Marie Rose folded his arms across his breast and closed his eyes. She knelt by the bed and she prayed for the repose of his soul and she prayed for his Mary, in Gloucester far away. She continued her supplications until day broke.

This is why Marie Rose made a certain answer when bolder visitors, seeing her ring revealed, inquired, "Ah, madame has been married?"

And Marie Rose replied, "For a very little while. A long, long time ago."

AN ECHO OF LOVE

GARSON KANIN

He stood by the window of the sitting room of his suite and looked down at the bug-people scurrying along Fifth Avenue. It was lunchtime, and the fact that he was still in pajamas and robe made him feel guilty. His breakfast—a pot of coffee—waited on the low table in front of the sofa. A copy of *The New York Times* and a tray holding his morning mail lay beside it. He glanced at the table and considered diving into the day. Not yet. He looked down into the street again.

"The public," he said aloud. "Bless 'em."

He poured a cup of coffee and settled easily into his morning routine: spreading the newspaper on the floor, sitting on the sofa's edge, turning the pages of the paper with his left hand and torturing his tongue with hot coffee from the cup in his right hand. A name, his name, sprang up. *Wesley Priest*. He read:

Theater Tonight

On with the New, a comedy by Wesley Priest. Presented by Hal Evers. With Joe Blake, Amanda Storrs, Susan Olefen, Blane Thomas and Girard Jeffers. Directed by Joseph Pulaski. Settings and costumes by Rene Lemaitre. Curtain at 7:45 p.m. Cort Theater, West 48th Street.

The announcement made it seem irrevocable. A perverse part of his brain had hoped, through the fitful night, that something might happen to stave off the event: illness, death, a fire, some thoughtful act of God.

He flipped through his mail. No phone messages. With his hand over his eyes, he organized his day.

Lunch with his ex-wife at 1:30. Leave here at 1:15. Lunch. An hour? More. She would be late. Make an appointment for three o'clock. Escape. Back here to dictate opening-night wires to Mrs. Donnell? Hold it. What time was the final run-through? Three. Perfect. Frances would have to understand that. Then the wires? No. Florist first. Then the wires. Ask Mrs. Donnell to stand by for last-minutes. Ask her to dinner. Here? No. A good, noisy, impersonal place. Frankie and Johnnie's. Yes. Reservation. Last great steak for some time to come. Be sure to reach the theater by seven.

A boat whistle sounded mightily, reverberating across Manhattan. Wesley smiled as he congratulated himself on his plan.

Out there on the Hudson his luggage was already aboard the *Queen Mary*. After tonight's performance he would thank the cast, the director and the management and go directly to the ship, which would sail at midnight. He had insisted upon a Saturday-night opening so that no reviews would be available until Sunday night, by which time he would be breathing pure sea air as he sped farther and farther away from the point of tension. Whatever the verdict, it would seem less important out there.

He felt so strong and in command as he went into the bathroom and began to prepare for the day.

Shaving turned out to be a problem, because his hands were shaking. He felt perfectly calm. Why, then, were his hands shaking? He spoke sharply to his face in the mirror—"Cut it out!"—and went on trying to shave.

He reviewed—not for the first time this week—the situation. This would be his ninth Broadway opening. Until now he had had one smash, two successes, one so-so and four failures. Not a bad record, better than most; but tonight's play was in a new key, and the question was: Would they take it from him? At fifty-one he was telling his first love story. Why not? He thought of his play, felt its strength and stopped shaking.

He was on his second tomato juice when Frances arrived. He glanced at his watch, and at her, but said nothing.

"Sorry," she said. "I'm in the middle of a nightmare day."

"Aren't we all?"

She kissed his cheek briefly and sat down. "What's that? A bloody mary?"

"No, just plain."

"Oh, Lord! Not again!"

The waiter approached. "Vodka martini," she ordered. "Double."

"Why not triple?" Wesley suggested.

Frances dismissed the waiter with a look and pointed her lighted cigarette at him. "Don't rag me, Wes. Not today. I'm in no mood."

"You're in *quite* a mood, far as I can see."

"I know your trouble. Opening night and all that. You have to wait till Monday morning to find out whether you're a genius or a bum. Poor boy! It's a strain, and I feel for you. Only don't take it out on me with those ever-so-sly jokes."

"Well, it's no compliment to me that you start banging on double martinis the minute you see me for the first time in—what?—four months?"

"Five."

"Five, then. And considering you've had one or two already."

"My, what a long nose you have, Grandma!"

"Yeah."

Frances giggled. "That damned chlorophyll chewing gum doesn't fool you, does it?"

The waiter served her drink, took her order. While Wesley ordered, she finished the drink and tapped her glass. "One more."

Wesley stared at her.

"Single," she added.

"See?" Wesley said as the waiter left. "You should have taken the triple."

"Why, dear?" she asked archly. "Is it cheaper that way?" He blushed and tried to smile when her drink was served.

"How do you feel about tonight?" she asked.

"The usual willies. It's a good play, though. And a good show."

"I heard you were very large in Washington."

"Yes," he said. "Philly too."

"Well, then?"

"Doesn't seem to count anymore. Out-of-town fuss. Anything can happen."

Lunch was served. "I need an extra ticket, by the way," Frances said.

"No," Wesley said.

"I need it."

"I got you three," he reminded her.

"It's for my third beau," she said, winking. "Wait till you see us."

"Question: Are you really going to my opening with three escorts?"

"Why not?" She shrugged. "Kicks, I suppose. Break the monotony. I may as well say it, lad; that's one thing I never knew with you."

They ate in silence for a while.

"What's with you?" she asked. "Got a girl?"

"No."

"What happened to You Know?"

"Well," he said. "You know."

She laughed, but stopped abruptly. "Poor guy. I'm sorry for you. You don't believe that, but I am, truly."

"Don't be."

"We none of us ever make it with you, do we? Never have. Never will."

"All right, Fra." His upper lip glistened with sudden moisture.

"Because we're all competing with Miss Perfect."

There were tears in her eyes. "Emotional release," she said. "Best thing in the world for the digestion."

She began to talk about her plans for a winter holiday. He nodded and made occasional sounds, but his mind was in another time, another place. . . .

. . . Miss Perfect. No. Miss Barr. Rebecca.

He was twenty-six, she a few years younger. They were employed by Columbia Pictures in Hollywood. He was a junior writer; she, a contract player. The art and business of films consumed their lives: stories and scripts and previews and options and tests and gossip and the Big Chance that lay a day ahead.

Rebecca Barr was unique. "A young Irene Dunne" was the casting director's quick label, but Wesley could not see it. Rebecca had her own sort of distinction. She reflected the joy and, at the same time, the terror of living. Every moment was of consequence to Rebecca, every person, place, thing. She was never bored, never boring. She had soaring ambition and poetic legs; an unmistakable, unforgettable laugh and a sense of wonder. Wesley loved her. She accepted his love humbly and with respect but made it clear that she could not, or would not, return it. He wooed her gently and waited. Her eyes—— You felt as though you could walk right into them. . . .

". . . Wes!"

It was Frances's voice. She went on. "Do you honestly think you fool me with all that automatic nodding and that ugly grunting? I know when you're not listening."

"Would you like me to repeat everything you just said?"

"No, thanks. I've just heard it."

He spoke softly. "Fra?"
"What?"
"I'll get you that extra ticket."
"I knew you would, honey."
"And I have to go. Run-through."
"Drop me?"
"Sure. . . . Check, please!"

He sat in the dark, almost-empty auditorium, watching the final run-through of his play. Without makeup and costumes it had an air of unreality; further, the director had told the company to accelerate the pace. "The audience'll slow you down tonight," he said.

The sound from the stage faded in Wesley's ears; the action became a kaleidoscope. He took advantage of the interlude to think.

Was Frances right? Was he doomed forever to fail with women because of Rebecca? Had he idealized her out of proportion to reality? The truth was that he and Rebecca had been the closest of friends, nothing more. But almost, once. . . .

. . . Arrowhead Springs. The enormous new hotel had just opened, and one of the studio heads had invited forty of his employees to a weekend party. Wesley and Rebecca had driven up together.

The company-party mood embarrassed them both, and amid the planned gaiety of the second evening they escaped, separately. Wesley overtook her by chance in the woods, half a mile from the hotel.

She turned when she heard his footsteps behind her, and he stopped.

"I hate being followed," she said testily.

"I swear," he said. "I had no idea."

"Sorry. I believe you." She held out her hand. He took it, and they continued the walk together.

"I'm one big exposed nerve tonight," she said. "What about this occasion? It's humiliating."

"Exhausting. Everybody's knocked out trying to show what a good time they're having."

"I'm glad you turned up," she said. "They say there are bears out here."

"Bears out here and wolves back there. You dazzlers lead one hell of a life."

"How come *you* sneaked out?" she asked. "Don't you care if your option gets picked up?"

"I'll never be missed," he said. "Not in that powerhouse clan."

She shivered. "We'd better go back. This damp."

"Here." He slipped off his jacket and put it on her. She spun gracefully, modeling it, and said, "We ought to live together. We could wear each other's clothes."

"I'm game."

She took his arm and held it tightly with both her hands as they walked back to the hotel.

"You're my best friend, Wes. A beguiling fella. I count on you."

He was grateful for the darkness that masked his instantly perspiring face.

She went on. "Don't think I don't think about it. I do. There are times I want it to be. But you're a serious guy, and I wouldn't dent you for the world."

"I think we should go to bed together and see what *that* tells us."

"I've considered that. But it would only make things worse."

"All right, then. Let's get married. And that's my final offer."

"I can't joke about it, Wes. It means too much. I'm flattered. And touched."

"But?"

"But."

"Give me one reason."

"No. Because the best thing in my life out here is your friendship, and if I told you—we wouldn't be friends anymore."

They had reached the hotel. She said, "Come on up to 732 in ten minutes."

"Gladly."

"Big Chief sent up a bottle of champagne. In a bucket. And just one glass."

"I'll have mine out of a toothbrush mug," he said. "Or out of your sneaker."

He went to his room, undressed, showered, put on fresh clothes and made his way to 732. He noticed that the room had taken on her personality. It was imaginatively arranged. A rare scent pervaded it. The flowers were artfully set. The lighting was soft and restful.

Rebecca pointed to a huge armchair. "That's where I planned for you to sit."

"I will if you promise to dolly in for a close-up once in a while."

She tossed a pillow to the floor. "I'll sit here," she said. "Will you open the champagne or shall I?"

"I've never opened a bottle of champagne in my life," he said. "Is that why you won't marry me?"

"Not exactly."

She went to the champagne bucket. He rose, went to her, turned her firmly and kissed her.

"Thank you," she said softly. "I enjoyed that. Now let me do the champagne."

They drank, and smoked, and talked in the open, intimate way they had found. Yes, he thought. This is the time. He made careful, practical plans.

They shared the sense of belonging together. Among all those who peopled this vast, remote hotel tonight, there was no one else for either of them. They shared interests, intentions and standards.

They had both begun in the theater, both hoped to return to it someday. His first play had failed, but his promise as a playwright had been noted by important critics. It had led to this job, which he would have turned down if he had been able to afford to. He had planned to write his second play on evenings and weekends, layoffs and holidays—but it had not worked out. The studio work was consuming and interesting, and his second play remained in note-book form for four years. It might never have been written at all if he had not been drafted early in 1941. When he was released from the Army in 1946 he had three plays in his footlocker. The second of these was his smash—but that night at Arrowhead Springs, the event which was to germinate the idea lay embedded in the future.

Rebecca was saying, "You see, the trouble with me is——"

"Cut!" he interrupted. "I never let anybody finish that particular sentence."

"Why not?"

"Always devious."

"Not this time."

"All right. I'll make an exception in your case, lady, because I'm hopelessly in love with you. I mean hopefully."

"The trouble with me is I'm a damn snob."

"I've never noticed it," he said, "and my hobby is noticing things about you."

"Part of it comes of being scared, I suppose. For all my noise, I think there's a good chance I'll never get very far on my own. That's why I feel the need to hang onto the up-theres."

"Why not the going-to-be-up-theres? Like me."

"Look at the ones I've been hooked up with so far. You know the list."

"Sure. I go over it every night before I go to sleep—planning murders."

"I don't admire myself. I'd change if I could."

"What is it you're saying? That I'm not important enough?"

"Well, you put it——" she paused.

"Crudely?" he suggested.

"No, but 'important' isn't what I mean."

"Dough?"

"It's some that, yes. I have expensive tastes."

"So if I were rich and up there, you'd love me."

"No, because if you were rich and up there you wouldn't be you."

He closed his eyes and gave his head a violent shake. "Put away those loaded dice. And give me another drink."

Pouring it, she said, "I know what I feel, but I can't put it into words."

"I can," he said.

"Of course. You're a writer."

"The words are 'bunk,' 'nonsense' and 'poppycock.' Also 'fiddlesticks.' "

She handed him his glass. "No. It's me—my weakness. My brother says I'm a product of my horrible upbringing. He says it's my mother's fault."

"Proposition," Wesley said. "Let's have a glorious love affair while I get rich and up there—and if I don't——"

"Yes?"

"You get a refund."

"Oh, Wes!" she said.

Their talk ended there. He decided later that jesting had been a mistake.

He had gone on to middling success as a screenwriter. She had become mired in supporting roles. They had remained close friends, but neither his position nor her aim changed appreciably.

A few weeks after he began his military service she wrote him about her marriage. The man, a Bostonian, was chairman of the board of the largest banking institution in New England, specializing in motion-picture finance. He was often in the news as a possible gubernatorial candidate. Thus overnight Rebecca outranked even studio heads and their wives. It meant a good deal to her when she and her husband visited California. At other times she dwelt in that exclusive world beyond the world. Wesley often came upon her photograph in *Vogue, Harper's Bazaar* or *The Illustrated London News.* She grew more attractive to him through the years and still played the leading part in his fantasies of a somehow future.

A few months after his first success he married Frances, who resembled Rebecca in form and spirit. Frances knew and did what she could to deepen the resemblance, but, the closer she came, the more poignantly was Wesley reminded of his failure. Still the marriage lumbered on, collapsing only after fourteen years under the weight of pretense and fatigue. . . .

. . . Applause. The run-through was over. The players took their rehearsed curtain calls and gathered on the stage to hear the director's final comments.

The producer approached Wesley as he stood putting on his overcoat. "Well, boyo," he said, "too late to get out of it now, what? Can I say one thing?"

"You bet, Hal," Wesley said.

"I've got no qualms. Not a one."

"All right," Wesley said. "I'll give you one of mine."

They shook hands, and Wesley left. Later, he dressed and had dinner with his secretary at Frankie and Johnnie's.

Mrs. Donnell was an attractive French widow of forty. Her husband had died shortly after he brought her, a war bride, to America, leaving her with an almost compulsive need to work; she seemed unhappy only when unoccupied. With her, Wesley discussed plans for meeting again in Paris in the course of coming weeks.

"But before," she said, "shall I phone you the reviews on Monday to the ship? Or Sunday if I know something?"

"Send them airmail-special to Claridge's," he said. "But just the good ones."

"That will be everything." She saluted him with her wineglass. "I feel it."

"Remind me to give you a raise."

"Very well." She took a notebook from her handbag and made a note, mumbling, "Remind W.P. give N.D. substantial raise."

Before leaving for the theater he swallowed two pills, tranquilizers. His doctor had advised them, provided he had nothing to drink, but in deference to Mrs. Donnell he had ordered a bottle of wine and consumed half of it. The combined effect of the wine and pills detached him from the evening, and he spent most of it at the back of the house, watching Frances and her three escorts from the moment they entered until, at the end, they sat applauding enthusiastically.

He forgot even the critics. Mrs. Donnell brought him, periodically, what seemed to add up to thirty glasses of water, and he spent a good part of the second act in the men's room.

The backstage crush afterward was familiar, as though it were a rehearsed part of the evening. "Darling!" Overpraise. "Baby!" An embrace. "Darling." Whispers. And one worried face.

In the taxi on the way to the pier he asked Mrs. Donnell, "What did you think—no kidding?"

"The best performance. The best audience."

"But you didn't see much of it, did you, Gunga Din?"

"Pardon?"

"Water boy. Joke."

"But each time you looked at me you have made a motion—so—for drinking."

"Is that why you kept pouring water down me?"

"Of course."

"I meant, 'Let's go out and get a drink.' "

"I'm sorry for my sign language so poor. But why then did you keep on drinking the water?"

"I couldn't think of anything else to do with it."

They laughed for three blocks. He thought her remarkably attractive. The best secretary he had ever had, by far. The day he found her she had been one of nine candidates. He had been working on an adaptation of a French play, and the agency had sent over all available bilingual secretaries. He had chosen Nicole Donnell by instinct. Neither her resume nor her interview personality was impressive, but he had felt relaxed only with her. A lucky day, he reflected. She was now an indispensable part of his life. He took her hand.

"Thanks for everything," he said. "All of a sudden I wish I weren't going."

"Don't then. Take the stateroom luggage off—and, in the hold, one trunk—nothing you need. They would return it as unaccompanied baggage, free."

He let go of her hand. "Don't encourage me, " he said. "I'm weak as water."

She saw him to his cabin, a spacious one on main deck, gave his steward a list of instructions and checked the passenger list. "No one," she said happily.

He walked her back to the gangplank, kissed her on each cheek and put his arms about her. A ritual. But this time, for the first time, he was aware of her breasts against his chest. As he let go of her she smiled, and they kissed again. While it was in progress, he realized not only that it was thrilling but that he had not kissed anyone in many months, and that this was the first time he had ever really kissed Mrs. Donnell, who had been with him for seven years. The kiss ended.

"Bon voyage," Mrs. Donnell said, and left the ship. At the bottom of the gangplank she turned and waved.

Wesley made his way to the smoking room, his favorite bar of the many on this ship. He had postponed reading the current weekly publications and Mrs. Donnell had provided him with a large envelope containing everything he usually read. He ordered an especially prepared bourbon old-fashioned, skimmed through *Variety* until sailing time and then went up to the sun deck and watched Manhattan Island recede. It seemed glamorous all over again, the heart of his world, and he had to remind himself that he was doing what he had chosen to do in order to keep from sinking into despair.

He reviewed the curious farewell he had shared with Mrs. Donnell. Tension, no doubt. Opening-night excitement. Overemotional. But it had never happened before. He gave up as the Statue of Liberty waved good-bye.

The air of the open deck had chilled him. He returned to the bar and continued to drink, switching to hot whiskeys. They were especially pleasant and efficacious, and by 1:30 a.m. he felt cured of his chill and of all other ills as well.

He engaged the smoking-room steward in a long conversation about the time changes which were made thrice daily—a twenty-minute advance each time—and realized contentedly that he would not know the correct time anywhere until the ship reached Southampton. Then he remembered that Mrs. Donnell had provided him with an extra watch for his left wrist which was to remain set at New York time. She's getting officious, he thought. There's such a thing as being overorganized. She went too far sometimes, like putting those laxatives in his medicine case. Hell. He saw that he was the only one left in the smoking room. He finished his drink hurriedly, got up feeling lightheaded, overtipped the steward and went to his cabin.

The cabin steward had followed Mrs. Donnell's instructions, and the room was prepared to suit Wesley's habits. A bottle of Malvern Water on the night table. A pad and three pencils. The book he was reading, James Joyce's *Ulysses*, and beside it a copy of Rolf Loehrich's *Secret of Ulysses* and a dictionary. Two pairs of pajamas—one heavy, one light; dressing gown, slippers—everything in place, including the Dramamine and sleeping pills on a piece of pink paper on which was typewritten, "*Important. Do not take if alcohol has been consumed. Important.*" Defiantly he took two sleeping pills, undressed, put on neither pair of pajamas, crawled into bed, and sank into deep, cavernous sleep.

He awoke with a hangover. Someone had opened one of the portholes. The sea air was bracing, but his head—— He rang, and soon the steward appeared bearing a tray on which stood a pot of coffee, a glass of tomato juice, a bottle of Worcestershire sauce, a vial of Alka-Seltzer and a tall glass of water.

"Good morning, sir. Lovely morning."

"What's all this?"

"Special instructions, sir. All in order?"

"O.K. What's your name, by the way?"

"Peacock, sir."

Peacock placed the tray beside Wesley, picked up the Worcestershire sauce, poured a teaspoonful and offered it. Wesley gulped. Peacock shook a few streams of the sauce into the tomato juice and, as Wesley drank, poured a cup of coffee and left the cabin.

Wesley felt better at once. He finished the coffee and showered: hot, warm, cold. When he came out he found Peacock preparing the Alka-Seltzer. Everything he wanted had been transferred to the night table by the bed he had not slept in . He got into the fresh bed and took the fizzing glass from Peacock, who went out and returned almost at once with four massive New York Sunday newspapers.

Wesley frowned. "You must have had these last night—before we sailed."

"Yes, sir."

"Mrs. Donnell."

"Yes, sir."

Wesley laughed. Peacock gave him his reading glasses. "Will that be all, sir?"

"I don't know," Wesley said. "You'd better ask *her*."

Peacock left, and he started on the Sunday papers, his delight in the comics tempered by the fact that the ship's roll had increased and he was beginning to feel squeamish.

There was a gentle knock and Peacock ushered in two people dressed in white.

"Doctor Morgan, sir."

"Good morning," said the doctor. "We just popped by to see if you might not want the nurse here to give you our new hypo against possible mal de mer."

"Sure," Wesley said.

"Righto," said the doctor. "Mrs. Donnell thought you might be wanting it."

The nurse came forward with her covered tray, and Wesley extended his arm.

"Your hip, please," she said.

"Yes," said the doctor, lighting his pipe. "Bottoms up!"

Wesley turned over.

110

The doctor's remedy was effective. His seasickness was gone in twenty minutes, but the shot made Wesley drowsy, and he alternated between sleep—dreaming wild and unfamiliar dreams—and reading the newspapers. At two o'clock Peacock brought him a chicken sandwich on Hovis toast and more coffee.

Sleep, read.

At 4:30 Peacock brought tea and cakes.

Read, sleep.

He was awakened by a messenger who brought him a radiogram. He tipped the boy a dollar (for luck) and got out of bed. He went to the open porthole, took a few deep breaths and opened the radiogram.

It read:

TWO CHEERS HAL.

Wesley sat on the edge of his bed and considered the message for ten full minutes.

What did it mean? Good Lord! No more plays with that bonehead! Two cheers. Did it mean that the general reaction was lukewarm? Or that so far there were two favorable reviews? Or that two reviews were good and the rest bad? Mixed notices—defined by George S. Kaufman as "good and lousy." He could pick up the phone and find out. No. But why, oh, why, couldn't that idiot have sent a clear, straightforward message?

The phone rang. "Mr. Wesley Priest?"

"Yes?"

"We have a radio call for you."

Noises in his ear—unearthly, magical, comical. Waiting, he stared at the message as if it were a riddle, hoping that the answer would break through if he concentrated long and hard. *"Two cheers Hal."*

Mrs. Donnell came on the phone. "Hello? Hello? Can you hear me? Can you hear me?"

"Yes."

"All is well." She seemed to be speaking from the ocean's depth. "All is well."

"Go on."

"Sorry to call. Sorry to call. Hal told me message. I worried it would confuse you. I worried it would confuse you."

"It did. It did."

"*Times* good," she said. "*Tribune* excellent. *Tribune* excellent. *Times* good."

"Listen, Nicole. Just say it once. I can hear you."

"I'm not so sure *I* can hear *you*. It sounded——You called me Nicole?"

"What else?"

"*Daily News* OK. Some reservation, but fine quotes. And that is all we have now. Carl says wire services good and affirmative hints from everywhere and for you not to wo-ah-leeoi."

"What?"

"Not to wor—not to worry."

"Oh."

"Congratulations. Congratulations. And don't forget my raise. Good-bye."

"Hello. Mrs. Donnell? Mrs. Donnell? Nicole?"

"Thank you," said the ship's operator. "Your party has left the line."

Smiling, Wesley reviewed the conversation, making notes on his pad.

Peacock came in with his dinner jacket, hung it up and began to lay out the rest of his evening clothes.

"Sir, Mr. Burke sends his compliments from the Verandah Grill and is looking forward to seeing you."

"I've just had some good news from New York, Peacock."

"Yes, sir," said Peacock as he left.

The Verandah Grill, although only half occupied, had never seemed so gay and handsome. "And how've you been keeping?" asked Mr. Burke, the chief steward.

"Fine, Mr. Burke."

"Got something new on, have you?"

"Very new. Last night. I've just heard it's a success. A great success."

"Well, then," Mr. Burke said, "you'll be wanting champagne. A half-bottle?"

"No," Wesley said. "I think it's good enough for a whole bottle."

Caviar, soup, guinea hen, salad, cheese and peach Melba, champagne all the way. He called for a cigar and brandy.

He went down to the cinema. The attraction was a new Peter Sellers film he had missed in New York, but he could not keep from dozing off now and then.

He was awakened each time by a girl's laugh—unforgettable, unmistakable—a laugh he had heard often before, but not for twenty years. Rebecca Barr's laugh. He reasoned that his ears were playing tricks on him. His ears and too much champagne. He left the cinema for the promenade deck, walked briskly for half an hour, felt sober, went back to the cinema, heard the laugh again, felt drunk again, went to his cabin and to bed.

When Peacock brought his breakfast the next morning, Wesley had only to glance at the festive little stack of radiograms on the tray to know that the news was still good, probably great. Failure, he had found, invariably bred silence.

The messages were from Joe Pulaski, the director, from Frances, from his agent, from the two stars and from the ingenue, who had made her first success; and best of all, from his friend the ticket broker, who cabled,

YOUR TICKET SO HOT HAVE TURNED
OFF HEAT IN HERE THANKS KIDDO JOEY.

He replied by radiogram to each message—extravagant, but, oh, well—and went to the gym, worked out, had a swim and a sweat and a massage. After lunch, on a heady impulse, he went to his cabin, got out a stack of his green-tinted writing pads, found his box of favorite pens and sat down, giddy with excitement.

"Act One, Scene One," he wrote, and continued to release in draft form a play he had been carrying within himself for more than a year. He worked steadily, in a zestful trance until tea was brought in. He worked while he had his tea and on through the dinner hour. At 9:30 Mr. Burke phoned to ask if he was coming up. Wesley said no and returned to his work. He did not stop until well after midnight.

He put the manuscript in a drawer and absently began his morning routine. Half an hour later he found himself dressed and ready for the deck. It was 12:45 a.m. Laughing at himself, he changed into a dark suit and went up.

In the smoking room he found himself thinking back on the shape of what he had composed. He began to drink to shut off the motor in his head—or at least to slow it down—and then he tried walking round and round the promenade deck. The glass-enclosed bow of the ship was in darkness at this hour, lighted only by the moonlight freed intermittently by swift-moving clouds. Several passengers stood here, and Wesley became increasingly aware of them each time he passed. He made a puzzle of it. Two couples. Three. And a single shape. Man? Woman? The fourth time around he identified the single one as a female—by scent. He made a side trip to the bar. Next time around, the girl was alone. He walked by slowly.

"Hello," she said.

"Good evening," he said and passed her. A few steps later he stopped and grasped the rail. His knees buckled.

The girl—or wraith—who had greeted him was the young Rebecca Barr. Inconceivable. He wanted to turn back and look but did not dare. He went once again around the deck.

The girl was still there when he got back—and still Rebecca. He heard her laugh, Rebecca's laugh, the one he had heard the night before in the cinema. At least *that* was explained.

She spoke. "You *are* Wesley Priest?"

"Yes," he said and fled.

In his cabin he tried to figure it out. Certainly he had not had all that to drink. Rule out plastered. He had been thinking of Rebecca a good deal these past few days, true enough. The power of suggestion? A girl who resembled her. Not so remarkable. But the look, the laugh, even the sound of her voice. Even the way she said his name. The way Rebecca had said it always. Wait. Rebecca had a daughter—but no. Not as grown up as this. Her daughter would be—what? Rebecca married in 1941. The child born '42 or '43, say. Twenty. Nineteen. Wow! Time. Daughter, then? If it is her daughter, she'll be listed under Follett.

He found the passenger list and studied it. No Follett. She was gone when he returned to the deck.

He searched the ship. Verandah Grill (at this hour a supper club), lounge, smoking room, library—he could not find her.

He went back to the Verandah Grill and drank, convincing himself finally that he had suffered an unimportant hallucination. He turned his thoughts to New York and his good fortune there. Suddenly he rose, went to a nearby table and invited a tall, lovely young woman to dance. He kept her in his possession for over an hour, returned her, and went to bed.

He laughed about it the next morning but decided, although it was a tempting story, never to tell it. He worked well, came to the end of a scene at one o'clock precisely and quit for lunch.

Waiting for his lamb chop, he went through the motions of scanning a magazine. Actually his mind was exploring aspects of his new project.

"I beg your pardon," Rebecca's voice said. "May I join you?"

He looked up. There before him, in indisputable flesh, stood his hallucination—Rebecca Barr, exactly as he had known her a quarter of a century before.

Words would not come. He tried to rise and pitched forward in a faint.

114

He came to in his cabin. Doctor Morgan, the nurse, Peacock and Rebecca were all there.

"All right now?" the doctor asked.

Wesley nodded. "What happened? Was I out long?"

"About twelve minutes," the doctor said. "Stand up. Walk about."

Wesley did so. "Fine," he reported.

The doctor and nurse left. At a nod from Wesley, Peacock went out quickly and closed the door.

Wesley faced his guest. "Who are you?" he asked. "I mean, who the hell are you?"

"Vanessa Follett," she said. "Shouldn't you go up and finish your lunch?"

"No."

"I feel awful. Spoiling it."

Wesley lit a cigarette. "You're Rebecca Barr's daughter."

"Well, yes. Rebecca Follett's. I wish you'd let me take you back to your lunch. And let me sit with you."

"How come you're not on the passenger list?"

"Oh. My other name. Vanessa Kemble. It's my stage name. Do you like it?"

"No. Yes. What's the difference?"

"After Fanny Kemble."

"How old are you, Vanessa?"

"Twenty-one and four days," she said. "Which explains everything, doesn't it?"

"All right," he said. "let's go up to lunch and start all over."

She ate heartily and talked passionately, in the manner of young actresses—and disturbingly, to Wesley, in the manner of her mother.

"She talks about you. Always has. Not in front of dad, though. That's what gave me the idea you were a beau of hers."

"Depends what you mean by 'beau.' "

"I mean lover."

"No," he said. "Never that."

"Oh, blast!" She filled her mouth.

"You eat like her," Wesley observed.

"Was she any good? As an actress?"

"I always thought so, yes."

"She says she was, but the only time I ever saw her was in an old movie on TV, and she seemed awfully affected to me. Of course it was a tiny part. A sort of society tart."

"Probably *Skyline*."

"Yes!" she cried. "That was the name of it. How'd you know?"

"I wrote it."

"Oh," she said. "Yes." She wet her lips. "I thought it was quite—wonderful."

"It's improved with age, then. It was lousy when we made it."

Vanessa laughed. It was *that* laugh.

They had coffee in the deserted main lounge. She leaned forward intensely.

"Finally," she said, "I just got tired of arguing—or rather of listening. So I made my plans. To wait until my twenty-first birthday and meantime to work and study and practice and coach and not tell them a thing about it. They thought I was a French major, for heaven's sake! I've loaded up on voice, speech; I dance, play piano, sing; three acting sessions a week—what's more, I'm good."

"And what are you doing on this ship?"

"Chasing you."

He put down his cup. "Me?"

"You're my connection. And when I read the squib in *Variety*—I read *Variety* every single week—about how you were going to take off right after your opening—well, it struck me that this ship was sailing the day after my twenty-first birthday, and it all seemed to be part of some great sensible plan. Foreordained."

"Does your mother know where you are?"

"Yes."

"And what else?"

Vanessa smiled and shrugged her mother's shrug.

"I'd like you a lot better," he said, "if you weren't so much like her."

"No, you wouldn't," she said.

Wesley spent the rest of the afternoon trying to keep from falling in ridiculous love. They walked the deck and talked. He found her listening. Rare. He found *himself* listening. More rare. At teatime he told her his memories of this very ship as a troop transport, and of wartime London. It struck him that that was about the time she was born. He buried the thought.

At 5:30 she led him to a secluded part of the promenade deck. "I own this particular piece," she said, indicating two deck chairs, well blanketed. "And I'm trained to sleep at this hour. Could you?"

"I'll watch you."

"Please try," she said. "Good for you."

They covered themselves, leaned back and joined hands. A few minutes later she was asleep. He reflected that it was the first time he had been alone since coming out of his faint. Smiling, he began to sort out his impressions. What an adventure! He reminded himself that he must keep his head. This creature was, after all, a child. Moreover, the child of a friend. So young, he observed, studying her in sleep. He saw her as Rebecca, saw himself as young, and fell asleep.

He woke to find Vanessa looking at him. "Good morning," he said.

"You're better-looking than you were," she said. "I mean, back years ago."

"How would you know?"

"I've seen pictures." She yawned and stretched. "The inevitable scrapbook all once-were actresses keep. More pictures of you in hers than anyone."

"What's the time?" he asked.

"Seven-thirty, ship's time. Are we having dinner?"

"Sorry," he said. "I'm meeting a few chums at Sardi's."

"To celebrate *On With the New*? Isn't it—stirring?" He looked at her quizzically and she explained. "I've had messages. And Mr. Burke told me about the whole bottle of champagne by yourself. I was there opening night, so it's no surprise."

"Thank you."

"This is a dopey question, I know," she said. "But how did you happen to shift into such different subject matter?"

"I suppose I wanted to try writing something I didn't think I could do. What you do when you're fifty ought to be different from what you did at thirty, for instance. It's easy to grow old—what's hard is to grow up."

They left the chairs and strolled. When they reached her cabin she said, "Come on in. I'm quick at this."

She made him a bourbon old-fashioned, omitting the sugar, adding extra bitters, and with a single cube of ice. He looked at it, surprised that it met his exacting specifications. She explained. "I watched you, first night out."

With no apparent sense of impropriety she showered, changed and arranged her hair and makeup for the evening. She moved in and out of the dressing room and bathroom, continuing their conversation. In less than twenty minutes she was ready.

In his cabin she had a drink while *he* changed. He was unable to bring it off with the same ease of style she had; nevertheless he enjoyed it.

Cocktails in the observation lounge.

"I remember the day you were born," he said. "The day after, I suppose it was. There you were in *The New York Times*. I didn't like you at all—the idea of you."

"But you've changed your mind since?"

"I've got no mind—that's what makes me a successful playwright. Imagination, experience, sweat. But no mind."

"Ridiculous. *The Day After Forever* was created by a first-rate mind."

"It ran three weeks," he said.

"It ran two years in my head."

"Thank you," he said softly.

Dinner in the Verandah Grill.

"Isn't it funny you've never met my father?" Vanessa said. "All these years."

"What's he like?"

"Sweet—and square. He looks at me and I can hear him thinking, *Did I have something to do with* that?"

Her instant transformation into another character, projected clearly and wittily, told Wesley that she might have talent, at that. "Did he?" he said.

"You should see the suitable types he turns up for me, endlessly. Junior executives. . . . Gosh, the food's good here!"

"You bet. Tell me some more about Rebecca."

"I don't know much about her. She's a sort of secretive character."

"Happy?"

"I suppose. She had one great summer, years ago, marvelous affair with——"

"Shut up!"

They ate in cold silence. She was blushing. "Well," he said, "you might as well go ahead now."

"No. He's awfully high up in the government, and I ought to be ashamed of myself, and I am."

They went into the cinema and sat in the back row, holding hands. The film, a mystery story, took itself too seriously. Half an hour was enough. They looked at each other, nodded and left.

They played bingo—and lost. They danced—and won.

At midnight they went up to the supper club, drank champagne and went on dancing. Wesley began to worry. The evening was drawing to a close, and he feared the coming hour. His heart was pounding, and his reason refused to operate.

They walked the deserted deck. Passing through the dark passage in the bow, he said, "This is where I first saw you last night and thought I was having a spell."

"I wondered why you wouldn't stop."

She was holding his arm with both hands, and he quivered, so clearly did the gesture re-create Rebecca by his side. And when, after a time, Vanessa said, "Mr. Priest, you're a beguiling man," he felt his face go damp. Since Rebecca no one had used that word to describe him. For a disconcerting while the girl beside him was more Rebecca than her daughter, time was a jumble, and he was someone else—that worried, pushing, toadying young man full of doubts and ambitions.

They reached the dark passage again. This time she slowed their walk.

"Tired?" he asked.

"No. It's just that I want to be kissed." She looked at him gravely.

He walked away, and she followed him. It was a long time before he spoke.

"When you get to be my age," he said, "you won't take things so lightly."

"I don't take them lightly now."

"You may be a minx, for all I know."

"I'm not sure what that means."

"Look it up."

"Where?"

"Well," he said, "I have a fine dictionary in my cabin. Let's both look it up."

He wished that he could have cut that last speech.

"Let's go to mine," she said, "where there are no dictionaries at all."

With a surge of dizzying feeling he wanted her more than he had ever wanted anything. At the same time he wanted to behave properly. The conflicting desires pulled in a tug-of-war.

Vanessa led him toward her cabin. The night steward sitting in the corridor said, "Good evening," and vanished.

She whispered, "Won't you come in? I'll make you some scrambled eggs."

She laughed, stepped into the cabin, held open the door, and he was drawn magnetically in. She closed the door. They stood in the blackness and she waited a full minute before turning on a light. She moved to the table and fixed two drinks. He said, "Not until I know who you are."

She handed him his glass and took a thoughtful sip from her own.

"My name is Vanessa Follett," she said, "and I'm sort of mad about you."

"Sort of."

"Really."

"Because I'm your one connection, as you put it a while ago?"

"It may have started that way, but this whole day—it's made it different. And I see now it's because I've thought and known about you, and seen your plays and admired them, and maybe too because my mother has told me that you were the one great mistake of her life."

He sat down heavily. "What's that got to do with it?"

"Everything and nothing."

She knelt before him and touched her forehead to his chest. "It isn't a crush. I've had crushes galore, and I know what they feel like, and this is different."

"Missy," he said, "I'm trying hard to do the right thing, but you are making it—arduous."

"I hope so." She moved away.

He followed and put his arms about her. "So far," he said, "you have provided the dearest few hours of my life. See you tomorrow."

"Wes!"

"What?"

"I won't sleep."

He left her and went to bed, but lay awake in a turmoil of thought. Audacious projections leading to apprehensions. Daring plans, then sickening reservations. Encompassing the whole was the idea of marriage. Two days ago he would have bet his fortune that such an idea could never again concern him. *What would they say? Rebecca, Frances? What did it matter?* He played with arithmetic, taking himself and his young wife many years hence. He thought of the ludicrous old husbands in *The School for Scandal, L'Ecole des Femmes, Desire Under the Elms.*

Why marriage? Call it a fling. The girl was of age and willing. Why not play the game and see? Circumstance appeared to be providing a monumental second chance. Why blow it?

He got up, dressed, put on his heavy overcoat and made his way to the open deck and cool night air. His head cleared. *Slowly now. Was this not the most dangerous period in a man's life? Was he attempting foolishly to latch on the coattails of time? Easy to make a fool of yourself. True. Equally easy to cheat yourself out of life for fear of making a fool of yourself. What is all this? I've known this gal for a day. No, longer. That's the trap. This inner churning is the old Rebecca affliction. Nothing to do with this child.*

He experienced a five-second sensation of having solved the problem, and went back to bed and to troubled sleep.

Peacock brought his coffee at eight. He drank it and set to work, but the subject of Vanessa swamped him. Last night's solution had been left behind in sleep. He wanted to see her, to hear her voice, to walk with her—above all, he wanted to ask her to marry him. *What if she refused? She probably would. No matter. Woo her, win her. How? With time and attention and tenderness and*—he felt a wave of nausea as the next weapons came to mind—*with money, position, importance, with what he could do for her.*

He took a shower and returned to his work but found himself blocked. On a fresh pad he began a long, exploratory statement of his theme. It was changing in his fingers as he wrote. Why? He became aware that he was aiming the new work at the new girl in his life. *The part of the daughter could have more importance, couldn't it? One of those parts with one good scene in each act and*—— He got up suddenly, went to the bathroom and brushed his teeth hard for ten minutes.

The phone rang. He looked at the clock. 12:45. "Yes?" he said.

"Lunch?"

"Good morning."

"I've been up for hours. Had two breakfasts and what they call elevenses, a swim and had my hair done. I'm trying to capture a rare man. All's fair."

"I wish you'd called earlier."

"I would have, but you told me you never talked to anyone in the morning when you were working."

"The observation bar? Ten minutes."

"I've found a new place. The cabin-class bar. Much jollier. Younger."

The pause which followed had a silent siren in it. "Good," he said. "So am I."

She laughed too hard. "Pick you up."

"No," he said as she hung up.

He put on his jacket and brushed his hair, and she entered. Instantly he knew that it was no longer a matter of Rebecca, but of this girl.

They drank sherry in Vanessa's newly discovered place. "I did an awful thing last night," she said. "I slept."

"Why's that awful?"

"Well, I'd rather have said to you, 'Not a wink.' "

"Why didn't you?"

"I don't lie."

"You'll learn. You'll have to."

"I won't to you. Not about anything. What about *you* and sleep?"

"Not much. Trying to figure out what to do about you kept me awake."

"I could tell you."

At lunch he asked, "Would you like some wine?"

"No, thanks," she said.

"Would you like to marry me?"

"No, thanks."

They ate two courses in silence. Smiling, she said, "I'm not going to marry for five years."

"All right," he said. "Will you marry me in five years?"

A wild, dramatic storm hit the ship without warning. Within fifteen minutes, lunching became precarious.

"Oh, dear!" she said. "This is embarrassing. I'm getting sick."

"Come on," he said.

She had turned pale and shiny. "I'd rather go alone."

"Nothing doing." He led her out. Waiting for the lift, he steadied her.

"Please go away," she begged.

"What's the matter with you?" he said, out of patience. "You're on a ship in a storm. You're *supposed* to be sick."

The lift arrived, and they made it to her cabin. She was grateful for his help.

Afterward she lay in her bed, pale and weary. Doctor Morgan came with the nurse and saw that the proper injection was given. The doctor and nurse went on to answer other calls. Wesley stood by Vanessa's bed and stroked her brow. "Hello, friend," she said.

"You'll probably sleep for a stretch. I'll stick around."

"My diary's in the top drawer there. I want you to know me."

"I know you."

"You know my mother. People—you—think we're alike because we look alike, but we're not, we're very different."

"All right," he said comfortingly.

"Please love me," she said.

When she fell asleep he went to his cabin, returned to hers with his manuscript and sat down to work. Here was an opportunity to retrieve the morning. Her gentle breathing soothed him, and her presence gave him strength.

He worked well until she awoke four and a half hours later. She sighed, stretching, and he came to the bedside.

"Feel just—oh, Lord—great!" she said. "I'm thirsty."

Wesley gave her a drink of water.

"When is it?" she asked. "Morning?"

"Seven-thirty p.m." he said.

"I'm hungry," she said with astonishment, and laughed. "I'm not sick at all. You took good care of me."

"Of course."

"Come here," she murmured.

"We'll have dinner," he said.

She sat up, looking so innocent in her schoolgirl's nightgown and with no makeup that he was unnerved. He began to gather the pages of his manuscript.

"Listen," she said. "I don't want to say it—I'm not entirely without what they call experience."

"I didn't think you were," Wesley said. "I'll be back for you in half an hour."

"I'll be ready. I said *ready*."

The evening was joyous. Many things made it so: her recovery, his mood (work had gone well) and hers, his determination to stop taking it all so big. And the sea was calm now.

The ship's festivities offered little to match their pleasure and they took no part. Instead they traded autobiographies. He thought it odd that hers took so much longer to recount than his.

At midnight precisely she put down her brandy and said, "Please, let's go down. Too many people are floating in here."

As they reached the main deck she said, "Ten minutes."

"All right," he said. He went to his cabin, showered and put on fresh clothes.

Twenty minutes after he had left her, he knocked at her cabin. She opened the door, and he stepped inside.

"You're late," she said.

The lights had been arranged: she wore a floor-length negligee. He looked around for flowers. Yes. He breathed the scent. Different. Better? He looked around for the champagne bucket, and it was there. He laughed.

"You're not laughing at *me*, are you?"

"Hardly," he said. "Would you like me to open the champagne? I know how to now."

"What do you mean, 'now'?"

"There was a time I didn't."

"You sound different. Boyish."

"I am." He turned to open the bottle. He did it slowly, willing her to come to him. It worked. When he felt her hands on his shoulders, he let the bottle go, turned and took her into his arms. He kissed her. She moved to him, forward and upward—her whole body responding. She trembled. His hands soothed her, and then he released her gently.

"Oh, my," she said, clinging to him. whispering. "I knew you'd be like this. Special and grand. Important."

He broke the embrace, moved away and filled two glasses. Turning, he found her sitting hunched over, her head in her hands, on the edge of the sofa. He offered her one of the glasses. She did not take it, but kissed his arm.

"Here," he said.

She took the glass. He sat beside her and they drank.

He spoke slowly. "Now when you say 'important'——"

"What?"

"That's the word you used."

"Are we going to be together?" she asked. "Please."

"Not please," he said, "but why."

"Because we want to."

"I do, because you're a dream—you're a lost time come again. I've got you all mixed up in my head with something I've missed most of my life—you're an echo of love. Of course I do—but the question is you. The why of you."

"I've told you."

"Tell me again."

"I'll sound silly compared to you."

"I'll do it for you. You're more Rebecca than you want to admit. You've had your first, some callow young man—you know there's more to it. You see yourself as not like the others. Someone—well, important."

She rose and moved away.

"Your mother. That summer. Someone high up in the government, you said. She's set you an example—the ol' lion hunter. Or should I say huntress?"

She returned with the bottle of champagne.

"Now you're following her example, whether you'll admit it or not."

"What you won't face is——"

"Don't interrupt. When you get to middle age, the future—the shrinking future—means more than ever. Because you've learned, my girl, that minutes aren't worth a damn—even days aren't all that important—it's the years that matter. So whatever you think I am—forget it. I'm not a character, or a personality, or even a somebody. I'm a man, trying to be. And what I can't be—won't be—is an object to satisfy your disgusting, still-alive, idiotic snobbery."

Carefully she refilled her glass and his.

"You're a snob, Vanessa. Like your mother. Except she admits it and you don't, and before you say anything—remember you told me you wouldn't lie to me. That, at least, is a good idea."

"I won't lie to you," she said.

"Fine."

"But *please* let's be together!"

He finished his drink. "I have to make an important call."

"I don't believe you."

"Thank you for a lovely evening. Better than lovely. Explosive."

He went to his cabin and placed the important call. It came through at 3:10 a.m. Mrs. Donnell was startled.

"What is it?" she asked. "Are you well?"

"I'm fine. Did I wake you?"

"What is it?"

"Change of plans. I'd like you to fly right over."

"Tomorrow?"

"Just so long as you're there to meet me when I land. You said good-bye so nicely, I want to see how you say hello."

In the pause that followed they both heard the operator ask, "Are you through?" Together and loudly they answered, "No!"

Mrs. Donnell said, "Box office nine thousand yesterday."

"Bring some of it with you. And listen, Nicole—about that raise——"

"The substantial raise?"

"I've got a better idea. Instead of a raise—now listen. Can you hear me?"

Silence.

"Sorry, sir," said a British accent. "But you are not connected."

"Well, connect me. It's urgent."

"Won't be for an hour, I'm afraid, sir. We don't have another rendezvous until then. Shall we try in an hour?"

"Yes!"

But the call did not come through. He tried all the following day, between abortive attempts to work, and remained in his cabin for the rest of the voyage.

Mrs. Donnell was waiting at Southampton when he disembarked, and his kiss said it all.

"Seven years," she said, her face flushed. "Why?"

"It's a long story," he said. "I'll dictate it to you."

They were married in Paris nine days later and spent their honeymoon in a small, perfect hotel two kilometers from Aix-en-Provence, Nicole's birthplace.

On their return to Paris they took Nicole's brother and his wife to Maxim's. It was a Friday evening, the gala, with everyone dressed up and on parade.

Wesley sat with his back to the dance floor, and Nicole on the banquette opposite him. All at once she frowned and put on her glasses. "There is a girl," she said. "Astonishing."

"Where?"

"She will pass again. She looks but exactly like the sketch in your study."

Wesley studied the mirror which reflected the dance floor. "By the way," he said. "Remind me to throw that sketch away."

"I already have," she said.

"You have?"

"Well—put it away. I always put her away when you are not there. I don't like the face. Ah! Look. Dancing with the blond boy. Is it not the same face?"

Wesley turned to look at the dancers and saw Vanessa. "Oh, yes," he said. "I see what you mean." He turned back to Nicole and smiled. "Come on, wife. Let's dance."

RUNAWAY HONEYMOON

OLIVER LA FARGE

The taxi driver, the bellhop, the desk clerk identified them on sight as hillbilly runaways, as though they had personal knowledge of them. The driver saw them first, of course, at the depot; the man trying not to look uncertain, the girl's bewilderment only thinly covered. The man was very young, yet a man; he was tall, well shouldered, obviously strong, and still a trifle too lanky for his strength. The girl was of good height, too, and well made, a strong girl, but her youngness was more pronounced, still in another category than his.

They were dressed in their Sunday best; the clothes themselves proclaiming it—her not-quite-fitting, not-quite-capturing-the-style homemade dress and her naive hat with too much on it; and his suit, little worn and also not quite fitting. It was visible in the way they wore them; not, in her case, the dress, which she wore with grace and enjoyment, but that hat, somehow uncertain of her head, as if hats were strange there. He made his suit appear stiff, the buttoned shirt collar and the necktie plainly oppressed him, and his small felt looked hard on his head. He had set the felt on square before they left the train, and from time to time his hand moved to it, making sure of its security. Each time, unconsciously, his hand moved it a trifle to the right, gradually approaching the slant at which he wore his broad and familiar straw hat, had worn it only the day before, getting in his father's hay.

Their baggage alone would have been enough to describe and

place them. There was a worn, cardboard valise, and another, new one, and a big, antique Gladstone bag, the dry, rubbed leather of which had broken through at two of the bending corners. The driver swung the grips into the front of the cab, opened the rear door and smiled at them, although he knew they might be too ignorant to tip.

The two sat stiffly. After they had gone a few blocks, she said, "My, but it's big and noisy."

She was thinking of more than she said, so that her tone clearly showed that this comment was favorable. The bigness, the noisiness, could hide them. They could turn back his father, whose menace had stayed just behind them all the way out of the hills, through the county seat, apace with the clicking race of the train, and even across the state line. She had thought about it on the train, even in the forgetfulness of sitting beside him in the curious, public privacy of the day coach, her shoulder touching his, their fingers intertwined. They had not left Charlesburg behind really, she thought, and where Charlesburg was, that iron, willful tyrant's power also reached out. What she saw through the taxi windows was too big, too strong, for Charlesburg. She felt safety, and when his hand found hers, she knew from his touch that he did too.

The taxi stopped before the hotel they had named because Mrs. Nottingham, the minister's wife, once had stayed there. That it had no doorman did not signify to them. When the girl saw their grips on the sidewalk, here where there was not the crowding or the grime of a station platform, on the neat, exact cement, confronting the big glass doors, for the first time she realized how shabby they were, and she had a moment of doubt that made her mentally review her clothing, the dress copied from a picture, and look quickly at the young man. She found him smart, stiff, correct, and she was satisfied as to her own raiment.

He paid the driver carefully, out of a change purse. They had three days before he must report for induction, and their small funds had to be made to cover those three days and all the travel at each end. Three days would create a fait accompli; three days would create something that could not be undone, that not even his father could eliminate or undo. He paid the driver, and then, having twice traveled a little distance into the world with his father and thus learned something of what was correct, he selected a dime and handed it over. The driver said "Thanks," without sneering, liking the couple, liking their innocence and reading correctly the careful handling of that worn purse.

They did not find the lobby shabby—quite the reverse. In his two previous journeys he had seen none better, and she knew only the River House at Sudden Bend, the county seat, not to stay in, but to sit in one of the lobby rockers briefly, shyly, after the special extravagance of a lunch in its restaurant. In this lobby were some amazingly comfortable-looking leather armchairs, a number of wicker chairs and a table on which was a pot with a green shrub in it. There were half a dozen tall ash trays, and no spittoons. At the far end was the desk, electric-lighted, and on either side of it a stiff, thronelike chair with embossed leather on the back and many small brass-headed nails. In one of these chairs the bellhop reposed, inert, estivating. To one side was the elevator, its doors open and beyond that, at the corner, a wooden staircase.

There was a door in the wall to the right, over which a lighted sign said *Olde Colonial Coffee Shoppe*. Beside the door a placard on an easel announced a roast-beef special and stated the meal hours. In the opposite wall was another door, open, which had above it the words *Ye Oak Taverne—Cocktail Lounge*. As they moved forward through the lobby, which was long enough to make its crossing an appreciable time with an increase of self-consciousness, the girl glanced sideways, to see all she could beyond that door without being caught gawking. In the lounge there was a blue semi-darkness punctuated by spots of soft light, and at the far end the rainbow of a jukebox, not then playing.

The desk clerk and the bellhop, neither of whom was young, identified them as the driver had. If clothes and possessions had not betrayed them, it was in their faces, more exposed now than in the station, where they had felt inconspicuous among the many people, the country look, hesitation, uncertainty and the underlying excitement which they believed they were concealing. The bellhop expressed his judgment by not moving to take their bags.

They stopped at the desk, the young man almost touching it, the girl half a stop behind him, still holding the new valise. "We'd like a room for three days," he said, his voice level despite the tremendousness of his words.

The clerk pushed the card and pen toward him. He, having foreseen this, having thought about it and mentally rehearsed it a dozen times on the train, took the pen calmly, and, as though he were not thereby changing the world, wrote "Mr. and Mrs. Jonas Hathaway." He hesitated only a moment before adding "Charlesburg," and omitted from his home address only the R.F.D. route. The girl watched this procedure with quiet admiration while at the same time her mind embraced the portentous written statement,

"Mr. and Mrs." Like that, clear and deep blue on the white card, visible, permanent, conclusive.

The clerk said, "You and Mrs. Hathaway already married or you fixin' to get married?"

The young man looked up with an expression of pure, stony anger that was a complete answer in itself. In that anger, in the sudden set of his jaw, she saw his father, and yet something different from that terrible man's rage, for this, which he had never shown in her presence before, was generous, with concern for her name and for keeping this precious occasion unsmirched, and strong as it was, it was controlled. As she watched him, and the clerk resisted an instinct to step back out of danger, he checked himself, and said mildly, "We're married." He started to draw the certificate from his breast pocket. His father would have been incapable of stopping himself like that.

Every minute, it seemed, she learned more of him, and each new thing deepened her love. She had thought she knew him thoroughly, since childhood—which she conceived of as long left behind her—yet in the running away, in the wedding, in the traveling, she never ceased learning him anew.

The clerk said, "That's all right, sir. No offense, but we have to be careful, especially with strangers from out of the state. What kind of room do you want?"

"What do they cost?"

"Without bath, from two-fifty; with bath, from three-fifty up." Then, in revenge for the moment of fear before the bright blaze of this country boy's eyes, he said, "But I guess you'll want the bridal suite. That's only twelve-fifty."

The young man stood motionless, slowly blushing, turned callow and helpless. Twelve-fifty was catastrophic, but he was the husband, the bridegroom, and this was their day, so he stood wrestling, knowing it impossible and feeling ashamed.

The girl said, "We don't want no suite, Jo. We just want a nice room."

Rescued, he relaxed, and the redness ebbed from his face. "That's right, a nice room with bath."

She touched his elbow. "Where we can look out and see the city."

The clerk smiled. He had had his moment and he was content. "You'll want a double bed, of course. Let's see." He turned and ran his eyes over the pigeonholes with their keys and scattering diagonals of letters and messages, in doing which he gave them a chance to shake off the impact of that casual reference to a bed. "There's a very nice room on the second floor, overlooking the street. It's four-fifty."

Jonas said, "That will do fine."

The clerk said, "Front, boy!" briskly, and the bellhop moved forward in torpor. The clerk handed out a key. "Two-oh-five."

The man took the baggage and led them to the elevator, gloomily anticipating no tip, or a dime, his face aloof, withdrawn. For the girl, the elevator was as new as taxis with clicking meters running up white numbers on a black ground, or the streets in spate of traffic, or the sight of a blue-dark cocktail lounge. She went to it curiously, her hand firm but easy on her husband's arm, then tightening when the door closed and they were shut in a too-small, bright room. The elevator wheezed and moved, then it stopped, causing a sensation in her stomach, and the door sighed open.

It was a very long corridor, red-carpeted over all its length, with a multitude of doors, over a dozen on each side. At the far end was the relief of a window; otherwise, after the enclosed magic of the elevator, one could imagine that one was in unfathomable interior recesses lost forever from sunlight. The bellhop stopped at 205, unlocked the door, opened it and went in, seeing no need to waste deference upon these two. He put the old, worn Gladstone on the rack, set the other two pieces beside it, opened the closet door, turned on the light in the bathroom, then opened the window, letting in heat and the dull, constant voice of the city, set the key on the bureau, and said, "Anything else?"

Jonas stared at him a moment, said "Oh," and took out the purse, thinking hard. His father had said you tip, and although he did not like this man, in whom he felt a mean hostility, he would do what was becoming, but he would not himself be mean nor yet foolish. He took out a fifty-cent piece, amazing the man and bringing about a change in him.

"Thank you, sir. You want anything—ice water, or drinks, or anything—just pick up the phone." He pointed to it, then left.

The bed dominated the room. To sit on, apart from it, there were a moderately comfortable, comfortably worn armchair, and a straight chair, facing and tucked up against the table, with the glass over its top, on which the telephone rested. There was a bureau, also with glass covering its top, under which lay several rectangles of paper telling of laundry service and the hours and offerings of the coffee shop and cocktail lounge. Of free space, there seemed to be hardly as much altogether as that occupied by the bed. What they needed was a sofa, on which they could sit together in decency, or else two approximately equal chairs, placed side by side, but there was neither, so they stood, embarrassed. After some seconds, the girl's mouth formed in determination, and with decisive motions she put her handbag on the table beside the telephone; then she removed her hat and placed it on the closet shelf. In so doing she took possession, she was the woman, and for now this was where she kept house, where she put things in their places. Her husband became less rigid. He followed suit with his hat; then took off his coat, without which he felt much more at ease, and hung it on one of the wire hangers in the closet.

These actions brought both of them close to the bathroom door, where the light attracted their eyes. The girl gasped. Jonas almost did the same. Traveling with his father, he had never been in a room with a bath, and the shabby lavatories he had known had not at all prepared him for this gleaming chamber, all tiled, the lower portion light green, with the huge shining tub, the mirror, the glistening, semitransparent shower curtain and the other fixtures. That there was a faint brown stain under the hot-water tap in the washstand was insignificant, nor did they notice that there was a tear in the shower curtain, but the girl saw, with a certain sense of relief, that the windowsill was grimy and should be wiped down. Like the bed, the bathroom proclaimed itself, and having it opening directly into their room seemed an indecency. They drew back and the girl closed the door firmly.

She moved to the window, drawn by the sounds of the city, feeling security in every evidence of its vastness. She looked down at the street, the twin rivers of cars and trucks, the people on the hard sidewalk. The sun was not yet down, but it was low, shining the length of the harshly straight roadway from the west to throw spidery, stretched-out caricature shadows of the walkers, which she watched with fascination. Down the block on the right was a moving-picture theater, and she reflected immediately that by going to it after, in a short time, they had eaten supper, they would solve what had begun to loom in her mind as a difficult problem of a gap in time—a period after eating when to sit in this bed-filled room together or to sit in the lobby publicly would be equally disagreeable in different ways.

She noticed a sudden appearance of colored light out of the corner of her eye, and looked to the left, to see an elaborated sign, its neon just turned on, which announced in curiously shaped letters, *The Canton Pagoda*, while simpler characters, red and blue across the windows, stated, *Chinese and American Food*, and *Chop Suey*. She had heard tell of Chinese restaurants, and it seemed to her that their voyage would have extended to farther places, the experiences would have been vastly deeper, her knowledge of the outside, great world enhanced, if Jonas would take her to eat there. Then she thought that being foreign, it would probably be too expensive for them, but there might be some moderately priced dish. There was a rectangle of white on the corner of one window, which, she thought, was probably a bill of fare, so that it would be possible to learn the prices without going inside. Jonas, she knew, would as lief have his hand cut off as walk into such a place, ask about cost, and then walk out without buying anything.

Up to then, she had been taken up with the business of running away, the fear of pursuit and the overwhelming fact of her wedding day. She had thought of the city in terms of protection that it might offer, food and shelter. Now the excitement of being in such a place, the explorations to be performed, the things to be seen, heard, tasted, crowded into consciousness. She decided that they should go down right away and walk a little in that crowded street; then that she would like to go into the cocktail lounge and find out what one was like, and try one of those complex, wonderfully flavored drinks that she had heard of. She knew only the taste of elderberry and dandelion wines, mildly hard cider, and vileness of one experimental sip of crude whiskey. She would taste a cocktail, and before that they would have found out whether the Chinese place was within their range, or whether they had better try the Olde Colonial Coffee Shoppe—but that special was no bargain—or perhaps somewhere else. In a city like this there would be many eating places, of many kinds and prices.

She was about to turn to her husband when she saw the dusty, gray, four-door sedan draw up in front of the hotel door. She drew in a sharp breath and froze, watching the big man get out, moving slowly, as was his way. So much heavier as he was, between his shoulders and Jonas's there was a strong resemblance.

She faced toward her husband and said, "Your pa's here. He just got out of his car."

The young man stared at her. "They won't let him up without we say so." He said it as if he wished to make it true, rather than really believed that anyone could turn his father back.

The girl reached decision suddenly and completely. "You better go down and tackle him."

He looked at her blankly. "No. I——" His voice trailed off.

"Jonas Hathaway, you go down and tackle him." She spoke firmly. "You got to sooner or later, and it might as well be now. And I ain't goin' to camp in this room, afraid to step outside. So you'd best settle it now." Then, in a gentler voice, "You can do it, Jo."

The young man nodded slowly. "I guess I can." He straightened, and his mouth set again, firm. Anyone would have been conscious of the hard jaw line. He put on his coat and opened the door; then he looked back, smiled wryly, and said, "Here goes. You can put up a prayer for me." He went out, shutting the door firmly.

She sat down in the armchair. His expression, his voice, his way of moving, during the last few seconds before he left, were clear in her mind. The telephone rang. She let it ring. He had gone down without being summoned, and nothing should be done that would allow any doubt of that. Her mind remained suspended until the ringing stopped; then, with the silence, she was thinking again. This was probably the best thing that could have happened, head on, right at the start. It was going to be all right; there was no question about that. Folding her hands in her lap, she offered up a prayer, for prayer was always suitable, but she was in no doubt. It was not only that the city had weakened, attenuated, diluted Mr. Hathaway, but that she knew Jonas's capabilities now almost better than he did. She was not in the least afraid. She sat calmly, waiting for her husband to return and take her out to walk in the city streets.

A WOMAN
BY CANDLELIGHT

SINCLAIR LEWIS

The heart of woman was hidden from Wilbur Cole; to him that secret beauty was as unfamiliar as great music. He was not hard, but he was young, and blind with first success. This January day he had finished his first trip as traveling salesman—as gripman for the St. Sebastian Wholesale Grocery Company.

He was a conqueror, and St. Sebastian was a city worthy to greet a conqueror's triumph. Snobs from the East, from Chicago and Eau Claire say that St. Sebastian is a scattering of dumpy buildings; but in the silo country we consider it oppressively grand.

It has twelve thousand inhabitants and a roundhouse and a state normal school.

To Wilbur Cole, reared in a farm shanty concealed only by a willow windbreak from the devouring prairie and trained in a cross-roads general store, St. Sebastian was a metropolis crammed with fascinating people—people who had six-cylinder cars and knew about dress suits and auction bridge.

As soon as he had reported to the office he began to wait for half past seven, when he would be able to go and call on Myrtle Hill-bridge, who wore a wristwatch and was the daughter of the head of the Hillbridge Farm Machinery Agency. He went to his room and tried to read the accumulation of St. Sebastian papers; but he fidgeted and spent an hour manicuring his nails, occasionally rushing to the window on the totally unreasonable chance that Myrtle might be passing. He pictured her, in the jumper and linen skirt she usually wore, as a combination of outdoor wholesomeness and city smartness. He saw clearly the triangle of cheek beneath each of her eyes. He would sit near her—this same evening!—just a few hours, now! Perhaps he would dare to touch her hand. Then she would become silent, and he would move nearer to her.

Though her house was luxurious, what did he care for the cabinet of cut glass, the lace table cover, or the expensive framed color photographs from Yellowstone Park, which proved that the Hillbridges had traveled? No; he would adore Myrtle if she were a squarehead on a cleared farm.

He could not sit through supper at his boardinghouse; to the grief of the landlady, he couldn't get down any of the lemon meringue pie. He wanted to be out and alone, thinking of the goddess. He may have been a bulky figure for a lorn lover, in the coonskin overcoat, sealskin cap, red flannel wristlets and knee overshoes of the region; but his chin was high and his breath made passionate puffs of steam as he tramped past the Hillbridge house, which he managed to do six several times. At first he went by on the theory that he was hastening to some important engagement a great distance off, and didn't even see the house. Then he half stopped, as though he were startled by the revelation of architectural charms in the front porch, which had turned columns and diamond-shaped shingles of red and green and yellow.

He was trying to keep himself from arriving before half past seven; but at twenty minutes past he could stand this exile no longer, and he rang the bell. . . . She herself was coming down the hall! He could see her shadow against the ground glass of the door. During the seven seconds while she put an inquiring hand up to her back hair and fumbled with the knob, he was boiling with anticipation. She was going to be more beautiful than he had pictured! She was going to look at him with tremulous shyness. Maybe she would be wearing the lovely yellow dress with that lace stuff at the neck.

He was frightened. He wanted to bolt. He wouldn't dare to look at her—much less touch her magnetic hand.

Then Miss Myrtle Hillbridge had opened the door and was saying:

"Oh, hello! Oh, it's Mr. Cole! Oh, I thought you were out of town! Oh, you must have got back!"

"Yes, I got back." He beamed fatuously.

"Oh! Oh, isn't it cold! Oh, do come in, so I can shut the door. Oh, you missed it, going away; we had the peachiest party at Hildy's! Oh, I wish I'd known somebody was coming tonight; I would have dressed up. Isn't this flannelette blouse dreadful! Oh, let me take your hat. Isn't it cold! Let's sit in the sitting room; it's so much warmer there. Papa and mamma have gone over to aunty's to play cribbage. Oh, did you have a good trip? Oh, let me tell you the latest—you mustn't tell a soul; it isn't supposed to be out—Bessie is engaged to Ben! Who would ever have thought it! Don't you think Bessie is a perfect fright in that pink charmeuse? Oh, listen; I've got a trade last for you."

"Well, I—uh—can I give you a compliment of my own for the trade last? I thought about you lots while I was on the trip. Say, by the way, I had a slick trip. I tell you, it's pretty darn' important—a fellow's first trip out on the road for a house. Of course I know the retail grocery business O.K., but I didn't know how it would be selling to dealers, but it went fine, and I landed a new customer for the house——"

"That's nice; it isn't a trade last at all unless it's something you heard somebody else say, all right, Mister Smarty; I won't give you my trade last at all. Oh, I must tell you about the funny thing that happened at Hildy's party: You know how her house is, with the dinky little conservatory—it isn't really a thing in the world but a bay window, even if Hildy does call it a conservatory—you know, on the dining room——"

As Wilbur had hoped, they were sitting side by side. He told himself that she was an "awful cute kid—not many girls can jolly a fellow along like this." Also, the Hillbridge house was of an even more gorgeous fancifulness than he had remembered, in its tapestry and velours rockers with carved arms, and the storm of light from the bracket lamps and from the electrolier of crimson, pearl and orange mosaic glass. But in the midst of these observations, so comforting to one recently returned from a round of smoking cars and uncarpeted hotels, Wilbur made two startling discoveries: He wasn't afraid of trying to hold Myrtle's hand, and he didn't want to hold her hand, anyway!

While she was confiding to him—but he mustn't tell a single soul!—that she could have snitched Ben from Bessie, Wilbur smiled politely, and nodded his head at regular intervals, and didn't hear a word she said.

He was wondering how he had lost all that exquisite fear of her. He wasn't in the least awed. To prove it he seized her hand.

She blushed and squeaked, though she let him keep the hand. But he did not wish to keep it. He was decidedly embarrassed by the possession of it. He did not know what to do with it. A plump hand—not a tingling electrode, but just an ordinary smallish hand, such as almost everybody had—seemed a foolish thing to be holding. Her knuckles were puffy and her fingers were fat, he noted.

She babbled, "My, but you are the fresh thing!" and he tried to live up to this new role as a perfect devil with the ladies by stroking her hand. A point in the setting of her small turquoise ring jabbed his finger. He carefully laid the hand down on the couch. She left it there for a moment, then took it back, drooping her head toward him and sighing in a pleased manner: "Oh, aren't you the bad one!"

He felt like different kinds of a fool and made an excuse to flee. She followed him to the door, and he combined an impression that he was highly honored with a desire to dodge.

His boardinghouse room seemed as bare to him as the hotels. In it he began to remember how warm and filled with curtains and newish furniture was the Hillbridge mansion, and again he saw Myrtle as something costly and beautiful.

Two days later, as he took the northbound train during the first gray blast of a coming blizzard, he was certain that he was longing for Myrtle.

II

Wilbur should have reached Gopher Prairie in seven hours, with a stop at Joralemon; but for twenty-four hours the train struggled in the blizzard. Between gusts it made a mile, two miles, gasped a little, balked, and stopped. Wilbur covered himself with his coonskin coat and a strip of coco matting from the aisle in the cold car and watched the outside world turn to roaring steam. Through the night he slept raggedly, and smoked till his throat was parched, and talked to the seven passengers and the trainmen till they reached religion and politics, and became personal.

The train was finally stalled three miles from Gopher Prairie. It would not move till the rotary plow dug its way through from Ferguston. The storm passed; the world was a level plain of snow, which covered the track from embankment to embankment, all achingly brilliant with sun from a blue porcelain sky. Farmers began to fight through with bobsleds. With his bags, Wilbur was bundled into the hay-covered bottom of a sled, and thus did he crawl into the town of Gopher Prairie.

The rows of two-story brick stores running off into straggling frame houses, which made up Gopher Prairie, were covered with snow like a counter of goods with a linen cover smoothly drawn across them. Lovely was the molding of the snow; it swooped in long curves from eaves to sidewalk; it was eight feet deep beside wind-break fences; it made of the squat buildings a series of Chinese pagodas. But none of this too-familiar beauty was interesting to Wilbur Cole. It meant only that he would be imprisoned here till the trains were running again. To north, south and east the service was shut off. Telephone and telegraph wires were down. There would be no mail, not one message from the world beyond the waste of snow, for two or three days. And Wilbur knew no one in Gopher Prairie. On his previous trip he had met two men in the grocery dealing with his house; but they had not warmed to him yet.

He stumbled along the paths that were being gouged through the drifts and spent an hour in the store. The clerks were affable, but they were too busy telling of their heroism in reaching the store to listen to his account of being stalled; and they did not invite him to supper. At last there was nothing to keep him from toiling to the hotel, mountain-climbing over drifts on the way.

He hoped to find a bunch of jolly fellow salesmen; but the only other guests at the hotel were a cranky old jewelry salesman who regarded himself as in some way an artist, as a superior person entitled to glance at you over his eyeglasses, together with a silent man who seemed to Wilbur to have no purpose whatever in existing except to monopolize the warmest hot-air register in the office.

A floor which has been scrubbed for so many years that the knots stand up out of the soft pine boards can be more desolately bare than a dirty floor scattered with different interesting things; and the hotel office was nothing but a waste of scrubbed floor, dotted by a desk of grained wood, a brown writing table decked with advertisements of the bus line, and a row of wooden chairs. Even less adorned was Wilbur's bedroom, its bureau listed to starboard, its one chair, and the bed with the dirty red comforter—which was so much like the other dirty red comforters in all the other hotel rooms on his route that it might have been a pursuing haunt.

He walked up and down the office, made halting efforts to get acquainted with the two morose salesmen and the sleepy night clerk, and crept out into the cold, to go to the movies. It was like ice water, that cold; he was gasping and struggling with it the moment he plunged into it. He made his way a block down to the movie theater only by darting in at stores to get another supply of warmth.

Over the theater was the sign "Closed tonight, acct. storm."

He struggled back to his room and made an occupation of getting ready to read. He did not undress—he took off his coonskin coat, and shivered, and hastily put the coat on again. He moved his chair two inches to the right, then an inch to the left, and sat with his feet on the bed. For two hours he solemnly read a two-days-old copy of the *Minneapolis News*. He turned the pages very carefully, exactly creasing the paper each time. He rattled it rather unnecessarily—the sound was cheerful in this room, surrounded by the bulky silence of the snowbound village. Now and then he looked up and said, aloud: "Let's see: Tomorrow the train might get through—I'll get to—— No, I don't suppose there'll be a train—wish I could see Myrtle and sit and jolly with her! Oh, this is a sweet life! Let's see; Larsen took two cases of apricots this time. . . . ." was comforted by his own voice. But he hadn't much to say. His brain felt dead as a bone, dead as the silence packed in about him.

He read every obituary and want ad in the paper. He considered the desirability of jobs as textile chemist, curtain hanger, Italian-Greek salesman, actuary, oxyacetylene welding expert, designer of little gents' garments, and bright boy. He learned the diverting news that "peas, Scotch, choice, 100 lbs., were 13.50@ 13.75"; that the "Fifth Race, for three-year-olds, selling, one mile and seventy years," would be run by an amazing company consisting of Garbage, Springtide Reverie, Oh You Kid, Tippytoes and Pink Suspenders; that "John Swan, Mary Ammond Swan, and their heirs-at-law, devises, and next of kin, and other persons, if any there be, and their names are unknown to the plaintiff," were warmly invited to a guessing party; that "deb 5s, etfs of dep, stpd"; That "1 do cvt 4s ser B55 55 55"; and that "J.B. Terrell as exrx & c of S.L. Barnes dec'd pltf."

In the midst of this last thriller he hurled the newspaper across the room and, as it fell in a shower of detached sheets, he cried:

"I want you so, my dear Myrtle——"

They are heroes, these salesmen and agents, who sit so quietly in trains and small hotels.

For all of another day the train service was interrupted, and Wilbur trudged through drifts, unnoticed, while about him were the shouting of men shoveling walks or driving horse plows down the street, and the laughter of children skiing. He managed to spend two hours in the grocery store, helping the clerks arrange a display of canned goods. As he returned to his hotel in the early darkness, he could see happy families in lighted homes, and the prospect of this second evening of loneliness was not boredom—it was fear.

He got to the hotel at five. He skipped when he heard the voices of Fred Oberg and two companions in the office!

Fred Oberg was one of the best known traveling men in the state. He was a practical joker, a teller of stories, a maker of love, and an inspired player of poker. His two companions were noisy of tie and laughter. They had got through from Curlew by bobsled, and they were going to make a night of it. Would Wilbur join them in a little game, with a few bottles, in Fred's room? Wilbur thankfully would. He sat down with these older, more poised men, and laughed with them. He sounded a little hysterical.

Now it is a rule of the road that young traveling men must be broken in, and there are certain tricks that may lawfully be played upon them, to the joy and righteous approval of all beholders. . . . Fred Oberg slipped out of the hotel. He went to the drugstore, next door, where there was a telephone. Fred Oberg could make his voice soft and feminine. . . .

While the other salesmen were encouraging Wilbur to tell them all about how successful his first trip had been, the telephone in the hotel office rang. It was a call for Mr. Wilbur Cole, said the night clerk, coughing and hiding his mouth with his hand.

Wilbur rushed to the telephone and heard a voice as of a large pleasant woman with a cold:

"Hel-lo-uh? Oh! Oh, is this Mr. Cole? Oh, Mr. Cole, this is Miss Weeks, the milliner. I just heard that you were in town. I am a cousin of Mr. Gasthof, of your firm. I'm so sorry to hear of your having to stay at that horrid hotel. Won't you come over and have a homy supper tonight? I'd just love to have you! I live over my shop, one block down Main Street, toward the depot."

Wilbur did a two-step down the office to the other salesmen, who grunted, "What's the excitement, little one?"

"I'm invited out for supper!"

"The deuce you are! Gwan! Don't believe you."

"You bet I am! Oh, you fellows can stick to the roast pork and apple sauce. Watch little Wilbur wade into the fried chicken!"

"Who's the fall guy?"

"Never you mind who it is."

"Gwan—tell a fellow."

"It's Miss Weeks, the milliner. She's a cousin of a friend of mine."

"The little Weeks? Oh, you lucky dog! Why, she's the swellest skirt in town."

"Is she—honest?"

"Is she? Why, don't you know her? Why, say, she's pretty as a magazine cover—nice and round and plump, and not a day over twenty, and lively——Say, I bet you have some evening! Now ain't that luck for you! Some men are just nachly born lucky."

Wilbur's cheerfulness was in no wise lessened by the envy

headlined in the faces of the two salesmen; and when Fred Oberg returned, and was informed of Wilbur's good fortune, Fred sighed that he wished he could make a hit with the ladies like that. Wilbur tried to look modest; but he cocked his hat over one eye and lit a cigar.

"Say, we got to help the boy dress up for the occasion," Fred tenderly proposed; and the three of them dragged Wilbur upstairs.

They insisted that he ought to wear a red necktie; and Fred produced from his grip a tie like a fireman's shirt. Solicitously Fred said:

"We got to brush your hair right, kid. Stand there in front of the bureau. I got a slick new patent hairbrush that shines 'em up like a St. Paul barber."

The three of them seemed to have a good deal of difficulty in getting just the right light on Wilbur's hair, and during an altercation as to whether he ought to stand on the right or left of the incandescent, they almost rended him.

"Ouch! Say, quit! Quit, I say! You're almost tearing my arm off," wailed Wilbur.

The salesman dropped his arms. In tones of deepest grief Fred Oberg protested:

"Gosh, that's what you get when you do your best to help a brother knight of the grip make a hit with a squab! All right, sir. Sorry we bothered you."

"Aw, thunder, Fred; I didn't mean to be ungrateful."

"Well, stand there then."

He stood there, while Fred brushed his hair with an instrument of torture which dug its claws into his scalp. Wilbur tried to look patient, though he winced at every stroke. One of the salesmen had a fit of coughing that sounded somehow like laughing, and Wilbur became suspicious.

"That's enough, Fred. You don't need to take my scalp off."

"Well, maybe I was digging in a little more than I had to; but I had to get even with you for swiping the swellest little chicken in town. But you're wise to all these roughhouse stunts, all right, Wilbur. You're going to make a great hit on the road."

"Well, I hope I'm not entirely a darn' fool," said Wilbur, much pleased.

One of them polished his shoes with a dirty handkerchief. Another offered him a drink from a pint flask of rye; but he politely refused. The three kept up their sighs of envy: A home supper with a peach! Oh, but Wilbur was the society favorite! And would Wilbur be so good as to join them in the poker game when he got back?

They accompanied him to the street door, bidding him hurry and not keep the fair one waiting.

Wilbur found Miss Weeks' Millinery Emporium in the Colby Block, a row of two-story brick stores adorned with a galvanized iron cornice. It occupied half of a shop, the other half of which belonged to a jeweler and optician. Beside the shop was a stairway, an incredibly broad and dark stairway, smelling of yellow soap. He stumbled up it, and stopped under a small incandescent, which showed the K.P. Hall on one side and an attorney's office on the other. Miss Weeks' rooms must be at the back. Through the darkness he felt along the wall, stumbled over a doormat, and knocked at a door.

"Yes?"—in a weary voice.

"Is this Miss Weeks' residence?" said Wilbur elegantly.

"Yes."

The door opened. He saw a woman three or four years older than himself, a tired-eyed, restrained, businesslike woman in a spinsterish blue-and-white wash dress. Gentle she seemed, but not round nor jolly.

"Miss Weeks?"

"Yes."

"This is Mr. Cole."

"Yes?"

"Wilbur Cole."

"Why—who were you looking for?"

"Didn't you telephone me at the hotel?"

"I'm afraid there is some mistake."

Then was Wilbur aware that down the hall was a rustle and a masculine giggle, as of two or three men. He was filled with fury that he had been tricked; that they had even followed, to watch him make a fool of himself. But he had to relieve Miss Weeks. She was holding the door tight, beginning to close it, looking anxious.

He spoke softly, so that his tormentors should not hear:

"I know what it is now. I'm new on the road—salesman—and some of the boys at the hotel were kidding me, and pretended it was you telephoning to invite me to supper. I don't care about myself—I can get back at them; but, honest, Miss Weeks, I'm terribly sorry it was you I had to bother. I guess maybe it must be kind of scary, living here alone; but don't be scared. I'll beat it now. It was a good joke on me—heh? You see, I been stuck in town, with the storm tying up the trains, and I was so proud of being invited to a home feed that prob'ly I boasted a little; so I guess I deserved all I got."

"You poor boy—you are only a boy—it was horrible of them!"

"Oh, I'm not a boy. I'm twenty-eight."

Her weariness smoothed out in a darting smile as she mocked:

"Oh, so old; so very old! I'm older than that myself."

"Say, sometime on some other trip, may I drop into the store and have a chat, and make up for those other fellows? But I know they didn't mean to get you in Dutch. They were just kidding—they're a wild bunch—but they don't mean any harm; and a fellow sure is ready for any kind of a jamboree to break the monotony when he's on the road."

"Yes." Her face lighted again, as though she had an inspiration.

"Well, good night."

"Wouldn't you like to really stay and have supper?"

"Do you mean it?"

"Yes. . . . I think I do."

As he followed her in, she banged the door shut with a sudden nervous energy and sighed:

"There! Let's shut out the loneliness. I know how it is at your hotels. I get that way myself, living alone; and I've never dared to invite a man to supper, because people gossip so here. But we'll forget all that tonight, and I'll see what I can scratch up for supper. I was going to have scrambled eggs and tea; but we'll have to have something grander than that—for company."

While she searched the cupboard he sat on the edge of a chair and clung to his cap. No man feels entirely abandoned to a situation so long as he keeps hold of that symbol of his royalty, his headgear. Wilbur would have felt more independent had it been a derby; but still, a sealskin cap was a solid masculine thing.

He was puzzled by her and by her living room. He told himself that she was like a schoolteacher. The room seemed bare. There was no carpet; only a large rag rug. The table was of reddish wood, with something like a double set of legs. It seemed to be the dining table as well as library table. There wasn't a real sideboard, with the beveled glass and brass handles, and rows of cut glass, which spelled elegance in St. Sebastian, but only another reddish-wood thing, very plain, with small glass knobs, and covered with a plain blue cloth, set with two brass jars.

The only chairs were black wooden things—not even rockers. He "liked them, sort of," he announced to himself; "they were kind of pretty, but awful plain and old-fashioned."

Most curious of all was the fact that the room was lighted only by candles.

Even on the farm they had had lamps, and every nice house in St.

Sebastian had so many electric clusters that you could read fine print in the farthest corner. Yet somehow it was "restful, the way the candlelight shone on the reddish wood, even if it was tabby."

"How do you like my candles and mahogany?" Miss Weeks interrupted his inspection.

"Oh, is that mahogany, that red wood? I've heard of that."

"Yes; my grandfather brought that table from Vermont to Minnesota. It's a gate-legged table."

"Oh, is it? I've read about them."

"Do you disapprove of my candles much? All my women friends here in Gopher tell me that candles are used only in the log cabins, way up North; but then an old maid needs a dim light to look attractive in."

"Oh, they're just envious. Don't get silver candlesticks like those in any log cabin, let me tell you! I like candlelight. It's—oh, it's——"

"Yes; it really is. Do you think you could stand some shirred eggs with canned mushrooms and some nice little sausages for supper?"

"That would be corking!" he breathed. He was telling himself, "I bet she's educated."

While she prepared supper he was uneasy. He did not feel that he had a right to be here, and he pictured Fred Oberg and his confederates waiting for him in the hall, possibly knocking at the door or sending a foolish message to him. He did not gain confidence till he sat opposite to her at supper.

She still seemed to him of the forbiddingly bluestockinged sort who "expected a fellow to be interested in suffrage and all that highbrow stuff." But his heart, which was so hungry for beauty without knowing that it was hungry, was pleased by her fine nose, her intelligent eyes, her quick and fragile fingers. He had a perplexed feeling that the supper table, with its four candles and thin china, was more impressive than even a Sunday dinner table of St. Sebastian. He tried to tell her his feelings:

"I've never been brought up to real pretty things much. I was raised on a farm; and then I got busy *mit* groceries at Jack Rabbit Forks; and then—oh, you know—a boardinghouse at St. Sebastian and out on the road. I guess I'm pretty ignorant about this decoration stuff, and so on and so forth, never being in the furniture line or anything."

"Ignorant? Heavens, so am I!" Her eyes glowed. He had a sense of impersonal friendship such as he had never known with women. She mused, while he was pleased by the turn of her wrist as she dropped lumps of sugar in his tea.

"Yes, I'm afraid I'm a bluffer about silver and candles. I talk so glibly about grandfather's table—it was his; but, just the same, dear old granddad died in the poorhouse, and I never was able to get his mahogany back till a few years ago. A farm? Heavens, child, I lived on a farm for eighteen years. And taught district school, and made the fires every morning, and sometimes scrubbed the floor. But I always wanted to handle pretty things; and so, when mother died and I didn't have to be a schoolma'am any more, I went to Winona and learned millinery, so I could play with pieces of velvet and ribbon and jet ornaments—and oh, things from Paris and Vienna, and all sorts of far, far-off places—long red feathers that make me think of the tropics—palms and parrots——"

"Yes, I know; I've always wanted to travel too."

They laughed at each other—friends now, these children of the new settlements. Because they did belong to the new settlements they could not keep up the strain of rhapsodizing. It didn't seem to Wilbur quite decent to talk about beauty. As though the label on a tomato can had any use except to make it sell! They gossiped about the blizzard, the governor, and the prospect for a good crop. Wilbur was permitted to smoke after supper, and he was in a state of fullness and friendly comfort, though not in any artistic fervor. But when she brought out a genuine Rue de la Paix hat ornament, set with brilliants, and laughed at herself because she could not bear to sell it, he began to confess that he had felt emotions in the presence of wild roses.

She read aloud a poem from a magazine—a slight verse with none of the boom and red-bloodedness of the verses he had approvingly read in newspapers. It concerned an English watering place and a seller of periwinkles. There was a line which Miss Weeks repeated: *"The 'winkie woman's coming in the twilight by the sea."*

Wilbur knew but little regarding periwinkles and the vending of periwinkles, and he had never thought of the sea except as a means of importing olive oil; but always he was enthralled by dusk, and wondered whether he wasn't a little "soft." Now he perceived that there might be others like himself.

He took leave in such a high mood of goodness and happiness as he had not known since Sunday afternoons on the farm. He thanked her for faking him in, and they shook hands at the door.

He crept into the hotel, avoiding Fred Oberg and his associated jesters. He could not endure the questions and rib-pokings with which they would soil his memory of the evening. Next morning the trains were running again, and he slipped away from town, the memory in his heart like something delicate and of pearl.

III

Through springtime and summer Wilbur covered his territory, not by train, but by a little runabout motor, such as traveling men were beginning to use everywhere. These were the good days of youth and first success, travel and discovery, dawns of starting and dusks of whistling arrival, great skies, and the vast and breathing land.

He issued early from frame hotels to rush to the garage and be chummy with the repairman, and wise about mixtures, and that heat pipe which was working loose. He started in the cool hour of dew and meadowlarks.

He drove from the larger towns to German or Norwegian settlements, each with a large brick church, a large saloon, a small smithy, with the smith in wooden shoes, and a hum of flies about the hitching posts in the street.

His laugh became more confident; his cheeks resumed the tan of farm days; his eyes, pale amid the brick red of his flesh, were calm with visions. He followed fenceless roads that were close in amid the grain, while overhead rolled the bellying clouds. He was alone most of the day, but he was not friendless now. The grocers had come to accept him; they liked his eagerness and truthfulness.

At one end of the route, which he covered once every two weeks, he had Myrtle Hillbridge for stimulant, and he was on first-name terms with her; he strolled with her beneath the lindens and box elders, and laughed a good deal, and pretended he was going to try to kiss her.

Midway on the route he had an inspiration in a Gopher Prairie milliner named Miss Weeks.

He could not again have supper in her rooms. The little town, with its poverty of melodrama, was hungry for scandal, and she clung to her immaculate reputation. She scorned herself for her timidity, she said; but there it was.

He called on her at the millinery shop and touched with his horny, blunt forefinger the bits of colored fabric she loved. They planned that someday, when he was the owner of a chain of five hundred grocery stores, they would buy a yacht and sail off to Hong Kong and the isles of the sea, and bring back carved ivory and dusky opals, and the feathers of cockatoos.

Most of this fancy was hers; it was she who, from her yearning study of magazines, had garnered the names that studded their game: Taj Mahal and Singapore and Colombo, Kioto and the Hotel du Chemin de Fer of Buitenzorg. His contribution was an insistence that the yacht should have stores of city food and enormous boxes of candy; and mahogany and candles, for which decorations he had come out strongly.

On a moonlit evening in August he begged Miss Weeks to walk out beyond the town to see the moon on the prairie.

He was excited; he was proud of her, as a treasure he had found. But he talked casually, trying to be very cultured. They passed a house on a hill. He knew it was a noble edifice, because it was like the Hillbridge mansion in St. Sebastian.

"That's an elegant place—don't you think so?" he said in selected accents of politeness and intellectuality.

"No; I'm afraid I think it's pretty ugly. It's—— Oh, I wish I knew something about architecture! I don't know why I don't like it, except that it looks to me like a fat woman with lots of paste diamonds, and too dressy, and a stenciled garden hat on top of that. It's so lumpy, and it's got scrollamajigs all over the porch; and that round tower is just silly—don't you think?"

"Yes, I guess—yes; that's so," he sighed.

He told himself that, after all, this monstrosity was not like the chaste Hillbridge mansion. But he knew it was.

"Our towns aren't beautiful—not yet. Maybe they will be when they stop trying to be showy."

"Yes I guess—yes; that's so. . . . Though, golly, the towns looked pretty good to me when I came off the farm. Oh, I'm an ignorant brat! I don't know how you can stand me."

"My dear, you're not! You're good and sweet and honest. It's myself who am ignorant. Look at me—old enough to be your grandmother; the perfect catty old maid, daring to criticize these towns that the pioneers built out of sweat and blood. And what am I? Just a small-town milliner, with half a shop—tinkering and making a few silly hats."

"You're not! You're not! You're—oh, so cultured and everything—— And you're young; you aren't hardly a bit older than me by the family Bible; and your—oh—your imagination is so young; and—— Oh, I don't know how to say it, but you know what I mean."

He put his arm about her shoulder, on a corner shadowed by a bank of lilac bushes. There was a hush, rhythmic with a distant chorus of frogs. The angel of quiet affection bent lulling wings about them. She patted his arm as they walked on.

The town broke off abruptly. One moment they were hedged in by one-story cottages; the next, with the town forgotten, they faced the splendor of the open prairie, brown and honest and elemental by day, but charmed now to an uplifted radiance. It was not a flat, dull plain, but dipping and winsome. Nothing save the stormy ocean could be so broad, so far-stretching to that pale shimmer of horizon.

They were on a slight rise, and they looked across ten miles of meadow and corn patch and fifty-acre wheatfields. The moon was still low and touched the veils of mist that rose from hollows. Beyond these apparitions the eye lifted till the spirit was swimming and dizzy with the sweep of the shining land. The groves of willows, the alder bushes marking a curving creek, and the eye of a slew were sparkling points on the plate of silver. The yellow light of a distant farmhouse stirred the poignant thought of home.

Unspeaking, with one strong emotion linking them, unconsciously hand in hand and their arms swinging together, they moved forward into that world of light. Their eyes were solemn. They passed from the road into a meadow. The long grasses whispered to their slow tread.

He ignored the heavy dew, which soaked his shoes, till he realized that he was not caring for her, and urged:

"Sakes alive! You'll catch your death o' cold. Let's sit on this gate."

He had spoken so softly that the charm was not shattered; and, swathed in glory, they perched on the three-barred wooden gate of a barbed-wire fence, which had been enchanted into a spider web. She sat on a lower bar and leaned her head against his knee. The faint pressure made him tender, conscious that she belonged to that wistful beauty.

He instinctively stroked her cheek. Slowly the full ecstasy of the holy hour welled in him till he could no longer be mute. He identified her with it, and demanded her.

"I've never felt—oh, so happy before! I don't want to ever lose you, dear. Can't we be married? I ain't—I am not worthy——"

She straightened up; stood by the fence.

"Boy, you don't love me! It's just moonlight and walking with a woman. You don't know what you want yet. I've always had such big visions of love that—— No, no, no! You wouldn't propose to me if it were a hot afternoon, a muggy, wilty afternoon, and we were walking down Main Street."

"But you do like me; and when we're both lonely——"

"Probably no one will ever love me as I want. Oh, why should they? What am I but a little hat trimmer, with a love for tea and cats!"

"You aren't; you are the one person I could love—if you could only understand how much I mean it!" And as he said it he knew he didn't quite mean it; he knew he was merely living up to the magic moment, and he listened to his own high-pitched voice going on in poetic periods unnatural to him: "Your soul shines like the prairie there; and when I look into your eyes I see all the fairy stories my mother used to read to me——"

"But, my dear boy, you don't want a lady reciter. You want a nice home and somebody to send out the laundry for you. That's all right! I understand. I often want a home myself. But I'm a funny old silly. Frightfully sentimental. So I distrust sentimentality. Wait. Think it over tomorrow. Oh——"

Suddenly she was crying, in sobs accumulated through years of loneliness. She crouched on the lower bar of the gate and hid her eyes against his knee. Her hat fell off and her hair was a little disordered. Yet this touch of prosaicalness did not shock him. It brought her near to him; made her not a moon wraith, but a person like himself. He patted her shoulder till she sat up and laughed a little; and they strolled toward the town.

The overwrought self that had sung of love was gone. But he felt toward her a sincere and eager affection.

Twenty-four hours later, back in St. Sebastian, he was calling on Myrtle Hillbridge. They put a humorous monologue record on the phonograph and laughed loudly over it and ate fudge; and he was perfectly sincere about that too.

IV

He was to spend two weeks in St. Sebastian, helping take stock. It was his longest stay there since he had met Miss Myrtle Hillbridge at a church social. On his first call he criticized the Hillbridge house to himself for having a foolish little tower and a battlement. He was uneasy in the glare of electric light falling upon bright green velours upholstery in Myrtle's parlor, and he decided that Myrtle's smooth cheeks were stupid in that hot shine. He thought of the gentle vividness of Miss Weeks' ever-changing face. But he reasoned with himself:

"Thunder, they can't everybody have the same kind of a house! ... Rats, they can't everybody be the same kind of a person! ... Miss Weeks is the finest woman I know; but Myrtle is a mighty jolly girl. ... Gosh, that's a funny record! I wonder if Myrtle has any of this jazz music."

He was invited to an Advertisement Party at Myrtle's, and by reason of much reading of magazines upon trains he won the guessing contest. He danced the fox trot with damages to the slippers of not more than one or two girls, and told a good story about the Chippewas at Cass Lake.

When the young married couples were departing, and the girls were being persuaded to let various young men take them home, Myrtle whispered:

"Don't go yet, Wilbur. Wouldn't you like to stay and help me eat up the rest of the cake and lemonade?"

She looked confidential; and he felt confidential and superior to the rest of the party as he whispered:

"Yes."

They sat in chairs drawn up to the polished expanse of the dining table and nibbled crumbs of coconut filling, and laughed at the rest of the guests. The least he could do was to hold her hand. This duty he performed to the perfect satisfaction of all immediately concerned. She hung her head; and, while she shyly traced the design on his cuff button with her finger, she murmured:

"Why am I so bad? Why do I let you hold my hand?"

He didn't know the answer, and he felt guilty that she was so moved by his caress. How could he, as a regular man, stop now when she was so innocently happy? He seized her hand more boldly; and, because the tension of the moment demanded that he should say something complimentary at once, he sighed:

"Pretty little hand!"

She glanced at him sharply and snatched away her hand.

"I don't believe you care a bit about holding my hand; and I'm not going to let you, either! You're nothing but just a lady-killer, going round playing make love."

"I am not, either!" he insisted, and tried to capture the hand again.

She would not let him, and informed him that she should never have yielded to his petition to be allowed to stay and finish up the cake if she had not supposed he would behave himself. He was crushed by her coldness and convinced that to hold the hand of Miss Myrtle Hillbridge was a very close approximation to heaven.

She sent him home; but relented at the door and let him kiss her good night, which he did with rapturous thrills, and went out exultant. When he got home, and began to smoke a cigar of triumph, he wondered whether Myrtle was entirely unwilling to be kissed. He informed himself that she was maneuvering, but that he was an ungrateful dog to think anything of the sort; that Myrtle would like to drag a promising young man to the altar, but also that she was just a kindly girl whom said ungrateful dog had sore offended; that she was more human than Miss Weeks, but that Miss Weeks' little finger was worth more than Myrtle's whole body. He repeated this highly consistent analysis over and over, and went to bed in a whirl of perplexity, out of which emerged only one fact—that he liked to kiss Miss Myrtle Hillbridge.

It was past one, three hours after the canonical bedtime in St. Sebastian, when he went to bed. He was sleepy next day, and all his opinions regarding women could have been summed up in "Drat them; they disturb a man's work!" But Myrtle called him up and invited him to drop in after supper. After having kissed the poor, trusting girl—why had he ever been such a scoundrel!—he couldn't be cold to her; and he thanked her ardently, though his warmest desire was to get to bed directly after supper.

He hoped that she wouldn't be too affectionate or talkative that evening. She wasn't. They sat on the front steps, upon flattened doughnuts of willow, leaning against the porch pillars; and they talked drowsily of Ben and Bessie, and of how admittedly superior Myrtle was to Bessie. He found himself kissing her good night at the gate, and he went home feeling bound to her.

Never, he meditated, could he tell her that he hadn't really meant those kisses. Why, it would break her heart! He had to go on now. . . .

How come he had kissed her again? He certainly hadn't meant to. He didn't understand. Well, anyway, it wouldn't be so bad to marry Myrtle. She was a splendid girl and a normal-school graduate. . . . But he plaintively wished he had met Miss Weeks earlier. He wondered, with excitement, why he couldn't correspond with Miss Weeks. Never thought of that before! . . . No; too late! . . . Besides all that—oh, that moonlight stuff was too highbrow for a jay like himself! Oh, well——

V

He was invited to supper at the Hillbridges'. It was a party meal, with olives and candied orange peel. Mr. Hillbridge treated Wilbur as one accepted by the established set in St. Sebastian. He asked him questions about the grocery business outlook, and boomed: "Have some more of the lamb, Wilbur, my boy. And don't you two young people go holding hands under the table there!" Mrs. Hillbridge smiled, and said, "Now, Chan!" to her husband; and, to Wilbur, "Don't mind him, Mr. Cole; he's a terrible joker."

Myrtle was moody, but she gave Wilbur secret smiles. And Mr. Hillbridge gave him a two-for-a-quarter cigar.

The Hillbridges were temporarily without a maid—most families in St. Sebastian are permanently temporarily without a maid. After supper Myrtle commanded her parents: "You two go off to the movies, and Wilbur and I will wash the dishes—won't we, Wilbur?"

Yes—Wilbur would, indeed; there was no sport he admired so much as the washing of party supper dishes. Mrs. Hillbridge protested for a suitable period, then winked at her husband and jerked her head backward at him; and they departed, leaving Wilbur in a comfortable fancy that this was his house and Myrtle his jolly little wife.

They laughed as they washed the dishes. He dropped some cold water down her neck, and she chased him about the kitchen, snapping the dish towel at him till he begged for mercy. They did not talk of solemn beauty or the misty plains; neither of silver nor of candlelight; but lustily sang together a pleasing melody:

> Oh, myyyyyy E-GYP-shun queen,
> You're the best I ever-rever-rever seen;
> And your winks put the jinx on the sphinx, so I thinks,
> My dreamun Ejup que-en!

"Isn't that a dandy song?" glowed Myrtle. "Oh, I'd die if I could just write one song like that! They say this man made a hundred thousand out of 'Poor Butterfly'; but I don't know—maybe it would be more fun to write movie scenarios. Oh, just think of being a scenario writer and going out to Los Angeles and meeting Douglas Fairbanks! Isn't he a peach! I wonder if he is married. I was reading—why, just yesterday—it was an advertisement in the paper, where you can learn to write scenarios in six lessons; and you get from a hundred to a thousand dollars apiece for them. Think of that! Maybe I wouldn't buy an automobile that would put it all over Doctor Julian's! But still, think of writing a song like that—My dreammun Ejup que-en!"

"Yes; that's so," Wilbur agreed.

It had been a good supper. He certainly did like corn fritters.

He contrasted this big kitchen, its enamel refrigerator, its cabinet, its new range, with the closet which Miss Weeks called a kitchen and in which she cooked one thing at a time on a kerosene burner.

It was good to be on kitchen terms of intimacy after months in bedrooms and offices of hotels. It was good to have Myrtle acknowledge that he was on such terms and to say, when they had gone out to the front porch: "Oh, do run in and get me a glass of ice water, Wilbur. You know where the icebox is."

He swaggered through the hall, the dining room, the kitchen, as though all this were his. He was no longer a farm boy on sufferance in the great mansion of the great city.

He cheerfully let the tap run cold, chopped ice, filled the glass, made the ice tinkle, switched off the kitchen light, started toward the hall—and stopped.

Someone, a block away, was playing a violin. The kitchen window was open; and as he looked from the darkened room he was conscious of a honeysuckle bush rustling in the yard, of slumberous trees and the quiet night while the music wound a thread of faint, fine emotion about him. And instantly he was identifying that mood with Miss Weeks; and he knew that he was doing it, and wanted to run away from the admirable young woman awaiting him on the front porch.

"It isn't Myrtle's fault—she's a lot better than I am. I'm a hound; but, Lord, I don't want to settle down yet! I don't want to look fat after supper, like Pa Hillbridge. I guess probably she is eight, maybe ten years older than Myrtle; but still, she's so much younger; and she always will be. I want to play yet, like a kid—like her."

"Her" meant Miss Weeks to him. "Her" would always mean Miss Weeks to him, he knew.

Myrtle was waiting. He trailed out to the porch. She was cuddled on the porch swing. She patted a cushion and said amiably:

"Sit here and be comfy."

Then, because he was afraid he would kiss her, he did kiss her, and felt himself to be a traitor and a fiend and a scared rabbit, all at once. Again he wanted to run. Also, he wished to kiss her. Suddenly he was standing beside the porch swing and listening to his own stammering:

"Oh, I mustn't kiss you—I mustn't—you're so good and bully; and—I guess I better go."

"I didn't—I didn't mind. I like you!" she whispered.

If she would only be angry—only tell him to go! He couldn't be churlish to her. But never again would he be so weak as to kiss her! She was a stranger to him; and always would be, though they were married with bell, book and candle. But he could say nothing. He was afraid of the serene power of commonplaceness in her. He could only stand in a cold numbness, wondering why he couldn't find anything to say.

"Wilbur, what is the matter?"

He did not answer; could not answer.

"Wilbur!"

Nothing.

She sat on the edge of the swing and stared at him. She drew an angry breath. He turned his head away. Then:

"Well, Mr. Wilbur Cole, if you think I am so crazy about you that I am going to stand for your being silent and queer and cranky, as if you had done me a favor by—by kissing me—and now you guess maybe you want to run along home, then I guess you have another guess coming, Mr. Wilbur Cole. You can go; and you can't go one bit too soon for me!" Her voice was round and resolute, young and hard.

He moved toward the gate.

"Wilbur!" It was a sound of relenting.

He turned back, and heard a queer vulgar little old man in him piping: "Darn it! I thought she was going to let me go now."

"Wilbur, don't you think you ought to apologize before you go? What is it, dear? Come, tell me the matter."

Terrified, he cried:

"I can't—not tonight. Oh, I'm so sorry, honey! You're sweet; and—I'll call you up tomorrow."

He bolted; and not for a mile did he slacken his half run.

He sat on a pile of ties overlooking a cindery railroad yard for three hours or more; and he was no longer young. He was suffering, and he was not enjoying the spectacle of himself. Youth makes a dramatic picture of itself as heroic in suffering. Past youth blames itself and wants either to heal or to cause the suffering of others.

The moon came up in its last quarter—riding like a wrecked galleon in a lost sea of grasses. It seemed to bind him to Miss Weeks, up there, sixty miles away. The night breeze was ever cooler and more fresh. He muttered:

"Gee! I'm free! It isn't too late now, no more. Myrtle, poor kid! Hope she gets a new beau in couple of weeks. . . . Bet she does, too. . . . Why don't I go? I'll do just that."

He walked sedately to the garage. He awoke an irate night attendant. He cheerfully filled the tank of his little car, and even took care to fill a grease cup. At three o'clock he started due north, toward Gopher Prairie.

He no longer blamed himself or justified himself. He merely growled:

"Bet there's lots of fellows get married when they don't specially want to—just drift along, and see they're expected to buy a ring; lots more than will ever admit it. Tell you, me, if I ever get married it's going to be—oh, like one of these here pilgrimages. Kind of religious. I've crawled up from a farmhouse attic to this little ole car, and I ain't going to stop with just being a solid citizen. No, sir! Read books. Not just selling talk, but music. Mahogany. Tropics. . . . Candlelight. . . . All that stuff. . . . Motor sure does run a lot better at night!"

The road was free of traffic and there was exhilaration in slashing through villages barren with sleep; in chasing an imbecile of a jackrabbit that hadn't sense enough to get out of the road, but kept ahead for half a mile, humping itself ludicrously in the circle of gliding light.

The darkness trembled; the fields awoke in choruses of insects; the tremendous prairie sunrise boomed across the land; the early goldenrod was cheerful beside a red barn; a meadowlark fluttered up to a fence wire and caroled—and Wilbur came riding into Gopher Prairie.

He ran up the stairs in the Colby Block, past the K.P. Hall; pounded at her door. Miss Weeks opened it—yet somehow it was not Miss Weeks.

Love had performed its old miracle of alchemy—this ordinary human face had been changed, somehow; to him it had become beautiful and imperishably young. She exclaimed:

"Why, what are you doing here? I thought you had to stay in St. Sebastian for two weeks."

"Huh? Just a moment—gee, out of breath! Do you know how pretty you are? Especially when you smile? Just ran up here to tell you I want to try that stunt of walking up Main Street on a hot afternoon; and twice in every block I want to tell you about you and me and all kinds of things—— Dear, will you listen? Will you?"

She searched his eyes; then stretched out her hands. There was a skylight in the hall. Morning sunshine fell upon the lovers.

THAT RYAN WOMAN

FRANK O'CONNOR

Mick Courtney had known Nan from the time he was fourteen or fifteen. She was the younger sister of his best friend, Dinny Ryan, and youngest of a family of four in which she was the only girl. He came to be almost as fond of her as her father and brothers were; she had practically lost her mother's regard by inheriting her father's looks. Her ugliness indeed was quite endearing. She had strong masculine features, all crammed into a feminine container, so that they bulged, and a stocky, sturdy figure. None of her features was really bad and her twinkling eyes were delightful, but they made a group that was almost comic.

Her brothers liked her spirit; they let her play with them while they were of an age for play; and, though she suffered from night panics and Dinny broke the maternal rule by letting her into his bed, they never told. Dinny would be waked in the middle of the night by Nan's pulling and shaking.

"Dinny, Dinny," she would whisper fiercely, "I have 'em again."

"What are they this time?" Dinny would ask drowsily.

"Li-i-i-ons!" she would reply in a bloodcurdling tone, and then lie for half an hour on his arm, contracting her toes and kicking spasmodically till the fit passed.

She grew up a tomboy, fierce, tough and tearless—fighting in Dinny's gang, which contested the old quarry on the road with the hill tribes from the slum area above it. And this was how Mick was to remember her best—a stocky little Amazon, leaping from rock to

157

rock, hurling stones in an awkward but effective way, and screaming deadly insults at the enemy and encouragement to her own troops.

He could not have said when she gave up fighting, but between twelve and fourteen she became the pious one in a family that was not remarkable for its piety. She was always out at Mass or diving into church on her way from school to light candles and make novenas. Afterward it struck Mick that it might have been an alternative to getting into Dinny's bed, for she still suffered from night fears, only now when they came on she grabbed her rosary beads instead.

It amused Mick to discover that she had developed something of a crush on himself. Mick had lost his faith, which in Cork starts a sort of excited flutter among the quiet ones of the opposite sex. She would be waiting at the door for him in the evening, and when she saw him would begin to jump down the steps one by one with her feet joined, her hands by her sides and her pigtail tossing.

"How are the novenas coming on, Nan?" Mick would ask with amusement.

"Fine!" she would reply in a shrill, expressionless voice. "You're on your way."

"I'll come quietly."

"You think you won't, but you will. I'm a fierce pray-er."

But though her brothers could ease the pangs of childhood for her, adolescence threw her on the mercy of life. Mrs. Ryan—a roly-poly of a woman who usually kept her arms folded, thus increasing the impression of curves and rolls—was still beautiful, and did her best to disguise Nan's ugliness.

"I'm no blooming beauty," Nan would cry with an imitation of a schoolboy's toughness, whenever her mother tried to get her out of the rough tweeds and dirty pullovers she fancied and into something more feminine.

"God knows you're not," her mother would say, folding her arms and studying her with resignation. "I suppose you don't want to advertise it, though."

"Why wouldn't I advertise it?" Nan would cry, squaring up to her. "I don't want any of your dirty old men."

"You needn't worry, child. They'll let you well alone."

"Let them!" Nan would say. "I don't care. I want to be a nun."

All the same, it made her self-conscious about friendships with girls of her own age. They, too, would have boys around, and the boys did not want Nan. Though she carefully avoided giving occasion for a slight, even the hint of one was sufficient to make her brooding and resentful. Suddenly and inexplicably she would drop some girl she had known for years, and never even speak of her again. It gave her the reputation of being cold and insincere, but—as Dinny in his shrewd way observed to Mick—she tended to make friends of older women and even of sick people, though even with these she was jealous and exacting.

Dinny didn't like this, and naturally his mother did not like it at all, but Nan paid no attention to their views. She had become exceedingly obstinate in a way that did not suit either her age or her sex, and it made her seem curiously angular, almost masculine, as though it were the psychological aspect of her ugliness. She had no shyness and stalked in and out of a room, swinging her arms like a boy. Her conversation changed, too, and took on the tone of an older woman's. It was not dull, but it was too much on one key—"crabbed," to use a local word—and it did not make the sharp distinctions young people's conversation makes between passion and boredom. Dinny and Mick could be very bored indeed in each other's company, but suddenly some topic would set flame to their minds, and they would walk the streets for hours, arguing.

Her father was disappointed when Nan refused to go to college. When she did go to work, it was behind the counter of a dress shop—a curious job for a girl with no great interest in clothes.

Then one night something happened that electrified Mick. As usual, he and she had been arguing while Dinny was out of the room. Mick—though without formal education—was an exceedingly well read man, and he had no patience with Nan's literary tastes, which were those of her aged and invalid acquaintances—popular novels and biographies that were the successes of a season. As usual, he made fun of her, and she grew angry.

"Ah, you never agree with anybody," she said, and went to look for the book they were talking of in the big bookcase.

Laughing, Mick got up and stood beside her, putting his arm about her shoulder as he would have done at any other time. She misunderstood the gesture, for she leaned back on his shoulder and turned her face up to be kissed. At that moment only did he realize that she had turned into a girl of startling beauty. He did not kiss her. Instead, he dropped his arm and looked at her incredulously while she gave him a reproachful grin and went on with what she had been saying.

For the rest of the evening he could not take his eyes from her. Now he could easily analyze the change for himself. He remembered that she had been ill with some type of fever and had come out of it white and thin. Then she had seemed to shoot up, and now he saw that during her illness her face had lengthened and, one by one, each of those awkward lumps of feature had dropped into place and proportion, till they formed a perfect structure that neither age nor illness could any longer quite destroy. It was not in the least like her mother's type of beauty. It was a translation of her father's masculinity, tight and strained and almost harsh. Already it had begun to affect her gait, because she no longer charged about a room, swinging her arms. And he wondered at the power of habit that causes us to live with people historically, with follies or virtues long disappeared from every eye but our own.

When Dinny followed him into the street, Mick began by being elaborately casual.

"Quite a change in Nan, isn't there?" he observed, flicking the ash from his cigarette.

"In who?" Dinny asked without interest. "Oh, Nan? Yes, that's since she was sick."

"Astonishing," added Mick, seeing that his casual tone would draw nothing from Dinny.

"Darn nuisance, as a matter of fact," Dinny said gravely.

"How so?"

"The house is overrun with fellows till you can't find a place to read."

Mick threw back his head and laughed heartily. Dinny was more affectionate than most brothers, and did not even object to a miracle or two if it made his sister happy, but he disapproved of revolutions in the home.

It proved a revolution for Mick as well as for him. For twelve months Mick had been going steady with a nice girl from Sunday's Well, and in due course would have married her. Mick was that sort—a creature of habit who controlled circumstances by simplifying them down to a routine—the same restaurant, the same table, the same waitress and the same dish. It enabled him to go on with his own thoughts. At the same time, whenever anything happened to disturb his routine, it was like a convulsion of Nature for him.

The transformation of his old admirer into a beauty was something of the sort. Gradually he dropped the nice girl from Sunday's Well and went more and more to the Ryans'.

Dinny had exaggerated the number of Nan's friends and suitors, but the change was there, all right. Mr. Ryan enjoyed it as proof that he had always been right about Nan's attractions. Mrs. Ryan had no such pleasure. Naturally, she had cared more for the boys, but the boys had not brought home attractive young men who had to flirt with her, and now Nan took an almost perverse delight in keeping the young men and her mother apart. Beauty had brought out what ugliness had failed to do—a deep resentment of her mother which at times went too far even for Mick's taste. She made up for it by what he thought an undue consideration for her father.

She had ceased to wear the rough masculine tweeds she had always liked, and to Mick's eye it was not a change for the better. She had developed a passion for good clothes without a taste for them. But if he disapproved of her taste in dress he disapproved even more of her taste in men. He and she argued about them as they had so often argued about other things. "Smoothies" he called them to her face, with a supercilious sniff.

There was Joe Lyons, the solicitor, a handsome, dark-haired young man who combined a knowledge of the right wines with an intellectual Catholicism; and Matt Healy, the butter merchant, who had a boat and talked about whisky and "dames." The pair of them could argue for half an hour without stopping, about how much you could get out of a particular car, or how quickly you could do the trip to Dublin, or which was the best hotel there. Obviously, Lyons despised Healy as a chatterbox, and Healy despised Lyons as a stuffed shirt, while Mick despised both of them equally. Intelligent discussion was impossible with them, for they both thought Mick something of a character and, when he tried to argue about religion or politics, they listened with an amusement that only made him angry.

"Mick," said Lyons, the kindlier of the two, resting an arm on Mick's shoulder, "you'll get wiser yet. Mind, I didn't say 'more intelligent'; I said 'wiser.' There is a difference."

Mick couldn't help being angry. He was hard-working but un-ambitious; too intelligent to value the things commonplace people valued, but too thin-skinned not to resent their scorn at his failure to do so.

Nan herself had no objection to being courted by Mick. She was still under the influence of her childish passion and it satisfied her vanity to be able to indulge it. She was an excellent companion, and would go off for long walks with him over the hills to the river, and then stop him when he wanted to be extravagant in the manner of her other young men.

"I'm a whisky drinker, Mick, but you're not a whisky buyer," she would say. "I'll have beer." But when he tried to become more serious, she countered with a bluff practicality that shocked him.

"Ah, what's the good of talking like that, Mick?" she asked. "Sure, you haven't a cent, and the way you're going on, you're not likely to make one."

"Why, is it a matter of cents?" he asked quietly, though he was stung by the good-natured contempt in her tone.

"What else is it?" she retorted. "As long as I remember my family, it's never been anything but quarrels about money and I don't want to be stuck with it."

"Well, if you marry Joe Lyons you'll never have to worry," he said, with a hint of a sneer.

"I didn't say I was going to marry him but if I were, I wouldn't be put off by what you think of him," she replied hotly.

"Why should you?" said Mick, feeling like a small boy, but unable to stop himself. "A fellow who reads Thomas Aquinas and can do a hundred in his new car."

"Ah, to listen to you, one would think it was a mortal sin to have a car," she said scoldingly. "Why can't you stop resenting people that have more than you?"

The worldly, middle-aged tone, particularly when linked with the Ryan push-and-go, could be exceedingly destructive. There was something else that troubled him as well, though he was not sure why. He had always liked to pose a little as a man of the world, and to talk frankly about sex, but Nan could sometimes shock him badly. There seemed to be depths of sensuality in her that were out of character and phase. He didn't know, he could not believe that she really intended it, but she could sometimes inflame him with some sudden violence or coarseness, as no ordinary girl could have done.

Then one evening when they were out together by the river he noticed a change in her. She had been spending a few days in Glengariff with Lyons, Healy and another girl, but she didn't want to talk of it, and he had the feeling that something about it had disappointed her. She was somehow different—brooding, affectionate, intense. She had pulled off her shoes and stockings and was sitting with her feet in the river, her hands joined between her knees.

"You know, Mick," she said, "you let Matt and Joe upset you too much. You should be able to pity them."

"Pity them?" he asked, laughing with surprise.

"If you weren't such a blooming agnostic, I'd say pray for them."

"Pray for bigger dividends for them?" he asked in the same tone.

"The dividends aren't much use to them," she said. "They're both bored. I like Joe Lyons because he has enough humility to know he's bored. Mind," she added in her enthusiastic way, "I like money, Mick Courtney. I like expensive clothes and flashy dinners and wines I can't even pronounce the names of, but they don't take me in. A girl that was brought up the way I was needs more than that to take her in. You mean more to me than the whole lot of them, if only you'd go do something."

"Do what?" he asked with interest.

"How do I know? I don't even care. I don't care even if you make a mess of it. It's not failure I'm afraid of. It's just getting stuck in the mud. Look at daddy. You mightn't think it, but he's a brilliant man, and he's stuck. Now he hopes the boys will find out whatever secret there is and do all the things he couldn't do."

"Yes," Mick said thoughtfully, answering himself rather than her. "I dare say I'm not ambitious. I know what you mean. But if it was the only thing that stood in your way, I dare say I could do something. It would have to be in Dublin, though. There's nothing here in my line."

"Dublin would do me fine," she said with satisfaction. "Mother and I would get on a great deal better at that distance."

Their engagement made a big change in Mick. He was, as I have said, a creature of habit—a man who lived by associations. He really knew the city in a way that few of us knew it, its interesting corners and queer characters, and the idea of having to change it for a place of no associations was more of a shock for him than it would have been for any of us. But though at certain times it left him with a lost feeling, at others it restored to him a boyish excitement and gaiety, as though the trip he was preparing for was some dangerous voyage, and when he lit up like that, he became more attractive, reckless and innocent. Nan had always been rather in love with him; now she really admired and adored him.

At the same time she did not discontinue her outings with her old beaux. In particular, she remained friendly with Joe Lyons, who was genuinely fond of her and believed that she wasn't serious about marrying Mick. He was, as she said, an exceedingly kind man, and was genuinely shocked at the thought that so beautiful a girl should even consider cooking and washing clothes on a clerk's income. He went to her father about it, and would even have gone to Mick himself, only that she forbade him. "But he can't do it, Nan," he protested; "he can't do that to you." This did not worry Mick in the least. He was a man who was almost devoid of jealousy. He was merely amused by her occasional lies and evasions, and even more by the fits of conscience that followed them.

"Mick," she would say feverishly, "when I said I was going to Confession last Saturday, that was a lie. I was out in Joe Lyons' car. He still won't believe but I'll marry him and I would, if only he had a brain in his head. Mick, why can't you be attractive like that?"

Mrs. Ryan resented it on Mick's behalf, though even more she resented his complaisance. She was sufficiently feminine to know that she might have done it herself, and to feel that she would need correction if she did.

It was Nan's father who really irritated Mick. When Joe Lyons had lamented Nan's decision to him, he had also pointed out that if Nan married Mick she could not be "received" in the best houses—a fate that worried him more than it worried her. But Mr. Ryan was thunderstruck by the threat. He had never really approved of the marriage, but it had not crossed his mind that it might ever imply Nan's exclusion from society—whatever that was.

He began to bully Mick about the future. The prospect of the Dublin job did not satisfy him in the least. He wanted to know what Mick proposed to do then. There were examinations a young fellow could take which would insure his chances of promotion. Mick mustn't let the grass grow under his feet. Tom Ryan would arrange it all and coach him himself.

Mick had no intention of letting himself be coached by his future father-in-law, and the more Mr. Ryan pressed him, the firmer he became on the subject. At first, he was amused and polite; then he became sarcastic—a weakness of his when he was forced on the defensive. Mr. Ryan—who was as incapable as a child of under-standing sarcasm—rubbed his bald head angrily and left the room in a flurry.

"I wish you wouldn't speak to daddy like that," Nan said in a hurt tone.

"I wish daddy would stop arranging my life for me," Mick said wearily.

"He only means it in kindness."

"I didn't think he meant it in any other spirit," said Mick, with a sniff. "I still wish he'd get it into his head that it's I who am marrying you."

"I wouldn't be too sure of that, Mick," she said angrily.

"Really, Nan," he said reproachfully. "Just because I don't like being pushed about by your old man."

"It's not only that," she said desperately. "It's just as well we've had this out because I'd have had to tell you later. I can't possibly marry you."

"But why?" he asked gently.

"Because I'm scared."

"Of marriage?"

"Of marriage as well."

"Of me, so?"

"Of marriage and you and myself," she said explosively.

"Afraid you may kick over the traces?" he asked with affectionate mockery.

"You think I wouldn't?" she retorted, her eyes narrowing and her face looking old and grim. "You don't understand me at all, Mick," she added. "You don't even know the sort of things I'm capable of. You're wrong for me."

Mick treated the scene lightly, as though it were merely another of their disagreements, but when he left the house he was both hurt and troubled. Clearly there was a side of her character which he did not understand, and he was a man who liked to understand things, if only so that he could forget them and go on with his own thoughts. He knew she was unhappy, and felt that it really had nothing to do with the subject of their quarrel. It was unhappiness that had driven her into his arms in the first place, and now it looked as though it were about to drive her out again.

He had assumed, rather too complacently, that she had turned to him because she had learned to see through people like Lyons and Healy, but now he realized that her unhappiness had nothing to do with them either. She was desperate about herself rather than them. She might, he thought, have been tempted too far. She was the sort of passionate girl who could very easily be lured into an indiscretion and would then react from it with loathing and self-disgust. The very thought that this might be the cause moved him to a passion of protective tenderness, and before he went to bed he wrote and posted an affectionate letter, apologizing for his mockery of her father and promising to consider her feelings more in the future.

In reply, he received a brief note which she delivered at his house while he was at work. She did not refer at all to his letter, but told him that she was marrying Lyons. It was a dry note, and to him it seemed full of secret malice. He left his own house and met Dinny on the way up to call on him. From Dinny's gloomy air, Mick saw that he knew all about it. They went for one of their usual walks, and only when they were sitting in a country public house did Mick speak of the breach. The scene lingered in his mind because of the country boys who came in and argued about the weather and racing.

Dinny was worried, and his worry made him rude, and through the rudeness Mick seemed to hear the voices of the Ryan family discussing the affair. They had never really cared for him as a husband for Nan but had been prepared to accept him just because she seemed to like him so much better than any of the others. But there was no question in their minds that she did not care at all for Lyons and was marrying him only in some mood of desperation induced by Mick.

"I can't imagine what it was," Mick said thoughtfully. "Your father started bossing me and I was rude. I apologized for that."

"Oh, the old man bosses us all and we're all rude," said Dinny.

"Beyond that, I can't think of anything," said Mick.

"And Nan won't tell," said Dinny. "So whatever it is, the harm is done. You know how obstinate she is when she takes an idea into her head."

"You don't think I should see her and have it out?"

"I wouldn't," said Dinny. "It'll only hurt you worse than you're hurt already."

Mick realized that Dinny—whatever his reasons might be—was advising him to quit, and for once he was in a position to do so. With the usual irony of events, the job he had been seeking in Dublin only on Nan's account was now his, and he would have to leave at the end of the month.

This—which had seemed to him an enormous break with his past—turned out to be the very best cure for his troubled mind, for, though he missed old friends and familiar places more than most people, he had the sensitiveness of his type to the novelty of a larger and more exciting city, and he soon ended by wondering how he could ever have existed elsewhere. Within twelve months he had met a nice girl and married her.

So entirely did Cork scenes and characters fade from his mind that it came as a shock to him to meet Dinny one fine day in Grafton Street. Dinny was on his way to England, and Mick at once invited him home. But before they left town they celebrated their reunion in Mick's favorite pub off Grafton Street. Then he could ask the question that had sprung to his mind on catching sight of Dinny's face.

"How's Nan?"

"Oh, didn't you hear about her?" Dinny asked in some surprise. "She's gone into a convent, you know."

"Nan?" said Mick. "Into a convent?"

"It surprised me too," said Dinny. "I fancy it surprised the convent even more," he added dryly.

"For heaven's sake!" exclaimed Mick "And the fellow she was engaged to? Lyons?"

"Oh, she dropped him inside a month," said Dinny with distaste. "I never thought she was serious about him anyway."

Mick went on with his drink, suddenly feeling embarrassed and strained. A few minutes later he asked, with the pretense of a smile, "You don't think if I'd hung on she might have changed her mind?"

"I daresay she might," Dinny replied sagaciously. "I'm not so sure it would have been the best thing for you, though," he added kindly. "The truth is I don't think Nan is the marrying kind."

"I daresay not," said Mick.

But he didn't believe it for an instant. He was quite sure that Nan was the marrying kind, and that nothing except the deep unhappiness that had first united and then divided them had kept her from marrying. But what that was about he still had no idea, and he saw that Dinny knew even less about her than he did.

The meeting had brought it all back and at intervals during the next few years it came back again, disturbing him. It was not that he was unhappy in his own married life; on the contrary, all its little commonplaces were a deep joy to him. But sometimes in the morning when he had kissed his wife at the gate, he would go swinging down the avenue of the little estate toward the sea, thinking of the girl who had seemed to have none of his pleasure in simple things and whose decisions all seemed to have been dictated by some inner torment.

And then one day, years later, he found himself alone in Cork, tidying things up after the death of his father—his last relative there. Suddenly he found himself plunged back into the world of his childhood and youth, and he wandered like a ghost from street to street, pub to pub, old friend to old friend, resurrecting other ghosts in a mood that was half anguish, half delight. His absorption in the familiar made him peculiarly susceptible to the poetry of change. He visited the Ryans and found Mrs. Ryan as good-looking as ever, though she moaned sentimentally about the departure of the boys and the disappointment of Nan.

Then, when she saw him to the door, she folded her arms and leaned against the jamb. "Wisha, Mick, wouldn't you go and see her?" she said reproachfully.

"Nan?" said Mick. "You don't think she'd mind?"

"Wisha, for heaven's sake why would she mind?" Mrs. Ryan said with a shrug. "Sure, the girl must be dead for someone to talk to."

Mick, thinking of what Mrs. Ryan had said, made up his mind to see Nan. The convent was on one of the steep hills outside the city, with a wide view of the valley from its front lawn. He was expecting a change, but Nan's appearance in the terrible convent parlor startled him. The frame of white linen and black veil gave her strongly marked features the unnatural relief of a fifteenth-century German portrait. And at the first glance he became convinced of an idea that had formed slowly in his mind through the years.

"Isn't it terrible I can't kiss you, Mick?" were her first words. "Come out in the garden where we can talk," she added.

Chattering on, she rustled ahead of him onto the lawn, and he knew that she was as pleased to see him as he to see her. She led him to a garden seat behind a hedge that hid them from the convent and grabbed his hand.

"Are you converted yet, Mick?" she asked eagerly.

"Do I look it?" he asked with a pale smile.

"You don't," she replied with a doubtful grin. "I'd know that agnostic look anywhere. But you needn't think you'll escape me all the same."

"You're a fierce pray-er," he quoted and she burst into laughter at the memory.

"I am, too," she added boyishly. "I'm a terror for holding on."

"A wonder you couldn't have held on to me, so," he said mockingly.

"Ah, that's different," she said with sudden gravity. "I suppose 'twas the way God came first." Then she looked at him out of the corner of her eye. "Or do you think I'm only talking nonsense?"

"I do."

"I'm not really," she said. "Though sometimes I wonder myself how I got here," she added ruefully. "And it's not that I'm not happy here. You know that?"

"Oh, I know," he said with a nod.

"You've changed a lot if you do," she said.

"Haven't we both?" he asked.

He had not needed her to say that she was happy nor did he now need her to tell him why. He knew that the idea that had been forming in his mind in the last year or so was the true one, and that what had happened to her was not something unique and outside his own experience. It was something that happened to others in different ways. Because of some inadequacy in themselves—poverty or physical weakness in men, poverty or ugliness in women—those with the gift of creation built for themselves a rich interior world; and when the inadequacy disappeared and the real world was spread before them with all its wealth and beauty, they could not give their whole heart to it. Uncertain of their choice, they wavered between goal and goal, were lonely in crowds, dissatisfied in the middle of noise and laughter, unhappy even with those they loved best. The interior world called them back, and for some it was a case of having to return or die.

He tried to explain his ideas to her, feeling his own lack of persuasiveness and at the same time aware that she was watching him keenly and with amusement, as though she did not take him seriously. Perhaps she didn't, for none of us can really feel, let alone describe, the interior world of another. They sat for close on an hour, and Mick refused to stay for tea. He knew convent teas and had no desire to spoil the impression that their meeting had left on him.

"Pray for me," he said with a smile as they shook hands.

"Do you think I ever stopped?" she asked mockingly.

He strode quickly down the shady steps to the lodge gate in a strange mood of rejoicing, realizing that however the city might change, that old love affair went on unbroken in a world where disgust or despair could never touch it, and would continue so till both of them were dead.

THE BONFIRE

JOHN O'HARA

Kitty Bull said the final good nights to the children, the final "no, no more stories" to the older two and paid a silent visit to the baby's room (for she firmly believed that a one-year-old can sense a break in his routine even when he is asleep). The cook and the maid were at the early movie in Southampton. The Bannings and their guests—a noisy cocktail party—had taken off for a dinner party in Wainscott, leaving all the lights on in the house next door but leaving, too, a merciful silence. The ocean was reasonably subdued, pounding the beach at long intervals and with only enough force to keep you from forgetting that it was there, that it had been angry most of the day and could be angry again.

She kicked off her Belgian slippers and went out and stood on the top of the dune. There was still enough light for a visibility of five miles, three miles, six miles. Make it three miles. It was about three miles to the Inlet, and she could see two white dots that would be fishing boats heading for the Inlet in a race against the coming darkness. The sand squishing through her toes made her wish she could run down and go for a brief swim, but she could not leave the house so soon. This was the first half hour, when Jeanie might be naughty and find some excuse to call her. She would pay no attention to the first call, and Jeanie might give up; but sometimes Jeanie would be insistent and repeat her call, louder and often, and disturb the other children.

She thanked God for the children. She thanked God. . . .

Now she could not see the white dots and she would have to suppose that the fishing boats had got inside the Inlet. The visibility, whatever it had been, was now to be estimated in yards, not miles, and far far out, where the horizon had been, there were three twinkling lights, the riding lights of three other fishing boats that she had not seen before. They would be out there all night and if she got up early enough—five o'clock in the morning—they would still be there, but at six o'clock they would be gone. They were professional fishing boats, bunker boats that filled their nets, loaded up, and returned to Islip or to Baltimore with catches that would be converted into some kind of fertilizer. That, at least, was what Jerry had told her years ago. Five years ago. Six years ago. *Seven* years ago, when they had first come to this house. Could it be seven years? Almost a fifth of her life? One wave, heavier than all the others had been, struck the beach like thunder and she picked up her slippers and went inside.

In her bare feet she went upstairs and stood outside the children's rooms and listened. There was not a sound from them. She opened the door of the baby's room. She could not see him, but when she caught the rhythm of his breathing she closed the door and went downstairs again. The first half hour was more than gone, and for a moment she thought of going for a swim; but that was something she had promised Jerry never to do. Never go in that ocean alone, but especially at night. He had never permitted her to go in alone at night even when he was there in the house, watching a ball game on the TV. It isn't a question of how good a swimmer you are, or of keeping your head, he had told her. Naturally you would have sense enough to conserve your energy, and try to keep the lights of the beach cottages in front of you. But who could see *you* in the dark? Never go in alone at night, he had said; and then one night a year ago, a little tight and just arrived from the hot city, he had broken all his own rules. He had stopped for dinner at Rothman's on the way down, and you did not stop at Rothman's if you were alone, but she guessed whom he had dined with. It was not a clever guess. It was not a guess at all. It was an assumption based as much on instinct as on the things she had heard. "I feel as if I'd been dipped in oatmeal," he had said.

"You've been dipping in something stronger than oatmeal," she said.

"A few. Not enough to do any damage. I'm going for a swim."

"I can't go for a swim. Doctor Mando said not to for a while."

"That's all right. I just want to dunk."

"Why don't you just take a shower?"

"Because I want to go in the ocean! My God, Kitty."

"Well, you're always the one that says——"

"I'm *not* planning to swim to *Brazil*. If you're going to make a federal case of it, I won't go in. But my God, Kitty."

"Oh, go ahead," she said.

She could have stopped him. For a year she had told herself that she could have stopped him, and many times during the second half of that year she had wondered why she had not stopped him. She had given in to him and to his irritability and his stubbornness, but had there not been some irritability, some jealousy, on her part? Four days later they found his body near the Inlet, confirming his identity through his dental history, an X-ray photograph of a shoulder he had broken in college, and physical measurements that matched his in the Navy files. It was he, all right, beyond any reasonable doubt, and it was not necessary for her to look at him. His mother and father had been perfectly wonderful, and so had his brother. The only unpleasantness had been created by his sister, when he had been dead six months.

"You don't mind talking about Jerry, do you, Kitty?" said Edna.

"Not a bit. Why?"

"Well, because he was always against going in the ocean at night. It was so *unlike* him."

"Your father brought that up. Your mother did too."

"I know they did, and you tried to stop him. I know that, too. But can you think of any reason why Jerry would do such a complete about-face? I mean, he was my brother and we were very close."

"I know."

"I adored him. I really did."

"I know you did, Edna."

"But I wasn't blinded to his imperfections," said Edna.

"He had a few. Who hasn't?"

"Yes, who hasn't? Francine Barrow, for instance. You know what she's saying, of course."

"Yes, I do. But I didn't expect you to repeat anything Francine Barrow said. Jerry didn't commit suicide over Francine Barrow. He didn't commit suicide over anyone or anything. He was quite tight that night."

"You might have thought the cold water would have sobered him up."

"It doesn't always work that way. In fact, almost never. Haven't you ever been to a beach party where there was a lot of drinking? I haven't noticed that going in the ocean sobered them up. Quite the contrary, in some cases. I remember one night when you were tight and you went in and came out without your bikini."

172

"I've never been allowed to forget that," said Edna.

"Well, I only bring it up now to show that cold salt water doesn't necessarily sober you up. Jerry himself said you were really bagged that night. And you were."

"I'm perfectly willing to change the subject, if that's what you want to do, Kitty."

"No, I'd rather have this out. I knew about Francine. It started the last few months I was having the baby, and it continued for the same reason after the baby was born."

"Did you quarrel with him about it?"

"We had some minor quarrels, not over Francine. Although I suppose that was at the bottom of it. I didn't like it. You wouldn't like it if Mike slept with someone else while you were in the midst of having a baby. My first two pregnancies were fairly simple, but not this one. I was having a hard time, and Jerry wasn't much help to my morale. I've always thought Francine was one of the worst tramps on Long Island anyway."

"So do I, for that matter."

"Well, then why do you help her spread that story? Jerry did not commit suicide. I would have known if he'd had any such intentions. The only reason he came down that night was because he was playing in a tournament at the National the next day. That was on his mind, not committing suicide."

"All right, Kitty. I'm satisfied. I'm sorry I had to bring this up, but I had to."

"Yes, I suppose you did," said Kitty, and the weariness in her voice surprised her. Acute grief had gone and now there was weariness that she had not suspected, and it remained with her for many months. It was much worse than the acute grief. The doctor had told her that she need not worry about having the strength to recover from her pregnancy and take care of the children. Nature is very reliable, he had said; when something like that happened to you, a shock, a dramatic episode, Nature responded. But when the acute grief began to wear off and the postponed weariness set in, that was the time to be careful. She went to see him, and because he was a good man she told him about her sister-in-law's conversation.

"I was afraid there'd be something like that," he said. "She hit you with it at just the wrong time. I'm going to send you up to the hospital for a G.I. series."

"Is that the barium thing? I haven't got an ulcer."

"Let's make sure," said the doctor.

She saw him again in a few days. "Now you can be glad I made you swallow all that barium," he said. "There's no sign of an ulcer."

"I knew there wouldn't be," she said.

"Did you indeed?" he said. He smiled.

"Well, I was right, wasn't I?" she said.

"Gloating, hey?" He had a pencil in his hand and he began sketching on a prescription blank.

"Now what, Doctor Mando? I always know there's something when you start drawing those little pictures. Are they my insides that you're drawing, or just anyone's?"

"You're pretty fresh. I think you're greatly relieved at my good news."

"Well, why shouldn't I be? I'd *hate* to have an ulcer. But come on, Doctor, what's on your mind?"

"*You* are, Mrs. Bull. Four cigarettes just since you've been here. I'm sure your internist has spoken to you about them. I *know* he has, because we had a conversation this morning. He had the first look at your X-ray pictures, you know."

"Yes, you two keep me up in the air like a shuttlecock."

"Badminton," said the doctor.

"Don't tell me I'm not going to be able to play games."

"No, that isn't what's on my mind. You can start swimming any time you feel like it, and golf or tennis, if you're planning to go south."

"I'm staying in New York, but there are places where I can swim and play squash."

"Exercise will be good for you. Doctor Randolph will tell you that, too."

"Fine, and now you tell me what's got you drawing those pictures."

He put down his pencil and sat back in his chair, his hands folded across his chest and reminding her of a spiritual adviser. "Is there any chance that you might be getting married fairly soon?"

"No," she said. "Is there any reason why I shouldn't?"

"On the contrary, there is every reason why you should, from my point of view."

"I haven't thought about it, at least not very much. And there's no man in the offing. Someday I suppose I will. Someday my prince will come." Suddenly, inexplicably, the sound of her words made her burst into tears. The doctor bent forward and gave her one of his large, hand-rolled handkerchiefs.

"Good Lord," she said. She dried her eyes and blew her nose.

"Mm-hmm," the doctor muttered.

"May I keep the handkerchief? I'll send it back to you," she said.

"Of course," said the doctor. He opened his desk drawer and took out a silver cigarette box. "I keep these out of sight nowadays. Have one?"

"Thanks," she said. He lit it for her. "I remember that lighter," she said.

"Yes, it's quite a beautiful piece of workmanship," he said. He looked at it and put it back in his pocket, and resumed his clerical attitude.

"It was the words of that song," she said.

"Yes, but it wasn't only the words of the song, Mrs. Bull. You know that."

"I do now. I hadn't realized that I was in any such state. But I guess I am, aren't I?"

"Be very strange if you weren't. I've known you pretty well these last six or seven years."

"Well, what do you suggest?" she said.

"I suggest that you start going out a little bit."

"In the hope of meeting some man," she said.

"Naturally."

"And having an affair with him, even if I don't fall in love with him?"

"You may have to wait a long time before you'll admit that you're in love with anyone."

"Yes, you're right," she said.

"In fact, you could conceivably go through the rest of your life without falling in love again."

"Yes," she said.

"Your husband left you three children, and the circumstances of his death. No other man will be able to make that deep an impression on you. On your life. On your memories. So don't expect anyone to."

"You didn't like my husband, did you, Doctor Mando?"

"That's not a very nice question to ask me, young woman. And I'm not going to answer it. But if he were my own son I'd still give you the same advice. You're in your early thirties and most of your life lies ahead of you. That includes having children, if you want any more. And you should, or those nice children you have now will become something that they shouldn't."

"What's that?"

"Walking reminders of your husband, of course. Making it impossible for you to start your new life. I hope you'll meet an interesting man and marry him and have children right away."

"I don't think that's going to happen," she said.

"It won't if you don't give it a chance," said the doctor. "Well, when do you want to see me again?"

"When do *you* want to see *me*?"

"In about three months. Miss Murphy will give you an appointment."

"Not till then? That's the longest I've ever gone without seeing you. Aren't you going to miss me?"

He smiled. "Yes, as a matter of fact I will. But it'll do you good to stay out of here for a while. Save you money, too."

"You're such a lovely man, Doctor Mando. You really are," she said.

"Of course I am," he said. "My patients are nice, too. Some of them."

"Me?"

"Go on, young woman. There are women waiting," he said. "And I have to clean out this ash tray."

There was no "interesting" man at any of the small dinner parties she went to. Among the new men there were the pitiers, depressing fellows who acted as though Jerry had died last week; there were the others who were so determinedly cheerful that they seemed to deny that Jerry had ever lived at all. Among the men she had known in the past there were the instant patriarchs, contemporaries of Jerry's who took it upon themselves to plan her life for her; and, not surprisingly, there were two who were ready to move into her life. One of them was a dirty talker, who had never talked dirty to her while Jerry was alive; and the other was Edna's husband, Mike, who had always looked at her from the edges of groups with a dumb lechery that he now expressed in terms of love. "I think you've always known how I felt about you, Kitty," he said.

"Not exactly," she said. It was malicious, drawing him out, but she had not forgiven Edna for her inquisition.

"Maybe not exactly, but you must have had some idea," said Mike.

"Some idea, more or less," she said.

"Invite me to dinner some night. Just me."

"Without Edna?"

"That's the general idea," he said. "I suppose you're going to say that's impossible, but it isn't."

"But it is. If I invited you alone, there could only be one interpretation of that. There isn't any other interpretation."

"Oh, I see. You mean that you'd be the aggressor?"

"Not only the aggressor, but—well, yes, the aggressor. The troublemaker."

"Would you go away with me? If we went in my car, I'd be the aggressor, if that's what you object to. What I'm trying to tell you is—we've gotten sidetracked with this aggressor talk. I want you to see me without Edna, without anyone. To get used to me. And if I can convince you—to marry me."

"Oh."

"I know you're not all that anxious to get married again so soon. But it would take time in any case. Unfortunately people don't just say 'I've had it' and end a marriage that way. But I've been in love with you for a long time. We would have had this conversation sooner or later, even if Jerry had lived."

"I wonder," she said.

"You needn't. He kept you pregnant most of the time or I'd have spoken up sooner."

"That was very considerate of you, Mike."

"Is that sarcasm?"

"Not at all," she said.

"The week after next I'm going to Pinehurst. Come with me. I'm taking my car because it's more convenient. I'm making stops on the way down and then circling back through West Virginia, Ohio, and Pennsylvania. I'll be in Pinehurst for three days, a business convention, and you probably wouldn't want to do that, but you could join me when the convention's over, and we could have the better part of a week together. The most I'd have to spend with my business acquaintances would be two or three hours a day, and you like to read. What do you say?"

"Oh, you know what I'm going to say, Mike. How could I nip off for a week, leaving three small children and telling the nurse that I'd be at such-and-such a motel?"

"You're so practical," he said. "What if I sent Edna away, that is, gave her a trip abroad?"

"I don't know. Yes, I do know. I think that when I'm ready to do anything in that department, I *am* going to have to be the aggressor. I'm the only one that will know when I'm ready—and I'm not ready now."

"That Jerry. He's still got a tight grip on you, hasn't he?"

"Or I have a tight grip on myself. One or the other, or maybe both."

"When you loosen up a little, will you let me know? I'm serious. You can trust me, you know."

"You mean if I just wanted to have sex?"

"Yes. Don't you ever want sex? You've had a lot of it. With Jerry, I mean."

"And for seven years with no one else. So, when the time comes—I'm awfully tired of the word—but I'll be the aggressor. I much prefer 'on the make.' "

"You'll never go on the make, Kitty."

"Except that I did with Jerry. I wanted him, I went after him, and I got him. And I've lost him."

She would have been more abrupt and far more cruel with Mike if she had not realized, midway in the conversation, that the conversation was useful to the clarification of her problems. Mike was in no sense a stimulating man, but he had helped her to see that the next man in her life would have to be one she chose. Whimsically she told herself that she owed something to Mike for his collaboration, and in that mood she thought of inviting him to spend a night with her. But he was a clod and he would be around again and again, believing himself to be in love with her and upsetting the lives of too many people. Nevertheless she felt better for having come even that remotely close. Very tentatively, a toe in the water, she was back in life once more.

It was enough to go on for a while, and there were other things to keep her busy. At home there were the children, uncomprehending of the mystery of death or, in the case of the baby, petulantly demanding that she keep him alive. The older two were forgetting about their father. Kitty put a cabinet-size photograph of Jerry in a silver frame and set it on a table in the living room of the New York apartment. It was two days before Jeanie noticed it. She stood in front of the picture for a moment, and Kitty waited for her comment.

"That's Daddy," said Jeanie.

"Yes. It's my favorite picture of him. Do you like it?"

"I guess so."

"But not very much," said Kitty. "What is there that you don't like about it?"

"He's so serious, Mum."

"And that's not the way you remember him? Well, that's because when he was with you and your little brothers he *wasn't* very serious. Nearly always laughing. Little jokes and so forth."

"Didn't he have jokes with you too?"

"Oh, yes. Lots of them."

"Tell me one," said the child.

"A joke that he told me? Well, let me think. A joke that he told me. There was one that Grandfather Bull told him. About an oyster?"

"Tell it to me."

"It's sort of a riddle. What kind of a noise annoys an oyster? Do you know the answer?"

"What?"

"A *noisy* noise annoys an oyster."

"Oh, that's old."

"It sure is. See if I can think of another. Most of his jokes with me were about people. I'll think of some and write them down so I won't forget them. And I'll see if I can find a picture of him smiling. Where shall we put it, if I find one?"

"I don't know. Over there, I guess. Mummy, can I watch TV after supper?"

"Nope. Before supper, yes. After supper, off it goes."

The older boy, Timothy, was only three, cheerful and strong and increasingly able to take his own part when his sister bullied him. The Irish nurse would say to him, "You're the man of the house, Timothy."

"I yam not a man. I'm a boy, silly."

"You'll be a man soon enough, then."

"You're silly, Margaret. You're silly, silly, silly. You think a boy is a man. *You're* a man. You have a moustache."

"For that somebody gets no pudding this supper."

"It isn't pudding, it's junket, and I hate junket. So yah!"

And there was the baby, now old enough to follow her with his eyes when he was serene and to scream for her and only her when he was not.

There was more money than she had expected, and many more lawyers to see. There were certain financial advantages to be gained by a delay in settling Jerry's estate. "This could drag on for another year at least," said her lawyer, "but we want it to. Now for instance, Mrs. Bull, there's the matter of your husband's insurance. He carried a lot of insurance, much more than young men usually do nowadays. But he could afford it, so he did. The interesting thing here is that we've been arguing with the insurance company about the circumstances of your husband's death. We feel that accidental drowning may change the picture to your advantage. On the other hand *they* feel—I have to say this—that the possibility of suicide alters the picture in their favor. The medical examiner's report said accidental death by drowning, but the insurance company is trying to inject the element of suicide, not because they think they can get away with it, but maybe in the hope that we won't collect anything extra, like double indemnity. Give and take, you know. That's their position. But they know perfectly well that we're prepared to go to court. And by prepared I mean that you have enough money without the insurance to not have to make a quick settlement. By the way, who is a Mrs. Barrow? Francine Barrow? She wasn't at your house the night your husband lost his life, was she?"

"No. She was a friend of his. And mine, I suppose. My husband had dinner with her early that evening, over on the North Shore. But she wasn't in our house. She's never been in our house."

"No, I shouldn't think so. In a very roundabout way we found out that the insurance company is basing its whole argument on some story of hers."

"Well, she's a congenital liar, among other things."

"That's a good thing to know," said Mr. Hastings. "You understand, Mrs. Bull, that if we collect a large amount of insurance, it'll go a long way toward paying your inheritance taxes. In fact we may come out a little ahead of the game. You'd have no objection to suing the insurance company, I hope?"

"None whatever," said Kitty. "Especially if Mrs. Barrow is on their side."

"When Mrs. Barrow understands a little better what could happen to her in court, she may not want to testify. I know if I were her lawyer I'd tell her to think twice."

"She doesn't embarrass very easily, Mr. Hastings. In plain language, she's a tramp."

"It's a curious thing, though, Mrs. Bull. There's something about a courtroom. The austerity of the furniture. The flag. The judge's robe. The strange language. It produces an atmosphere that's the next thing to a church, and it's intended to. And a woman like this Mrs. Barrow, although she may be shameless in her everyday life, when she gets in court a remarkable change comes over her. They fight like the devil to stay respectable. The insurance companies have very good lawyers. None better. And I seriously doubt they'd want her to testify. In short, Mrs. Bull, her lawyer will advise her to shut up, and the insurance lawyers won't want her. But I have to give you the whole picture, to explain why we're moving so slowly."

"I'm in no hurry," said Kitty.

"That's good, that's fine. I'm sorry you have to come down here so often. I could save you some of these trips. There's probably a notary public in your neighborhood."

"I like coming down here. It's almost that same atmosphere you just described, the courtroom. And it makes me feel useful, as though I were doing it for my children. Although I'm not."

"Yes, you are," said Mr. Hastings.

"Well, maybe I am," she said. "But doing things for them is the same as doing them for myself. It's what I like."

She put on a sweater and went out again and sat on the top of the dune. There were stars but no moon and down the beach at someone's cottage—she was not sure whose—there was a sizable bonfire and moving about it, like comical figures in some pagan rite, were the members of a beach picnic. They were too far away to be recognizable, even to be distinguishable as to sex. It seemed to be a fairly good-sized party and she was glad that the noise they would make was no closer to her house. It was a party of the young, that much she could determine by their frenetic activity. A great deal of running about, chasing, and, as she watched, two of the figures picked up a third figure by the hands and feet and carried it to the ocean and dropped it in. This might go on all night. It was at the McDades', the only cottage in that section that would be having that kind of party for the young.

The young. *She* was young. She had been a young wife, she was a young widow, and people like Doctor Mando continually called her "young woman." She would still be young, really, when those children now asleep in her cottage would be having beach picnics like the McDades'. She was old to them now, as a parent is old to all young children; but to Jerry's father and mother she was so young that they had worried about her ability to cope. She was too young to have been invited to any of the Bannings' noisy parties. She was only four or five years older than some of the members of the McDade picnic. Angus McDade was twenty-six. George Lasswell was twenty-six or seven. Harry Stephenson had been one of Jerry's favorite golfing companions. They would all be at the McDades' picnic.

Something got her to her feet, and she knew what it was. She denied it angrily, then admitted it so that she could dismiss it. It was a word that had first come up in her conversation with Mike, and the word had stayed with her. Aggressor. Well, she was not quite being an aggressor if she was being drawn to that beach bonfire like a moth to a flame. They would be nice to her, they would offer her food and drink, and they would admire her in the ways that she was used to being admired. She would sit with them and drink beer out of a can and smoke a cigarette and in a little while they would start singing and she would sing with them. She would only stay a little while.

She kicked off her slippers. It would make her seem more like one of them if she arrived in her bare feet. She walked down to where the sand was hardest, at the dry edge of the beach that was not being licked by the tide. She turned and headed toward the bonfire, and she was almost very sure of herself, and her step was light. She did not feel that she was leaving footprints on the hard sand.

It was a long way, and she could make out the figures before she could hear them. She was so close to the ocean that its sounds were all she could hear for the first fifty yards, the first seventy-five yards, the first hundred. And then the voices began to penetrate the sounds of the ocean. She walked on and the voices grew more distinct, the voices of young women and young men, a harsh and frightening chorus of people who did not want her. She stopped to listen. Now she could hear baritone derision and alto contempt and soprano coquetry answered by the baritone derision, and though they were ignorant of her existence they were commanding her to stay away.

She turned and for a terrifying second her eyes, so long focused on the bonfire, looked into blackness. She could not move. Then she looked up at the sky until she could see a star, and then there were more stars and to her left were the lights of the cottages on the dunes. She ran all the way home.

THE FLOOD

CONRAD RICHTER

It's gone now, receded and dried up, so that amid all the peace and plenty long since dwelling on its shores, you can hardly find a living trace of it, save in the history books, the war colleges and in the Gettysburg words of Abraham Lincoln. And yet once not so long ago that flood flowed like a tide of blood two thousand miles across the country, dyeing rivers, engulfing farms, climbing mountains and penetrating the quiet valleys between. It even reached its long red arm across the endless plains of Texas, and if you look sharp, you may still see it there as it was then, sweeping from saddle to saddle, and from remote ranch house to ranch house, pulling men from horses and lonely pallets and starting them toward the distant front.

That's what it had done to Coe Elliot. Rigged out in his newly sewn suit of gray, he stood in this Texas town room with the alien young woman at his side, and in front of them the gaunt circuit preacher with a fierce look on his face and the open Book in his veined hands.

The preacher's voice grew sterner, "Coe Ellyit, do you take this lady, Bethiah Todd, as your lawful wife till death do you part?"

Now he was in for it, Coe thought. He would ride a thousand miles to get at those fool Yankees who reckoned they could tell the South what it had to do. He would leave his herd of longhorns scattered over the Nogal plain and his half dugout in the little Mexican settlement on the flat between the river and his spring. But riding the ninety miles in to town yesterday and day before, he had wished he

183

had a woman to leave behind, somebody to think of him when he was away and to come back to when the war was over. And that was a funny thing to wish, for white women were scarce as prairie chicken's teeth out in this new Texas country.

"I do," he said, and anybody, knowing Coe or not, could have told from that hard, tanned face that he would keep his word.

The gaunt Texas preacher turned to the girl. The blight of his eyes was on her. You could see he had nothing for this marriage. He might have Christian pity on her for her plight, but that was as far as his religion bade him go.

"Bethiah Todd, do you take this man, Coe Ellyit, as your lawful husband till death do you part?"

That's the way she had looked, Coe told himself, when they had brought her to town with the oxen and wagon after the Comanches had ambushed her father. They had got him at the river, with a cedar pail in one hand and a tin cup in the other, and they had nigh split his head open with their scalping. He was a plowman from Kentucky, out here for free land. He was big and shut-mouthed and dark, they said, and his daughter was little and slight and white as milk in her red dress against those jetty-black oxen. But now she was shut-mouthed too. Her little wisp of a face was set and her lips tight at what had overtaken her. Her eyes were dead and hopeless.

She had no place to go, Coe Elliot had thought with pity when he saw her, and he had spoken before he had weighed it.

"I can give you a home at the ranch," he had told her. "The Mexican women will look after you till I get back from the wars. And if I don't come back, everything I got is yours as my widow."

Bitterly she had looked at him then, and in bitter silence consented. And that was the way she answered the preacher now. If she gave him ever a plain word, like "yes" or "sir," it was too low for him to hear it. The preacher looked at her, and finally at Coe, who nodded him to go on.

"Then, with the authority invested in me by the Church of Christ," he declared, "and by the Confederated States of America, I declare you man and wife."

It was mighty quiet in that room now. Nobody made a move to kiss the set little face of the bride.

"All I got to say, Miz Ellyit, you got a mighty fine man," the preacher told her. It was plain that was all he intended to say. He turned away as if in disapproval of the whole business.

"Well, I reckon Miz Ellyit and me'll start for the ranch," the groom took hold of things to say. "We got only five hours till sundown, and steers are mighty slow."

The room kind of froze like the first skim of ice on a slough. The preacher turned around with the half-written marriage paper in his hand. "You're going up there today?"

"I ain't got much time," Coe said pleasantly. "I got to get back or they'll have those Yanks licked before I get a chance at 'em."

Nobody said anything for a little. At the end, the preacher spoke for all. "Couldn't you get there quicker and safer with a team and buggy, Coe?"

"I take it Miz Ellyit wants her fixens along," the bridegroom said. "She has too much in that wagon for a buggy to pack. And anything my wife wants, reverend, she can have."

"Certainly, Coe, certainly," the preacher boomed in his great voice, but his eyes looked sad and dull. "May you move in the protecting shadow of the Lord's wing all the way."

Coe stole a quiet look at his wife. She stood there like she was deaf to what was being said, and if she wasn't, she was too slight to do anything about it one way or the other. Her eyes never changed when the women wished her a safe journey. And when he hoisted her up to the wagon seat, she felt small and light in his hand as a cured calfskin. But there was a touch of rawhide in her, too, he reckoned, as he tied his mare, Tally, to the strange tailboard.

Far sooner would he have sold the oxen and put horses to the wagon. But he reckoned it might please her to have some creatures she could call by name around the ranch while he was away. Now those ponderous beasts started, hard of horn and soft of eye and muzzle. Some oxen, their owners claimed, were mighty smart walkers, but to Coe the best were like these, slow as land turtles, moaning a little as they let their shoulders into the pull, moving first one foot, then the other. Up the dusty street they went, the wagon lumbering after, the wheels dragging, the spokes turning slow as clock hands. He could see the town folk in their doors and windows, waiting to see the Kentucky plowman's daughter go by, fresh-orphaned and as fresh-married, setting out in a hard and savage world, sitting alone on her high seat while her cowman groom in his spurred boots walked the ground. But Coe didn't mind. He was in no great hurry to get there, for this was his wedding trip, the only time with his bride he'd get. Soon as he landed her at the ranch, he'd have to light out for Houston. Let folks wonder at him if they would. This was his honeymoon. You did queer things when you took a woman. He just hoped no Confederate soldier would happen along to see him plodding on foot in his short-cut cavalry jacket.

A prettier spot for a bride and groom you hardly could find than what he picked for the night. This was no camp along the trail for late travelers to stop and join them. He had turned the oxen off the wheel tracks. Down in a basin behind a long butte, he halted them. The land spread around like a saucer, soft and green with grass, while all the rolling knolls in the distance were stained with violet mist. Quickly he picketed the mare, unyoked the oxen, hobbled them and turned them loose. In a shake he had a fire of low cedar snapping, and the scent of his bacon and coffee stung the crystal-clear evening air. This was nothing. Men always cooked for their womenfolk out on the range. But she never came down from the wagon seat.

"You want to eat up there?" he asked gravely, and passed up the tin plate and cup.

He turned his back with a plainsman's politeness. The tin cup was half empty when it came down, but the plate had hardly been touched.

"You ought to had eat something," he told her sternly, like a husband should, but she only sat her wagon seat, staring out over the wild land. He stood there, stiff and clumsy, holding the cup in one hand and plate in the other.

"If you don't want to eat, couldn't you drink the rest of the coffee?"

Her lips moved no more than when the K-town preacher had put the solemn question. But she turned her head. And that was all he got from her—a turn of that slight head for "no," and a nod of that white face for "yes."

"Anything special I can get for you?" he persisted.

A slow turn of the head.

"You feeling all right?"

Not a move from her, neither yes nor no, just a long look at that wide horizon.

"You like this country out here?" he asked hopefully.

She turned on him such a suddenly bitter and terrible face that he felt all his hopes go out of him.

"Well, you better take a little walk before it gets too dark on you," he said kindly. "I'll fix up your bed this end of the wagon. You don't need to be scared of me. I'll have my bed on the ground."

But when he looked again, all the bright mist had gone from the distant hills, and a grayness from a low bank of clouds was creeping over the broad land.

Before closing his eyes, he could smell the rain coming. More rain. It had been raining most of the week. All night he heard the heavy drops pelting wagon top and sideboards. When he looked out along the tongue, he could see heavy lightning playing far ahead. It seemed to hang in that one spot all night. It was too far away to hear the thunder. Just before daylight, he crawled out and rolled up his bed. He didn't want any stray rider to come along and carry the news back to town that the groom had slept under the wagon.

That was a mighty strange day for a bridegroom, he told himself, driving a span of oxen through the rain, walking beside them through mud and puddles, with your bride sitting on the seat above you and never a spoken word between. Sometimes he fell a little behind, so his eyes could study her. What kind of a "creetur" had he married, sitting there with a face white as gyp rock, in a bright red dress above those jetty-black oxen? What was the name of the place she hailed from, he wondered, and had she brother or sister back there? Why, he didn't even know how old his bride was. Neither would she eat and neither talk. He had heard that women were mighty hard to brand. Now he knew that you might brand them, but they were a long sight harder to break or gentle.

Halfway to noon he remembered the ox hobbles left behind, and he rode back on his mare to find them. The hobbles were gone, but he found where fresh hoofs of two unshod ponies had cut this way and that across the wet camping ground. More than once he took to the mare that day, to sit gravely in the saddle and scan the four horizons. Behind them, K-town had already vanished behind the mesa. Ahead, the nester settlement along the river was still too far away to see. And if any red Comanche pair still followed the wagon, they kept themselves in some arroyo hidden in that blue expanse of sun and rain-streaked plain.

The river had looked much higher when they had come back to it that morning. Last night's rain in the upland country was starting to come down, bringing the Texas earth with it. And it was still raining. All the time they stopped at noon, while the mare cropped and the oxen grazed greedily side by side, as if still in the yoke, looping up the tufts of buffalo grass with their long tongues, the river kept steadily rising. It rained again that night, and next morning, when they started out, the river ran bankfull beside them.

They entered the long *cañada* about noon. For an hour or two they crawled along with the higher mesa land on either side and the river winding like a dark snake between. The sun was halfway down the western sky when something made Coe look around. Back where they had passed on dry land only a few minutes before, a thin, dirty stream was spilling over the bank, lapping a little farther as he watched, trickling into the wheel tracks and running down the trail.

"Come on! Buck and Berry! Step up!" he called, swinging his dead father-in-law's whip.

They had only a mile or two to go until the steep escarpment softened and a draw led up to the mesa. But the great plodding beasts never hurried. You could add ton after ton to their load, and they would pull it as long as the wagon would hold it. They would moan softly and lean their stout shoulders into the bows, their tails would twitch and the wheels would be dragged through hell and damnation. But they wouldn't move any faster. Not for flies or whiplash.

The river was still rising. From every up-country arroyo, wash and fork came the dark tide that could get through the wide *cañada* intake above faster than it could get out of the narrows below. Each time Coe looked around, he could see behind them a chocolate lake spreading, backing up, pushing ever closer to their heels. In the end, the water spread out on the trail ahead, widening and deepening until the team was in it, moving in one continual splash.

Up to now, those stolid, heavy-footed beasts had made little of the water, save to look down at it with their soft, wondering eyes. But once surrounded by it, a change came over them. They had waded many a ford. But they could always see the trail rising up the bank on the other side. Now they moved through an endless lake, and there was no trail to see either here or ahead. Their pace slowed, their great horned heads swung cautiously from side to side, and when the water at last touched their bellies, they stopped dead. No shouting or beating could stir them. There they stood, immovable except for their swaying horns, while the flood slowly rose to engulf them, first their dewlaps, then their gaunt black thighs, and finally the bows of the yoke itself. The water began pouring through the cracks of the wagon. Coe climbed in and piled his wife's goods to the rear, the most valuable on top out of reach of the wetness.

All the while his mare at the tailboard stood covered to her breast. Her eyes were rolling, and now and then she threshed about, backing as far as she could with her neck outstretched, trying to slip her halter. He would have to watch her or she might hang or drown herself.

He looked around for his wife. In all this waste of muddy water, she was drawn up tight as a jackknife. She had clutched her red skirts from below, so they wouldn't be fouled by the water, and now she sat there, small and rigid, her petticoats held between her knees. Her cheeks were like tallow and her small neck mighty hollow and thin. She was sure showing the long strain. With the little she ate and all she went through, it didn't seem like she could go it much longer.

"It ain't safe for you on shore alone, Bethiah," he told her. "But if you get on the mare behind me, I'll ride you up to the Sugareet till I get your wagon there."

She was staring at the oxen. She shook her head. She wouldn't leave her dead pap's jetty-black span, you could tell that. It showed how much he knew about women. A girl could be little and slight as if the wind would blow her away. She could be worn thin to a frazzle, and just when you figured she would go to pieces, she stiffened up and you couldn't break her.

Well, his wife couldn't sit there on the seat all night, he told himself. When he saw a board or plank coming down on this side, he waded the mare out, caught it with his hands or rope and laid it across the front end of the wagon box. By early dusk he had enough, and on this ill-assorted frame he threw down her bed and unrolled it.

"You better get some rest while you can," he told her.

That was a night he wouldn't forget easy, black as pitch, with the rain coming down and the unseen flood all around them. He tried his bed on the narrow seat, but it wouldn't lay right, and he sat there most of the time, listening to the water lapping at the wagon box, feeling with his hand to see how high it had risen. Now and then, some floating object struck the wagon softly and went on. When it was quiet, he could hear the oxen moving their heads in the bows, this way and that, this way and that, all the night through.

When dawn broke, he looked out on a wide and lonely scene. The *cañada* swam from escarpment to escarpment, while out in the center the current rolled with such power that it lifted in riffles above the rest of the flood. It had risen during the night. His mare's neck was nearly covered. She seemed exhausted and half drowned. Her wild eyes rolled toward either shore, but the oxen stood unchanged. The water flowed over their jetty-black backs. All you could see of them was their rhythmically moving heads sticking out of water, and that's the way they stood the whole day, without grass or grain, refusing to budge, although from time to time the heavy wagon seemed to lift from the ground and float of itself in the tide.

It rained fitfully most of the time, but the water rose little higher. This was the crest, Coe told himself. An endless assortment of flotsam was coming down now—posts, gates, loose clapboards, drowned cattle and sheep, and pole roofs from adobe walls that had become mud and collapsed. A nester's chicken coop went by in the current, and what looked like a buckboard with the top of its seat bobbing out. He stood out on the tongue and roped a cedar tub, which he hauled in to the wagon. It was a very pretty tub, handmade, with alternate red and white cedar staves, but his bride showed it no interest.

At the very top of the flood, a nester's cabin came down. It was made of pine logs that could be cut on the big mesa above Sugareet. He saw it first far up the river. Now it sank, partly covered by water, and now it reared up like it was on springs. He studied hard at it when it came close, but he couldn't make out whose it was, for a cabin sure looked different standing at its homeplace than floating down the river. It went on by, and at the sharp bend swept so wide with the current, it stuck on the shallow wagon side. Coe took his dead pappy-in-law's Kentucky rifle from its buckskin loops on the wagon bows. He'd carry it with him down the river, just in case. He could see back to the wagon all the time.

When his mare waded out, he found it wasn't the whole cabin. It had broken off three or four logs from the ground. The door was still there. The water had swelled the puncheons fast, and that was what had grounded the cabin. He couldn't budge the door, only the little loft shutter. He stood on his saddle and stuck his head in. That was a mighty strange sight in a cabin, to look down from the loft hole into gurgling water, with shelves and stools floating around inside. The flood had eaten out the mud chinking, and the current flowed through the logs like it was cribbing.

A bolster lay across one loft corner, with a pile of clothing beyond, and he reached out a hand to rummage through it. Then he saw all had been laid to keep something from rolling to the loft hole. It was a white baby, a couple of months old.

Must be the Cartwright cabin, he told himself. The babe lay flat on its back, its pinched face toward the roof. Coe studied it a long time before he saw the mite of a mouth twitch.

Now what did he have to come down here for and stick his nose in this cabin, he told himself. He had enough trouble on his hands without a babe. Now he couldn't go off and let it lay! Nor could he ride it on to some woman in Sugareet, for his wife wouldn't go. How he hated to go back and give it to her! She was miffed at him enough, without knowing he had a sick and starved babe to give her, a nameless orphan to tend, one that couldn't lift a finger to wait on itself and would likely die on her hands. Then she'd sull toward him sure. But what could a man do? He could only break it to her easy as he could.

He covered up the bundle so she couldn't see what it was, rode back to shore, up and out to the wagon.

"That was the Cartwright cabin went by, Bethiah," he started in, mighty sober. "Jim's off to the army. His woman must have tried to get out for help and was drowned. I can't see no other way, or she'd have been down the river with a posse after what she left behind."

"Drowned?" his wife whispered, and that was almost the first word she had said to him. Her face was bitter, as if this was just another proof of the horror of this wild Texas land.

190

"I reckon you better ride along behind me now. I got to get this to Sugareet sure," he said gravely.

Her dull eyes rested on the bundle.

"It's her babe," he said.

"Drowned too?" she whispered.

"Mighty near," he agreed.

Her face twisted and grew cruel. "You mean it's still alive?"

"It was a little while ago."

"Coe Elliot!" she cried, sitting up. "Give it here to me!"

He handed over the bundle, staring at her. Now what do you suppose got into her? You never could make out women. About the time you figured you knew how they'd take to something, they'd take it a different way. He watched her lift the cloth off that small face. Those tiny eyes squinted from the daylight, the peaked face screwed up and the pale lick of a mouth started to cry.

"It's suffocated and most starved!" she cried at him. "Coe Elliot, go out and get it some fresh milk!"

Now wasn't that just like a woman, he told himself. Why, a cowman never got a taste of milk, unless he had a family and his wife kept a tame cow in the corral. He rode grimly up to the mesa on this side, where he had seen some Bar Cross T calves with their mammies not far off. He could tackle a cow here and still keep his eye on the wagon. Those cows looked peaceful enough grazing there in a bunch like a V, heads all one way, but he felt glad no cowhand was around to watch him.

Oh, he roped his cow easy, and his mare did what she could to keep the rope tight, but the mare had to dodge when that longhorn made a rush for her. And when the cow wasn't after his mount, she was swinging at him. He couldn't get a drop till he took a couple of dallies around a cedar with his rope and snubbed the cow fast. Then, while it bawled and jerked and kicked, his hands manfully did their bidding. The canteen mouth was mighty small, but he got what precious white wetness he could and hustled back to the wagon with it.

His young wife shook the canteen. "Is that all you got?" she cried.

"Ain't that enough?" he stammered.

It was the look she gave him, he told himself, that sent him across the river—a provoked, exasperated, belittling look for him as a milker. Anything bad that came out of this now was her fault, for he had nothing to say. Already that bunch of cows he had tackled on this side had drifted out of sight of the wagon. But a few grazed on the other side. They looked like grains of sand up on the escarpment. He could keep an eye on the wagon from there. She told him to take a tin cup along. He could milk into it better, she said, and pour from that into the canteen. He took it silently from her hand, but the rifle he left behind. It would be mighty unhandy swimming the deep channel.

Once out in the swift current, his eyes swept the rim of the escarpment ahead. The cap rock above him dipped with arroyos and was tufted with cedars. He had seen no fresh sign on the wagon side of the river, and if that pair of red devils that followed them lay up there with their ponies picketed in some hidden draw, he couldn't help it. He hadn't wanted to come on this side. He had no choice. It might be too far for a good shot from up there to the wagon, but it was mighty close range to where he was putting himself now.

Even then he wouldn't make like he cared when it first happened. All he heard above the snorts and splashes of his swimming mare was a noise like the breaking of a distant corral bar. At the same time, he saw, just a little ahead of him, a gush of water rise from the river. It stood up for a moment, spinning like a top.

He had his cap-and-ball pistol in his belt, twice looped around his neck to keep it from the water, but all he could make out was a puff of black smoke floating away from the rim of the mesa. Then, nearer on the escarpment, another puff came. He could see the smoke before he heard the report. Almost at once, his mare sank and was gone, leaving him struggling in the water.

Well, it had happened like he thought, he told himself, and tried to swim back to the wagon. But the river bore him away. The main current ran as if something had given away in the narrows below, and all the water was going out. He kept his head above with difficulty. He hung to a piece of floating gatepost with one hand and worked for the wagon side of the river with the other all the time, but he was being swept downstream. When he saw it was hopeless, he raised up in the water as far as he could and tried to see Bethiah. He couldn't see her. Last thing he made out before the current swept him around the bend was two red riders swimming their ponies for the wagon. After a little, he heard what he never wanted to hear. The shots rang loudly several times along the bed of the water and echoed from escarpment to escarpment.

Far below and very far spent, he dragged himself out and stood in the shadow of a rock, blowing. All he could hear when he got his breath was the low gurgle of water and a curlew calling dismally as it flew over the flood in the dusk.

Once he thought that he heard a horseman climbing the dim mesa. His pistol lay at the bottom of the river, but he still had his knife. He took the benefit of every shadow and bush as he made his way up the river. He could now see the wagon in the deepening gloom, a lone, desolate dot surrounded by the wide water. Save for the specks of oxen, it hadn't a sign of life about. But when he grew closer, he thought he smelled smoke, and as he came abreast on the shore, there rose a faint, sinister glow of red in the wagon.

Wading out in the darkness, he could tell the river was definitely lower. Now that the worst had happened to him, the flood was going down. The oxen must be still alive, he reckoned, for he could hear the constant creak of yoke and coupling ring. Once he felt sure he saw the moving shadow of someone against the wagon sheet. It looked like a woman.

He splashed loudly, so if Bethiah were there she might be warned of his coming. Instantly, a rifle cracked from the wagon and a bullet sang near him.

"Bethiah!" he called.

"Why didn't you say who it was?" she called back sharply. In a little while he pulled himself up over the front wheel.

That was a picture under the wagon sheet he reckoned he'd never see in this life, Bethiah and the babe big as life and kicking. His wife had set a dutch oven on a plank and had a low fire of wagon wood going in it. She must have opened her trunk, for she had changed her red dress for a blue homespun one. As he climbed in, she knelt there by her pappy's rifle while she boiled coffee and fried bacon. Her bedroll had been spread on the boards. On it a tin cup and plate for him had evidently just been laid. And down there in the water, awatching everything, was the babe. She had bedded it in the cedar tub. And now that tub kept floating around the wagon box, rocking like a cradle in every little wave their movements in the wagon made.

"I might 'a' killed you like I did that red devil," she scolded.

He looked at her. Her slight little face with its black hair parted in the middle and pulled down on both sides didn't look like she could take her part or stand her ground. But he knew better now.

"What happened to the other one?"

"He didn't stay," she said briefly.

Little by little, as he put out the fire, she told how she stood behind her pile of barrels and boxes to fire out of the wagon. She vowed she was going to get that other devil, for he had put an unsightly bullet hole in her trunk, and that meant through some of her best fixin's. She'd have done it, too, for she could reload faster than he could. She had often done it for her pappy. But he turned tail and ran.

Coe sat there mighty quiet while they ate their supper, hardly daring to look at her, lest she see the respect in his eyes. Mostly he watched the babe in the tub swimming around the wagon. He had left a small, lone coal for light. So this was how a man felt when he was married, he told himself, with his wife cooking for him and setting beside him to eat while their young one drooled to itself close by. This was something to carry off in his mind with him to the war, something to come back to afterward. And if she could take care of a ranch like she could a wagon, he'd have something to come back to when it was over. "Water's goin' down fast," he told her when they finished. "That young one's tub'll ground in a minute. If this keeps on, the trail will be free by midnight. Maybe then we can get your oxen agoin'."

The moon was just coming up as she washed the dishes and fed the babe for the night.

"You might as well get some sleep till the water's down," he told her. "I don't expect that long-haired feller to bother you any more tonight."

She didn't say anything right then. But when he went to get his bed, she said he needn't bother. She said it, looking the other way. It was mighty narrow for a bed out there on the wagon seat. He could sleep better here on the platform, if he wanted to. Her bed, she allowed, was wide enough for two.

LIGHTNING NEVER STRIKES TWICE

MARY ROBERTS RINEHART

Camilla Rossiter was in the early forties when the lightning struck her. Later on she was to wonder whether a better simile would not have been going over Niagara Falls in a barrel, but perhaps this was a mistake. One has some volition about a barrel, or at least some time to worry while it drifts along before it drops; and in her case she had had neither. So far as she could tell, everything was as usual, and then—if you like the barrel idea—suddenly she was dropping through space, and no way to stop and get out and go somewhere.

It was the unexpectedness which hurt. It had always seemed such a satisfactory marriage. At dinner parties, when someone would state that there was no such thing nowadays, someone else was sure to say, "Well, look at Camilla and Jay Rossiter." That always ended the discussion, so it could go back to Roosevelt and taxes, as usual.

Camilla herself had always thought she was a happy woman, and that things would go on as they were until the end of time. She was a simple woman, so she took that for granted. Not Jay, of course. She never took Jay for granted. Indeed, she had developed quite a pucker between the eyes from keeping him contented and watching to see if everything was all right. However, all women did that, she thought, and Jay was very much of a man. Everybody said that, too, and Camilla always remembered with a thrill the time the housemaid turned out to be a thief, and, when discovered, locked herself in the attic with the flat silver and Camilla's wristwatch in a suitcase.

Jay was superb then. He got a hatchet from the cellar and

threatened to break down the door if it wasn't unlocked at once, and when the girl came out he held her firmly until the police came. Camilla was filled with admiration for him that day, although she was just a trifle sorry for the girl, who turned out to have a sick mother, and a sweetheart who had planned the job for her. But Jay got her five years, and everybody in the courthouse was very deferential to him. This did not surprise Camilla, naturally. It was simply Jay having things the way he wanted them, as usual, and being looked up to by the community, also as usual.

She had never really got over her surprise that he had married her. He knew so many things, such as the law and how to keep the score at baseball games and what the figures meant on the financial page. She herself always felt small and unintelligent beside him, and she always blushed when they played bridge and she had to count the rule of eleven—Jay insisted on the rule of eleven—when she had to count it on her fingers.

"Any eight-year-old child could do better than that," he would say, coming home in the car.

She took it all meekly, and there were, of course, other times that made up for it. Sometimes when she was dressed for a dinner and went to see Jay give the final touches to his white tie—after throwing two or three on the floor—he would turn around in his shirt sleeves and give her a complacent glance of approval.

"You're looking very pretty, my dear," he would say, if the tie had finally tied properly, "I've got a very pretty wife." And he would look at her not only with approval but with a faint surprise, as though he had just remembered her.

She was still pretty in an anxious sort of way at forty-two, when the lightning struck. She had never cut her hair, because Jay hated short-haired women, and in the evenings she wore a good bit of pale blue, because he liked it. She loathed it herself. It made her feel obliterated, so to speak. But she wore it, although other women were wearing strong colors that year.

"How quaint, Camilla!" they would say, and she would shiver inside.

But she was pretty and appealing, and on the way home, if they had not played cards and Jay reached over and took her hand, she would wonder what other women saw in the men they had selected, and would look like anything but a woman with a married daughter and Jay, Junior, at college.

It had never occurred to her that she was submerged, as J.J.—short for Jay, Junior—put it later. It seemed quite natural to her that Jay's clothes took most of her closet space as well as the closetlike space he called his dressing room, and to order only the food he liked.

"We might have onion soup," she would say to the cook in the morning. "Mr. Rossiter likes it." Or: "Do have the roast very rare. Mr. Rossiter said the last one was overdone." And that night she would dutifully eat her onion soup, although it gave her indigestion, or play with the rare meat which sickened her, and Jay would sit back at the end of the meal and light a cigarette and glance comfortably at her across the candles.

"Very nice dinner, my dear," he would say, his handsome square-jawed face relaxed and contented. Then he would look around the dining room, at its well-polished silver on the sideboard, at the shining old mahogany, at the low flowers on the table—he liked them low, so he could see Camilla when he talked to her—and last of all at Camilla. And she would know what was in his mind—that this fastidious living, these flowers and candles, the neat waitress in her black and white, and perhaps even Camilla herself, were the proof to him that he was a man in a world of men, and successful beyond most of them. When the dinner had been particularly Jay-ish, he would put his arm around her as they went out.

"Pretty good little housekeeper, aren't you?" he would say.

"I aim to please," she would answer demurely, and feel very happy although rather undernourished.

It had never occurred to her that between the hours of nine a.m. and six p.m.—except, of course, on Sunday—she knew nothing about him at all. As to his being Jay-ish, it was Jay, Junior, who had coined it. To J.J. his father was Jay-ish when he came home after a good game of golf, or had won a case, or descended the stairs in his evening clothes, very impeccable, and stood erect in the hall while Gertrude put him into his overcoat and handed him his hat and gloves. Camilla remembered the first time she had heard the word.

"Jay-ish?" she said. "Why, J.J., what on earth do you mean?"

"Complacent," he said, grinning at her. "Good-looking. Prosperous. Smug. Center of the world. That sort of thing."

"That's unkind, J.J. He is a good father to you, and you know it."

"Sure he is," said J.J. "I forgot that. Good-looking, good lawyer, good husband, good father. Mother, doesn't it pall on you?"

"Never," said Camilla firmly. "And if this is what you learn at college——"

There were actually tears in her eyes, and J.J. saw that he was tearing down something she had built up over quite a number of years, and kissed her.

"After all," he said cheerfully, "he's Jay-ish twenty-four hours a day, but you've only got it evenings and Sundays. It's a break for you."

"You talk as though you hadn't any proper feeling for him."

"Good Lord, mother! Of course I have. It's only—well, I'm fond of you in my own way"—he grinned at her—"and I'd like to see you being something more than the accompaniment while he sings."

"That's nonsense," said Camilla firmly. "He knows more than I do. If I defer to that——"

"Oh, hell," said J.J. "You know a lot he never heard of. Let's stop this. Who started it anyhow?"

She put that conversation out of her mind. Life was a fixed and definite thing. When one day she found a few gray hairs in the mass which Jay had refused to let her cut, she accepted them as she accepted the fact that the clothes nowadays went on over the head, so that one dressed and then had to do one's hair, which was always awkward, and sometimes almost impossible when that hair was long. But Jay did not like them. He came in one night when she was brushing her hair under the hard light of her dressing table and stood staring down at them.

"Don't tell me you're getting gray, Camilla."

"We're not children anymore, Jay dear."

He stood behind her for a moment, looking first at her and then at himself in the mirror. His face was rather like the face she had seen when he stood outside Mary's door with the hatchet, or like whoever it was—Camilla was vague on history—who had commanded the waves to stand still, or the tide to come in, or something. Then he bent down and examined his own head, which showed no gray at all.

"We're certainly not old," he said stiffly, and straightened himself, as though—instead of the tide or waves, or whatever it was—it was time itself he was defying. Something about his attitude and his voice roused what little spirit he had left her, and perhaps she was a trifle malicious when she said in her soft voice:

"It's queer that you haven't any. You are eight years older."

"Seven and a half," he said shortly, and turned and went out of the room.

There was a change in him after that. Nothing you could put a finger on. Camilla, having accepted her graying hair, which was rather beautifying than otherwise, forgot all about it. But Jay began to play more golf than usual, and one day he sent home a scale and had it installed in his bathroom. After that she could hear him moving the weights in the mornings after his bath, and one day he ordered no fattening foods at dinner, and she and the cook went almost frantic trying to feed him well without butter or sugar or starch. Camilla almost starved during that period, and quite often the look he cast around the dining room after dinner was more nearly a glare. But he did lose weight, and if Camilla lost it, too, he did not notice.

"Down to a hundred and seventy-five," he said one day. "I'll bet I could wear the clothes I was married in."

Camilla's wedding dress would have hung on her, but she said nothing, and some time later she heard him rummaging about. When he came down, he had on his ancient morning coat—he still had it; he kept all his old clothes—and by letting out all his breath he could button it.

"Perfect fit," he said. "Another couple of months and I'll be back to my weight in college."

He was so boyish about it that she smiled, although another couple of months of the diet and she would have to stand twice to make a shadow. He did look younger, however, although that did not worry her. He was faithful to her. She knew that, although it was a long time since, unless she coughed, he had really known that she was in the next bed.

"It's a dirty game," he would say. "This thing of giving your wife a diamond bracelet out of remorse as a peace offering! Besides——"

"What, Jay?"

"Well, a man's a fool to let himself in for that sort of trouble. I see enough of it in my business."

Not a sign of the lightning then. A clear sky and the sun by day, and the stars by night. Onion soup—not fattening—and rare roast beef and raw wild ducks that turned Camilla's stomach in the shooting season. Jay eating an apple every night before he went to bed and taking a liver pill Wednesdays and Saturdays. New clothes to fit his new figure and still nothing to give to the Thrift Shop. An occasional check to Milla, who was going to have a baby, but a slight sense of grievance at her, as though by so doing she had played him an unfriendly trick. Otherwise no clouds in the sky, save for now and then a weekend out of town on business, and a Monday morning grouch as a result.

If the weekends gradually increased, she did not notice it. When he was about, she catered to him, and when he was away she thought of him. There were one or two mental pictures of him that she particularly cherished. One of them, of course, was the day they were married in her father's garden. They had built an altar there, and, what with the rector in full canonicals and the assistant rector and the women's dresses and the garden flowers, the scene had been most impressive. Only, in the very middle of things, a bee had tried to settle on Jay's handsome nose, and he had had to slap at it. Over and over, it came back, and at the end he looked faintly dazed; as though he had hardly known he was being married at all. And another was the time they were riding together, and his horse had thrown him in the middle of a creek. He had merely sat there, looking surprised, and he had been furious when she laughed. He had never ridden since.

There were one or two others. She did not know why she remembered them, but probably it was because they reduced him to the level of common humanity.

There were other memories, of course; very sacred ones, such as the evening after Milla's wedding, and something he had said then. J.J. had gone back to school, and the house was fairly orderly once more. The caterer's men had taken away the gilt chairs for the reception, the furniture was in place again, and except for the odor of the flowers—which smelled like a funeral—it might have been any evening. She had taken off her blue taffeta dress and put on something loose, and was slipping her feet into low-heeled slippers when Jay came into the room.

"Well, that's over, thank God," he said. "I've been looking at the presents. She got a lot, didn't she?"

"More than she can use."

"Well, after all, why not?" he demanded. "We've given enough. And we count in the community. Why fool ourselves about that? If a man does his best, it's bound to tell in the end."

J.J. would have called that Jay-ish, she thought. Nothing about her. Nothing about Milla and her joyous youth. But she dismissed that as *lèse-majesté*, and he surprised her then by putting an arm around her.

"Just you and me now, my dear," he said. "We'll have to stick pretty close, won't we?"

And she had turned her face up to him as a sunflower—or almost any other flower, or vegetable, too, for that matter—to the sun, and her eyes had filled with tears.

"I've been so frightfully happy with you, Jay," she said huskily. "I was sitting here, thinking about our own wedding. Do you remember? And the bee?"

He looked bewildered.

"What bee?" he said. "What's a bee got to do with it?"

II

It was a year after Milla's marriage that he told her one night that he would like the divorce. Just like that. Just the way he would ask for a clean handkerchief. "D'you mind getting me a handkerchief, Camilla?" It would have been easier, possibly, if he had shouted, as he did when the studs were not in his dress shirt or the car was late. But not at all. He stood very calmly on the rug in front of the library fire, and looked exactly the way he used to look when J.J.'s school report was bad.

"You and I must talk this over, J.J. If you think I'm going to pay good money for your education and then let you go ahead and throw it away——"

It was rather like lightning, and he stood like Jove, or whoever it was, pitching his thunderbolt. For there had been no preliminaries at all. They had been out to dinner and, so far as she could remember, he had eaten a normal meal and afterward had played a normal game of bridge. In the car, coming home, he had been rather quiet; but then, he often was quiet unless he was telling her, without rancor, where she had thrown away a game here or there.

Actually, she had thought he looked more than usually handsome that night; and sitting back in her corner of the car, she had glanced now and then at his fine profile. The only thing unusual she had noticed was that he had said nothing about her dress, which was new and, of course, pale blue.

"What? Another blue dress?" Milla had said when she saw it. "Why in the world don't you let me go with you when you get your clothes? Blue again, for heaven's sake!"

"Your father likes it, Milla."

Milla, however, had gone rather silent after that.

So, leaning back in the car, she thought of Milla.

She had her baby now, a little thing with tremendous lungs, but very sweet for all that. Camilla did not feel like grandmother, but there it was, and Jay had said that they would have to stick pretty close. Well, they were doing it. She felt warm and happy, but she knew better than to put that feeling into words, so she slipped her hand into his and he held it for a moment. Then he let it go, and the next moment he was looking at the back of the chauffeur's head—only a dark silhouette ahead of them—and saying:

"Why on earth don't you tell Smith he needs a haircut?"

There was no way of knowing then that Smith needed a haircut, but that was like Jay. He would see something and take note of it, and then bring it out when nobody expected it. Which was precisely what happened when they reached the house. He turned into the library and stood there while she slipped off her evening coat in the hall, and she was surprised to hear him say, through the open door:

"Do you mind coming in for a few minutes, Camilla?"

"I'd better heat your milk first."

A glass of hot milk at night had been a part of his diet, and he still kept it up. But he did not want it, it appeared.

"Hot milk?" he said, with an edge to his voice. "I tell you I have something important to say, and you babble about hot milk."

From his voice, one would have gathered that Camilla's habit was to babble, but she was accustomed to things of that sort.

"In a second," she said, and stood for just about that instant of time in front of the hall mirror, smoothing her hair. What she saw was really very nice, and certainly slim enough, in all conscience, and she felt pretty and almost young when she turned away and went in. And Jay looked at her with eyes that never saw her at all, and said:

"Camilla, I don't want to hurt you, but I'd better say this and get it over."

"Say what, Jay?"

"I want a divorce."

Just like that. No preamble. No explanation. A clean surgical cut and then it was all over. Or was it? For she was merely looking bewildered.

"Are you joking?" she asked uncertainly.

"Do I look as though I am joking?"

She looked at him then. In the firelight he appeared much as usual—as though what he wanted was not a divorce at all, but his clothes sent to the cleaner's. His voice was odd, however, so she took a long breath and said:

"I see. You want a divorce. But what for? I don't——"

"What does any man want a divorce for?" he said impatiently. Then it dawned on her.

"You're not telling me you want to marry again? At your age! I don't believe it."

"I'm not Methuselah!"

Her chief feeling was one of intense amazement. Perhaps she would suffer later. She supposed women did suffer over things like this. She even supposed that Jay had expected her to faint—which she had never done—or to go into hysteria. All she did, however, was to sit down and try to stop the queer feeling that her brain was whirling inside her skull.

"Then there is another woman?" she managed to say.

"What do you think I'm telling you?"

"And—you're in love with her?"

"Do we need to go into that?"

She did not speak at once. She sat in her chair, looking up at Jay on the hearthrug and trying to see him as the chief figure of some great passion, a man capable of tragedy and pain, ready to cast the world away for love. All she saw, however, was Jay, who wore holes in the heels of his socks and took a liver pill on Wednesdays and Saturdays and liked his breakfast eggs turned.

The first words she said were apparently inconsequential:

"I suppose it's Milla's baby."

"Don't be an idiot. What has Milla's baby to do with it?"

"It made you a grandfather."

"It didn't make me senile. Look here, Camilla; if this is the way you are going to treat a serious thing, a vital thing——"

"Oh, don't orate, Jay," she said wearily. "If you want a divorce, you'll get it. You always get what you want."

He looked as if a pet canary had turned and bitten him.

"I had hoped you'd be reasonable about this thing, Camilla. After all, you're a sensible woman. As to getting what I want, you've always had what you wanted, haven't you?"

She got up. Her long blue dress trailed about her and hid her shaking knees.

"I've always had what you wanted me to have. There's a difference," she said carefully. "I suppose you have it all worked out, so why discuss it? And I suppose we'll do the conventional thing too. You'll sleep in your dressing room tonight, and tomorrow you'll go to the club. I'm rather inexperienced in such matters, but that's usual, isn't it?"

He stared at her. This was not the Camilla he knew at all. She was letting him go lightly, easily, without a struggle. It hurt his pride, and it demanded assuagement.

"It isn't," he said, "as though I really meant anything to you. I haven't meant anything to you for years."

And to her eternal credit, she used what amounted to her last breath to move to the door, and pausing there, to throw a barb instead of a sop.

"I wouldn't say that, Jay," she said gently. "You've supported me."

Then she went out of the room, leaving him staring after her as though he had never seen her before.

He was still astounded when, having put out the lights, he went upstairs that night. He was loaded with words, things he had meant to say to her. Kindly things, of course, such as still being fond of her and intending to see that she was well provided for. Even an explanation or two, such as the immorality of two people living together after they had grown apart, and also just how she had lost him, and so on. He liked things clean-cut and in the open. He had the exact amount of her alimony fixed in his mind as he climbed the staircase.

Unluckily, Camilla had shut her door and locked it, and was inside along with all his pajamas and his dressing gown. He stalked into his dressing room, so-called, and surveyed it with distaste, but at last he went to the mirror and surveyed himself. What he saw was a man going through hell for the sake of his first real love; a tired man, but certainly not Methuselah; a man worn with the struggle of supporting a wife who did not appreciate him and two children who simply used him as a source of signed checks.

Then very carefully he took out his wallet and extracted from it the picture of a youngish woman on a horse. She held what was apparently a cocktail glass in her hand, and there was the tail of a hound in the immediate foreground.

He refused to get out his glasses to see it properly, but he knew it by heart anyhow.

Dear Mae. Darling, gay, high-spirited Mae. All that money, and unspoiled. A child of Nature and the open fields.

As a sudden afterthought, he remembered his riding boots, which he had not used for years, and looked about for them. But they, too, like his pajamas, were in Camilla's room, and Camilla had locked her door and gone into the silence. Reluctantly he put away the picture, and crawling into the bed, which was too short for him, prepared to sleep in his skin; an outraged figure which grew cold toward morning and practically forgot the great passion in a severe attack of goose-flesh. He had no idea where the blankets were kept, but at daylight he wandered stealthily along the hall, searching for the closet, and it was Gertrude who, coming down early with a toothache, caught a glimpse of him there and fled with a squeal.

That settled it; and when, having ascertained that the hall was clear again, he crept back to his dressing room, he merely took a hot bath to warm himself, and, having dressed and shaved, proceeded to pack what he could find. True, most of the things he wanted were in Camilla's room, but she had apparently had a warm and comfortable night and was still sleeping.

Before going, however, he left a note for her. It began without preamble:

I am going to the country for a couple of weeks and shall need the usual things. Please send suitcase to club.

J.R.

P.S.: Also my riding boots.

Camilla was apparently still sleeping when he left, and Gertrude failed to appear. The cook served his breakfast and had forgotten to turn his eggs, and he left his home for the last time like almost anything but a great lover. Nor were things better at the club. His room looked exactly like all the other rooms, and when he had time—it was still early—to realize that he had taken his first step toward his life's real happiness, he found it extremely hard to think about it at all. The situation was not improved by the discovery that he wore one black and one blue sock and had no others with him, and, all in all, the only passion observable in the Jay Rossiter who stalked into his law office at 8:30 that morning and found his secretary sitting on his desk chewing gum was one of pure fury.

He sent out for a pair of socks and looked over his mail. Then he got a long-distance number in the hunting country in Virginia, feeling quite sure that the operator at his switchboard was listening in, and held a brief conversation with a lady obviously just roused from sleep.

"Is that you, Mae?" he said with dignity.

"Darling! But what an hour! I've just gone to bed."

"Sorry," he said stiffly. "I just called to say that it's all right. I'll take the night train."

"Darling! I can't believe it. Was it terrible?"

"Not at all," he said. "Some details still to be arranged, but that's all."

The telephone operator took off her earphones and looked at the office boy.

"I win," she said briefly. "She's got him."

"Holy mackerel!" said the office boy, and reluctantly produced a quarter from his pocket.

III

Back at the house, Camilla lay, still stunned, in her bed. She had a feeling that her world had suddenly shot her off into space and that she was whirling there alone. She had not slept all night, and when she heard Jay slam out of the house, she got up and looked at herself in the mirror, as though she had to reorient herself among the world of the living. What she saw was not comforting—a woman who had lost her girlishness overnight, and whose swollen eyes looked out from a blotched and certainly fortyish face.

She crawled back into her bed. On the next one lay Jay's pajamas, and she wondered briefly how he had slept without them. On a chair was his silk dressing gown, and beneath it his slippers. It seemed incredible that he was not inside them, shouting to know what had happened to the hot water, or why the devil the laundress couldn't learn to do his shirts. And she wished now that she knew something about the other woman, so that she could have something to hate.

That was the most cruel thing of all. She had nobody to hate. She could form no mental picture at all. She could not see Jay with his arms around anything but empty space.

She ran over all the women she knew. Jay had shown no interest in any of them, so far as she knew. Most of them bored him almost to violence.

"Lot of empty-headed fools," he would say. "All they want is a man to support them, clothes and dancing and nightclubs. Exhibitionists, too, showing as much of their bodies as they dare. Indecent exposure, that's what it is."

No, it would be none of them. It would be some brilliant woman, a woman with brains who would further his ambitions. She herself had not been clever. All she had done was to try to make him comfortable. It was, however, very difficult to visualize a woman's brains. She remembered a picture in her schoolbooks long ago, showing a head with queer convolutions inside it, but, outside of that, all she could remember was the calves' brains at the butcher's shop, and Jay had never allowed them in the house.

She cried now and then, but she was too stunned for many tears. She felt weak, as though she had had a long illness, and when Milla called up the next morning to report on the baby, she could hardly lift the telephone. The baby, it appeared, was fine and had gained six ounces. For just a moment she hated the baby, because of what it had done to her.

"That's fine. Your father's gone away, Milla."

"On a trip? Well, take a good rest, darling," said Milla, and hung up.

She lay back resenting that. Why did both J.J. and Milla think that life had been difficult with their father? As though she needed a rest. As though he was not the very pattern of her life. She could have lost a leg, she thought grimly, and missed it less.

The house was very still, as though there had been a death in it. Did the servants suspect, she wondered? Were they shut in the pantry now, whispering together? She lay back, her long hair loose on the pillow, and wondered how she was to get Jay out of the house. All those clothes of his, she thought wearily. His desk and the papers in it. His golf clubs and his pipes and the humidor for his cigars. Even his bed. His bed would have to go.

It seemed terrible, now that she had lain in her own for twenty years and tried to shut out the sound of his eating his nightly apple. Even with a hand over an ear and the other ear buried, she could hear it crunching. It seemed silly, too, for her to have resented his refusal to let her read in bed. What did that matter? What did anything matter but that he was gone?

It was only later, when the full significance of his note dawned on her, that she began rebuilding the woman in the case from this new angle. Boots. She rode. She was a big angular woman who rode horses and played good golf. Jay would ride, and that would keep his stomach down. But Jay hated horses. What strange things love did to a man! And with the thought of Jay being in love with another woman the tears came, and she began to cry again.

Afterward she thought she had wept for weeks. Milla came and sat in the dark room, going now and then for a fresh handkerchief for her and telling her not to be so silly.

"After all, mother," she said, "it isn't as though you were old, you know. Why don't you get yourself a boyfriend and step out a little?"

"How can you talk like that, Milla?"

Milla moved impatiently.

"You make me sick, both of you," she said in her brisk young voice. "You're incurable sentimentalists, both you and father. Father gallivanting around with a love affair at his age, and you mourning like a sick dove! If you could see yourselves! You're like a picture of the Nineties."

Camilla passed that over for what was the real question in her mind. So real that she sometimes felt that it was burning a hole there.

"But who is it, Milla? Who is it?"

Milla, however, was as much in the dark as she was. "He's been mighty secretive about it, whoever she is," she said. "Of course, he always was secretive."

"Not with me."

Milla laughed.

"Most of all with you, darling."

It wasn't that Milla was not sorry for her, she knew, but, like all her generation, Milla was a realist. You made your life with a man or you didn't. In case you didn't, you merely began all over again; with another man, if possible. It didn't bother you to see his shaving brush—which Jay had forgotten—or the chair he always sat in or his empty bed. You simply got rid of them and went out and got a new permanent or a new hat or a new husband, and started again.

J.J., however, was different. He came home, when Milla sent for him, in a white heat of anger, and confronted his mother, pale with indignation.

"The old fool!" he said. "The old fool! After the way you've submerged yourself all your life for him!" He was proud of that word, for all his fury. "Who is this woman, anyhow?"

"I don't know."

"Well, I'll know, and darned quick. Mind you, I don't want him back. He can go, and be damned to him. But he's got to look after you. I'll make him pay through the nose, if it's the last thing I do on earth."

"I don't want his money, J.J."

"Well, you're going to get it anyhow."

She felt less lost with J.J. around the house, slamming doors and sitting across the table from her at meals. She fed him roast beef medium and no onion soup whatever, and when she mended his socks, it was comforting to find that he wore them out at the toes instead of the heels. She wondered dully sometimes whether, after all, it was really Jay she missed, or merely a man about the house.

He was out a good bit, however, and one day he disappeared and was gone for twenty-four hours. Then one evening he came home and, standing tall and indignant in front of her, told her that he had got what he called the dope.

"She's a widow," he said. "He's been settling her estate for her, and there's a lot of it to settle. I gather she fell hard for him the minute she saw him, and she's done most of the courting. Her name's Barker, if that interests you, and her first name is Mae. Get that, mother, M-a-e."

She sat very still, trying to see Jay calling another woman "Mae." Dearest Mae. Mae darling. My own Mae. It was too bad that she knew the very words he would use. They were all in his old letters to her upstairs. It was too bad that she should know exactly how he would put a strong well-cared-for finger under this Mae's chin and tilt her face for a kiss. It was too bad that he still had no secrets whatever from her. But J.J. was still talking. The Barker woman had a house in Newport and a place in Virginia where she hunted. She was there now, having a house party.

"You know, mother. Ride all day and drink all night. And in the morning they ring a bell and everybody goes back to the room where he belongs."

"Please, J.J."

Anyhow, it appeared that his father was there now and—still according to J.J.—it would do no harm if he fell off a horse at a fence and broke his neck. She looked up incredulously.

"He is hunting? Are you sure?"

"Saw him myself," he said, grinning. "Hid in the corner of a field, trying to look like a rabbit, and he darned near went over me. If ever I saw a man scared when he took that jump——"

"But he did take it," she said, not without pride.

"Sure he took it. He had to. The horse did, and he had to go along."

That indeed was J.J.'s idea of the whole situation. Mae apparently was taking the fences and Jay was going along. It did not sound like him, but then men do queer things when they set out to prove to themselves that they are as young as ever they were. J.J., however, held out no hope. Mae had money and, in his vernacular, was pretty glamorous into the bargain. She had Jay in a bag, and the thing to do was to forget the whole mess and begin again.

She thought that over later on. Begin again! How did one begin again? She tried to see a strange man in the house, a sort of hypothetical husband, but she shivered at the thought. It had taken her twenty-odd years to know Jay, and then it turned out that she had never known him at all. Twenty-odd years of onion soup and rare beef and watching Jay at bridge when she played a hand. He had a way of leaning back and glancing around the room when she made a misplay, as though his very eyes could not endure the torture to which she was subjecting him. As to a strange man eating an apple in the other bed, or later on snoring loudly——

She felt a fresh pang of homesickness at that. So many nights she had known that he was there, safely beside her, because only a completely deaf woman could have doubted it for a second.

One thing she could do, and, after that talk with J.J., she did it at once. She got Jay out of the house. She packed innumerable trunks and suitcases with those old garments of his and sent them to his club. Then, with the first real closet room she had had since her marriage, she sat down and simply waited for the next step.

She had, however, a faintly malicious feeling when she learned that Milla was going to have another baby. Let Jay ride all he wanted and jump fences if he could. He was more and more a grandfather. . . .

Jay was indeed jumping fences at that time. Mae had no use for men who didn't hunt, so, every day when he turned in his horse, he prayed that it would die in the night.

It never did, however, so he would follow the field, letting the brute go where it wanted; and on coming in, he would put his stiff bones in a long hot bath and take ten grains of aspirin, and dress the part of the great lover for the evening, with arms and legs so stiff that he could hardly get into his trousers.

Not that great lovers were in any real demand in Mae's establishment, he discovered. There was no time. Either one was risking sudden death outside or one was drinking in a crowd, or eating the same way, or playing bridge for high stakes until God knows when. But Mae was a great girl. She was a wonder, and after marriage she would settle down. She was easy to get along with too. She did not seem to mind if, in the middle of telling her what a great girl she was, he suddenly yawned.

"Poor old darling!" she would say. "Go on up and take a nap."

"Nonsense! I don't want a nap."

Now and then they went into the ballroom and danced. Jay had been a good dancer, but now his knees were always stiff and—while he preferred standing up to sitting down—he sat out quite a few dances. Mae would drag him out, however, and for a few minutes, as he held her, he would see himself as young and gay and deeply in love. It never occurred to him that in some ways Mae was merely a younger edition of Camilla, plus a faint odor of the stables and an ability to stay up all night and be fresh as paint the next morning; and that what he was actually doing was setting the clock back ten years. Or the calendar, or what have you.

Mae was loving enough, of course, when she had to be, but there were always people around, or servants. One fell over servants in every corner, and, like the house party, they seemed never to go to bed. And she was proud of him. She never got over being proud of him.

"Let me look at you, darling. You're so wonderful to look at. I wish these people would go, and leave us alone."

They would go, of course, but it always turned out that there were others coming. The beds never really got a chance to cool off. It was hardly decent, he sometimes thought. And after the first week, he actually got to dreading her knock on his door in the early morning, when he had just settled down and his bed had stopped taking fences.

"Get up, darling. It's a perfect morning for a ride."

He would get up, hurrying as fast as his stiffened muscles would let him, and after a while it would be fine to be riding beside Mae on some country trail, knowing how much she loved him and how well she understood him. Not that she always did what he wanted. One day he told her he would like to see her in a pale blue evening dress, and she said that was the only time he had shown his age.

It was about that time that he began to feel slightly bilious, and to take bicarbonate of soda at odd moments. But he stayed—stayed until, his law partner having made the arrangements, Camilla had started for Reno. Then he went back to town, to his dreary room at the club and a Turkish bath or two to get the alcohol out of his system.

Camilla was still on the train while he lay in the hot room—a Camilla cheered on by J.J. and Milla, but a Camilla who felt as though life had ended at forty-two and had a faint hope that the train would fall off a trestle.

"Good-bye, mother. And don't be silly."

"Good-bye, darlings. I'm all right. I'm perfectly all right."

Nothing happened to the train, however; and after she grew accustomed to it, Reno was not so bad. Was quite gay, indeed. Most of the people she met were excited and pleased about being free again and starting life all over. Of course, they had not been married to Jay, but still, there it was. They seemed to have no idea of everything being over. Quite a lot of them intended to remarry at once, which made her shiver. But quite a lot of them liked her, and even admired her looks and her clothes.

She was surprised, too, to find that they thought her bridge was very good; and she learned to knit. She would sit in the lobby of the hotel in the evenings, knitting an afghan for the new baby, and watch the gaiety going on around her. But she did not join in it. She still felt too much like an extracted tooth, and there were nights in her room upstairs when the very silence wakened her out of a sound sleep, as though Jay had stopped snoring and might be dead. She would find herself sitting up and listening, with her heart pounding.

Otherwise she supposed everything was as well as might be. She had some money of her own, and Jay was ready to pay substantial alimony. But she had nothing to think of and very little to hope for. One day, on impulse, she walked into a beauty shop and had her hair cut off and a permanent wave put in. Then she went utterly berserk and had a facial and bought some rouge and a lipstick. She had never used rouge before, and the very pallid lipstick of the Jay days had always been hidden among her handkerchiefs.

That night she made up her face—very delicately, of course—and hardly knew herself in her mirror. Her eyes, however, were still rather like those of a dead fish, and when she looked at her hands, the left one looked almost naked without her wedding ring. The finger had shrunk under it, as happens in such cases, and she herself felt shrunken.

One day a very nice man named Browning asked her if she would take a drive and have dinner somewhere. She went, but she felt, somehow, that it was highly improper. He was very quiet, however, and she ended by enjoying it. She slept that night, too, what with the fresh air and having eaten more because there was someone across the table. She had always hated eating alone.

After that they often drove, and one day he asked her if she thought that two halves could ever make a whole again. It was some time before she understood what he meant. Then she colored and said "No," very firmly.

He eyed her.

"It's as bad as that, is it?" he said. "What a rotten married life you must have had!"

"Not at all. I was perfectly happy until——"

She cried then, and he drew her head down on his shoulder and patted her. That, however, reminded her of Jay when they were first married, and did not help a great deal; and Mr. Browning, whose first name was Ted, had a queer look in his ugly, kind face when he let her go.

"The human heart is a damned nuisance, isn't it?" he said, and hummed softly to himself on the way back.

She went home soon after that. The proceedings had taken only a few minutes, and on the way back in the train she tried to realize that she was free again. She did not feel any more free, however, than an amputated leg, and when Milla met her at the station and admired her hair and her clothes and made a quite unusual fuss over her, she felt a little sick at her stomach. At the house, her room looked empty and bare without Jay's bed, and she found herself staring at the place where it had stood. Like running a tongue into the place where a tooth has just gone, she thought drearily.

"Now, please, mother!" said Milla. "Stop looking like that. Just remember that you're free, white and forty, and better looking than you've ever been."

"Forty-two," said Camilla with her devastating honesty. "All right, darling. I'll try to forget and start again, although just what I am to start——"

"Start living," said Milla. "You never have lived, have you?"

All of which was well enough, save that Jay would not let himself be forgotten just then. The wedding had been announced, and that very day there was a news picture of Mae in an ermine coat entering the Metropolitan, and a piece of an overcoat beside her which presumably was Jay. But Mae still had no reality to Camilla, and as time went on she remained merely a newspaper picture surrounded, according to the press, by orchids, horses, butlers, footmen, limousines and people. Hundreds of people. Thousands of people. After her simple fashion, Camilla sometimes wondered just when Jay was doing his courting. Which was not unlike what Jay himself was thinking at the time.

It was during that interval that Camilla developed a sort of psychosis. This was that people had liked her because of Jay, and that now nobody cared about her. As a result, there was a long blank when she went nowhere and saw nobody, and when she slipped bleakly into the comfortable ways of lonely women. She no longer had to get up for breakfast with Jay, so she had a tray in bed and the morning paper. Jay had always read it at the table before, and, as often as not, had carried it downtown with him also. And she avoided every contact with the past. When Milla's new baby came, she stayed in the hospital until it was over, and then had a nurse telephone Jay. He came up, but she was gone before he arrived, so that was all right.

It was a day or two later that Milla said, quite suddenly:

"Father looks dreadful. He's jaunty. Good Lord, how jaunty! It would make you sick! But he looks dreadful!"

Camilla felt as though a hand had clutched at her heart.

"What do you mean, dreadful? Not sick, Milla?"

"Sick of her. Sick of the whole mess, if you ask me. He's too old," she said, with the brutal callousness of youth. "He gets up early in the morning and rides in the park with her; he works all day at the office; and I'd like to bet he hasn't been in bed at a respectable hour for six months. It's written all over him. He can't sit still. He can hardly sit at all, for that matter. If ever a man hated the thought of a horse, he's it."

"He must like her." She tried to make her voice casual.

But Milla was not even sure of that. She had gathered a surprising amount of information about Mae. How she hated being alone and had a party or went somewhere every night. How she had a book with sketches of her clothes, so she could look at it and decide what to wear. How she had a secretary to seat her dinners, and a sunken bathtub, and even how her bed was on a dais and had peach-colored curtains falling from a gilt crown on the wall.

"I'd love to see him in it," she said vindictively. "What do you bet he wants them baby blue?"

Camilla was scandalized.

"No matter what he has done," she said primly, "he is still your father."

"That's your fault, not mine, mother dear," said Milla wickedly.

The last thing she heard Milla say as she left was that Mae had a mean temper, and, glory, how she would like to see the first real fight. But Camilla went home very anxious. She wanted Jay to be happy. She had never really felt bitter about him; all she had had was a sense of failure, that she had not held him. Now she was anxious. She went into the house, where the front door never slammed now when he came home in a bad humor and where nobody shouted because there was a button off a shirt, and, stopping in front of the hall mirror, inspected herself.

Just so had she stopped that night when he had called her into the library and told her that he wanted a divorce. She had wanted to get his hot milk, but he had not given her a chance. He had not even broken the thing to her gently. She had gone in, in that sickening pale blue dress, and he had dismissed her. Like a servant.

Suddenly she was angry—angry and affronted. She threw up her head, and walking into the library, picked up the first cigarette of her life and deliberately lighted it. It nearly choked her, but it was at last a gesture of defiance for Jay—as definite as though she had put her thumb to her nose at him.

IV

Jay was to be married in a week or two, when one day she met him face to face in a downtown hotel. Ted Browning had come to town and asked her to lunch with him, and—still carrying the flag—she bought herself a new hat and tucked an orchid or two in her furs and went to meet him. She looked very pretty and surprisingly young that day. Not because she was meeting Ted, but because the whole thing really was rather like going over Niagara Falls in a barrel. Nothing could stop it now. And all at once Jay was in front of her, holding out his hand and saying:

"Aren't you going to speak to me, Camilla?"

She was so shaken that she trembled. Part of it was shock, of course, as though the barrel had hit a rock. All the memories that lay between them, for one thing—the big ones and the little ones—the onion soup, and the day Milla was born and he'd wanted a boy, and the fuss when the roof leaked, and the time J.J. was almost drowned and they'd had to roll him over the bottom of a boat. But the rest was sheer surprise, for what she remembered about him—and she remembered plenty—had little to do with this dapper individual who looked all his age, and more, and who was staring down at her as though she was somehow strange to him.

"I'm sorry. I didn't see you."

He had her hand now and was holding on to it. A sort of desperate clutch, she thought, although he was smiling and there was a fresh carnation in his buttonhole.

"You're looking wonderful," he said, eyeing her. "I don't know when I've seen you looking so well."

"Thanks. I'm splendid."

But there was a curious look on his face; and suddenly she realized what it was. He had thought of her all this time as wan and grieving for him, and now, seeing her as she was, he was shocked and astounded. She smiled again, conscious of her new hat, her short hair, her general air of smartness and well-being. Smiled and released her hand.

"I've got to go," she said cheerfully. "I'm lunching with a man, if I can find him."

"A man?" he said sharply. "What man?"

"Good gracious," she thought, "he's being Jay-ish again. I'm glad the children aren't here." She was quite calm on the surface, however, and she looked him straight in the eyes.

"That," she said pleasantly, "I should regard as strictly my own affair."

She had the feeling, as she went on, that he had not moved, but was staring after her as she went briskly along on knees that still were shaking wildly under her.

Ted Browning proposed to her again that day, offering her his simple heart, his sturdy body and his rather considerable worldly goods. But the meeting with Jay had confused her.

"I'll be good to you, my dear. You know that."

"Yes, I know that."

"It's no, anyhow? Is that it?"

"I'm afraid so, Ted. You see, I can't get over feeling married to someone else."

Because that was the final effect of that meeting on her. She still felt married to Jay. She lay in her bed that night with her book and realized that he had brought an upsurge of memories with him. She did not love him anymore, but the chains were still there. And he had not looked happy that day. She was quite confident that he was neglecting his liver, for one thing.

She could not sleep, and after a time she went downstairs to the kitchen and heated herself a glass of milk. The kitchen was brilliantly clean and tidy, and she sat there thoughtfully sipping. After all, why should she worry about him? It was his liver now.

She yawned and went upstairs to her bed.

It was two days later that she returned from a bridge party to find Gertrude all of a twitter in the hall and gesturing wildly toward the library.

"He's in there, ma'am."

"Who's in there?"

"Mr. Rossiter."

She turned to the hall mirror and automatically straightened her hat. Gertrude was watching her, and so she took out her vanity case and powdered her nose also.

"Has he been here long?" she asked.

"About half an hour, ma'am."

Well, let him wait. Let him stew in his own juice, as J.J. would have said. Why should she hurry for him? He had let her wait long enough. All those months—— And what did he want? What could he want of her now? He had killed her. Was it true that men always came back to the scene of a crime?

Nevertheless, she was brightly casual when she opened the door and went in. He had no imagination, she thought, or he would not have been standing, just as he had stood that night long ago, in front of the fireplace. In the dim light it might have been the same scene they were reenacting, only now——

"Well, Jay!" she said. "How nice of you to come."

He did not offer to shake hands. He merely stood there, jauntily dressed and with a flower in his lapel, and seeming to be puzzled.

"I hardly seem to know you, Camilla," he said finally. "You've changed somehow."

"I've cut my hair. Maybe that's it," she offered.

"You're not like yourself."

"No? Well, that may be for the better."

He frowned.

"Look here," he said. "Do you have to be flippant? I came here for a serious talk, and I'm damned if you don't seem to think it's funny."

A serious talk. He had said something like that before. She smiled.

"Funny? Oh, no, Jay. There was never anything funny about you."

And that, she suddenly realized, was the truth for once. There was nothing funny about him. He had no humor. He had never thrown back his head and really laughed in all his life.

"I'm sorry," she said, more soberly. "Do sit down. Would you like a highball?"

"No," he said, with sudden violence. "I don't want a highball. I never want anything to drink again. I never want to see a horse again either. Or people. Or parties. Or nightclubs."

"I thought you looked bilious," she said companionably. "You always show it in the whites of your eyes. Well, maybe when it's all over and you can settle down——"

"I'm telling you it is over."

She was too stunned for speech. She sat there looking up at him, and she saw that he was still the same Jay; only now he wanted pity and comforting instead of onion soup and his eggs turned. But she knew, too, that there was nothing left in her of either pity or comfort.

"You mean that you are not marrying her?" she managed at last.

"That's what I said."

"I'm sorry, Jay."

"There's nothing to be sorry about," he said. "It is a mutual arrangement. She is a very fine woman." [Of course! He would never admit a mistake.] "But she's considerably younger than I am, and she likes gaiety. I'd rather not discuss that part of it."

She felt a cold chill going down her spine, and the backs of her knees felt suddenly hollow.

"Then what did you come to discuss, Jay?"

He looked more like his old self then—a trifle condescending, but reasonable. He had always said he was a reasonable man. He cleared his throat.

"After all, Camilla, we know each other. We like the same things." She lifted her eyebrows at that, but he did not see it. "And I've never forgotten you. I—I've often thought of you. Of course, you've had the children, but still——"

"But still I'm lonely? Is that it? Jay, are you proposing to come back to me?"

"I thought we might at least discuss it," he said stiffly. "After all, you're a sensible woman, and in a sense this is my home. I'm uncomfortable at the club, and the food's bad. Besides, we lived together happily for a good many years. If we can see eye to eye in this—— You were a good wife to me, Camilla. Don't think I don't appreciate it."

To his amazement, she looked horrified. Suddenly she knew what this would mean. Her dearly bought peace, her small comforts, even Ted Browning—whether she married him or not—and against all that, this Jay in front of her, still incredibly Jay-ish, still a good citizen, still handsome, if slightly shopworn, and now offering to take her back after—well, after dropping her over the falls.

She leaned over and took a cigarette.

"And what sort of a husband do you think you have been to me, Jay?" she said quietly.

He did not answer. He was staring at the cigarette in her hand.

"Since when did you take to that?" he demanded.

It was her turn not to reply. She sat back in her chair and looked at him. So this was Jay, back again. And she did not love him. She did not even like him. He was pompous and arrogant and incredibly naive. Suddenly she found herself laughing out of sheer relief.

"Oh, Jay, Jay!" she said. "And to think that I once thought I was in love with you!"

He was staggered. For almost the first time in his life he had nothing to say. She got up and moved over to him.

"Listen," she said. "I don't want to hurt you, but you can't throw me away and keep me too. I thought I missed you, but I don't, Jay. I'm very happy without you. Happier than I ever was with you."

"I don't believe it."

"It's true, believe it or not. You know, Jay, lightning doesn't strike twice in the same place."

He eyed her suspiciously.

"What's that got to do with it?"

"You blasted me once. You'll never do it again."

"What sort of talk is that?" he said furiously. "You don't look blasted. You never looked better in your life." He took a step toward her. "Camilla, are you thinking of marrying another man?"

"Well, yes and no," she said reflectively. "I can marry again if I want to. I may, someday. But that has nothing to do with you, Jay. I just simply don't want you back."

He stood staring at her as though he could not believe his own eyes, and then, to her surprise, there crept in from the hall the delicate and familiar aroma of onion soup. It reached him, she knew, for she saw him lift his head and give a wild and haunted look around the familiar room. Then he turned on his heel and went out.

She was entirely calm and rather interested, and she went to the window to see the last of him. She had expected the front door to slam, but it did not; and what she saw as he left the house was a man, still handsome but past middle age, who moved stiffly, as though his muscles hurt him, and who gave every indication of being a gentleman on his way to a bad club dinner and a dreary club bedroom. Not only for that night but for all the nights to come.

She viewed him with complete detachment, as though the very

closing of the car door had shut away both him and her memories. Then she made a little gesture, as though she was drawing her house comfortably about her. Like a barrel. A soft, well-padded barrel.

Gertrude was waiting in the hall, and she turned and spoke to her.

"What on earth is the cook doing with onion soup?" she asked. "She knows I can't eat it."

"I'm sorry, ma'am. It isn't soup. We were having a bit of liver and onions in the kitchen."

Well, that was life too. The shadow for the substance, or whatever it was. It was enough that Jay had thought it was onion soup and had had to leave it behind, just as she had left a lot of things a long time ago.

She went into the library and picked up the evening paper. The front page said that the marriage was off, and there was quite a lot about it. On another, however, there was a belated picture of Jay taking a fence in Virginia, with a look of agony on his face and every possibility that he would never hit the saddle again.

She looked at it, quite unmoved. It was nothing to her whether he hit the saddle again or not. He was nothing to her. She was sorry, but she could feel nothing about him whatever. She could not even hate him. It seemed rather pathetic, she thought, that he had not left her anything even to hate. He was gone, and he had not left anything.

But he had, at that. There was something on the floor, and she saw that it was the flower from his lapel. She looked at it for some time. Then she got up and carefully dropped it into the ashes of the fireplace.

PARIS IS THE PLACE FOR YOU!

WILLIAM SAROYAN

Dear old Katey kid: Come to Paris as soon as you can. Don't put it off until you are a year older, because Paris may be different in a year, and I don't think you ought to miss the way it is now.

Everything is people in Paris. The people keep saying "Ah" and "Oh la-la" to one another all day and all night. No matter what time you go to bed you will hear somebody in the street saying "Ah" or "Oh la-la" in a loud voice to somebody else. I wish I knew a little more French than I do, so I could begin to guess what this is all about.

I know it's about tomatoes now and then, because I saw a little old lady buying fifty francs' worth of little old tomatoes from a young movie star at a pushcart on a narrow street, and after the little old lady had come out with her "Oh la-la," the movie star put back a bad tomato and put in a slightly better one. The little old lady wagged her head at his audacity in trying to give her a bad tomato, handed over her coin and went down the street, whereupon the movie star said "Ah" and made a famous French face. I call him a movie star because I've seen him in the six or seven French movies I've seen so far. All of the people in the French movies appear to have side jobs selling tomatoes from pushcarts in the streets. The French people want their movie heroes that way. And that's one of the things I want you to come over and enjoy.

The French seem to believe that if there is anybody who isn't handsome enough to be in a movie, then there isn't anybody who *is* handsome. They don't like their movie heroes to be better-looking than the rest of the people.

Everybody in Paris believes he either is in a movie or could be if he wanted to, and everybody acts as if he had just turned down a big part in a movie because it wasn't as much fun as being in the full-time movie he has always been in.

I think this particular movie, which is a very pleasant one, is coming to an end, though, and may be over next year about this time. And who knows what the next movie is going to be like?

You're not a kid anymore, although I've got to call you "Katey kid" because I've always called you that, and my Della has been dead five years, and your Edward has been dead two, and our kids have all grown up.

I don't mind saying I'm sixty-six, although I can't understand how I ever got to be so old all of a sudden. Wasn't it just last year that both of us graduated from Fremont High School in the same class?

I'm not asking you to come over and be my bride, either, in case you're thinking that that's what's in the back of my head. The only thing in the back of my head is that for all of my sixty-six years, Paris has got me thinking I'm sixteen again, and I believe it'll get you to thinking you're sixteen again too.

Now, as you may remember, when I *was* sixteen, I spoke to you about our getting married, and you asked for a little time to think it over. You felt there was plenty of time—and, of course, there was. There were fifty years of time for me, for instance, but now all of that time has been used up, but at least once a year—in October, because that was when I brought up the matter the first time—I've thought it over. *Old Katey kid, what's she up to now, I wonder?*

This time I would rather you didn't ask for time to think it over, because I have this feeling that the movie is going to change, and I don't think you ought to miss this part of it, which seems to be the best part.

It's late September now, and October will soon be here. Bring your money, of course. It would be silly for me to pretend I could afford to pay your way and then pay your expenses after you got here. I live like a king on thirty dollars a week, which is what I get in the mail the first of every month, the retirement pay of an ex-English teacher at Fremont High School, and I just couldn't pay for anything else out of that. But I know you get more than that in the mail the first of every month from Ed's insurance. With that extra money, you could buy some of the things that Paris is famous for—hats, shoes, perfumes. I know you could live like a queen on your money.

I live a little down the hill from a place called Pigalle, in what you might call the slums, only nobody here does that. Everybody believes he is in the same movie that everybody else is in, and everybody believes his own neighborhood is the best in the city.

The name of my street is *Rue de la Victoire*, and I am at No. 127, third floor, front two rooms, no elevator, but you don't need an elevator. The people in the building are all fine people who say "Ah" and "Oh la-la" to one another all the time. I haven't learned any real French yet, but after all, I've been here only six months. I wanted to be sure I wanted to stay before trying to learn the language; but now that I know I want to stay, I'm taking lessons from the old man who lives on the floor just below mine, who used to be a gardener but has been retired for more than twenty years.

He wrote his age on the back of an envelope the other day, and it was eighty-eight. I couldn't believe my eyes, for he doesn't look that old at all, except for his big white mustache. He gets around nicely, too, although he doesn't take the Metro very much because he doesn't like crowds. The Metro is short for *Metropolitain*, the name of the subway.

You can get around very nicely for a very small amount of money and you can get there much swifter than by a taxi, for instance. I take a taxi once in a while, but not too often. Why waste the money? The people of Paris don't like to waste money.

The man's name is Lebeque. The first thing he wanted to teach me was to count, which I am now able to do. And then he taught me the days of the week. I always know what day it is. Today is *samedi*, for instance, Saturday.

The two rooms cost me, furnished, three hundred francs a day, or about sixty cents. Well, they're worth it. They're not exactly enormous rooms, but I have all the room I need and then some. The kitchen is small, but it *is* a kitchen, and I get out some pretty good cooking in there.

Now, the other day, the lady who occupied two other rooms on this floor, also overlooking the street, was taken at her own request to a home because she didn't want to look after herself any more. Since her departure I've visited her rooms and I know you would love them and be perfectly at home in them. The rent, I am sorry to say, is a little higher than mine—three hundred and fifty francs a day, or seventy cents; but the rooms are really worth the difference—better furnished, more suitable for a lady, and just a little more spacious too, with more light, on account of an extra window.

So if you came to Paris and liked the rooms and took them, there you'd be at that end of the third floor, and there I'd be at this end;

and if it was October at the time, we might just take it into our heads to walk to the Opera—not to go inside or anything, I mean to the place where the Opera is—and from there we could walk on to the Louvre, where all the great paintings are, but again we wouldn't need to go in. I think it costs half a dollar, but once you are in there, there is enough to see to keep you there all day. We might go to the Louvre together, starting early one morning and leaving at closing time. We'd take our lunches, of course, as many people do.

But if we didn't go in, we could visit the Tuileries, which is a famous garden, full of chestnut trees, little lakes with kids sailing boats on them, and a lot of statues of various kinds. We could walk around in the garden—it's very big, you understand, and we could sit and talk and notice the statues and watch the kids and the other movie stars or we could just listen to them and try to guess what they're saying.

At the other end of the garden is the famous *Place de la Concorde*, where there is an Egyptian obelisk that is always nice to see from far off or from very near, and then comes the famous *Avenue des Champs-Elysees*, a great place for promenading.

We could have fun, Katey kid; and don't think for a moment I don't know I'm being a little forward about it. But why shouldn't I be? I don't believe you'd rather I weren't, as a matter of fact. You only live once, and there comes a time when it just doesn't do not to be forward, or at any rate a time when it is no longer necessary to be overcautious. That time came for me five years ago when Della died.

I really didn't know what kind of a time I had come to, but little by little I began to find out. I don't blame my kids for being busy with their own lives. When they were little I was pretty busy with mine, I guess, but as long as Della was there with me they visited us regularly. The wives of my three boys were always bringing stuff along, and the husbands of my two girls were always doing that too, and even some of their kids, my grandkids, brought stuff along—a little painting, or something made in shop at school.

For all I know, it may be that way with you too, now that old Ed has been gone for two years, or maybe it's only *beginning* to be that way. Well, take my advice and don't wait until it goes too far. Just remember our talk in October fifty years ago and come to Paris. Just remember I remember you as if you were the pretty girl you were then, which you are.

But why Paris? Why not California, for instance, or Florida? Well, I really don't quite know how to put it, but if you're going to go away, I say go away, go far away and be gone, be truly gone.

I didn't write to anybody for a month, because I didn't want anybody to misunderstand—which is easy for kids to do. But after a month, I decided to write to every one of them—sons, daughters, their wives, their husbands, and their kids. I even wrote to kids I know can't read, and every letter went into its own private envelope, because that would please each of them. And I believed soon the replies would begin to come. Just a letter in the box downstairs with my name on it, instead of only the check every month. Nothing fancy—"Hello, Pop, got your letter: glad to hear all goes well. Good-bye, Dan." Or Dorothy.

I wrote a new letter every day describing life in Paris in a kind of humorous vein, and so by the time I had written to everybody, more than two weeks had gone by, and I believed the replies would begin to appear in the box downstairs.

Every morning I looked into the box. At last one letter came, from my grandkid Helen, who is now eleven, I think. George's second kid. They say she's a little slow, only they put it another way, but I'm not going to put it that way at all. She wrote the letter in print, and it must have taken her a long time. "Dear Grandpa: Thank you for your letter. I love you. I miss you. Come and visit me tomorrow, please. Helen." I never received a letter that made me prouder.

I'm crazy about the people of Paris, of course. They are really a lot of fun—so enthusiastic, so full of noise and life, so outspoken, so charming, really, and every one of them is like a hero in a movie; but at the same time I miss my own people a little. The trouble is, so many of the people I miss—well, they're gone. I even miss some of the people I never cared for, because if they *weren't* gone and if I happened to see them, I would at least remember that we knew one another long ago, even if we didn't care for one another.

Now, with October coming on, I just don't want to be quite so far away from everybody I ever knew, and the one person I want most of all to be not too far away from is you. So come on over, and let's start October together; let's have the whole month together. I know Paris is the place for you, just as it's the place for me, and we'll have nothing but happy times all over the whole great city.

Of course, I'm not going to mail this letter, just as I haven't mailed the other six or seven I've written to you during the past three months, but that's only because the letter's not quite good enough.

But one of these days, I'll write a letter that I know *is* good enough and I *will* mail it; and even if you don't come to Paris, or even if you don't answer it, I'll be glad you received it and read it, because the fact is, Katey kid, I love you, I have always loved you, I will always love you. Your old rejected suitor.   *John Copley*

LOVE IS A PROUD AND GENTLE THING

DOROTHY THOMAS

"No, Rosie," Mrs. Timble said, knitting fast to reach a good stopping place in her ribbing. "I'll go! When I see the mailman stop, and think there may be a letter from Jim in the box, I can't bear for any hand but mine to touch it!"

"All right, Mrs. Timble," Rosie said, and slipped out of her coat and held it for Mrs. Timble to get into. "Better wear Mr. Timble's boots; the path's not broken yet."

She ought to go right on picking over the navy beans, Rosie knew, but it was hard to get busy at anything when someone else went down to the gate to get the mail, to see if there was a letter from Jim. All morning she had worked with her ear tuned to the coming of the mailman's car, but Mrs. Timble had taken up her post by the living-room window, her knitting in her plump hands, waiting, too, and so Rosie had been denied the satisfaction of going out for the mail, even after she had put on her coat.

"Well, Rosie," Mrs. Timble said, when she came puffing in, stamping the snow from Mr. Timble's boots, "I had a feeling I'd hear from my boy today and I did! 'Twas all I could do to keep from opening the letter right out there at the box. Jean and Sonny would have come from school and found me frozen, the letter in my hand, a snowbird on my ear, in this weather, now wouldn't they?" Mrs. Timble could be very gay about a letter from her boy, when she held one in her hand, and was ready to share her gaiety and possibly some crumbs from the letter with Rosie. "Oh," she said now, "I used to think, when he was in school, his letters meant everything, but I didn't know! A letter from camp, that may bring word that he's going to the ends of the earth, means a thousand times as much. Here, Rosie, you want the paper?"

Mrs. Timble settled into the little kitchen rocker, still in Rosie's coat and Mr. Timble's boots, and tore open the letter.

Rosie knew the newspaper was handed her with the thought, *I'm not forgetting your feeling for Jim, that has persisted despite my trying to tell you a hundred times, as subtly and kindly as I could, that Jim will never give you a thought. Be a good girl, Rosie, and look at the paper, and don't let anything you may be feeling show in your pretty gray eyes and dim my joy in my boy's letter.*

Rosie laid the folded paper by the pan of beans on the kitchen table. A postal card fell from it, and Rosie stooped to pick it up.

Mrs. Timble, reading her letter, cried, "Oh, thank heaven!"

"What is it?" Rosie asked, and then bowed her head and looked down at the card in her hands.

Mrs. Timble did not look up. "Just a dear, good letter, Rosie," she said, as she might speak to Sonny, had he overheard her saying, "We'll have ice cream for supper."

"Rosie," she said, when she had finished reading the one-page letter, "do you know, is Mr. Timble out at the barn?"

"Yes, he's in the cow barn," Rosie said.

"Well, I'll just run out while I'm still in my coat—oh, it is your coat, isn't it, Rosie?—and read him Jim's good letter."

Mrs. Timble got up and made a little dancing turnabout before her hand settled on the doorknob. Her mouth was rounded in the happy O she kept for family surprises. "He's fine," she said to Rosie, tossing her first crumb. "Jim's just fine!"

Rosie, through the kitchen window, watched Mrs. Timble go along the packed path toward the barns, saw her take several little hop-skips, all but fall in her husband's big boots, then go on more carefully, taking her little pigeon steps, the letter held high in one hand, the envelope in the other.

Rosie looked down at the card in her hand, and was astonished to find it was addressed to her, and in Jim's handwriting. The card had lain hidden in the folds of the paper, unseen by Mrs. Timble's bright eye. It read: "Dear Rosie: Won't be long now. How about roasting Rufus with plenty of stuffin'? Jim."

He was coming, then. He was coming home, and he must be coming soon, that he would ask that they roast and stuff Rufus, the other turkey gobbler. Rosie had felt sure that nothing less than his being made a sergeant, or the promise of a leave and a trip home could have brought such joy to his mother's face. That was the news that Mrs. Timble had, understandably, of course, to share first with Jim's father—he was coming home! She would run upstairs quickly, before Mrs. Timble came in again, and hide the card away with the five other cards Jim had written her, from school, in the three years she had been the Timbles' hired girl.

She put the card in her apron pocket and said aloud, into the kitchen quiet, "Don't go starting taking anything for granted now. He likes roast turkey, not you!" She remembered how she had walked on air when his first card had come, just before Thanksgiving, the first year he had been away at school. When he came home for the holiday and greeted her with his same kindly "How are you, Rosie?" she had seen how foolish she had been to hope that his remembering to send her a card meant that he liked her better.

Summers, when he came home for the whole vacation time, his mother hovered about in the kitchen a few days, to make sure that Jim had taken no special notice of how much prettier, how much more a lady, with his mother's careful and patient training, Rosie had grown to be, and then had, apparently, felt safe about him and given up her vigil. Jim never teased Rosie as his younger brother, Sonny, or the hired men did; never threw water on her or chased her with grasshoppers. Always his eyes met hers with the same kind and level look; always his voice was just as appreciative when he said, "Thank you, Rosie," when she filled his iced-tea glass at table. Each time he came home she tried hard to fight down the hope that he might now find her greatly changed—with all she had learned about housekeeping, about talking well, behaving well, and about looking lovely—from the awkward child he had gone to fetch from her folks' wretched place up in the hills that summer day when she was seventeen. But each time Jim had seemed to take her very much for granted as the hired girl in his parents' household. Yet she found much to treasure, remembering.

Now Jim was coming home, and Mrs. Timble would come in and tell her he was coming, and she would suggest the sacrifice of Rufus, and the happy work of getting ready for Jim's coming would begin. When would he come? Sunday likely. Day after tomorrow! They would have to fly around. His sister Jean would help, and Sonny too. The beef roast they had planned for Sunday dinner and the plain white cake she had baked would never do now. There must be Rufus with "plenty of stuffin'," and the fine chocolate cake with the frosting Jim liked.

Rosie was putting the beans on to cook when Mrs. Timble came in. "Oh, I'm so happy I'm foolish," Mrs. Timble cried, clapped her hands, then folded them and blew on them to warm them. "I'm like that woman my Aunt Nellie tells about—the one, you know, who got so excited she put the roast in the bassinet and the baby in the oven! That's what happens to me when I hear from my Jim!"

Rosie managed a smile, though the baby in the oven had long lost any horror for her. "What do you want me to do first, Mrs. Timble?" she asked.

Mrs. Timble got out of Rosie's coat and hung it in the little hallway off the kitchen. "I think, Rosie," she said, "I'll change my mind and not have that roast beef for Sunday. I think chicken or turkey would be nicer."

"Rufus," Rosie said confidentially, "with plenty of stuffing." Evidently Mrs. Timble wanted to string out the telling of Jim's coming as long as she could.

"Yes, Rufus," Mrs. Timble said, looking away toward the bare orchard trees and laying her pink fingers against her lips as though to give the secret they held a pat. "I just asked Mr. Timble to catch Rufus for us. Rosie, I've a little surprise for you!"

Why was she wasting so much time, when there was so much to do, Rosie wondered.

"We thought—I thought, rather—that it would be nice to let you go home for over Sunday to see your folks."

Rosie sat down quickly on one of the kitchen chairs and stared up at Mrs. Timble, her gray eyes wide with hurt and bewilderment.

"We don't let you go home often enough," Mrs. Timble said, looking away to the orchard again. "You've not been home since the Sunday after Christmas; you must be homesick."

"I'm never homesick," Rosie said.

Mrs. Timble gave her a quick glance that said plainly, "Now, don't be trying, Rosie; that's not like you."

"All right," Rosie said. "If you don't need me." It could only mean that Mrs. Timble wanted her out of the way while Jim was home.

Mrs. Timble clapped her hands together and said cheerfully, "Now, let's see, Rosie; I've asked Herb to get Rufus and to pick him for us. Is there hot water for scalding? I'll dress the turkey."

"I'll dress it," Rosie said.

"No, Rosie," Mrs. Timble said gently. "I want to dress it with my own hands." Then seeing she might, with that sentimental phrase, have given away the secret, she said quickly, "How would you like to make your chocolate cake, Rosie, before time for Mr. Timble to take you home?"

"When is he planning to take me?" Rosie asked hollowly.

"Oh, whenever you get the cake baked, I guess. I want him to go in time to pick up the children at school. My, Rosie, when I think of Jean being away at college next year, if our world keeps so we can send her, my heart bleeds—yes it does!"

She turned and smiled on Rosie piteously, asking her sympathy for her heart's bleeding a year hence. She could send Rosie away when Jim was coming home on leave, and still look so wistful about Jean's going away to college! It was hard, Rosie found, to remember, in such moments, how reasonably little her happiness meant to Mrs. Timble in comparison to that of her children, and how wonderfully good Mrs. Timble had been to her over the years, teaching her with such kindness and patience, making her almost one of the family, denying her nothing except the right to hope that Jim might sometime fall in love with her.

Alone in the kitchen a moment, Rosie took another quick look at the postal card, and then set about making the chocolate cake.

She had to go home! In the years and months Rosie had found it increasingly harder, with each visit, to go home. It was not that she did not love her folks—she did. It was that their life was no longer hers; that she could in no way, except to share her wages with them, be a part of it. There was always so much she saw to be done in the miserable little house that she hadn't the time or the means to do, so much she would like to do for her brothers and sisters, her weary, overworked mother and even her cranky, grudging father. Theirs simply was not her home anymore. The Timble place was home.

Mr. Timble came in with the wing-drooping turkey, and said to his wife, "Well, Fernie, you say you want me to pick this bird for you, with all you have to do?"

Mrs. Timble gave him a dark, hushing look, reminding him of her warning to keep the news of Jim's coming from Rosie.

He got quite red and stood shuffling his feet on the grain-sack mat at the kitchen door.

"Well, chocolate cake!" he said. "Fernie, why don't you stick around sometime and catch on when Rosie is making a cake, eh?" He took a spoon and helped himself to a taste of the cake dough, winked at Rosie, and then, seeing the sad look in her eyes, sobered and said, "So, you're going home for over Sunday, Rosie?"

How gently he asked. He was like Jim in his kindliness, or rather Jim was like him.

"I expect her folks miss her," Mrs. Timble said. "And why shouldn't they? She's a dear, good girl. . . . Yes, you are, Rosie!"

"Not good enough," Rosie said, under her breath, and went into the pantry, on the pretense of getting another sieve of flour, but actually to get a better hold on her feelings.

When the cake was out of the oven and frosted with the icing Jim liked best, Rosie went up to her room and quickly got into the good blue flannel dress that Mrs. Timble had helped her make before Christmas, and tied a blue-and-rose kerchief about her head. She would dress for Jim's coming, even though she was not to see him, and wear her best. She put clean everyday clothing into a bundle and went downstairs and out to the kitchen, where Mr. Timble was waiting, ready to take her home.

It was plain that conscience and her natural kindliness were at work in Mrs. Timble. Possibly Mr. Timble had said, "I can't see why, Fernie, you're packing Rosie off like this, just when you need her help badly. You know what it would mean to the kid to be here when Jim comes." And Mrs. Timble had said, likely, "You do too know why, Herb Timble. It's because she's like she is about Jim. You know, a boy, coming home from camp like that, is apt to fall in love with whatever pretty girl is handy."

Rosie had happened to overhear such a talk between them before Christmas when there had simply been too much work for her to be spared, and the danger of Jim's finding her in the house when he came home from school for the last time had to be met.

"Well, all set, Rosie?" Mr. Timble asked. "Come on then; that's quite a drive up there. Don't know whether we can get through even." Mrs. Timble gave him another of her telling looks. "Don't you dare bring her back home!" it said. Then, "Rosie, with the turkey and chocolate cake we'll not need that beef roast and that plain cake you made. I had Herbert put them in the car for you to take home to your folks, along with bread and some canned stuff."

In the car Rosie sat very straight, looking at the grayed skyline, the plain cake in a cardboard box on her lap. She had not wanted to take the food, but it was not fair, she reminded herself, to rob her family of the treat of having it. To take it, even with Mr. Timble's having put the basket into the car for her, hurt her pride. She wondered at that pride, that it should have come to be, and wondered why she wasn't too proud, now that she had learned to feel pride, to love Jim, to love him so utterly and lastingly, when his mother made it so plain that, though she was a nice, good girl who had done very well in the years she had been with them, she wasn't half good enough for Jim, and he, himself, in the language of her home, had "never paid her any special mind."

Rosie remembered the night Sonny, to tease her, when he was wiping dishes for her in the kitchen, had started to sing in a mock-sad falsetto, a song that he had learned from the radio, that went:

*"Jim never sends me pretty flowers
Jim never cheers my lonely hours,"*

that ended:

"I'll go on carrying the torch for Jim."

Rosie, though she knew the song was sung to plague her, felt that it was sadly true, and had remembered Jim's first year in school, and how homesick he had been, and the flower and the ginger cookies she had put in the pocket of his shirt when she ironed it, just to say she was thinking of him, and how he had remembered to say, when he came home, "Thank you, Rosie, for the things you put in my laundry. That was mighty nice."

But Mrs. Timble had not liked Sonny's singing the song called Jim. She had come out to the kitchen and had given Sonny a good shake, and said, "I don't like that song! The sentiment is unworthy of real love. It's degrading. Love should be proud!"

Now, driving home and away from Jim's coming, Rosie thought about love and mused, "Maybe it should be, but what if it just isn't?"

"What just isn't, Rosie?" Mr. Timble asked, and Rosie realized that, in the strength of her feeling, she had spoken aloud.

"Love," she said softly. "Maybe it is supposed to be proud, but I think, if it is real, it just has to be however it is, and if it isn't proud it just can't help it."

Strange that she should speak of love like that to Jim's father and not be overcome with confusion. It was riding quietly beside him for so long without talk that made that possible.

"When I was in school," Mr. Timble said, "we had a way of reading a lot of poetry, and I got to liking it. What you just said puts me in mind of some lines I read not so long ago. I'll see if I can remember them."

He raised one of his gloved hands and scratched his head while he tried to remember, and then said slowly:

*"Love is a proud and gentle thing, a better thing to own
Than all the wide impossible stars over the heavens blown.
And the little gifts her hands give are careless given or taken
And though the whole great world break, the heart of her is not shaken."*

"That seems to be all I can recall of it right now."

"It's pretty," Rosie said. "Will you say it again, so I can get it, too, by heart?"

"Sure," Mr. Timble said obligingly; "and maybe the rest will come back to me."

When Rosie had the lines to memory, she said them over and over silently to herself, and found some comfort in them.

"Proud and gentle." That was what love was, all right. Being proud meant so much besides feeling better than someone else, in something one had or was.

"Oh, my darling Nellie Gray, up in heaven there they say——" Mr. Timble was singing to himself as they left the highway and took to the hill road. "My Rosie, I wonder if we can make it!" he said. "You folks up here in the hills don't get out much when there's snow, do you?"

"No, guess we don't," Rosie said. She was coming home, and already, on the hill road, she was one of her folks to Mr. Timble.

"Looks like we're going to make it," he said. "This is the worst of your hills, isn't it?"

They're not my hills, Rosie found herself wanting to protest. *I don't belong here anymore. I'm just going home on a visit*, but she was silent.

When her home came in view and she saw there was only a footpath up to the kitchen door, she said, "Let me out here, Mr. Timble, and I'll run up. The road's not broken, and you'd be sure to get stuck."

When she was out in the snow, he handed her the basket of food, the cake box and her bundle of clothes, and said, "Here, hadn't I better go up with you, Rosie? You can't carry all that stuff, can you?"

"Sure I can, easy," Rosie said, and smiled up at him bravely. She couldn't bear for Mr. Timble, well as he knew how it would be, to come up to the house with her and see the cluttered dooryard, the dirty children, the disorderly kitchen, and hear her mother's complaints.

"Here," Mr. Timble said. "Wait a minute, Rosie." He scratched his head again and added, "I got it—'twas on the edge of my mind all the way up this hill. I've got it, not all of it, but the end:

> *"And the little things that love gives after shall be as they were before,*
> *For life is only a small house—and love is an open door."*

"Thanks," Rosie said. "Thanks for bringing me up, Mr. Timble, and thanks for that."

"Don't mention it," Mr. Timble said, and then, wanting, Rosie was sure, to say something that told her he knew she knew of Jim's coming, and that he was sorry things had to be as they were, "We'll miss you!"

Rosie was only halfway up the slope when three of the children came leaping and yelling, and the basket was snatched from her hands.

"Rosie!" the youngest cried. "Guess what we've got! A little black kid in the tub in the kitchen. A nanny goat had twins and wouldn't claim this one!"

In the low-ceiled, dingy kitchen Rosie's mother said, "Come here to the light, Rosie, and let me look at you. My, you look nice! Where'd you come by that pretty wool dress?"

"Mrs. Timble helped me make it," Rosie said, "before Christmas."

"Well, do tell! I bet you, Rosie, she's got you picked out for that big boy of theirs, that they treat you so good. . . . Hit the nail that time; look at her blush!"

"Yah," her father joined in. "How's that young fellow they've kept agoing to school after he was a man grown? If he's had his eye on you, Rosie, why wasn't he home, workin' and layin' by to marry you? Oh, he went in the Army, didn't he? Well, how's he like it?"

"Jim's fine," Rosie said. "They had a letter from him just today."

"And how about you? Ain't you his girl? Did you get a letter too?"

"I'm not his girl," Rosie said. . . . "Ma, it's warm in here. Can't we have the windows open?"

"Will you hear that?" her father asked. "Can't breathe the air her folks do, she's got so tony! Wants the windows opened in the dead of winter. Next thing it'll be, 'Pa, build a fire in the front room!' And she'll have us all herded in there, wasting wood with two fires in the house, while she mops and sweeps out here in the kitchen!"

"Well, leave her do as she wants," he mother said. "She's the only one among you cares whether I drop in my tracks! If the little girls could grow up and hire out in homes where they'd treat them like those folks treat Rosie, that'd be all I'd ask. . . . Go on, boys, and get in more wood."

When she had cleaned and filled the lamps, Rosie carried one in and set it on the front-room table near the stove, and said to her mother, "Come on now, ma; you come sit down and mend or something. If you'll all stay in there, I'll mop up the kitchen, and then I'll peel potatoes to go with the roast, and we'll have a good supper."

"Those words sound good," her mother said. "Nobody but you ever says the like to me, Rosie! Supper? Why, that's going to be a regular Sunday dinner of a supper! . . . You kids mind Rosie, and stay in here and keep out from under her feet while she mops."

When she had finished mopping the kitchen floor and had got the potatoes on to cook, Rosie looked in on them all in the front room, to say, "Will you all stay out a little longer, folks? I want the kitchen."

"What you going to do?" one of her brothers asked. "Stir up another cake, Rosie?"

There was wondering pride in her in his voice, under his teasing.

"I'm going to wash," Rosie said, "and get back in my good dress."

In the kitchen Rosie took a small tub from its nail on the wall and partly filled it with water from the teakettle and got quickly out of her clothes and washed, with the black kid watching her with his soft dark eyes from over the edge of the tub in the corner.

Working, she had managed to keep from thinking too painfully about the Timbles, about "home" and about Jim. Now she could let her heart ache with wondering how it was with them all.

Mrs. Timble's right, Rosie said to herself. *You got to start from the time you were born, and slant your whole life to it, to be right for somebody like Jim; you can't hope to do it in a little old three years.*

She got back into her blue dress and went in her bare feet across the still steaming kitchen floor, and swung open the creaking door and stood looking up at all the "wide impossible stars." The crisp winter-evening air felt good on her warm cheeks and her throat.

"Impossible" didn't mean really out of question, the way it seemed to say, but just unlikely, in the way her ever having come to live with the Timbles and to know and love Jim was impossible. She thought she had never seen the stars more wonderfully bright. "It ain't ever going to get me anywhere, looks like," she said to the coming night, "unless just to love is to get somewhere. I can't be the only one not getting to see, one more time, one who's going away, to come back we don't know when. I'll do my work down there and I'll wait, and if my loving him is impossible, it is wonderful, too, and good. It's the best thing there is, and it can't hurt Jim, or his folks, or anybody, for me to keep it."

Someone was coming up the path from the road—a neighbor, likely—to see her father. The road up to the house was too deep with snow to be driven on, and he had left the car at the foot of the hill. The man had a longer, quicker stride than any neighbor Rosie remembered. He took no heed of the tracks she had made when she came in the afternoon. Then he raised his arm and waved to her.

"Jim!" she cried, when she was sure it was he. "Jim!"

Forgetful of her bare feet and of everything but the joy of seeing him, Rosie ran down to meet him.

"Jim, what is it? What's happened?" she asked.

"Rosie," Jim said, and took her by the arms and looked down into her face, "you're so little! I thought you were taller!"

"Oh, I am," Rosie said. "I am, Jim. It's that I'm barefoot."

"Well, for gosh sake, you are! Whatever for, Rosie?"

He picked her up then—picked her up in his arms and carried her toward the open kitchen door, where the pale lamplight spread as far as it could across the goat-trampled snow.

"Jim, why did you come?" Rosie asked. "Has something happened down at home?"

"Yes, something happened," Jim said. "I came home and you weren't there, Rosie, and it wasn't home without you."

"Jim, do your folks—does your mother know you came for me? Did you tell her you were coming to bring me home?"

"She knows by now, for I told dad. I went out to the barns with dad, and I told him I'd like to take the car and go get you, and that we'd be back for supper. Can you come now, Rosie? Where are your folks? This is the only time I ever saw this kitchen empty."

"The folks are in the front room. Let me down, Jim."

The little black goat was out of his tub and came skidding across the still-damp floor to put his cold muzzle against Rosie's foot.

Jim set Rosie down in a chair. She reached for her stockings, turning a little from the lamplight and from Jim.

"Don't shut the door, Jim, please," she said.

"All right, Rosie, but won't you be cold?"

"I want the stars," Rosie said, and slid her foot into a shoe. "Your father was going to tell your mother that you were coming for me, Jim?"

"Yes," Jim said. "You know, Rosie, I was kinda wondering, driving up here, if the folks didn't send you home so I'd see, when I came, what it was like without you. Can you come now, Rosie? Can't we go in and tell your folks I'm taking you back with me? Then, if you want to, I can bring you up tomorrow."

"I don't know that I ought to go," Rosie said. "You've come home, and your folks will want—just your folks. I've seen you. You were good to come for me, Jim, and I'd love to go, but——"

"Come. Let's go tell your folks!"

"Well, dinner's ready and in the oven," Rosie said. "They don't need me."

"Then that's where they and I differ!" Jim said.

When they had told Rosie's folks good-bye, they went down the path to the car, their shadows long and together on the snow.

Rosie pressed her mittened hands hard together and looked up at the stars. "Your mother, Jim," she said—"your mother is so good and kind. She's done everything for me. She wants everything right and wonderful for you."

"I'd like everything right and wonderful for myself," Jim said. "It took me a long time to tumble to it, Rosie, but I love you! These last few years you've been just a part of my life that was a mighty good life, a part of my life back home. I've known I loved you, though, loved you like everything, Rosie, since I went back after Christmas, and more all the time since I've been in camp."

Jim had come for her, and now he was telling her that he loved her. She looked up at him, wordless with wonder, with pure happiness. Now he drew her to him and kissed her. No worlds set them apart anymore. Love was something they shared at last, and was a wondrous "proud and gentle thing."

Then Rosie remembered Jim's mother—remembered her sending her away, because only the best in the world was good enough for Jim, and thought how she would be waiting for Jim to come home. Jim would not understand, would not like it at all, if he ever knew that his mother had sent Rosie away when he was coming home, and would never quite forgive her for it if he ever knew. But of course he wouldn't ever know.

"Jim," Rosie said, "I'll go if you'll do something for me."

Jim smiled down on her. It was so strange to see Rosie lifting her gray eyes to his and saying "Do something for me"—Rosie who was always hurrying to do something, just the very best she could, for somebody else.

"What is it, Rosie?"

"If, when we go home, you'll not say anything about this. If we can just go on like we always have, and——"

"You don't love me, Rosie?"

"Oh, Jim, I do!" Rosie said. "But now you've told me, and I'll have it to know and to remember all the time, that you love me, I can go on. You'll write me letters now, and I can wait until you come home. I can go on helping your mother and learning, and——"

Jim kissed her again. "Rosie," he said, "our love isn't something that belongs to, that depends on, other people—on the folks or anybody else. It's ours. I told dad I loved you; I told him I was going to ask you to marry me tomorrow, if you will, Rosie. Dad was pleased. The folks think the world and all of you, Rosie; don't you know that?"

"Oh, Jim," Rosie said, "that's too wonderful to be true. If I were anybody else, any other girl, I could feel like that about love—that it's ours and not your folks'—but, Jim, your mother gave me a place in your home and was so good to me, made my life like new and taught me everything. I owe it to your mother, Jim, not to do something she wouldn't want me to do! Let's be sweethearts, Jim! Maybe in a year, maybe by the time you come home, I'll have learned enough to be ready to be a good wife to you, Jim; to make you proud of me—make your mother proud of me, even."

"Let's go home now, Rosie," Jim said. "We can talk about it as we drive along. I couldn't be prouder of you, Rosie, than I am."

Rosie could not talk, though, as they drove along. There wasn't any way to tell Jim how this would be for his mother. She thought of all that Jim's coming home meant to Mrs. Timble, how she had planned for it, counted on it, and had wanted to have just his family there to greet him—wanted that badly enough to send Rosie away. Would Mrs. Timble know and would it count for anything that, with no proper bringing up, with everything to learn in those three short years, she had had it in her heart, even when Jim was telling her that he loved her, was asking her to marry him, to treasure the trust the boy had in his mother, and keep it whole for her, to remember his folks and care about their feelings and their wishes?

When they got out of the car, Mr. Timble came to meet them. He put his arm about Rosie, kissed her cheek and said, "I'm glad you're home, Rosie." Then, "I told your mother, Jim."

"Oh," Rosie breathed, and was glad of Jim's steadying arm about her.

"She cried a little," Mr. Timble said, "the way women do—the way Fernie does, anyway—at your having gone and grown up, I guess, at your going into the Army and your wanting to marry, and then she said, 'Well, Herb, now that we know, now that we come to think about this, it isn't one woman in a thousand has the chance to raise her son's wife, to have her in her home, helping her, day by day, and to know that she's loving and true, and just as nearly good enough for him as it would be possible for a girl to be. It's not like she was a stranger, a girl that we didn't know. She's Rosie!' Put the car up and come on in the house, kids."

While she waited for Jim at the garage door Rosie looked up at the stars, and when he came to her he said, "What is it, Rosie? Is it the starlight? Is it that we're home? You look so pretty and proud!"

The kitchen door was flung open and the light shone across the snow.

" 'Life is only a small house,' " Rosie whispered, " 'and love is an open door.' "

Mrs. Timble stood in the doorway. "Rosie," she said, "with Jim coming home, and the turkey to baste, and a wedding to get ready for tomorrow, I don't know whether I'm afoot or horseback! . . . Jim, dear, will you and your father go into the living room, where I don't have you to look at and talk to, and then maybe, if you'll help me, Rosie, if you'll help me, daughter, we can get supper on the table!"

WEDDING RING

STEWART TOLAND

It was the peddler man made them know how poor a folk they were. Mostly they just drifted, not wanting more than was their lot. Then the peddler man came walking by and opened up his pack.

White ware he carried. Pots and kettles and tin ovens and fry pans, they stuck out all over his back, shining like purest silver, and singing a little silvery song as he swung the pack onto the puncheon floor. The pack was half the largeness of a feather bed, and it rolled out a world of treasures. Needles, and cologne, and red-top boots, and piece goods—red-flannel, and domestic, and calico—and tucking combs and corset stays, and a wedding ring and shining as bright as life should be.

And there was death. Mourning pins and veiling and shrouding, and coffin nails made in little gold crosses, as though just lying under a row of them could point your way to heaven. There was Bibles and butter molds and seed. There was even more than that. Oh, it was an ache to look at all the pretties spread about, and not to have any for your own. Or for the one you loved.

Everence Lile looked and looked. But it was Miss Beth he watched. He saw the things she touched. Tucking combs and a butter mold—and the wedding ring. She didn't pick them up as if maybe she might be buying; she just felt of them to know what they were like, and that was enough.

She was so small; in all that crowd of folk kneeling round the peddler's pack there wasn't no one as dainty as she. She was like a flower growing there. And her eyes were flowers, too, they were as pale as violets born too late. And she had been born too late. And he had been born too late. For their land and their people was all worked out.

For this place was called the Hungry Hill. And that was what it was. They didn't even wish anymore. They just looked to see what it was other folk had, then went back adrifting, going out to sit in the sun, and remember how things used to be. No one saying nothing, for there wasn't nothing left to barter with, not even words.

Everyone left but Miss Beth and Everence Lile, kneeling there before that golden wedding ring. They were promised. They were to be married come falling weather if his corn patch made enough to bread them through the winter. So being promised, it seemed almost like that ring was made for them. It was their ring, even though they couldn't have it.

"Miss Beth," Everence whispered, "I would buy that for you if I could. You know that, don't you? And the tucking combs too."

She knew. For she had loved him, and he had loved her, ever since they could remember, though they hadn't never told each other so. Hereabouts love wasn't something you talked on. It was something you knew without knowing it at all. So she smiled at him, and that was answer enough.

The peddler man laid the butter mold in her lap. It was a round pound, and carved deep into the bottom was a woman's hands waiting to take this goodness of the world and mold it the way it should go.

"There's a butter buyer coming to the county seat every Saturday. It wouldn't take too many weeks of butter to buy that golden ring."

"We don't have no cow."

"Then catch you one of the wild ones roaming the far hills and plant you a pasture." He laid a bag of seed in her lap. "You feed your cow up and she'll bring you cash money every week. Cream money and butter money, and everything you could ever want for."

"My ma said that once, long ago, she asked pa to try for milk and butter, but pa wouldn't listen." She laid a scattering of seed in Everence's hand. "I haven't right to ask, but if I did ask for pasture and cows and fine fat chickens, and a way to make us a farm place, would you listen?"

He only stared at the seed in his hand. And he didn't answer.

And she said, "I want it should be different for us, Everence. Oh, please, do you think you could make it be?"

240

Different. But this was a land where people did as their fathers did before them. Their fathers planted grain, until Western grain came to market cheaper than their own. They turned to cattle. And by and by Western beef, juicy and good eating, came, meat every Thursday, and there wasn't no room for hill-ranged beef that had climbed into muscles to make its way. They planted grass to fatten them up. And watched it die. Some mortgaged their homes to make pasture, and watched their homes die too. This wasn't grassland. It was hill land and tree land. But all the trees were cut and gone, and the corn patches were about used up, for the land had grown poor, and the people was poor. There was nothing left. Nothing but their home for a hundred years and more. And they loved it. Could anyone understand that? Men loving hungry land? They wouldn't go away, even though every year the game was scarcer and the corn bushels fewer, and they ate a little less than they ever had before. Still, it gave them roof against the night. It was home. And the trees were growing again. In twenty-five years the sawmills could come back. That was what they were waiting for—the trees to grow. When that day came there'd be cash money for everyone. Once more in their lives they could have anything they wanted. And maybe that would be soon enough. But by then all her young life would be gone.

In the Seven Hills of Wisdom a woman's place is keeping her home. It isn't telling a man how to make his way. But she couldn't stop. Not with all those pretties staring at her that she couldn't never have. "It seems like we oughtn't just wait for tomorrow. We ought somehow to help it be a good day. Our folk tried for grass, and failed. But that don't say we couldn't try again, and make crop on it. The seed might be fatter this year, and the sun a warmer goldness."

The peddler man knew about the fathers, and why this hill was so hungry a place. "There's new ways to do. Fertilizers that'll make grass grow even on a tin roof. Now, if you bought yourself some fertilizer——"

Everence Lile flung the seed in his face. "It ain't right," he stormed, "for you to lay all this tempting in our women's way!" And he said what his pa said before him, "These hills wasn't made for grass and milk and butter. They wasn't made for nothing but a home, and for folk to make the most of what little they got, and not try to go against the Hand of God or be above their raising. We been born too late. It's our lot to find our way not easy and you can't change the things that are to be. There ain't no sense a man goin' to debt just to watch a beast grow poor just to lose his land and have no place on this earth to call his own."

He stopped and let the storm within him die, and then he hunted out the only pride they had left. "I got seed that knows this land better than you. I got corn to make my bread, and that's all the prayers says we got coming. Just to give us this day our daily bread."

He turned and went out the door and sat down with the menfolk drifting along in the sun because they and the land was all worked out. Only the bread was left.

Miss Beth tied the sacking fast and laid it and the butter mold down. She curtsied to the peddler man and walked away. But at the door she turned to look once more. The tucking combs were tortoise-shell with like a great brown wave curling over them. And the gold of the wedding band was brighter than any gold had ever been. It was like a promise.

"Where," she asked, "do the rich people live who buy these things? Where, peddler man, do you come from?"

"There's rich folk everywhere, and I've walked all the way from the sea."

"It must be they have better land than we." But when she went out the door, it wasn't the land she looked at. It was the people. The old men who were old, and the young men who were old, and the women who were no more than their men made them be. Beth walked to her cabin and the tin trunk, and got out her marriage quilt. It was new-pieced. And folk did tell as how the dream you dream beneath a new-made quilt always comes to be. She had been saving her dream for her marriage night. But maybe this was more impor-tant—her young man drifting his life away.

So when good dark came, Miss Beth laid down beneath her new-made quilt. She held the candle close, and looked and looked. All the little stitches made in feather darts, all the little stitches marching to her heart. It was made wide enough for two and to last a long life. It was made for her marriage and all the years after. It would grow as old as she grew old, and they would be buried together. She wouldn't be afraid to die with it to warm her grave, for all the living she would ever know would be wrapped up in that quilt. Now she was asking just how it would be.

Miss Beth snuffed the candle and closed her eyes. And slept. She dreamt of the sea where the peddler men got their treasures—of brown tortoise-shell waves beckoning in the sun. She dreamt of a man—it was only the darkness of him she saw, and he came to a golden wedding ring, and he seemed to walk on it like it was a golden road. It lay there like a promise. And the dream said that was what it was. It said it wasn't so about her hill, about their being born too late. For no one ever was. For there was a road to Promise for every man, and for every man somewhere there was a treasure. He only had to search for it and find it. That was what the dream said, as plain as dreams can be. And just then the walking man came to the end of the golden road by the tortoise-shell sea, and he turned and smiled at her. And it was Everence Lile.

It was then she woke. She was frightened, and searching for the morning. It lay between the logs where the chinking had blown out. It lay in her heart, this beginning of a day. And she wondered had she dreamt a dream or had she known it all along—how he had to go away. She cried then.

But when all her tears were gone she went to tell him of the dream. She carried the quilt all down her hill there where the ferns grew tall as fawns, there where the sunshine slept. It never came in the deepest hollows; this was where the noon shadows lived, falling from the clouds. This was where the water dripped, little rills and laughters of it falling down the cliffs. This was where the mosses hung like jewels from every stone, and where a man never walked alone. All his years, and the years before piled high against his door, like leaves falling from the nevermore.

But one of these things that used to be was made of dreams. So she stood in the path and called through the morning mists, "Everence Lile!"

The echoes answered, and the waterfalls. And he came and listened. She didn't tell him of her doubting—that maybe it wasn't a dream at all. The sea was the combs she wanted. The golden road was the ring she wanted. And the man was the man she loved. She knew he wasn't no-count, that wasn't why he drifted along with all the rest. It was only he didn't know what to do. For everything he knew had failed.

She laid the quilt in his arms so he could know the dream was real. "I heard the words as plain as whippoorwills. They said as how no one is ever born too late. That for every man somewhere there is a road to Promise. That on that road for every man there is a treasure. He only has to search for it and find it."

A woman couldn't tell her man when or what to plant or how to make his way, for these were his. His heritage. A man being lord and master. But she could tell him of the dream she found in the dark of the night.

A lovely light came over the hollow; it seemed to touch his face, a sort of glowing, as Everence Lile said the words again, "For every man there is a road to Promise. And on that road, for every man there is a treasure." And he was believing it. Because he wanted to. It was not too strange nor hard a thing to do. When all you've known is something told, it's as easy to believe a dream as that the world is round and old. They both are only something one has been told.

Finally he said, "I think it just might be, and I should like to see if I can find where the Promise waits for me." He smiled on her, so new, so shy a smiling. "I will find my road, and I will turn it around and bring it back to you. Did the dream say that this could be?"

"It didn't say, but every road has many turnings and no road truly ends."

"Except the ones that ride down to the sea."

"I dreamt of the sea. That was where you walked, and when you got there you smiled at me. Maybe that was what the dream was telling me. That you'll find your treasure in the sea."

She only gave him a dream. She didn't know what it was she really gave him. And he didn't know. Not then.

All over the hill, folk stood beside the trail to watch him go. They gave him a poke of journeycake to last a month and a day. They gave him their blessing, and then they let him go into the shadows and the lonely places of their hearts. For they were sure they would never see him again. Not even Miss Beth, who was promised, and had had her promise stole away as she waved good-bye to where he had been.

He saw a snowbird beckoning him on. He saw a gray fox sitting on a rock. He saw where the bobcat slept.

And the first man he came to, he said, "Can you show me the road to Promise?"

And the man said, "Promise? I ain't never heard of the place."

"Maybe it's near the sea."

"Ah, the sea! That's down yonder a thousand miles or more away."

And Everence Lile walked on and out of his Hills. And he met another man, and he said, "Can you show me the road to Promise?"

And the man said, "Promise? I never heard of the place."

"Maybe it's near the sea."

"Ah, the sea. I saw a sea gull once. It had come from a long ways off. It laid down here and died. Nothing lives well away from its home."

Everence Lile walked on. He saw a phoebe beckoning to him. He saw a moccasin sunning on a bank. He saw flatland without one hill. And houses as tall and white as clouds. And people who had whatever they wished. But nowhere was there a place for him.

He hunted and hunted, and he was no different than he ever had been. And he was afraid. Maybe men were like turtles, and wherever they went they took their houses and their hungers, and what a man was, he was, and couldn't never change. And then he was even more afraid, and he tried to run from himself.

When an old man sitting by a crossroads called, "Why are you in such a hurry? This day is as long as any other day!"

Everence Lile stopped. "I'm looking for the treasure there is for every man. For me it's near the sea. Do you know where the sea might be?"

The old man and his one tooth laughed, and he pointed down the path. "That's the marsh road, boy, and no one takes it, for it leads only to the sea. And all the treasure you'll find is sand and shells, and the wrecks of ships and men. That's all the treasure there is in the sea. I know. For when I was young I walked that road and I sailed the Seven Seas."

The Seven Seas. He listened to it, and he listened. And he liked the sound of that. And he said, "I come from the Seven Hills." And it was a magic. The fear died and left his eyes. For where else would the promise be for a boy from the Seven Hills but in the Seven Seas? And he turned and ran down the marsh road, for he had waited so long it was long enough.

He saw a marsh mouse climbing a reed. He saw a bald eagle hunting the curve of a creek. But the sun had set and the sky turned black with silver mists before he came to the loneliness that was the sea. It was a strange smell. And a stranger sound. A hissing and a slithering, like something alive reaching and reaching for what it couldn't never have. And he wondered, *Is the sea like me, reaching for what I won't never have? Is this what the dream was telling about the sea and me?*

He walked over the sand to where the sand was wet, and he watched the waves come and break and crash. They fought each other and themselves, and were no more in the end than they were in the beginning. Clouds ripped and tore at the sky. There was wind up there and rain, and all he could see was the whiteness of the sand and the whiteness of the breaking sea. For hours he walked along the shore, and in all this loneliness beside the water's edge he found less than nothing at all. It was as he said—the roads that ended were the ones that ended in the sea. And here was the sea, and the road was done, and he hadn't found no promise anywhere along it.

Suddenly he was very tired. And he thought of the sea gull and how tired it had been, and it had lain down and died. "NO!" he cried. When a strange thought came to him—how even the roads that came to the sea didn't always end. Because you could ask the sea to open and make a way for you. It had before. It was in the Book.

So he stood where the sea and the sea winds were, and he said, "Sea, is there a way for me?"

It didn't gather up in a mighty wave and roll away. But just then those queer, scuddy little clouds that had been flirting across the sky all night danced round behind the moon and let it shine out bright. And it was a wondrous sight. This was wider than he had known wideness could be. And then he saw the ships out there where there had been blackness before.

One was closer than all the rest. It lay just within a silver path the moon had laid across the sea or the sea had made to hold the moon. It was as plain a road as any road could ever be. He had never seen a ship; he did not know about masts and sails, or waves and worms and rot, and winds loosed upon an ocean. He did not know about the men who sailed the seas. He only knew he had asked the sea for a way, and the way had been shown to him.

Everence Lile stepped into the sea. It was cold. But not so cold as mountain waters even on a summer's day. It tore at him, and then it seemed to help him on his way. He had swam all his life, for the Dark River curled below his hill, and it was swift and cruel and wide. He had never heard of sharks and rays and barracuda, all he'd ever heard about was whales, so he kept his eyes upon the moon road and he was not afraid.

He swam until his breath was a pain inside, and his arms too heavy to lift. He swam until he saw masts like naked trees against a winter's sky. Two were bare, except for swinging ropes, but the third had a sail spreading white as though a giant cabbage moth rested there. The winds made music in the masts. It was such a lovely song they sang. There was no hint of sadness. No warning to tell him to go away, and he never thought of that, for the silver road came just to here, and laid down on that ship.

There was a lantern burning on the ship, and the sides of it were black, with gold letters. *The Lassie* was what they said, but he did not see any of this. Only the figure of a woman rising above him out of the sea. She looked so real. Almost for a moment he thought she was, with her arms outstretched to help him, and give him rest. A tangle of ropes hung down beside her trailing into the sea, and he climbed them and clung there, dripping and shivering and plunging with her and her ship. Because it must be her ship, she was part of it. She was carved of wood; he could see that now—she was made of wood, and white as milk. Her dress swirled as though it blew with the wind. Her hairs was braided round her head. And her eyes—they were Miss Beth's eyes. He looked and looked. They held the same measure of softness and strength. They held the silence and the secrets of the Hills. They were Miss Beth's eyes, as blue as violets born too late. It was very strange.

But his hands were cold and much too numb, and he was so tired.

He crawled up the ropes and over and onto the deck. There was no one there. Only a great wheel creaking in its ropes. Only the lantern burning bright. He walked to the small house near the middle of the ship and opened the door.

Smells tumbled out. Such a many and a mixing he could not sort them out. The smell of oil and onions and tobacco and men. Of wood and salt and sweat and rum and rot. And fever. He climbed down the tiny stairs and into a room like he'd never seen before.

Its walls were curved and its ceiling low, and there were round glass windows here and there, and along the walls hung books and boots and coats and ropes and things of brass. There was a great table covered with maps and a book and a gun. There were more things in this room than in all the houses on his hill. There was a lantern hanging from the ceiling sliding to and fro, and its shadow swung with the swing of the ship, and under the lantern there was a great chair, and in the chair there was a man.

He had black shining boots, and black shining pants, and above that he was red and naked as a newborn mouse, save clear across his chest was painted the picture of a ship—a great ship of four masts and near half a hundred sails. His chin hung down against his chest and almost touched the ship. He had a white scraggly fringe of beard like a fallen halo, and eyes as black and dull as rotting plums.

The lantern swung with the swing of the ship, the wood groaned and creaked, and Everence stood and wondered whether the man was dead.

And the man stared at this boy dripping on his rug, and finally the fevered lips said, "Are you quick or are you dead? Because if you're quick, I'm glad you've come. And if you're dead, you're not too soon."

"Why would I be dead?"

"Because every seaman is allowed this. He is allowed one vision before he dies. It is always so. When he is deserted by all the living, then the dead rise out of the sea to help. Every man who dies alone upon the sea has this one more chance to talk and dream. You are dripping on my rug, so you are risen out of the sea. You are the dead come to help where all help has gone."

"I am living." He held his arm. "Here, pinch me for yourself." The seaman pinched, and pinched hard, and Everence laughed, "I am not made of oak or stone or jewels that you can pinch so hard."

"Jewels!" The man rose out of his chair in his fury. "That is why I sit like this! That is what my crew took—all the China silk and all the ivory and amethyst and jade! Thieves and mutineers and murderers! They went away to make themselves rich, and left me to die alone!"

He sobbed. "I would have stopped them, but I could not reach my gun! I could not walk!"

Everence gentled him into the chair.

"Where is there water and onions? I will make you a poultice."

The black eyes wavered and wandered and were not sure. "Are you really living or are you only my dream?"

"I am living."

"Then where is your ship? We must get to it while there is time."

"Time for what?"

"For living. What kind of a sailor are you that you have not noticed the glass?"

"I am no sailor. I have never before seen a ship or even seen the sea. I swam here. I was so tired I almost wished to die just to give me rest, but there was a sea gull died once far from home, and he would not let me rest. Now I am here where I was meant to be. I know it's so because the sea laid a path just especially for me."

The old man listened to the wind. "Boy, there's a cork ring; take it and swim for shore. It won't matter how tired you are; the ring will carry you. The cold would kill me, but there might be time for you to reach the land before the sea turns upside down."

"Why should the sea turn upside down?"

"Because that's a barometer there, and it tells of a great storm that is nearly here. Because without a crew to sail *The Lassie*, she won't ride it through. She'll be sunk, and everything aboard her."

Everence Lile touched the barometer with its needle and its glass and the winds painted on its face. He looked at the old man so red with fever. Everence found a barrel of water and smelled out the onions. He made an onion poultice, and he made an onion tea.

And the old man said, "Go, boy. You do not know how deep is the sea. Go while there is time. The dead will come and care for me."

Everence picked up the cork ring and went into the night. The wind cried in the masts. All the music was gone. It was crying there now like the world was lost. And the water, from here, was mean and black. Looking at it, he could know how deep was the sea. He could save himself, but what would he save? Someone who'd left a man in mortal trouble. He, who knew how sad and lonely a place was trouble. Besides, it couldn't be. The sea was too large; nothing could turn it upside down. It was the fever made the man talk so of his doom. The fever was the danger, not a storm.

He went back down the stairs and watched the barometer fall. Every now and then he changed the poultice, and the old man woke enough to drink, and then he'd sleep again. He cried in his sleep. He said his name was Captain Noah. He said he would be glad to rest.

Everence listened to the wind, and he listened to the waves. It's a strange sound waters make when pounding at a wall. A thumping, like a heart that has lost its beat. And then suddenly it was more than that. The waters were a pounding and a crashing and a hissing, not only at the sides of the ship but clear across the top. He clung to the wall and watched through a window, and he saw the sea rise to bury the ship.

It was green. Green water up there where the sky should be. The sea was turning upside down. It seemed to come so slowly, as though it hadn't quite made its mind how devouring a thing it should be.

And then the waters fell. The ship shuddered with it, and screamed, and pitched down and down. And then somehow staggered up again. And he was alive, with life enough left to live this over. And over again.

He turned from the window and clung to the table that was nailed fast. The chair had crashed against it, and Captain Noah was awake.

"You did not go," he said. "Didn't you believe me?"

"Not at first. And when I did, still I would not go. I couldn't leave you to die alone. Most especially when it was my fault. The storm, I mean. I brought it."

And Everence Li¹ , with the waters and the winds and the ship screaming around them and the lantern flickering like their lives, told how he was born too late, after all the good things were used and gone.

"The sea made a road for me as plain as any road could be. But at the end of the road a storm is waiting for me. It must be it came along with me, for we on the Hungry Hill were born to misfortune. It must be no matter how far you run, you cannot change the things that are to be."

"You could have changed this. You didn't have to stay and die. You could have run from the sea and left the storm behind you."

"Could I? Or would the storm have gone with me?"

They waited. There wasn't anything else to say.

A green sea came, so great and terrible a one the hooks popped off the walls and the coats and cloaks flung out and around like lost souls, and down to join the stew of things rolling on the floor. And they heard the scream of a mast as it split and crashed to the deck.

"She's breaking up," Captain Noah said.

"I wish I could live," Everence whispered. "I wish I could live long enough to say good-bye. For now they won't never know. They might even think I've forgot." He watched his shadow. "If only men were big as their shadows hanging on a wall, then I could take this ship and ride it through the storm." He begged, "Isn't there something we could do? Some secret you have learned in all your years that would help us ride it through?"

"There are no secrets and there's nothing we can do. And I am old and I am tired, and it's taking too long for me to die."

They sat there waiting from this wave to the next, to the time when there wouldn't be any more. Everence crawled to the window and watched and in the morning he saw the white lady with her arms outstretched as though to give him rest. He said, "Your lady is like someone I love. There's such a pleasantness about her lips, and a softness to her eyes, and strength."

"She was carved for my wife. And my wife was a wonderful woman." Captain Noah sat there smiling at things that used to be, as he waited for the waves to break up his ship.

Everence Lile looked at the lady. And the strangest stirring stirred within him. For it seemed as if she spoke. And the words she said were, "Why are you dying?"

She hadn't said them at all, not with wooden lips. It was the way her arms were made, the way she dipped into the waves and pushed them away from her ship. As if all by her lone, if she tried long enough and hard enough, she could push all the Seven Seas away.

He looked at his own arms. And he knew he wasn't dying because he believed in a thing so much as to set it right. A drowned man was as dead as one with lung fever. So he wasn't dying to save a life. He was dying because he wasn't doing nothing at all. He hadn't held up one hand against the storm, because a man who should know had said there wasn't nothing to be done. And he believed him. Like he'd believed his pa and his grandpa, and all the years before him.

He stared at Captain Noah, and he knew they were both alike—the man from the Seven Hills and the man from the Seven Seas. Drifting along the tide of things that are to be, and finding less than nothing at all. He looked at the white lady pushing at the seas. He heard Miss Beth telling him a dream.

He said, "Captain Noah, what if your lady wasn't just carved of wood and out there drowning in the waves? What if she was in here, living still? Would three be enough to sail your ship?"

"The masts are gone. Haven't you counted them as they fell? And how would we hold the wheel with green seas breaking over your deck? I am too old and you are too young, and my wife weighed ninety pounds."

"Then we would wait to drown. Is that what she would let you do?"

He didn't answer. They crouched there, clinging to the table, as the ship dropped out from under them. For that was the way it seemed. And without knowing it at all, Everence knew they had come in the trough of a terrible wave. And he said, "This is the beginning, and the end of me." And when the waters struck, it seemed the ship must split in two.

Everence screamed at Captain Noah, and he pointed to his chest, "This is the ship that is going to drown—the one you loved enough to paint upon your flesh!" He snatched at the flesh as though he would rip it off. "And your lady, all that's left of her, your pretty white lady, will rot and never see the day again! And for this I am deserting you!"

He pushed his lips against the old man's ear and screamed against the storm, "You are alone! All the living have deserted you! You said the dead would take your care! I leave you to the dead! You said every man who dies alone upon the sea has a vision, one more chance to talk and dream! And she's come! I've heard her knocking at the door!" He listened and he looked. "She's come to tell you how to save her ship! For it is her ship! You hear? It isn't yours to drown, it is her ship! And she knows the way!"

He crouched there, weeping, beside Captain Noah. "What is that she says? I cannot understand. She loves you, and she loves her ship, and it is to you she speaks. What is it would she do to save you both? All I can understand is that she has come to help you try again."

Captain Noah looked round the cabin, and saw no one. He listened, and heard only the voice of the storm. He stared at this boy from nowhere, and wondered what it was he knew. He said, "She loves me? You think she loves me still? How can she when she's dead, and only made of wood?"

"Her ship lives, and her husband, and they are a part of her. And when part of you is living, how can you be dead?"

They sat there staring at each other, and looking worlds and worlds away. And Everence said, "You didn't hear her speak, but if you had, what was it would she say? What way would she find for you?"

Captain Noah remembered. "It's something sailors do when sailing round the Horn. We did it once long years ago, in a night of storm when all seemed lost. We were young then, and not ready yet to die. Almost I had forgot. But I think she would remember this. It is better than nothing at all. She would tell me to make oil bags and hang them to the rigging."

They did. They sewed sailcloth bags large enough to hold a quart or even two, and filled them full of oil. Every bit of cloth and every bit of oil there was in the cabin and its lockers. And with the sail needle they punched holes so the oil dripped out like a silent rain.

They tied rope about Everence's waist, and they opened the cabin door between the crashing seas, and he clung and he was pounded and near drowned. The water was like mountains crawling all around. But he hung the bags in the twisted rigging, and with his arms plunging in the icy waters, he thought of the white lady pushing at the Seven Seas as though all by her lone she could push them away. He tied himself to a broken mast and watched the oil pour out on those troubled waters. And all around the ship, little by little, a calmness came. It was very strange.

And the troubled waters within him grew still and ebbed away. And Everence Lile knew they would never rise again. For he had found his road to Promise and his treasure in the sea.

And he brought it home, this thing that had never been away. He came to Miss Beth's door, and in the dooryard he tied a cow and her calf. And the sourwood sled they pulled piled high with bags of fertilizer—the kind that would make grass grow even on a tin roof. And on her door stone he laid a box of chicks and a butter mold and a bag of seed. He laid all the things she'd asked, if she asked for, would he listen.

Miss Beth opened her door and stood there in the sun. In good time he'd tell her of Captain Noah and the cash money he'd given to Everence for saving his ship. When he hadn't, Everence knew he hadn't saved it at all. It was a woman's hands. It was a man having a woman so deep in his heart he knew the things he didn't know at all.

Everence said, "Miss Beth, I found the road to Promise."

She stroked the cow and the little red calf. She read the printing on the fertilizer. She knelt and held the chicks and the butter mold with a woman's hands carved deep into the bottom to take the goodness of the world and mold it the way it should be. She opened the bag of seed and found tucking combs. Tortoise-shell with like a great brown wave above them.

"I found my treasure in the sea." He knelt before her. "I found it wasn't a dream you gave to me. It was only the will to try again. That was the treasure I found in the sea. That a man with a woman living deep in his heart can know the things he doesn't know, and do the things he cannot do, for she will help him try again, even though it seems there ain't no use. And that, I reckon, is treasure enough for any man."

And Everence Lile dipped into the bag of seed and brought out a golden wedding ring as bright and shining as life should be. And she smiled on him. And that was answer enough.

A NIGHT FOR LOVE

KURT VONNEGUT, JR.

Moonlight is all right for young lovers, and women never seem to get tired of it. But when a man gets older he usually thinks moonlight is a little too thin and cool for comfort. Turley Whitman thought so. Turley was in his pajamas at his bedroom window, waiting for his daughter Nancy to come home.

He was a huge, kind, handsome man. He looked like a good king, but he was only a company cop in charge of the parking lot at the Reinbeck Abrasives Company. His club, his pistol, his cartridges and his handcuffs were on a chair by the bed. Turley was confused and upset.

His wife Milly was in bed. For about the first time since their three-day honeymoon, in 1936, Milly hadn't put up her hair in curlers. Her hair was all spread out on her pillow. It made her look young and soft and mysterious. Nobody had looked mysterious in that bedroom for years. Milly opened her eyes wide and looked at the moon.

Her attitude was what threw Turley as much as anything. Milly refused to worry about what was maybe happening to Nancy out in the moonlight somewhere so late at night. Milly would drop off to sleep without even knowing it, then she would wake up and stare at the moon for a while, and she would think big thoughts without telling Turley what they were, and then she would drop off to sleep again.

"You awake?" said Turley.

"H'm?" said Milly.

"You decided to be awake?"

"I'm staying awake," said Milly dreamily. She sounded like a little girl.

"You think you've been staying awake?" said Turley.

"I must have dropped off without knowing it," she said.

"You've been sawing wood for an hour," said Turley.

He made her sound unattractive to herself because he wanted her to wake up more. He wanted her to wake up enough to talk to him instead of just stare at the moon. She hadn't really sawed wood when she'd slept. She'd been very beautiful and still.

Milly had been the town beauty once. Now her daughter was.

"I don't mind telling you, I'm worried sick," said Turley.

"Oh, honey," said Milly, "they're fine. They've got sense. They aren't crazy kids."

"You want to guarantee they're not cracked up in a ditch somewhere?" said Turley.

This roused Milly. She sat up, frowned and blinked away her sleepiness. "You really think——" she said.

"I really think!" said Turley sharply. "He gave me his solemn promise he'd have her home two hours ago."

Milly pulled off her covers, put her bare feet close together on the floor. "All right," she said. "I'm sorry. I'm awake now. I'm worried now."

"About time," said Turley. He turned his back to her, and he dramatized his responsible watch at the window by putting his big foot on the radiator.

"Do—do we just worry and wait?" said Milly.

"What do you suggest?" said Turley. "If you mean call the police to see if there's been an accident, I took care of that little detail while you were sawing wood."

"No accidents?" said Milly in a small, small voice.

"No accidents they know of," said Turley grimly.

"Well—that's—that's a little encouraging," said Milly.

"Maybe it is to you," said Turley. "It isn't to me." He faced her, and he saw that she was now wide awake enough to hear what he had been wanting to say for some time. "If you'll pardon my saying so," he said, "you're treating this thing like it was some kind of holiday. You're acting like her being out with that rich young smart aleck in his three-hundred-horsepower car was one of the greatest things that ever happened."

Milly stood, shocked and hurt. "Holiday?" she whispered. "Me?"

"Well—you left your hair down, didn't you—just so you'd look nice in case he got a look at you when he finally brought her home?"

Milly bit her lip. "I just thought if there was going to be a row, I didn't want to make it worse by having my hair up in curlers."

"You don't think there should be a row, do you?" said Turley.

"You're the head of the family," said Milly. "You—you do whatever you think is right." She went to him, touched him lightly. "Honey," she said, "I don't think it's good. Honest I don't. I'm trying just as hard as I can to think of things to do."

"Like what?" said Turley.

"Why don't you call up his father?" said Milly. "Maybe he knows where they are or what their plans were."

The suggestion had a curious effect on Turley. He continued to tower over Milly, but he no longer dominated the house, or the room or even his little barefoot wife. "Oh, great!" he said. The words were loud, but they were as hollow as a bass drum.

"Why not?" said Milly.

Turley couldn't face her anymore. He took up his watch at the window again. "That would just be great," he said to the moonlit town. "Roust L.C. Reinbeck himself out of bed. 'Hello—L.C.? This is T.W. What the hell is your son doing with my daughter?' " Turley laughed bitterly.

Milly didn't seem to understand. "You've got a perfect right to call him or anybody else, if you really think there's an emergency," she said. "I mean, everybody's free and equal this time of night."

"Speak for yourself," said Turley grandly. He was overacting. "Maybe you've been free and equal with the great L.C. Reinbeck, but I never have. And what's more, I never expect to be."

"All I'm saying is he's human," said Milly.

"You're the expert on that," said Turley. "I'm sure I'm not. He never took me out dancing at the country club."

"He never took me out dancing at the country club, either," said Milly. "He doesn't like dancing." She corrected herself. "Or he didn't."

"Please, don't get technical on me this time of night," said Turley. "So he took you out and did whatever he likes to do. So, whatever that was, you're the expert on him."

"Honey," said Milly, full of pain, "he took me out to supper once at the Blue Mill, and he took me to a movie once. He took me to *The Thin Man*. And all he did was talk, and all I did was listen. And it wasn't romantic talk. It was about how he was going to turn the abrasives company back into a porcelain company. And he was going to do all the designing. And he never did anything of the kind, so that's how expert I am on the great Louis C. Reinbeck." She laid her hand on her bosom. "I'm the expert on you," she said, "if you want to know who I'm the expert on."

Turley made an animal sound.

"What, sweetheart?" said Milly.

"Me," said Turley impatiently. "What you're an expert on—me!"

Milly made helpless little giving motions Turley didn't see.

Turley was standing stock-still, winding up tighter and tighter inside. Suddenly he moved like a cumbersome windup man. He went to the telephone on the bedside table. "Why *shouldn't* I call him up?" he blustered. "Why shouldn't I?"

He looked up Louis C. Reinbeck's number in the telephone book clumsily, talked to himself about the times the Reinbeck company had gotten him up out of bed in the middle of the night.

He misdialed, hung up, got set to dial again. His courage was fading fast.

Milly hated to see the courage go. "He won't be asleep," she said. "They've been having a party."

"They've been having a what?" said Turley.

"The Reinbecks are having a party tonight—or it's just over," said Milly.

"How you know that?" said Turley.

"It was in this morning's paper on the society page," said Milly. "Besides," she continued, "you can go in the kitchen and look and see if their lights are on."

"You can see the Reinbeck house from our kitchen?" said Turley.

"Sure," said Milly. "You have to get your head down kind of low and over to one side, but then you can see their house in a corner of the window."

Turley nodded quizzically, watched Milly, thought about her, hard. He dialed again, let the Reinbecks' telephone ring twice. And then he hung up. He dominated his wife, his room and his house again.

Milly knew that she had made a very bad mistake in the past thirty seconds. She was ready to bite off her tongue.

"Every time the Reinbecks do anything," said Turley, "you read every word about it in the paper?"

"Honey," said Milly beseechingly, "all women read the society page. It doesn't mean anything. It's just a silly something to do when the paper comes. All women do it."

"Sure," said Turley bleakly. "Sure. But how many of 'em can say to themselves, 'I could have been Mrs. Louis C. Reinbeck'?"

Turley made a great point of staying calm, of being like a father to

Milly, of forgiving her in advance. "You want to face this thing about those two kids out there in the moonlight somewhere?" he said. "Or you want to go on pretending an accident's the only thing either one of us is thinking about?"

Milly stiffened. "I don't know what you mean," she said.

"You duck your head a hundred times a day to look at that big white house in the corner of the kitchen window, and you don't know what I mean?" said Turley. "Our girl is out in the moonlight somewhere with the kid who's going to get that house someday, and you don't know what I mean? You left your hair down and you stared at the moon and you hardly heard a word I said to you, and you don't know what I mean?" Turley shook his big, imperial head. "You just can't imagine?"

The telephone rang twice in the big white house on the hill. Then it stopped. Louis C. Reinbeck sat on a white iron chair on the lawn in the moonlight. He was looking out at the rolling, lovely nonsense of the golf course, and, beyond that and below, the town. All the lights in his house were out. He thought his wife Natalie was asleep.

Louis was drinking. He was thinking that the moonlight didn't make the world look any better. He thought the moonlight made the world look worse, made it look dead like the moon.

The telephone's ringing twice, then stopping, fitted in well with Louis's mood. The telephone was a good touch—urgency that could wait until hell froze over. "Shatter the night and then hang up," said Louis.

Along with the house and the Reinbeck Abrasives Company, Louis had inherited from his father and grandfather a deep and satisfying sense of having been corrupted by commerce. And like them, Louis thought of himself as a sensitive maker of porcelain, not grinding wheels, born in the wrong place at the wrong time.

Just as the telephone had rung twice at the right time, so did Louis's wife Natalie appear as though on cue. She was a cool, spare Boston girl. Her role was to misunderstand Louis. She did it beautifully, taking apart his reflective moods like a master mechanic.

"Did you hear the telephone ring, Louis?" she said.

"H'm? Oh—yes. Uh-huh," said Louis.

"It rang and then it stopped," said Natalie.

"I know," said Louis. He warned her with a sigh that he didn't want to discuss the telephone call or anything else in a flat, practical Yankee way.

Natalie ignored the warning. "Don't you wonder who it was?" she said.

"No," said Louis.

"Maybe it was a guest who left something. You didn't see anything around, did you, that somebody left?"

"No," said Louis.

"An earring or something, I suppose," said Natalie. She wore a pale blue, cloudlike negligee that Louis had given to her. But she made the negligee meaningless by dragging a heavy iron chair across the lawn, setting it next to Louis's. The arms of the chairs clicked together, and Louis jerked his fingers from between them just in time.

Natalie sat down. "Hi," she said.

"Hi," said Louis.

"See the moon?" said Natalie.

"Yup," said Louis.

"Think people had a nice time tonight?" said Natalie.

"I don't know," said Louis, "and I'm sure they don't either." He meant by this that he was always the only artist and philosopher at his parties. Everybody else was a businessman.

Natalie was used to this. She let it pass. "What time did Charlie get in?" she said. Charlie was their only son—actually Louis Charles Reinbeck, Junior.

"I'm sure I don't know," said Louis. "He didn't report in to me. Never does."

Natalie, who had been enjoying the moon, now sat forward uneasily. "He is home, isn't he?" she said.

"I haven't the remotest idea," said Louis.

Natalie bounded out of her chair.

She strained her eyes in the night, trying to see if Charlie's car was in the shadows of the garage. "Who did he go out with?" she asked Louis.

"He doesn't talk with me," said Louis.

"Who is he with?" said Natalie.

"If he isn't by himself, then he's with somebody you don't approve of," said Louis.

But Natalie didn't hear him. She was running into the house. Then the telephone rang again and went on ringing until Natalie answered.

Natalie held the telephone out to Louis. "It's a man named Turley Whitman," she said. "He says he's one of your policemen."

"Something wrong at the plant?" said Louis, taking the phone. "Fire, I hope?"

"No," said Natalie, "nothing as serious as that." From her expression, Louis gathered that something a lot worse than that had happened. "It seems that our son is out with Mr. Turley's daughter somewhere, that they should have been back hours ago," said Natalie. "Mr. Turley is naturally very deeply concerned about his daughter."

"Mr. Turley?" said Louis into the telephone.

"Turley's my first name, sir," said Turley. "Turley Whitman's my whole name."

"I'm going to listen on the upstairs phone," whispered Natalie. She gathered the folds of her negligee, ran, manlike, up the stairs.

"You probably don't know me except by sight," said Turley. "I'm the guard at the main-plant parking lot."

"Of course I know you—by sight and by name," said Louis. It was a lie. "Now what's this about my son and your daughter?"

Turley wasn't ready to get to the nut of the problem yet. He was still introducing himself and his family. "You probably know my wife a good deal better'n you know me, sir," he said.

There was a woman's small cry of surprise.

For an instant, Louis didn't know if it was the cry of his own wife or of Turley's wife. But when he heard sounds of somebody trying to hang up, he knew it had to be on Turley's end. Turley's wife obviously didn't want her name dragged in.

But Turley was determined to drag it in, and he won out. "You knew her by her maiden name, of course," said Turley. "Milly— Mildred O'Shea."

All sounds of protest at Turley's end of the line died. The death of protest came to Louis as a shocking thing. His shock was compounded as he remembered young, affectionate and pretty, mystifying Milly O'Shea. He hadn't thought of her for years, hadn't known what had become of her.

And yet, at the mention of her name, it was as though Louis had thought of her constantly since she'd kissed him good-bye in the moonlight so long ago.

"Yes—yes," said Louis faintly. "Yes, I—I remember her well." He wanted to cry about growing old, about the shabby ends brave young lovers come to.

From the mention of Milly's name on, Turley had his conversation with the great Louis C. Reinbeck all his own way. The miracle of equality had been achieved. Turley and Louis spoke man to man, father to father, with Louis apologizing, murmuring against his own son.

Louis thanked Turley for having called the police. Louis would call them too. If Louis found out anything, he would call Turley at once. Louis called Turley "sir."

Turley was exhilarated when he hung up. "He sends his regards," he said to Milly. He turned to find himself talking to thin air. Milly had left the room silently on bare feet.

Turley found Milly heating coffee in the kitchen on the new electric stove. The stove was named the Globemaster. It had a ridiculously complicated control panel. The Globemaster was a wistful dream of Milly's come true. Not many of her dreams of nice things had come true.

The coffee was boiling, making the pot crackle and spit. Milly didn't notice that the pot was boiling, even though she was staring at it with terrible concentration. The pot spit, stung her hand. She burst into tears, put the stung hand to her mouth. And then she saw Turley.

She tried to duck past him and out of the kitchen, but he caught her arm.

"Honey," he said dazedly. He turned off the Globemaster's burner with his free hand. "Milly," he said.

Milly wanted desperately to get away. But big Turley had such an easy time holding her that he hardly realized he was doing it. Milly subsided at last, her sweet face red and twisted.

"Won't—won't you tell me what's wrong, honey?" said Turley.

"Don't worry about me," said Milly brokenly. "Go worry about people dying in ditches."

Turley let her go. "I said something wrong?" he said. He was sincerely bewildered.

"Oh, Turley, Turley," said Milly helplessly, "I never thought you'd hurt me this way—this much." She cupped her hands, as though she were holding something precious. Then she let it fall from her hands, whatever her imagination thought it was.

Turley watched it fall. "Just because I told him your name?" he said.

"When—when you told him my name," said Milly, "there was so much else you told him." She was trying to forgive Turley, but it was hard for her. "I don't suppose you knew what else you were telling him. You couldn't have."

"All I told him was your name," said Turley.

"And all it meant to Louis C. Reinbeck," said Milly, "was that a woman down in the town had two silly little dates with him twenty years ago, and she's talked about nothing else since. And her husband knows about those two silly little dates too—and he's just as proud of them as she is. Prouder!"

Milly put her head down and to one side, and she pointed out the kitchen window, pointed to a splash of white light in an upper corner of the window. "There," she said, "the great Louis Reinbeck is up in all that light somewhere, thinking I've loved him all these years." The floodlights on the Reinbeck house went out. "Now he's up there in the moonlight somewhere—thinking about the poor little woman and the poor little man and their poor little daughter down here." Milly shuddered. "Well, we're not poor!" she said. "Or we weren't until tonight."

The great Louis Reinbeck returned to his drink and his iron lawn chair. He had called the police, who had told him what they had told Turley—that there were no wrecks that they knew of.

Natalie sat down beside Louis again. She tried to catch his eye, tried to get him to see her maternal, teasing smile. But Louis wouldn't look.

"You—you know the girl's mother, do you?" she said.

"Knew," said Louis. He hunched over.

"You took her out on nights like this?" said Natalie. "Full moon and all that?"

"We could dig out a twenty-year-old calendar and see what the phases of the moon were," said Louis tartly. "You can't exactly avoid full moons, you know. You're bound to have one once a month."

"What was the moon on our wedding night?" said Natalie.

"Full?" said Louis.

"New," said Natalie. "Brand-new."

"Women are more sensitive to things like that," said Louis. "They notice things."

Louis surprised himself by sounding peevish. His conscience was doing funny things to his voice because he couldn't remember much of anything about his honeymoon with Natalie.

He could remember almost everything about the night he and Milly O'Shea had wandered out on the golf course. That night with Milly, the moon had been full.

Now Natalie was saying something. And when she was done, Louis had to ask her to say it all over again. He hadn't heard a word.

"I said, what's it like?" said Natalie.

"What's what like?" said Louis.

"Being a young male Reinbeck—all hot-blooded and full of dreams," said Natalie, "swooping down off the hill, grabbing a pretty little town girl and spiriting her into the moonlight." She laughed teasingly. "It must be kind of godlike."

"It isn't," said Louis.

"It isn't godlike?" said Natalie.

"Godlike?" said Louis bitterly. "I never felt more human in all my life!" He threw his empty glass in the direction of the golf course. He wished he'd been strong enough to throw the glass straight to the spot where Milly had kissed him good-bye.

"Then let's hope Charlie marries this hot little girl from town," said Natalie evenly. She stood. "Let's have no more cold, inhuman Reinbeck wives like me." She shuddered. "Let's face it," she said, "you would have been a thousand times happier if you'd married your Milly O'Shea."

She went to bed.

"Who's kidding anybody?" Turley Whitman said to his wife. "You would have been a million times happier if you'd married Louis Reinbeck." He was back at his post by the bedroom window, back with his big foot on the radiator.

Milly was sitting on the edge of the bed. "Not a million times, not two times, not the-smallest-number-there-is times happier," said Milly. She was wretched. "Turley—please don't say anything more like that. I can't stand it, it's so crazy."

"Well, you were kind of calling a spade a spade down there in the kitchen," said Turley, "giving me hell for telling the great Louis Reinbeck your name. Let me just call a spade a spade here, and say neither one of us wants our daughter to make the same mistake you did."

Milly went to him, put her arms around him. "Turley, please, that's the worst thing you could say to me," she said.

Turley turned a stubborn red, was as unyielding as a statue. "I remember all the big promises I made you, all the big talk," he said. "Neither one of us thinks company cop is one of the biggest jobs a man can hold."

Milly tried to shake him, with no luck. "I don't care what your job is," she said.

"I was gonna have more money than the great L.C. Reinbeck," said Turley, "and I was gonna make it all myself. Remember, Milly? That's what really sold you, wasn't it?"

Her arms dropped away from him. "No," she said.

"My famous good looks?" said Turley with grand irony.

"They had a lot to do with it," said Milly. His looks had gone very well with the looks of the prettiest girl in town. "Most of all," she said, "it was the great Louis Reinbeck and the moon."

The great Louis Reinbeck was in his bedroom. His wife was in bed with the covers pulled up over her head. The room was cunningly contrived to give the illusion of romance and undying true love, no matter what really went on in the room.

Up to now, almost everything that had gone on in the room had been reasonably pleasant. Now it appeared that the marriage of

Louis and Natalie was at an end. When Louis made her pull the covers away from her face, when Natalie showed him how swollen her face was with tears, this was plainly the case. This was the end.

Louis was miserable—couldn't understand how things had fallen to pieces so fast. "I—I haven't thought of Milly O'Shea for twenty years," he said.

"Please—no. Don't lie. Don't explain," said Natalie. "I understand."

"I swear," said Louis, "I haven't seen her for twenty years."

"I believe you," said Natalie. "That's what makes it so much worse. I wish you had seen her—just as often as you liked. That would have been better, somehow, than all this—this——" She sat up, ransacked her mind for the right word. "All this horrible, empty, aching, nagging regret." She lay back down again.

"About Milly?" said Louis.

"About Milly, about me, about the abrasives company, about all the things you wanted and didn't get, about all the things you got you didn't want. Milly and me—that's as good a way of saying it as anything. That pretty well says it all."

"I—I don't love her. I never did," said Louis.

"You must have liked the one and only time in your life you felt human," said Natalie huskily. "Whatever happened in the moonlight must have been nice—much nicer than anything you and I ever had."

Louis's nightmare got worse, because he knew Natalie had spoken the truth. There never had been anything as nice as that time in the moonlight with Milly.

"There was absolutely nothing there, no basis for love," said Louis wonderingly. "We were perfect strangers then. I knew her as little as I know her now."

Louis's muscles knotted and the words came hard, because he thought he was extracting something from himself of terrible importance. "I—I don't suppose she is a symbol of my own disappointment in myself, of all I might have been," he said heavily.

He went to the bedroom window, looked morbidly at the setting moon. The moon's rays were flat now, casting long shadows on the golf course, exaggerating the toy geography. Little flags flew here and there, signifying less than nothing. There was where the great love scene had been played.

Suddenly he understood. "Moonlight," he murmured.

"What?" said Natalie.

"It had to be," said Louis. He laughed, because the explanation was so explosively simple. "We had to be in love with a moon like that, in a world like that. We owed it to the moon."

263

Natalie sat up, her disposition much improved.

"The richest boy in town and the prettiest girl in town," said Louis—"we couldn't let the moon down, could we?"

He laughed again, made his wife get out of bed, made her look at the moon with him. "And here I'd been thinking it really had been something big between Milly and me way back then." He shook his head. "When all it was was pure, beautiful, moonlit hokum."

He led his wife back to bed. "You're the only one I ever loved," he said. "An hour ago, I didn't know that. I know that now."

So everything was fine.

"I won't lie to you," Milly Whitman said to her husband, Turley. "I loved the great Louis C. Reinbeck for a while. Out there on the golf course in the moonlight, I just had to fall in love. Can you understand that—how I would have to fall in love with him, even if we didn't like each other very well?"

Turley allowed as how he could see how that would be. But he wasn't happy about it.

"We kissed only once," said Milly. "And if he'd kissed me right, I think I might really be Mrs. Louis C. Reinbeck tonight." She nodded. "Since we're calling spades spades tonight, we might as well call that one a spade too. And, just before we kissed up there on the golf course," said Milly, "I was thinking what a poor little rich boy he was, and how much happier I could make him than any old cold, stuck-up country-club girl. And then he kissed me," said Milly, "and I knew he wasn't in love, couldn't ever be in love. So I made that kiss good-bye."

"There's where you made your mistake," said Turley.

"No," said Milly, "because the next boy who kissed me kissed me right, showed me he knew what love was, even if there wasn't a moon. And I lived happily ever after, until tonight." She put her arms around Turley. "Now kiss me again the way you kissed me the first time, and I'll be all right tonight too."

Turley did, so everything was all right there too.

About twenty minutes after that, the telephones in both houses rang. The burden of the messages was that Charlie Reinbeck and Nancy Whitman were fine. They had, however, put their own interpretation on the moonlight. They'd decided that Cinderella and Prince Charming had as good a chance as anybody for really living happily ever after. So they'd married.

So now there was a new household. Whether everything was all right there remained to be seen. The moon went down.

THE QUIET MAN

MAURICE WALSH

Shawn Kelvin, a blithe young lad of twenty, went to the States to seek his fortune. And fifteen years thereafter he returned to his native Kerry, his blitheness sobered and his youth dried to the core, and whether he had made his fortune or whether he had not, no one could be knowing for certain. For he was a quiet man, not given to talking about himself and the things he had done. A quiet man, under middle size, with strong shoulders and deep-set blue eyes below brows darker than his dark hair—that was Shawn Kelvin. One shoulder had a trick of hunching slightly higher than the other, and some folks said that came from a habit he had of shielding his eyes in the glare of an open-hearth furnace in a place called Pittsburgh, while others said it used to be a way he had of guarding his chin that time he was a sort of sparring-partner punching bag at a boxing camp.

Shawn Kelvin came home and found that he was the last of the Kelvins, and the farm of his forefathers had added its few acres to the ranch of Big Liam O'Grady, of Moyvalla. Shawn took no action to recover his land, though O'Grady had got it meanly. He had had enough of fighting, and all he wanted now was peace. He quietly went amongst the old and kindly friends and quietly looked about him for the place and peace he wanted; and when the time came, quietly produced the money for a neat, handy, small farm on the first warm shoulder of Knockanore Hill below the rolling curves of heather. It was not a big place but it was in good heart, and it got all the sun that was going; and, best of all, it suited Shawn to the tiptop

265

notch of contentment; for it held the peace that tuned to his quietness, and it commanded the widest view in all Ireland—vale and mountain and the lifting green plain of the Atlantic Sea.

There, in a four-roomed, lime-washed, thatched cottage, Shawn made his life, and, though his friends hinted his needs and obligations, no thought came to him of bringing a wife into the place. Yet Fate had the thought and the dream in her loom for him. One middling imitation of a man he had to do chores for him, an ex-navy pensioner handy enough about house and byre, but with no relish for the sustained work of the field—and, indeed, as long as he kept house and byre shipshape, he found Shawn an easy master.

Shawn himself was no drudge toiler. He knew all about drudgery and the way it wears out a man's soul. He plowed a little and sowed a little, and at the end of a furrow he would lean on the handles of the cultivator, wipe his brow, if it needed wiping, and lose himself for whole minutes in the great green curve of the sea out there beyond the high black portals of Shannon mouth. And sometimes of an evening he would see, under the glory of the sky, the faint smoke smudge of an American liner. Then he would smile to himself—a pitying smile—thinking of the poor devils, with dreams of fortune luring them, going out to sweat in Ironville, or to bootleg bad whisky down the hidden way, or to stand in a bread line. All these things were behind Shawn forever.

Market days he would go down and across to Listowel town, seven miles, to do his bartering; and in the long evenings, slowly slipping into the endless summer gloaming, his friends used to climb the winding land to see him. Only the real friends came that long road, and they were welcome—fighting men who had been out in the "Sixteen": Matt Tobin the thresher, the schoolmaster, the young curate—men like that. A stone jar of malt whisky would appear on the table, and there would be a haze of smoke and a maze of warm, friendly disagreements.

"Shawn, old son," one of them might hint, "aren't you sometimes terrible lonely?"

"Like hell I am!" might retort Shawn derisively. "Why?"

"Nothing but the daylight and the wind and the sun setting like the wrath o' God."

"Just that! Well?"

"But after the stirring times beyond in the States——"

"Ay! Tell me, fine man, have you ever seen a furnace in full blast?"

"A great sight."

"Great surely! But if I could jump you into a steel foundry this minute, you would be sure that God had judged you faithfully into the very hob of hell."

And then they would laugh and have another small one from the stone jar.

And on Sundays Shawn used to go to church three miles down to the gray chapel above the black cliffs of Doon Bay. There Fate laid her lure for him.

Sitting quietly on his wooden bench or kneeling on the dusty footboard, he would fix his steadfast deep-set eyes on the vestmented celebrant and say his prayers slowly, or go into that strange trance, beyond dreams and visions, where the soul is almost one with the unknowable.

But after a time, Shawn's eyes no longer fixed themselves on the celebrant. They went no farther than two seats ahead. A girl sat there. Sunday after Sunday she sat in front of him, and Sunday after Sunday his first casual admiration grew warmer.

She had a white nape to her neck and short red hair above it, and Shawn liked the color and wave of that flame. And he liked the set of her shoulders and the way the white neck had of leaning a little forward and she at her prayers—or her dreams. And, the service over, Shawn used to stay in his seat so he might get one quick but sure look at her face as she passed out. And he liked her face, too—the wide-set gray eyes, cheekbones firmly curved, clean-molded lips, austere yet sensitive. And he smiled pityingly at himself that one of her name should make his pulses stir—for she was an O'Grady.

One person, only, in the crowded chapel noted Shawn's look and the thought behind the look. Not the girl. Her brother, Big Liam O'Grady of Moyvalla, the very man who as good as stole the Kelvin acres. And that man smiled to himself, too—the ugly, contemptuous smile that was his by nature—and, after another habit he had, he tucked away his bit of knowledge in mind corner against a day when it might come in useful for his own purposes.

The girl's name was Ellen—Ellen O'Grady. But in truth she was no longer a girl. She was past her first youth into that second one that has no definite ending. She might be thirty—she was no less—but there was not a lad in the countryside would say she was past her prime. The poise of her and the firm set of her bones below clean skin saved her from the fading of mere prettiness. Though she had been sought in marriage more than once, she had accepted no one, or, rather, had not been allowed to encourage anyone. Her brother saw to that.

Big Liam O'Grady was a great, rawboned, sandy-haired man, with the strength of an ox and a heart no bigger than a sour apple. An overbearing man given to berserk rages. Though he was a churchgoer by habit, the true god of that man was Money—red gold, shining silver, dull copper—the trinity that he worshiped in degree. He and his sister lived on the big ranch farm of Moyvalla, and Ellen was his housekeeper, a good cook, a notable baker, and she demanded no wage. All that suited Big Liam splendidly, and so she remained single—a wasted woman.

Big Liam himself was not a marrying man. There were not many spinsters with a dowry big enough to tempt him, and the few there had acquired expensive tastes—a convent education, the deplorable art of hitting jazz out of a piano, the damnable vice of cigarette smoking, the purse-emptying craze for motorcars—such things.

But in due time, the dowry and the place—with a woman tied to them—came under his nose, and Big Liam was no longer tardy. His neighbor, James Carey, died in March and left his fine farm and all on it to his widow, a youngish woman without children, a woman with a hard name for saving pennies. Big Liam looked once at Kathy Carey and looked many times at her broad acres. Both pleased him. He took the steps required by tradition. In the very first week of the following Shrovetide, he sent an accredited emissary to open formal negotiations, and that emissary came back within the hour.

"My soul," said he, "but she is the quick one! I hadn't ten words out of me when she was down my throat. 'I am in no hurry,' says she, 'to come wife to a house with another woman at the fire corner. When Ellen is in a place of her own, I will listen to what Liam O'Grady has to say.'"

"She will, by Jacus!" Big Liam stopped him. "She will so."

There, now, was the right time to recall Shawn Kelvin and the look in his eyes. Big Liam's mind corner promptly delivered up its memory. He smiled knowingly and contemptuously. Shawn Kelvin daring to cast sheep's eyes at an O'Grady! The undersized chicken heart, who took the loss of the Kelvin acres lying down! The little Yankee runt hidden away on the shelf of Knockanore! But what of it? The required dowry would be conveniently small, and the girl would never go hungry, anyway. There was Big Liam O'Grady, far descended from many chieftains.

The very next market day at Listowel he sought out Shawn Kelvin and placed a huge, sandy-haired hand on the shoulder that hunched to meet it.

"Shawn Kelvin, a word with you! Come and have a drink."

Shawn hesitated. "Very well," he said then. He did not care for O'Grady, but he would hurt no man's feelings.

They went across to Sullivan's bar and had a drink, and Shawn paid for it. And Big Liam came directly to his subject—almost patronizingly, as if he were conferring a favor.

"I want to see Ellen settled in a place of her own," said he.

Shawn's heart lifted into his throat and stayed there. But that steadfast face with the steadfast eyes gave no sign and, moreover, he could not say a word with his heart where it was.

"Your place is small," went on the big man, "but it is handy, and no load of debt on it, as I hear. Not much of a dowry ever came to Knockanore, and not much of a dowry can I be giving with Ellen. Say two hundred pounds at the end of harvest, if prices improve. What do you say, Shawn Kelvin?"

Shawn swallowed his heart, and his voice came slow and cool: "What does Ellen say?"

"I haven't asked her," said Big Liam. "But what would she say, blast it?"

"Whatever she says, she will say it herself, not you, Big Liam."

But what could Ellen say? She looked within her own heart and found it empty; she looked at the granite crag of her brother's face and contemplated herself a slowly withering spinster at his fire corner; she looked up at the swell of Knockanore Hill and saw the white cottage among the green small fields below the warm brown of the heather. Oh, but the sun would shine up there in the lengthening spring day and pleasant breezes blow in sultry summer; and finally she looked at Shawn Kelvin, that firmly built, small man with the clean face and the lustrous eyes below steadfast brow. She said a prayer to her God and sank head and shoulders in a resignation more pitiful than tears, more proud than the pride of chieftains. Romance? Welladay!

Shawn was far from satisfied with the resigned acceptance, but then was not the time to press for a warmer one. He knew the brother's wizened soul, guessed at the girl's clean one, and saw that she was doomed beyond hope to a fireside sordidly bought for her. Let it be his own fireside then. There were many worse ones—and God was good.

Ellen O'Grady married Shawn Kelvin. One small statement; and it holds the risk of tragedy, the chance of happiness, the probability of mere endurance—choices wide as the world.

But Big Liam O'Grady, for all his resolute promptness, did not win Kathy Carey to wife. She, foolishly enough, took to husband her own cattleman, a gay night rambler, who gave her the devil's own time and a share of happiness in the bygoing. For the first time, Big Liam discovered how mordant the wit of his neighbors could be, and to contempt for Shawn Kelvin he now added an unreasoning dislike.

Shawn Kelvin had got his precious red-haired woman under his own roof now. He had no illusions about her feelings for him. On himself, and on himself only, lay the task of molding her into a wife and lover. Darkly, deeply, subtly, away out of sight, with gentleness, with restraint, with a consideration beyond kenning, that molding must be done, and she that was being molded must never know. He hardly knew, himself.

First he turned his attention to material things. He hired a small servant maid to help her with the housework. Then he acquired a rubber-tired tub cart and a half-bred gelding with a reaching knee action. And on market days, husband and wife used to bowl down to Listowel, do their selling and their buying, and bowl smoothly home again, their groceries in the well of the cart and a bundle of second-hand American magazines on the seat at Ellen's side. And in the nights, before the year turned, with the wind from the plains of the Atlantic keening above the chimney, they would sit at either side of the flaming peat fire, and he would read aloud strange and almost unbelievable things out of the high-colored magazines. Stories, sometimes, wholly unbelievable.

Ellen would sit and listen and smile, and go on with her knitting or her sewing; and after a time it was sewing she was at mostly—small things. And when the reading was done, they would sit and talk quietly in their own quiet way. For they were both quiet. Woman though she was, she got Shawn to do most of the talking. It could be that she, too, was probing and seeking, unwrapping the man's soul to feel the texture thereof, surveying the marvel of his life as he spread it diffidently before her. He had a patient, slow, vivid way of picturing for her the things he had seen and felt. He made her see the glare of molten metal, lambent yet searing, made her feel the sucking heat, made her hear the clang; she could see the roped square under the dazzle of the hooded arcs with the curling smoke layer above it, understand the explosive restraint of the game, thrill when he showed her how to stiffen wrist for the final devastating right hook. And often enough the stories were humorous, and Ellen would chuckle, or stare, or throw back her red, lovely curls in laughter. It was grand to make her laugh.

Shawn's friends, in some hesitation at first, came in ones and twos up the slopes to see them. But Ellen welcomed them with her smile that was shy and, at the same time, frank, and her table was loaded for them with scones and crumpets and cream cakes and heather honey; and at the right time it was she herself that brought forth the decanter of whisky—no longer the half-empty stone jar—and the

polished glasses. Shawn was proud as sin of her. She would sit then
and listen to their discussions and be forever surprised at the knowledgeable man her husband was—the way he would discuss war and
politics and the making of songs, the turn of speech that summed up
a man or a situation. And sometimes she would put in a word or two
and be listened to, and they would look to see if her smile com-
mended them, and be a little chastened by the wisdom of that
smile—the age-old smile of the matriarch from whom they were all
descended. In no time at all, Matt Tobin the thresher, who used to
think, "Poor old Shawn! Lucky she was to get him," would whisper
to the schoolmaster: "Herrin's alive! That fellow's luck would
astonish nations."

Women, in the outside world, begin by loving their husbands; and
then, if fate is kind, they grow to admire them; and, if fate is not
unkind, may descend no lower than liking and enduring. And there is
the end of lawful romance. Look now at Ellen O'Grady. She came up
to the shelf of Knockanore and in her heart was only a nucleus of
fear in a great emptiness, and that nucleus might grow into horror
and disgust. But, glory of God, she, for reason piled on reason,
presently found herself admiring Shawn Kelvin; and with or without
reason, a quiet liking came to her for this quiet man who was so
gentle and considerate; and then, one great heart-stirring dark o'
night, she found herself fallen head and heels in love with her own
husband. There is the sort of love that endures, but the road to it is a
mighty chancy one.

A woman, loving her husband, may or may not be proud of him,
but she will fight like a tiger if anyone, barring herself, belittles him.
And there was one man that belittled Shawn Kelvin. Her brother, Big
Liam O'Grady. At fair or market or chapel that dour giant deigned
not to hide his contempt and dislike. Ellen knew why. He had lost a
wife and farm; he had lost in herself a frugally cheap housekeeper; he
had been made the butt of a sly humor; and for these mishaps, in
some twisted way, he blamed Shawn. But—and there came in the
contempt—the little Yankee runt, who dared say nothing about the
lost Kelvin acres, would not now have the gall or guts to demand the
dowry that was due. Lucky the hound to steal an O'Grady to
Knockanore! Let him be satisfied with that luck!

One evening before a market day Ellen spoke to her husband:
"Has Big Liam paid you my dowry yet, Shawn?"

"Sure there's no hurry, girl," said Shawn.

"Have you ever asked him?"

"I have not. I am not looking for your dowry, Ellen."

"And Big Liam could never understand that." Her voice firmed. "You will ask him tomorrow."

"Very well, so, *agrah*," agreed Shawn easily.

And the next day, in that quiet diffident way of his, he asked Big Liam. But Big Liam was brusque and blunt. He had no loose money and Kelvin would have to wait till he had. "Ask me again, Shawneen," he finished, his face in a mocking smile, and turning on his heel, he plowed his great shoulders through the crowded market.

His voice had been carelessly loud and people had heard. They laughed and talked amongst themselves. "Begobs! The devil's own boy, Big Liam. What a pup to sell! Stealing the land and keeping a grip on the fortune! Aye and a dangerous fellow, mind you. The same Big Liam! He would smash little Shawn at the wind of a word. And devil the bit his Yankee sparring tricks would help him!"

A friend of Shawn's, Mat Tobin the thresher, heard that and lifted his voice: "I would like to be there the day Shawn Kelvin loses his temper."

"A bad day for poor Shawn!"

"It might then," said Matt Tobin, "but I would come from the other end of Kerry to see the badness that would be in it for someone."

Shawn had moved away with his wife, not heeding or not hearing.

"You see, Ellen?" he said in some discomfort. "The times are hard on the big ranchers, and we don't need the money, anyway."

"Do you think Big Liam does?" Her voice had a cut in it. "He could buy you and all Knockanore and be only on the fringe of his hoard. You will ask him again."

"But, girl dear, I never wanted a dowry with you."

She liked him to say that, but far better would she like to win for him the respect and admiration that was his due. She must do that now at all costs. Shawn, drawing back now, would be the butt of his fellowmen.

"You foolish lad! Big Liam would never understand your feelings, with money at stake." She smiled and a pang went through Shawn's breast. For the smile was the smile of an O'Grady, and he could not be sure whether the contempt in it was for himself or for her brother.

Shawn asked Big Liam again, unhappy in his asking, but also dimly comprehending his woman's objective. And Shawn asked again a third time. The issue was become a famous one now. Men talked about it, and women too. Bets were made on it. At fair or market, if Shawn was seen approaching Big Liam, men edged closer and women edged away. Someday the big fellow would grow tired of being asked, and in one of his terrible rages half kill the little fellow as he had half killed other men. A great shame! Here and there, a man advised Shawn to give up asking and put the matter in a lawyer's hands.

"I couldn't do that," was Shawn's only answer. Strangely enough, none of these prudent advisers were amongst Shawn's close friends. His friends frowned and said little, but they were always about, and always amongst them was Matt Tobin.

The day at last came when Big Liam grew tired of being asked. That was the big October cattle fair at Listowel, and he had sold twenty head of fat, polled-Angus beeves at a good price. He was a hard dealer and it was late in the day before he settled at his own figure, so that the banks were closed and he was not able to make a lodgment. He had, then, a great roll of bills in an inner vest pocket when he saw Shawn and Ellen coming across to where he was bargaining with Matt Tobin for a week's threshing. Besides, the day being dank, he had had a drink or two more than was good for him and the whisky had loosened his tongue and whatever he had of discretion. By the powers!—it was time and past time to deal once and for all with this little gadfly of a fellow, to show him up before the whole market. He strode to meet Shawn, and people got out of his savage way and edged in behind to lose nothing of this dangerous game.

He caught Shawn by the hunched shoulder—a rending grip—and bent down to grin in his face.

"What is it, little fellow? Don't be ashamed to ask!"

Matt Tobin was probably the only one there to notice the ease with which Shawn wrenched his shoulder free and Matt Tobin's eyes brightened. But Shawn did nothing further and said no word. His deep-set eyes gazed steadily at the big man.

The big man showed his teeth mockingly. "Go on, you whelp! What do you want?"

"You know, O'Grady."

"I do. Listen, Shawneen!" Again he brought his hand clap on the little man's shoulder. "Listen, Shawneen! If I had a dowry to give my sister, 'tis not to a little shrimp like you would get her. Go to hell out o' that!"

His great hand gripped and he flung Shawn backwards as if he were only the image of a man filled with chaff.

Shawn went backwards, but he did not fall. He gathered himself like a spring, feet under him, arms half raised, head forward into hunched shoulder. But as quickly as the spring coiled, as quickly it slackened, and he turned away to his wife. She was there facing him, tense and keen, her face pale and set, and a gleam of the race in her eyes.

"Woman, woman!" he said in his deep voice. "Why would you and I shame ourselves like this?"

"Shame!" she cried. "Will you let him shame you now?"

"But your own brother, Ellen—before them all?"

"And he cheating you——"

"Glory of God!" His voice was distressed. "What is his dirty money to me? Are you an O'Grady, after all?"

That stung her and she stung him back in one final effort. She placed a hand below her breast and looked close into his face. Her voice was low and bitter, and only he heard: "I am an O'Grady. It is a great pity that the father of this my son is a Kelvin and a coward."

The bosses of Shawn Kelvin's cheek bones were like hard marble, but his voice was as soft as a dove's.

"Is that the way of it? Let us be going home then, in the name of God!"

He took her arm, but she shook his hand off; nevertheless, she walked at his side, head up, through the people that made way for them. Her brother mocked them with his great, laughing bellow.

"That fixes the pair of them!" he cried, brushed a man who laughed with him out of his way, and strode off through the fair.

There was talk then—plenty of it. "Murder, but Shawn had a narrow squeak that time! Did you see the way he flung him? I wager he'll give Big Liam a wide road after this. And he by way of being a boxer! That's a pound you owe me, Matt Tobin."

"I'll pay it," said Matt Tobin, and that is all he said. He stood wide-legged, looking at the ground, his hand ruefully rubbing the back of his head and dismay and gloom on his face. His friend had failed him in the face of the people.

Shawn and Ellen went home in their tub cart and had not a single word or glance for each other on the road. And all that evening, at table or fireside, a heart-sickening silence held them in its grip. And all that night they lay side by side, still and mute. There was only one subject that possessed them and on that they dared speak no longer. They slept little. Ellen, her heart desolate, lay on her side, staring into the dark, grieving for what she had said and unable to unsay it. Shawn, on his back, contemplated things with a cold clarity. He realized that he was at the fork of life and that a finger pointed unmistakably. He must risk the very shattering of all happiness, he must do a thing so final and decisive that, once done, it could never again be questioned. Before morning, he came to his decision, and it was bitter as gall. He cursed himself. "Oh, you fool! You might have known that you should never have taken an O'Grady without breaking the O'Gradys."

He got up early in the morning at his usual hour and went out, as usual, to his morning chores—rebedding and foddering the cattle, rubbing down the half-bred, helping the servant maid with the milk in the creaming pans—and, as usual, he came in to his breakfast, and ate it unhungrily and silently, which was not usual. But, thereafter he again went out to the stable, harnessed his gelding and hitched him to the tub cart. Then he returned to the kitchen and spoke for the first time.

"Ellen, will you come with me down to see your brother?"

She hesitated, her hands thrown wide in a helpless, hopeless gesture. "Little use you going to see my brother, Shawn. 'Tis I should go—and not come back."

"Don't blame me now or later, Ellen. It has been put on me, and the thing I am going to do is the only thing to be done. Will you come?"

"Very well," she agreed tonelessly. "I will be ready in a minute."

And they went the four miles down into the vale to the big farmhouse of Moyvalla. They drove into the great square of cobbled yard and found it empty.

On one side of the square was the long, low, lime-washed dwelling house; and on the other, fifty yards away, the two-storied line of steadings with a wide arch in the middle; and through the arch came the purr and zoom of a threshing machine. Shawn tied the half-bred to the wheel of a farm cart, and, with Ellen, approached the house.

A slattern servant girl leaned over the kitchen half door and pointed through the arch. The master was out beyond in the haggard—the rickyard—and would she run across for him?

"Never mind, *achara*," said Shawn, "I'll get him. . . . Ellen, will you go in and wait."

"No," said Ellen, "I'll come with you." She knew her brother.

As they went through the arch, the purr and zoom grew louder and, turning the corner, they walked into the midst of activity. A long double row of cone-pointed corn stacks stretched across the yard and, between them, Matt Tobin's portable threshing machine was busy. The smooth-flying, eight-foot driving wheel made a sleepy purr and the black driving belt ran with a sag and a heave to the red-painted thresher. Up there on the platform, bare-armed men were feeding the flying drum with loosened sheaves, their hands moving in a rhythmic sway. As the toothed drum bit at the corn sheaves it made an angry snarl that changed and slowed into a satisfied zoom. The wide conveying belt was carrying the golden straw up a steep incline to where other men were building a long rick; still more men were attending to the corn shoots, shoulders bending under the weight of the sacks as they ambled across to the granary. Matt Tobin himself bent at the face of his engine, feeding the fire box with sods of hard black peat. There were not less than two score men about the place, for, as was the custom, all Big Liam's friends and neighbors were giving him a hand with the threshing—"the day in harvest."

Big Liam came round the flank of the engine and swore. He was in his shirt sleeves, and his great forearms were covered with sandy hair.

"Hell and damnation! Look who's here!"

He was in the worst of tempers this morning. The stale dregs of yesterday's whisky were still with him; and he was in the humor that, as they say, would make a dog bite its father. He took two slow strides and halted, feet apart and head truculently forward.

"What is it this time?" he shouted. That was the un-Irish welcome he gave his sister and her husband.

Shawn and Ellen came forward steadily, and, as they came, Matt Tobin slowly throttled down his engine. Big Liam heard the change of pitch and looked angrily over his shoulder.

"What the hell do you mean, Tobin? Get on with the work!"

"To hell with yourself, Big Liam! This is my engine, and if you don't like it, you can leave it!" And at that he drove the throttle shut and the purr of the flywheel slowly sank.

"We will see in a minute," threatened Big Liam, and turned to the two now near at hand.

"What is it?" he growled.

"A private word with you. I won't keep you long." Shawn was calm and cold.

"You will not—on a busy morning," sneered the big man. "There is no need for private words between me and Shawn Kelvin."

"There is need," urged Shawn. "It will be best for us all if you hear what I have to say in your own house."

"Or here on my own land. Out with it! I don't care who hears!"

Shawn looked round him. Up on the thresher, up on the straw rick, men leaned idle on fork handles and looked down at him; from here and there about the stackyard, men moved in to see, as it might be, what had caused the stoppage, but only really interested in the two brothers-in-law. He was in the midst of Clan O'Grady, for they were mostly O'Grady men—big, strong, blond men, rough, confident, proud of their breed. Matt Tobin was the only man he could call a friend. Many of the others were not unfriendly, but all had contempt in their eyes, or, what was worse, pity. Very well! Since he had to prove himself, it was fitting that he do it here amongst the O'Grady men.

Shawn brought his eyes back to Big Liam—deep, steadfast eyes that did not waver. "O'Grady," said he—and he no longer hid his contempt—"you set a great store by money."

"No harm in that. You do it yourself, Shawneen."

"Take it so! I will play that game with you, till hell freezes. You would bargain your sister and cheat; I will sell my soul. Listen, you big brute! You owe me two hundred pounds. Will you pay it?" There was an iron quality in his voice that was somehow awesome. The big man, about to start forward overbearingly, restrained himself to a brutal playfulness.

"I will pay it when I am ready."

"Today."

"No; nor tomorrow."

"Right. If you break your bargain, I break mine."

"What's that?" shouted Big Liam.

"If you keep your two hundred pounds, you keep your sister."

"What is it?" shouted Big Liam again, his voice breaking in astonishment. "What is that you say?"

"You heard me. Here is your sister Ellen! Keep her!"

"Fires o' hell!" He was completely astounded out of his truculence. "You can't do that!"

"It is done," said Shawn.

Ellen O'Grady had been quiet as a statue at Shawn's side, but now, slow like doom, she faced him. She leaned forward and looked into his eyes and saw the pain behind the strength.

"To the mother of your son, Shawn Kelvin?" she whispered that gently to him.

His voice came as cold as a stone out of a stone face: "In the face of God. Let Him judge me."

"I know—I know!" That was all she said, and walked quietly across to where Matt Tobin stood at the face of his engine.

Matt Tobin placed hand on her arm. "Give him time, *acolleen*," he whispered urgently. "Give him his own time. He's slow, but he's deadly as a tiger when he moves."

Big Liam was no fool. He knew exactly how far he could go. There was no use, at this juncture, in crushing the run under a great fist. There was some force in the little fellow that defied dragooning. Whatever people might think of Kelvin, public opinion would be dead against himself. Worse, his inward vision saw eyes leering in derision, mouths open in laughter. The scandal on his name would not be bounded by the four seas of Erin. He must change his stance while he had time. These thoughts passed through his mind while he thudded the ground three times with iron-shod heel. Now he threw up his head and bellowed his laugh.

"You fool! I was only making fun of you. What are your dirty few pounds to the likes of me? Stay where you are."

He turned, strode furiously away, and disappeared through the arch.

Shawn Kelvin was left alone in that wide ring of men. The hands had come down off the ricks and thresher to see closer. Now they moved back and aside, looked at one another, lifted eyebrows, looked at Shawn Kelvin, frowned and shook their heads. They knew Big Liam. They knew that yielding up the money, his savagery would break out into something little short of killing. They waited, most of them, to prevent that savagery going too far.

Shawn Kelvin did not look at anyone. He stood still as a rock, his hands deep in his pockets, one shoulder hunched forward, his eyes on the ground and his face strangely calm. He seemed the least perturbed man there. Matt Tobin held Ellen's arm in a steadying grip and whispered in her ear: "God is good, I tell you."

Big Liam was back in two minutes. He strode straight to Shawn and halted within a pace of him.

"Look, Shawneen!" In his raised hand was a crumpled bundle of greasy bank notes. "Here is your money. Take it, and then see what will happen to you. Take it!" He thrust it into Shawn's hand. "Count it. Make sure you have it all—and then I will kick you out of this haggard—and look"—he thrust forward a hairy fist—"if ever I see your face again, I will drive that through it! Count it, you spawn!"

Shawn did not count it. Instead he crumpled it into a ball in his strong fingers. Then he turned on his heel and walked, with surprising slowness, to the face of the engine. He gestured with one hand to Matt Tobin, but it was Ellen, quick as a flash, who obeyed the gesture. Though the hot bar scorched her hand, she jerked open the door of the fire box and the leaping peat flames whispered out at her. And forthwith, Shawn Kelvin, with one easy sweep, threw the crumpled ball of notes into the heart of the flame. The whisper lifted one tone and one scrap of burned paper floated out of the funnel. That was all the fuss the fire made of its work.

But there was fuss enough outside.

Big Liam O'Grady gave one mighty shout. No, it was more an anguished scream than a shout:

"My money! My good money!"

He gave two furious bounds forward, his great arms raised to crush and kill. But his hands never touched the small man.

"You dumb ox!" said Shawn Kelvin between his teeth. That strong, hunched shoulder moved a little, but no one there could follow the terrific drive of that hooked right arm. The smack of bone on bone was sharp as whip crack, and Big Liam was stopped dead, went back on his heels, swayed a moment and staggered back three paces.

"Now and forever! Man of the Kelvins!" roared Matt Tobin.

But Big Liam was a man of iron. That blow should have laid him on his back—blows like it had tied men to the ground for the full count. But Big Liam only shook his head, grunted like a boar, and drove in at the little man. And the little man, instead of circling away, drove in at him, compact of power.

The men of the O'Gradys saw then an exhibition that they had not knowledge enough to appreciate fully. Thousands had paid as much as ten dollars each to see the great Tiger Kelvin in action, his footwork, his timing, his hitting; and never was his action more devastating than now. He was a thunderbolt on two feet and the big man a glutton.

Big Liam never touched Shawn with clenched fist. He did not know how. Shawn, actually forty pounds lighter, drove him by sheer hitting across the yard.

Men for the first time saw a two-hundred-pound man knocked clean off his feet by a body blow. They saw for the first time the deadly restraint and explosion of skill.

Shawn set out to demolish his enemy in the briefest space of time, and it took him five minutes to do it. Five, six, eight times he knocked the big man down, and the big man came again staggering, slavering, raving, vainly trying to rend and smash. But at last he stood swaying and clawing helplessly, and Shawn finished him with his terrible double hit—left below the breastbone and right under the jaw.

Big Liam lifted on his toes and fell flat on his back. He did not even kick as he lay.

Shawn did not waste a glance at the fallen giant. He swung full circle on the O'Grady men and his voice of iron challenged them:

"I am Shawn Kelvin of Knockanore Hill. Is there an O'Grady amongst you thinks himself a better man? Come then."

His face was deep-carved stone, his great chest lifted, the air whistled through his nostrils; his deep-set flashing eyes dared them.

No man came.

He swung around then and walked straight to his wife. He halted before her.

His face was still of stone, but his voice quivered and had in it all the dramatic force of the Celt:

"Mother of my son, will you come home with me?"

She lifted to the appeal, voice and eye:

"Is it so you ask me, Shawn Kelvin?"

His face of stone quivered at last. "As my wife only—Ellen Kelvin!"

"Very well, heart's treasure." She caught his arm in both of hers. "Let us be going home."

"In the name of God," he finished for her.

And she went with him, proud as the morning, out of that place. But a woman, she would have the last word.

"Mother of God!" she cried. "The trouble I had to make a man of him!"

"God Almighty did that for him before you were born," said Matt Tobin softly.

THE TWEED COAT

GEORGE WESTON

She was very gentle and very quiet. Indeed, you would have been surprised at some of the books she read.

"I like books," she once told herself, "that make the breath come faster; books that lift you out of yourself and throw you all around."

You wouldn't have thought it if you had known her only by her name and appearance. Her name was Miss Abby Bronson, of Bronson's Cove—a village consisting of a store, a church and a dozen houses, near the Connecticut shore of Long Island Sound—and she belonged to the D.A.R. and was always picked upon by the central committees of New London whenever a drive was organized that took in the southern counties. But if you had known that her forefathers had not only been ministers, but had been captains and whalers as well, with at least one generation carrying on a snappy sideline of privateering against the peace and majesty of King George III, you might have guessed that this had something to do with her choice of current literature.

Adventure—that was what Miss Abby craved between her book covers; adventure and action, with a heavy villain thrown in for good measure; a villain who was always sure to get beaned before he was through. And if the hero was a private, say, she didn't think any worse of him for that; or if he had killed a few of the cardinal's men in fair duels; or even if now and then whole countrysides trembled and babies crawled under the beds at the mere mention of his name.

"If Henry only had a bit of that in him," she sometimes told herself with a touch of wistfulness, "he'd get along a whole lot better than he does now."

At the time our story opens, she was thirty-five years old; and a party of tourists, passing her flivver in the road, winked at one another, and one of them said, "Did you ever see such a precious little old maid in all your life?"

And truth to tell, Miss Abby did look a bit thoughtful that afternoon as she turned her car out of the Bronson Road and headed for New London.

On the seat beside her were a number of papers tied together with ribbon—among them a printed prospectus of the Pan-Oriental Oil and Rubber Company and a letter addressed in Miss Bronson's own writing to that same company, and stamped by the Post Office Department, "Fraud Order. Return to Sender."

"I'm sure there's some mistake though," she told herself as she jogged along. "He had such a good face. And if Henry just writes them a letter on his legal letterhead——"

It was a quarter to five when she reached New London and turned up State Street—an hour which she had chosen in the hope that she and Henry might have dinner together and go to a movie before she started back home.

"But at that, I'll probably have to drop him a hint," she thought as she climbed the stairs and rapped upon a door which bore the sign "Henry J. Farnsworth, Attorney."

"Come in!" cried a deep voice inside, after a pause which might be described as ponderous.

Miss Abby did two tricks then which she had gleaned from literature. She first bit her lips to make them red, and then she rubbed her cheeks to make them pink, and then—feeling that quickening of the breath which was always like the wine of life to her—she opened the door and quietly stepped inside.

II

It was a large, old-fashioned office in which she found herself; but for all its size and length of life, there was an unmistakable flavor of failure about it. The safe in the corner, for instance, was too small for prosperity; and one could see that the name of a previous owner had been painted out and "Henry J. Farnsworth" lettered in its place. And instead of overlooking the street, the windows opened on a bricked-in court—an office without anteroom or offspring—no businesslike beauty tapping industriously at her typewriter—no boy to rise from his interrupted labors of punching holes in summonses and complaints and trying to look as though he were studying law. And the railway map of the United States upon the wall—that was clearly a hangover from a former tenant; and so were the cupboards, and possibly the old-fashioned copying press in the corner. In fact only the desk looked successful—an opulent, flat-topped affair in dull oak; but if you had been there, you might have guessed that the effort to acquire the desk hadn't been far from exhausting. At least the chair didn't match it, but was an ancient swivel effect in imitation walnut, and it had a decided list to starboard whenever relieved of its human ballast.

And yet, again if you had been there, you might have thought that the occupant of the chair could easily have graced a better office; that far less likely looking lights of the law had whole bevies of beauties tapping away like so many bright-eyed woodpeckers in Athenian groves; whole schools of boys to bob up before you in the outer passage and bar the way to the inner precincts. For even when he was seated in the walnut whatnot, one could see that Henry J. Farnsworth, Attorney, was not only tall but was well calculated to impress, having the Websterian forehead and that austere touch of dignity which is generally associated with those who have rubbed the back of fortune and have acquired the golden palm. High forehead under an arch of hair, dark brows and rather somber eyes, firm chin and tightly closed lips; and having learned that last item of the catalogue, you may possibly wonder whether this was the reason why Henry in his fortieth year had been outdistanced by many a legal chatterbox who had not yet turned twenty. All his life he had practiced that silence is golden, so that now, when he tried to spread a little silver, he generally found that his tongue was stuck behind his teeth and that younger squirts of the law with the gift of gab were putting it all over him.

"Hello," he said, gravely rising when Abby entered and shifting one of the other chairs for her.

"Hello, Henry," she said in a low voice, her breath still coming fast as she drew near to him.

But he neither strongly crushed her in his arms nor held her hand and muttered in trembling tones, "If you only knew how good it is to see you!"

Instead, he kissed her—kissed her, it might be said, legally, on her cheek, looking all the time as though he were thinking of the definition of "torts" and the time required to file demurrers in an action in the Supreme Court.

So, seeing this was all, Miss Abby sat down, her breath now nearly normal again, and told about her experience with the Pan-Oriental Oil and Rubber Company. Henry listened austerely; and after he had read the papers, he briefly delivered himself.

"Guess you've been stuck," said he. "I'll look it up—these people, I mean—and let you know in a few days for sure."

She would probably have defended her judgment more eloquently if it hadn't been for the manner of Henry's dictum—which might have reminded you of a pail of cold water being thrown on a robin. So, bit by bit, her chirping grew feebler.

"How did you come to do it?" asked Henry, again speaking austerely, when she had quite shut up.

"Because I needed the money so," she said. "The Bronson church has got to have a new steeple, and we're 'way behind on our foreign missions, and I've got the loveliest idea of fixing up the old Pennypacker place and making it a sort of a camp for city children—you know—one of the fresh-air funds. And—and——"

She didn't finish that, because, you see, she couldn't very well tell him that she had invested her own seven thousand in the Pan-Oriental Oil and Rubber Company, hoping that in a few months—perhaps even in a few weeks—she would be able to go to Henry and say, "You dear, loyal, faithful old thing, you, waiting for me all these years because you don't feel that you are making money enough yet to get married on! See this fortune which I have made—through a miraculous stranger who was guided by Providence to my door? Well, now there's more than enough for both of us; so please don't let's wait any longer, dear, because every year now I am getting a year older; and if we don't look out, we shall wait so long that—well, you know what I mean."

So instead of saying that, she said, "Well, anyhow, I hope it'll turn out right. I don't know why, but I don't feel the least bit worried." And perhaps to chide him, because he looked so dour and quiet, she said quite gaily, "It hasn't taken my appetite either. I think I'll have dinner in the city tonight for a change."

Of course he asked her then to have dinner with him; and later, as she had hoped, they went to a movie. But not once all evening did Henry make her breath come faster; not even in the darkened theater did he once touch her hand or even lean over so that her shoulder touched his in that heartwarming contact which has been known to lovers since long before the human race could sing or speak.

"Poor Henry," thought Miss Abby as she rolled for home alone, along toward half-past eleven. "He seems so worried lately, and so awfully quiet. And when he paid for the dinner, I noticed he had only a few dollars left. Of course he's always been quiet, like a nice big St. Bernard; but tonight—oh, I don't know, he didn't even wag his tail!"

A dark thought, and a rather dreadful thought, came to her then—one of those thoughts which sometimes come to daughters of Eve when they first begin to picture themselves as left upon the shelf.

"I wonder if it was because of the money," she thought, staring ahead into the darkness. "I wonder if—if I have lost it—if that's going to make any difference to him!"

In the uncertain light of the car, her face looked pinched, as though one of the gentler masks of tragedy had been slipped over it. It was at that moment that she noticed the car that was stopped by the side of the road ahead.

"Spooners," she told herself. "M'm—I'd like to see Henry."

She left the thought there, her attention attracted by a man who stepped out from behind the other car and lifted up his hand in mute appeal for her to stop.

"Like fun I will!" thought little Miss Abby, drawing from current literature and opening the throttle wide. "You may get a man to stop; but you won't get me!"

But just then, the flivver swerving a little, her headlights shone full upon the man in the road, and she saw that one of his arms hung by his side, the hand streaked with red; caught, too, the pallor of his face, the look in his eyes.

"Of course if you're hurt——" she thought. And putting on both her brakes, she stopped—stopped just in front of the man in the road—stopped warily for all that, with her engine running and ready to start it if anything looked like a trap.

III

He was a youngish man—the man with the stain on his hand—that is to say, he was about thirty-five, which, you may remember, was Miss Abby's age too. Moreover, he was tall, dressed in a tweed coat and flannel trousers of a rather precious cut, and a Panama hat woven as fine as many a piece of linen. He was standing, half leaning, against one of his front fenders, the light of Miss Abby's car falling well upon him; and underneath his coat she noticed was a green and gray sweater—a lightweight affair with a zigzag pattern—while his buckskin shoes, more dimly seen, had those rakish lines which are vaguely reminiscent of the yachtsman—toe caps cut like fish's tails and side leathers scalloped into waves.

There was also in his features a faint hint of the sea—blond hair, such as might once have crowned a Viking, a keen chin like the cutwater of a cruiser, and an aquiline nose which looked as though it had often smelled the weather when the sea was running wild. His car, she also noticed, was a Penguin Twelve, the length of its hood suggesting the speed and power within.

"I beg your pardon, madam," he said, taking off his hat and swaying a little, "but I wonder if—if you could get me to a doctor. I—you see, I've been hurt."

His voice sounded thick, his words now and then almost unintelligible; and although they were on the lonely stretch of road that led from the main highway to the Cove, Miss Abby straightway abandoned all suspicions of a trap. For one thing, she had just noticed the steady drip-drip which was falling from the injured man's sleeve; and not only that, but there was something in his manner, in the pathetic politeness with which he had removed his hat before speaking, which had gone straight to her heart.

"Why, of course I will," she said, opening the door and stepping out; and thinking there had been an accident, she continued, "What have you done? Cut yourself on the glass?"

"No," he said. "I—I think I'm shot. Some—somebody trying to hold me up, but I got away."

"They are doing that on the Shore Road every once in a while," she nodded. "That's one reason I was in two minds about stopping to help you when I saw you signal."

"Two—two other cars went by—wouldn't stop."

"Well, in a way, of course, you can't blame them, can you?" she gently asked. "But, gracious, if you'd stood here much longer——"

By that time she had seen more clearly how badly he had been hurt—had seen, moreover, that she must work and work quickly or he might soon be beyond any doctor's power to help him.

"We've got to stop it bleeding," she said. "Let me help you take your coat off and we'll put a bandage on."

The coat slipped easily from his shoulders, and the door of her own car being open, Miss Abby threw it on the back seat. She rolled back the sleeve of his sweater then and uncovered a wicked-looking furrow which stretched from his wrist to his elbow.

"We need something long for this," she said. "Now wait a moment, please, and you mustn't look."

Turning her back to him, she tore off the bottom hem of her slip—a stout wide band of silk—and was soon winding this around his arm above the wound—winding it as tightly as she could pull it and finally splitting the end of the bandage and tying a surgeon's knot.

"There!" she said. "That's stopping it, see?"

286

"You're awfully—good," he said, more thickly than before. "Two—two others. They wouldn't stop."

"Now I'll help you in my car," she said, "and we'll go to Stonington. There's a doctor there and you'll soon be all right. But wait a minute; do you want to lock your own car first? Where are your keys? I'll do it."

"Never mind," he said. "Hole in gas tank, I think. Anyhow she—she stopped——"

He was obviously growing weaker; so without delaying further she helped him in her car by the side of the driver's seat, and then slipping under the wheel herself she stepped on the pedal and they started for Stonington.

"Are you all right?" she anxiously asked, as the flivver gained speed. "Are you comfortable?"

"I—you——" he said in a sleepy voice.

He was beginning to lurch a little, though, as if he didn't have the strength to sit straight; and after a few moments' hesitation, Miss Abby resolutely put her right arm around his shoulders to hold him steady.

"If Henry only saw me now!" she couldn't help thinking.

And then all at once it came to her—the thrill of the adventure—an adventure which needn't take second place to anything which she had either read or seen on the screen. Midnight and a holdup. A wounded man, and the Pharisees who wouldn't stop. And then she—daring much, perhaps too much, stopping on a lonely road, giving first aid, and now riding through the night with her arm around a romantic-looking man with a keen chin who might have died if it hadn't been for her.

"And the funny part of it is," she thought, "just before I saw him, I was thinking to myself that not once tonight had Henry moved me, not once had he made my breath come faster. And then all at once——"

The injured man settled his head drowsily against her shoulder, one of his hands unconsciously patting her arm.

"Mamma's li'l' baby," he murmured. "Mamma's li'l' bright-eyed lover——"

"He's delirious," thought Miss Abby, and perhaps that was why she tightened her arm around him.

"I love you—love you," he murmured. "Nicest—beau'fulest—ever lived——"

Miss Abby's breath came faster and faster.

"Oh, if I can only get him better!" she thought, with shining eyes.

IV

Doctor Grinnell didn't think much of it—being roused out of his comfortable bed for an accident case, accident cases being proverbially poor pay; the patient, as a rule, being more interested in getting damages than paying for the pleasure of being sewed up in a doctor's chair.

"Accident?" he grumbled down the speaking tube. "Who is this?"

"This is Miss Bronson—Abby Bronson—and a man's been shot. I found him by the side of the road and I've got him here in my car."

"All right," grumbled the good physician, knowing quite well by that time that he would never get a cent for it. "I'll be down in a minute."

"Who is it?" asked Mrs. Grinnell in a sleepy voice, curious, but not wanting to get too wide-awake.

"Abby Bronson," said Doc.

"What's she want?"

The doctor made a professional jest, meaning to get a bit of fun out of it, if he got nothing more.

"What?" demanded Mrs. Grinnell, sitting up in bed, wide awake in a moment.

"Well, anyhow, she's got a man in her car," said the good physician. "I'll tell you about it when I come up."

Miss Abby had driven into the doctor's driveway, so that when he opened the door and turned on the porch light, he was able to see his prospective patient through the window of the flivver.

"What's the matter with him?" he asked opening the car door. "Unconscious?"

"Pretty well, I guess."

"M'm—let's feel his pulse."

He seemed to have trouble finding it.

"Shot, you said?" he asked.

"Yes; he was held up. There's an awful gash, beginning at his wrist. I tied it up as well as I could."

"You were with him when he was shot?"

"No, no!" said little Miss Abby hastily. "I was coming back from New London and he signaled me from the side of the road."

"I see. Well, you seem to have tied him up good, and he'll have to go to a hospital anyhow. So why not run him over to Westerly? It'll only take a few minutes; and I'll phone ahead and they'll have everything ready for you. Then if they have to probe for the bullet, they can do it a whole lot better than I can here."

Miss Abby briskly nodded, proud that she had made a good job of her bandage and anxious now to get her patient to the hospital as quickly as she could.

"Thank you ever so much, doctor," she said, slipping back under the wheel again. "I'll get him right over there."

So with one thing and another, it was pretty late when little Miss Bronson finally reached her home at Bronson's Cove that night. At the hospital they had discovered that the injured man had a second wound—the bullet which had plowed his arm evidently entered the side of his chest as well—and she had waited in the office until the night nurse had told her that he was resting quite comfortably—"everything considered, of course." Indeed, it was after two o'clock when Miss Abby ran her flivver into the miniature garage back of her house, and she was about to turn out the lights when she caught sight of something unusual on the back seat of the car.

"That's funny," she thought. "What is it?"

She opened the door of the car and reached it out; and the moment she saw it, she knew what it was—even though she was holding it upside down. It was the tweed coat which the wounded man had been wearing when she had first seen him—the coat which they had taken off so that she could bandage his arm; and just as she was reaching over for the collar to hold it properly, a sumptuous-looking wallet of pigskin tumbled out of an inside pocket—a sumptuous-looking wallet of pigskin with corners of polished gold.

V

Almost in haste Miss Abby replaced the wallet in the coat; and then, after locking the garage, she carried the coat into the house and laid it on the kitchen table and lit a lamp preparatory to going upstairs.

"I guess I'd better take the coat up with me," she thought, "especially with that big wallet in the pocket."

So she carried it up, the lamp in one hand and the coat in the other, her breath coming somewhat faster again at the thoughts which arose to her mind.

"It's just like him, somehow," she thought, looking down at the coat and thinking of the blond-haired, keen-chinned stranger to whom she had played Good Samaritan that night. "You'd almost know it was his, just to take one look at it."

Which was a woman's thought, and you'll have to get from it whatever you can.

She began to undress, though slowly—her thoughts still busy with the adventures of the night; but whichever way her memories turned, they always came back to when she was taking the owner of the tweed coat to Doctor Grinnell's office and his head was resting on her shoulder—— "I love you—love you—nicest—beautifulest—ever lived——"

"Of course he was delirious; I know that," she told herself with a slight flush of her cheeks. "But I can't imagine Henry saying that, even when delirious."

Her thoughts turned then to the car—the Penguin Twelve—which they had left by the side of the road.

"He must be awfully rich," she thought. "It's funny I never wondered before who he was. I guess I must have been too busy. But even at the hospital I couldn't begin to tell them who he was—and maybe his folks are just being worried sick because he doesn't come home. His mother, or—or—or—or even his wife, though I don't believe he's married," she hurriedly added. "He didn't look married, somehow, and you can nearly always tell."

Which again was a woman's thought, and you'll have to get from it whatever you can.

"But married or not, I think his folks ought to know," she presently continued, brushing her hair by that time and standing sideways at the mirror so she could look down at the coat which was draped on the back of a chair. "A man with a car like that—he's almost sure to have a phone, and it's the least I can do to call his people up and tell them where he is."

She was pretty sure, she knew, to find his name and address in one of the pockets of the coat—a card—a letter—his automobile license— even his driver's license—it was almost sure to be there somewhere.

"Of course it sounds awful, looking in anybody's pocket," she uncertainly continued; "but in a case like this, where they'd probably want to rush right over to the hospital——"

She picked up the coat then and sat on the side of the bed with it; and noticing that one of the sleeves was damp, she tucked it in as far as the elbow, this giving that coat a crippled look which made her feel quite weepy.

"Yes, and he may lose his arm too," she thought, her nose smarting. "But oh, wasn't he brave! It must have been hurting him dreadfully, but he didn't even pull a face. Just sat there with his head against my shoulder. 'Love you—love you—nicest—beau'fulest——' "

She did weep a little then, and when that was over, and she had blown her nose, she resolutely nodded her head and began exploring the contents of his outside pockets. There was a pack of paper matches, a silk handkerchief without a monogram, the end of a lead pencil, the metal seal of a bottle; but that was all.

"I'd hate to open the wallet," she thought, turning the coat over. "Perhaps there's a letter or something like that in the inside pocket."

But when she looked, there was only the wallet—fat and sumptuous and gleaming at her from its polished gold corners. It was one of those long affairs which are kept closed with a strap, and when she unfastened the buckle, the thing almost grunted like a fat man who has loosened his belt; and the wallet, opening in her hand like a book, showed each of its sides filled well nigh to bursting with a sandwich of orange-colored bills, each one a masterpiece of the engraver's art, and each one instructing the Treasurer of the United States to pay to the bearer on demand——

"Oh-h-h, what a lot of money!" gasped Miss Abby. "I don't believe I ever saw so much in all my life!"

Disregarding the money at first however—more intent upon finding clues of identity than certificates of the Treasury—she opened a leather pocket that had been fashioned in the inside of the flap, hoping to discover some card, some letter; but the only article in it was a girl's picture—the picture of a blonde with a halo of hair and a pair of eyes which coyly looked up from under her lashes as though expressing "M'm-m-m!"

Now little Miss Abby was dark, and between the blondes and the brunes there is a feud which probably goes back to the dawn of human history. So Miss Abby should at least be partly excused for her next remark, and the blame placed where it properly belongs—that is to say, upon heredity.

"A frizzy blonde!" she scoffed to herself. "You'd have thought he'd have more sense!"

But even at that, there was something gentle in her scoffing—the note which you sometimes hear in a mother's voice when she would make excuses for her first-born son.

"She probably looped him in before he knew it," she thought. "Everybody knows how bold they are."

The picture bore the name and address of a New York photographer, and from that again Miss Abby strengthened her case.

"A Broadway beauty!" she told herself, with a quite indescribable accent. "I thought it was funny, the way she rolled her eyes."

As though to express the way she felt, she turned the picture face down on a chair by the side of the bed, and thereby disclosed a line of writing on the back of the photograph.

"All Yours, M'leen," she read.

"Didn't I know it?" Miss Abby demanded of herself, almost angry in her unquestioned virtue. "Pushy! Common! The very idea, writing like that on the back of a photograph!"

At that, walking primly, she carried the picture to the other side of the room and put it on the shelf behind the clock.

"Anyhow," she thought, "I don't have to telephone you!"

She returned to the wallet then, but there was nothing else in it—absolutely nothing else except the money.

"A hundred-dollar bill!" she thoughtfully told herself, looking at the top of one of the sandwiches. "Isn't it pretty? I never saw a hundred-dollar bill before."

It was some little time before she did it; but knowing human nature as well as you do, you have probably already guessed that after a while she looked at the next bill, to see if that was for a hundred dollars too.

"Oh-h-h!" she gasped then, seeing the noble figure "1000" in each of the top corners. "I—I wonder if it's real!"

But she didn't have much doubt of that. Perhaps it was because of the appearance of the keen-chinned stranger whom she had taken to the hospital, perhaps because of the Penguin Twelve which he had been driving. In any event, little Miss Abby suddenly became cautious, looking over at the windows to make sure that the shades were tightly drawn and then locking her bedroom door, after first listening for any suspicious sounds downstairs. Then, almost tiptoeing back to her bed, she took out both the sandwiches and counted them, her eyes growing rounder and rounder and her fingers trembling a little before she was through.

"Eighty-five thousand dollars!" she gasped then. "What—what—what on earth am I going to do with it!"

It was at least easy to see that she could do nothing with it that night except to hide it; and so, after a while, she took it to her closet and put it under the lining of an old hat—a hiding place which she had sometimes used before. But after lying awake for more than an hour, she went to the closet and got the wallet and put it under her pillow, one of her hands around it under cover of the bedclothes.

This, she presently found, was a much more satisfactory place than the hat. It seemed to bring the wounded Knight of the Keen Chin more closely to her, and finally growing drowsy, she could feel his head against her shoulder again, could hear once more his gentle "Love you—love you—nicest—beau'fulest—ever lived——"

It was daylight when she awoke in the morning; and as though she had decided in her sleep just what to do, she threw a dressing gown over her shoulders and went straight down to the phone in the hall.

"Hello!" she said, after she had got her number. "Is this the Westerly Hospital? This is Miss Abby Bronson, of Bronson's Cove. I brought a young man to the hospital last night. He had been shot. . . .Yes, that's the one. Can you tell me how he is this morning, please, and whether I can come over and see him for a few minutes?"

For as long as it might take you to count ten slowly, she stood at the telephone, listening to the answer from the other end of the wire; and when it was over, she hung up the receiver and placed her arm against the wall and buried her face in the angle of her elbow.

"Dead—he's dead!" she whispered to herself, and straightway fell into the strangest fit of weeping.

VI

More and more clearly, then, Miss Abby saw that she must find out who he was. There was not only the matter of the wallet, but the hospital wanted to know his name and address so they could get in touch with his family.

"Of course if no one else turns up, I shall look after him myself," she thought. "But surely there ought to be some way of finding who he was."

All at once then it came to her, as solutions, elusive at night, will often come when Aurora trots her horses into view.

"His car of course!" she suddenly told herself. "We can tell who he was from his number!"

She lit the fire then and put on the coffee—the chores of life demanding attention, no matter what mountains may fall. And after she had washed her face in the coldest of water, and dressed and had her breakfast, she rolled her flivver out of its miniature garage and headed for the New London road, riding carefully over the ruts in front of Tillinghast's store and then getting a good run for the hill that led to the church.

As she passed the church, Old Gooseberry the Invisible must have stepped upon the running board, for she suddenly found herself thinking in the craziest way, "It wouldn't take much of that money to fix the steeple."

Of course she banished the thought as soon as it entered her mind; but at least it had found the way in.

Next she began wondering if Henry could help her with the number of the Penguin Twelve.

"If I telephoned him the number," she thought, "he'd know how to find whose car it was."

And here again Old Gooseberry, blithely cloven-hoofing it after the flivver, must have bobbed up on the running board again.

"Henry often says that if he could afford a better office it wouldn't be long before he had a good practice."

But here suppression was easier than in the matter of the steeple, for although she wasn't openly conscious of it, the tight-lipped Henry seemed queerly out of the picture that morning, extinguished, eclipsed by the memory of a keen-chinned stranger for whom she had stopped on the edge of the road after two Pharisees had passed by on the other side.

"Oh, well, anyhow," she thought, as she neared the scene where her adventure had started the night before, "I'll soon be there now, and I guess I'll find out something."

As a matter of fact, she found out more than she expected. As she neared the stranded Penguin, she saw a motorcycle standing by it; and drawing still nearer, she perceived a state cop standing at the back of the car and making an entry in his notebook.

Little Miss Abby hesitated, Old Gooseberry babbling away; but then, holding her head unusually high, a touch of color on each of her cheeks, she stepped on the brake and stopped.

"Good morning," she said to the cop.

"Good morning," said he, somewhat gruffly, she thought, and went on writing in his notebook.

Evidently that was all he meant to say; so, swallowing hard, Miss Abby started again.

"I beg your pardon," she said, "but can you tell me whose car this is?" And seeing that he was staring at her without answering, she added, "I was coming past here last night, and the gentleman had been held up and shot. So I took him to the Westerly Hospital, and—and—they want to know his name and address so they can telegraph his family."

"You mean he's dead?" said the cop, staring harder than ever.

Miss Abby nodded, meanwhile whispering to herself, "Now you're not going to cry. You know you're not going to cry."

The cop whistled—not only whistled but snapped his fingers too.

"Well, I'll be jigged!" said he. "Jerry thought he plugged him, but wasn't sure!"

"Jerry?" she asked, wondering. "You mean the man who shot him?"

"Sure! Some shot, too, in the dark, at that speed. Clipped the side of his gasoline tank too; that's what must have stopped him."

This time it was Miss Abby's turn to stare. Instead of expressing indignation, the cop seemed to be holding some sort of jubilee at Jerry's marksmanship.

"Have you got this man Jerry?" she asked in a colder voice.

"Got him? What do you mean—got him?" demanded the cop. "He's my buddy at the barracks, and we've been after this bird for the last six months."

When he said the word "bird" he pointed to the Penguin Twelve, but Miss Bronson knew that quite a different bird was meant.

"Do you know who he was?" she asked, cold tone giving way to faintness. "The—the gentleman who was shot last night, I mean?"

"Know who he was? Sure, I know who he was," said the cop. "Blondy Dykmann, one of the busiest little booze runners on the Sound!"

Miss Abby's next question was a long time coming; but when it finally did come, it must have sounded rather peculiar to a stranger.

"Has he—has he any family, do you know?"

"Family?" repeated the cop, going back to his staring.

"Yes," she said; and catching herself in time, she added, "I thought I told you the hospital wanted to know."

"Search me," he said. "They tell me he lived in New York somewhere when he was home, but I guess that wasn't often."

He took her name and address, then, because she had carried Blondy to the hospital; and when that was done, Miss Abby started back for the Cove.

"I shall have to watch the papers," she thought. "They'll tell his address. And as soon as I know where his family lives——"

She made a vague gesture then, her memory turning to the picture of the frizzy blonde which was back of the clock in her bedroom.

"I wonder if that was his wife," she mused. "I—I wonder what she'd do with all that money."

VII

The first thing Miss Abby did with the money when she reached home was to hide it—certainly not with any idea of keeping it, but so that it wouldn't be stolen from her before she could turn it over to its rightful owner. And truth to tell, she hid it rather ingeniously, screwing the money tightly inside a pint jar, placing this pint jar inside a large pickle jar, covering it with piccalilli, pouring melted wax over it and then placing it in the back row on her hanging shelf in the cellar.

Three times that day she telephoned the hospital, asking if anything had been heard from Mr. Dykmann's family, and each time the answer was the same.

"We'll phone you as soon as we hear, if you like, Miss Bronson," said the girl on the other end of the wire, the last time Miss Abby called.

"Thank you," she said. "I'd like it very much, if you would." But no phone message came.

After supper, Miss Abby rolled out her flivver again and went to New London, where she bought a copy of all the late evening papers that she could find. Nearly all of them had a story of Eric—Blondy—Dykmann's death after a breathless duel with the state police, most of the shots being fired when both pursued and pursuers were going more than seventy-five miles an hour; and although some of the stories were long ones, none of them told where he lived, other than to say New York, and none of them made any mention of his family.

One of the stories ended, "So far, Dykmann's body has not been claimed by relatives; and if nothing is heard by Thursday, it will be buried in the local potter's field."

"It will not!" thought little Miss Abby, her breath coming faster.

Again she thought of getting in touch with Henry; and again she didn't; Henry still seeming remote, almost as though he had never been.

"And anyhow," she thought, "he wouldn't understand."

On the way home she made a face—a wry grimace—as though life, that inscrutable doctor, had just given her a bitter pill to swallow.

"That blonde," she thought—"the photographer could give me her name and address. I guess I'll have to see her after all."

Time, you see, was getting short. That day was Wednesday, and if nothing was heard by Thursday——

"I could take the boat to New York tonight," she thought. "It doesn't sail till eleven." But she would have to hurry. "If there'd only been something else in that coat!" she thought. "Of course I can get the tailor's name; he might be able to tell me something."

So, as soon as she got home, she copied the tailor's label that was underneath the hanger, and then took the girl's picture from behind the clock.

"Isn't it funny," she told herself. "The more I see her, the more I hate her."

Then Justice raised blindfolded head.

"I know," nodded little Miss Abby, hurriedly turning to pack her bag. "She—she may have claims on him, even—even if they aren't married. Men sometimes fall for a girl like that—fall awfully, dreadfully hard."

But all the same, she decided to go and see the tailor first.

The tailor's name was a noble one, Caesare Napoleon, and whether or not he descended from the great Bonaparte, he had an appearance which was not without its elements of grandeur. As soon as Miss Abby saw his shop, dark and cool, its windows draped with the current weaves, her heart went "Pitter-patter-pitter-patter," and she thought to herself, her breath coming fast, "This is where the tweed coat was made. This is where he often came to be measured and fitted."

She went in. On one side of the shop was a cutting counter; and back of this counter, as soon as her eyes became accustomed to the gloom, she saw a tall, elderly Italian rippling a pair of Gargantuan shears across a bolt of striped blue flannel. He was very bald and very yellow, and for some reason which is hard to tell he looked incredibly wise—like one of those old mandarins, perhaps, who read The Seven Ineffable Flowers of Knowledge while most of the rest of the world was eating raw meat and painting their bodies blue. Perhaps his mustache had something to do with this—an enormous gray festoon which he had trained into the shape of a drooping horseshoe and which lifted him at once above the common run of men.

"Good morning," said Miss Abby, her breath coming faster.

"Good morning, madam," he said, with Old World courtesy, but still rippling the shears as he looked at her—looked at her as though with a veil over his eyes and departing not the breadth of a hair from the soap line he had drawn upon the cloth.

"I have called," she said, "to see if you can tell me where one of your customers lives—a gentleman named Eric Dykmann."

Without replying, and yet certainly without refusing to reply, he turned the cloth and started his scissors winging in a new direction.

"He was—he was a tall—a tall gentleman—as tall as you," she bravely continued, "with light hair and—and blue eyes and a keen chin. And—and you once made him a tweed coat—not very long ago—a tweed coat, with a herringbone pattern, and pretty shades of brown and dark red in it."

At that, Caesare pushed the cloth aside and stood up straight, resting the points of his shears on the counter, as a gallant warrior might rest the point of his sword upon the floor.

"You knew him, madam?" he asked, still with the veil over his eyes.

"Yes."

"And you know—the other night——"

"Yes," she said in a lower voice, when he finished his question

297

with a discreet lift of his eyebrows. "I was one of the last who was with him."

Without speaking, Caesare walked to one of his tables and came back with a bolt of tweed.

"Thees is the cloth of wheech the coat was made?" he asked, descending into vernacular for the first time.

"No," said little Miss Abby, still speaking faintly.

"Thees?" he asked, turning and drawing a smaller piece from the shelf.

"Yes," she said.

"I see you know him," he nodded, the veil lifting from his eyes. "The coat was ver' near new."

"You knew him well yourself?" Miss Abby asked.

"I knew him ver', ver' well. Cer-tain-lee. He come in here some-time for a suit of clothes and I say, 'Meester Dykmann, I wonder eef you like to help Italian hospital.' One word enough, madam. His hand in his pocket, like that. And once when I fit him, a Salvation Army come in on a tambourine. 'Caesare,' he say, 'you geeve her a dollar, I geeve her a five.' And right away queeck seex dollars she make-a the bells ring."

Miss Abby breathlessly nodded.

"Yes," she said, "he would do things like that."

"The cheeldren all like him, too—not for the penny, I mean—not cheap. But they smile when he pass and say, 'Good morning, Meester Dykmann,' and when one of the Silmerman cheeldren she break-a the hip and she no sets good, Meester Dykmann he sends her to a special hospital for seex months, and now no more she walks heepety-hop, heepety-hop, but straight in a march like me."

Miss Abby's cheeks were bright with color; and if you had seen her, you might have guessed that she wasn't far from setting up a hero in her mind.

"Where did he live?" she asked.

Caesare told her.

The next question was more difficult.

"Is he married—do you know?"

At that, Caesare took up his shears again and began to look at the soap lines on the flannel.

"A costomer's private affairs, madam," he said—"you onder-stand. I know leetle about them. But eef you ask me, I theenk not; or eff he was, I never hear about her. But where I tell you, he had a ver' fine place; and the janitor's wife she can tell you more, for she looks after his rooms."

At that he began rippling his shears again; and after Miss Abby had thanked him, she went to the address which he had given her and inquired for the janitor's wife.

"I think she's up in Mr. Dykmann's apartment, isn't she, Joe?" asked an enormous woman with a tiny wisp of hair who was mopping the tiled floor.

"Yep," said the elevator boy, busy at the brass work around his cage. "Fifth floor, Apartment 57. Want to go up?"

So little Miss Abby went up, thinking to herself, "He often went up here."

At Apartment 57, she stood by the door nearly half a minute before she felt she could ring the bell.

"Somebody's ringing the doorbell," she then heard a woman's voice saying inside. "Will you go?"

"Ye-ah," said someone else—a sleepier, younger voice. "I'll go."

There was the creak of a board, the turn of a lock, and the door opening, Miss Abby suddenly found herself face to face with M'leen, the girl whose picture she had discovered in the wallet.

IX

It would have pleased you, if you could have seen it—the contrast between those two at the door. M'leen was wearing a kimono of cubist design, irregular patches of startling colored silks; and her hair, like Mr. Kelly's trousers, looked as though it had been slept in. Miss Abby, on the contrary, was wearing a black tailor-made suit and a neat black hat—a neat black hat under which not a single lock of hair was out of place. M'leen had rings on nearly every finger and her shoes were of champagne-colored satin, with dark red heels. Miss Abby's only jewelry was a cameo brooch—the Arch of Titus, with a bit of the Colosseum—and her shoes were of an old-fashioned material which was once called leather, the heels both unrelieved by joyous shades. And finally M'leen looked sleepy, as though she had attended a late party the night before—a theory which was at least partly confirmed by the appearance of the hall behind her, while in her eyes was that slightly staring, slightly glassy look which at one time in our history was sometimes seen upon convivial gentlemen who on the previous evening had done something or other with the wassail bowl, or whatever the unregenerate phrase was.

"Hello," she said, staring curiously. "You ring?"

"Yes," said Miss Abby; and after a few moments' pause, she added, "I wonder if I could see you for a few minutes." And in a lower voice, "I was a friend of Mr. Dykmann's, and I understand he lived here."

Possibly the light-haired girl wouldn't have made the mistake if she hadn't been up so late the night before; but in Miss Abby's lowered voice, her black dress and her obvious embarrassment, she thought she detected a rather amusing thing.

"A lady friend of Blondy's," she announced over her shoulder; and nodding the visitor to come in, she led her down the hall with less sleepiness than she had shown before—led her with an air that said, "This ought to be pretty good."

Miss Abby followed M'leen into a front room—one of those rooms which might be described by the phrase "richly furnished." The walls, for instance, were nearly covered by oil paintings; and in one corner was a marble miniature of the Statue of Liberty, holding an electrolier in her hand, only instead of the lamp being shaped as a torch, it was like a purple bunch of grapes. And there were upholstered chairs, and a moose's head, and a crystal chandelier, and one of those long, deep davenports which are almost as long as a Pullman sleeper and yet so low to the ground that you have to be careful how you sit down or your chin will strike your knees. In the center of the room was a baize-covered table, from which a brisk-looking woman was moving a pile of plates and a chafing dish—Miss Abby guessed that she was the janitor's wife—while on the davenport, in a dark silk dressing gown, lay another sleepy girl with an empty coffee cup on the rug beside her, and her boyish form draped over an adjoining chair.

"Sit down," said M'leen.

"Thank you," said little Miss Abby, and seated herself by a bookcase which somehow didn't seem to match the rest of the room—a bookcase in which was a copy of the *History of Civilization*, for instance, and Carlyle's *French Revolution*, and a set of Dickens which looked as though it had been much read.

"This is a friend of Blondy's," continued M'leen, turning to the girl on the couch, and then looking back at Miss Abby she asked, "What did you say your name was?"

"Miss Bronson," said Miss Abby in her quiet voice.

"Pleased to meet you. . . . This is my friend, Trixie MacDougall. Perhaps you saw her in *Mamma, Be Good*."

Trixie was sitting up by then—a wise little madam with a humorous mouth—and noticing Miss Abby's black dress, she said, "Honest, you gimme a scare. I thought at first you might be Blondy's wife."

Miss Abby's heart gave such a jump.

"No," she said, "just a friend."

At that, M'leen winked over at Trixie; and watching her chance, Trixie winked back at M'leen.

"You live in the city?" continued M'leen.

"No; in Connecticut—on the Sound."

"He was often there," nodded M'leen. "I guess that's how you met him."

"Yes," said Miss Abby; and possibly thinking it was about time that she asked a few questions herself, she went on, "You spoke of—of Mr. Dykmann's wife. Was he married, do you know?"

"No," said M'leen; and beginning to enjoy herself, she added, "I don't know whether you noticed it yourself, but believe me, he always kept his fingers crossed."

That time Miss Abby caught the wink, and although she made no sign, she dimly began to catch its significance.

"Do you know anything about his family—his brothers and sisters, I mean—or—anybody belonging to him?"

"Nope," said M'leen. "Nothing doing there either. He told me once he was brought up in the Sheltering Arms, and all his folks was dead."

"The Sheltering Arms?"

"Ye-ah. An orphan asylum over in Rahway. We drove over once and he gave all the kids a treat."

"He was some little treater, believe me," said Trixie, "but I guess we had our last party on him last night. . . . Oh, hello, Sleepy-Head," she continued, looking toward the doorway. "Meet Miss Brown— one of Blondy's friends—from the country."

Miss Abby turned to look at a tall, dark man with a bulging forehead and a preternatural gravity of manner. He had evidently just shaved, but was still in his shirt sleeves; and Miss Abby recalled that before he appeared, she had heard a door open and shut along the hall.

"Come and sit here, Teddy," said M'leen, making room on the side of her chair.

Miss Abby watched her in her quiet way—watched the newcomer seat himself and M'leen's arm go curving around his shoulder, and then she arose and said, "Well, I must be going."

"Sorry we couldn't do more for you," said M'leen.

"Oh, that's all right," said Abby.

She paused then, having noticed for the first time a framed photograph by the side of the bookcase—the picture of a smiling, keen-chinned man who looked as though he was always sure of himself.

"I suppose—all his things here will be sold," she asked.

"Yes," said M'leen, more sharply than she had spoken before. "But that will have to go to pay his bills. We phoned the hospital as soon as we heard about it, but he had only a few dollars on him. Those cops who shot him took care of that, all right."

"Oh, I wasn't thinking of that," said Miss Abby, always in her gentle voice. "I was only wondering if—if you would care to let me have this picture of him."

"Why, sure," said M'leen, winking at the others again, "if you think it's going to do you any good now."

"Thank you." She took it, pausing meanwhile to glance at the titles of the books on the shelves. "He often sat here, didn't he?" she asked.

"Ye-ah," said M'leen, in some surprise, her hand still caressing Teddy's shoulder. "That was his favorite corner—when he was home."

"I thought so."

She left then, M'leen and Teddy following her to the door; and while she was waiting for the elevator in the empty hallway, Miss Abby heard a muffled burst of laughter from the apartment which she had just left—a muffled burst of laughter and the voice of Trixie saying, "Did you ever see anything funnier in your life?"

They might not have been so mirthful, however, if they had seen and heard Miss Abby a few days later when the latter was telling Henry Farnsworth how she wanted him to make up her will. You may remember Henry—Henry the Backward—with his Websterian forehead and lack of practice, his dark eyes and firmly closed lips—he who could never make Miss Abby's breath come faster. She had written him from Bronson's Cove, asking him to call "on a matter of business," and although he had kissed her when he came in—kissed her in his legal manner—they both seemed relieved when that was over and the conversation began. He hadn't been in long when he noticed the new photograph on the shelf—a photograph backed with flowers—but, true son of the Nutmeg State, he instinctively turned and whittled at something else.

"I see they're starting work on the steeple of the church," he said.

"Yes," said Miss Abby. "It's needed doing for a long time."

"And I noticed a fresh grave as I came past. Anybody around here?"

"No," said Miss Abby in her quiet voice. "It's a Mr. Dykmann, I think; and I understand his friends are going to give him quite a beautiful monument. And somehow it started me thinking, and I believe I'll make my will, Henry—especially as I'm going away for quite a while, and there's no telling what may happen before I get back."

She was dressed that afternoon in an apricot dress—a shade which went well with her hair and eyes—and looking at her with a glance of surprise, it might have struck Henry of the Websterian forehead that he would have to travel a considerable distance to find a nicer view.

"I didn't know you were going away," he said, trying not to look at the photograph on the table.

"Yes," she quietly nodded, her hands folded in her lap.

"But, say, that's going to make it pretty lonely for me."

"You won't mind."

"Won't I?" He struggled for speech then and finally found this: "Why, Abby, you're all I've got!" This he said quite loudly, and as though it hurt him too.

Just for a moment, then, Miss Abby thought her breath was coming faster.

"You hide it well," she gently railed him.

"Hide it well? Of course I do! Don't I have to? But just you wait till I'm making enough to get married on, and I'll show you!"

"Show me what?"

"I'll show you how I love you of course! What else?"

"Yes, you will!"

It was evenly said, but there was a faint note of derision in her voice which brought him to his feet quicker than any other flick which she could have given him. She, too, arose, as though in alarm; but whether it was alarm or not, she couldn't disguise from herself the fact that her breath was coming faster.

"I'll show you now if you like," he said, his voice none too steady.

"You sit down," she told him.

He did it slowly, but Henry sat down—Henry the Backward still, you see.

"You understand, though, don't you?" he said—the silent photograph still spurring him on.

"Understand what?"

"Any time you want to take a chance on living in debt half the time——"

Little Miss Abby demurely nodded.

"And now," she said, "I'll tell you the way I want to make my will."

Whereupon he grew more businesslike, and drew pencil and paper out of his pocket.

"Twenty-five thousand dollars," she said, "to the Sheltering Arms, of Rahway, New Jersey."

"How much?" he asked, looking up with startled eyes.

"Twenty-five thousand. And another twenty-five to the Lexington Hospital for Crippled Children."

Henry wrote on, his mouth opening a bit, too, as well as his eyes. Of course there were other instructions, and when she was through, she said, "Another thing, Henry, I wish you'd make me up a list of good investments. Mr. Dawson, of the Westerly Bank, is making a list of suggestions, and I'd like to compare the two."

"How much do you want to invest?" he asked.

"About eighty thousand dollars," she said in her quiet voice.

He said a queer thing then, as he arose to go—a very queer thing for a counselor learned in the law.

"You make me feel like a bum," he said in a husky voice.

"Why, Henry!" she protested. "What a thing to say!"

"You do, though," he said, and bit by bit, all his Websterian plaster seemed to be falling from his laths, and left him showing a much more natural-looking framework.

"But I don't see why I should," she said.

"You—you who have so much," he told her, "and me—I have so little."

It was the way he said it, more than the words, which touched her—the humble, despairing tones of a lover who has no thoughts of either torts or demurrers—and again Miss Abby's breath began to come faster.

"He's getting better," she thought. "That's twice."

"Well, good-bye," he said, holding out his hand and still speaking as before. "I'll have the will ready tomorrow."

"But, Henry," she said, all innocence in a moment, "don't you want to kiss me good-bye?"

"Want to?" he said. "I'll show you whether I want to!"

And indeed he showed her to such good purpose that he had been gone nearly five minutes before Miss Abby's breath returned to normal.

"He'll do," she thought.

She turned to the picture, then, which was smiling at her from the table—smiling at her with keen-chinned amusement.

"Thanks—to you," said she.

And still the picture smiled at her—the smile of a man who was always sure of himself. And if you had been there a few minutes later, it might have struck you that it was also the smile of a man who could always be sure of the gratitude of the happy-eyed Miss Abby, who was changing the flowers that stood behind his picture on the shelf.